Sunlight and Shadows

A Josefina Classic
Volume 1

by Valerie Tripp

★ American Girl®

Questions or comments? Call 1-800-845-0005,
visit **americangirl.com**, or write to Customer Service,
American Girl, 8400 Fairway Place, Middleton, WI 53562.

Printed in China
15 16 17 18 19 20 21 LEO 10 9 8 7 6 5 4 3 2

Grateful acknowledgment is made to the following for permission
to quote previously published material: p. 99—Enrique R. Lamadrid
(excerpt from "Las mañanitas/Little morning song" in *Tesoros del espíritu:
A portrait in sound of Hispanic New Mexico,* University of New Mexico Press,
© 1994 Enrique R. Lamadrid); p. 112—University of Oklahoma Press
(verse published in *The Folklore of Spain in the American Southwest,* by
Aurelio M. Espinosa, edited by J. Manuel Espinosa, © 1985 University
of Oklahoma Press, Norman, Publishing Division of the University).

Grateful acknowledgment is made to María C De Baca, Las Vegas, NM, for
permission to quote the verses appearing on pp. 154, 156, 167, 168, and 169,
originally published in the booklet *The Christmas Season* by Elba C De Baca.

Cover image by Michael Dwornik and Juliana Kolesova

Cataloging-in-Publication Data available from the Library of Congress

To my husband, Michael,
and my daughter, Katherine,
with love

To my mother,
Kathleen Martin Tripp,
with love

To Granger William Tripp
and Paige Elizabeth Tripp,
with love

Beforever™

The adventurous characters you'll meet in
the BeForever books will spark your curiosity
about the past, inspire you to find your voice
in the present, and excite you about your future.
You'll make friends with these girls as you share
their fun and their challenges. Like you, they are
bright and brave, imaginative and energetic,
creative and kind. Just as you are, they are
discovering what really matters: Helping others.
Being a true friend. Protecting the earth.
Standing up for what's right. Read their stories,
explore their worlds, join their adventures.
Your friendship with them will BeForever.

TABLE *of* CONTENTS

1   Primroses 1

2   Abuelito's Surprise 17

3   A Gift for Tía Dolores 35

4   Josefina's Idea 48

5   Light and Shadow 64

6   Turning Blankets into Sheep 79

7   Rabbit Brush 92

8   The First Love 102

9   Christmas Is Coming 117

10 Where Is Niña? 133

11 The Silver Thimble 147

12 La Noche Buena 158

Inside Josefina's World 172

Glossary of Spanish Words 174

Josefina and her family speak Spanish, so you'll see some Spanish words in this book. You'll find the meanings and pronunciations of these words in the glossary on page 174.

Remember that in Spanish, "j" is pronounced like "h." That means Josefina's name is pronounced "ho-seh-FEE-nah."

Primroses

 osefina Montoya hummed to herself as she stood in the sunshine waiting for her three sisters. It was a bright, breezy morning in late summer and the girls were going to the stream to wash clothes. Josefina's basket was full of laundry to be washed, but she didn't mind. She enjoyed going to the stream on a day like this. The sky was a deep, strong blue. Josefina wished she could touch it. She was sure it would feel smooth and cool.

Josefina liked to stand just in front of her house, where the life of her papá's *rancho* was going on all around her. From here, she could smell the sharp scent of smoke from the kitchen fire. She could see cows and sheep grazing in the pastures. Yellow grass rolled all the way to the dark green trees on the foothills of the mountains, and the mountains zigzagged up to the sky.

She could hear all the sounds of the rancho: chickens clucking, donkeys braying, dogs barking, birds chirping, workers hammering, and someone laughing. The sounds seemed like music to Josefina. The wind joined in the music when it rustled the leaves on the cottonwood trees. And always, under it all, was the murmur of the stream.

Josefina shaded her eyes. Even from this far away, she could see Papá. He sat very straight and tall on his horse. He was talking to the workers in the cornfield near the stream. The rancho had belonged to Papá's family for more than one hundred years. All those years, Papá's family had cared for the animals and the land. It was not an easy life. Everyone had to work hard. Some years there was plenty of rain so that the crops grew and the animals were healthy. Some years there was not enough rain. Then the soil was dry and the animals went thirsty. But through good times and bad the rancho went on. It provided everything Josefina and her family needed to live. It gave them food, clothing, and shelter. Josefina loved the rancho. It had been her home all the nine years of her life. She believed that it was the most beautiful place in all of New Mexico and all of the world.

Josefina was dancing a little dance of impatience to go with the song she was humming when her oldest sister, Ana, came outside to join her.

"Josefina," Ana said. "You remind me of a little bird, singing and hopping from one foot to the other like that."

"If I were a bird," said Josefina with a grin, "I could have flown to the stream and back twenty times by now. I've been waiting and waiting for you! Where are Francisca and Clara?"

Ana sighed. "They're coming," she said. "They couldn't agree on whose turn it was to carry the washing tub."

Josefina and Ana looked at each other and shook their heads. They were the eldest and youngest of the four sisters, and they got along beautifully. But Francisca and Clara, the middle sisters, often disagreed. It was always over some silly little thing. They reminded Josefina of goats she had seen ramming into each other head-to-head for no particular reason.

When the girls appeared at last, it was easy to see who had won the argument. Francisca, looking pleased with herself, carried only a basket of laundry balanced on her head. Clara, looking cross, carried the large copper washing tub.

Josefina put her basket into the copper tub. "I'll take one handle of the tub, Clara," she said. "We'll carry it between us."

Clara said, "*Gracias*." But she sounded more grumpy than grateful.

Josefina knew a way to cheer her up. "Let's race to the stream!" she said.

"Oh, no . . ." Francisca began to say. She didn't like to do anything that might muss her clothes or her hair.

But Josefina and Clara had already taken off running, so Ana and Francisca had to run, too.

The sisters flew down the dirt path that sloped past the fruit trees, past the fields, and to the stream. Josefina and Clara reached the stream first, plunked the tub down, kicked off their moccasins, and ran into the shallow water. Then they turned and scooped up handfuls of water to splash Ana and Francisca, who shrieked with laughter as the water hit them.

"Stop!" cried Francisca. She held up her basket to shield her face.

"Now, girls," Ana scolded gently. "We've come to wash the clothes that are in our baskets, *not* the ones we're wearing!"

Josefina and Clara stopped splashing. They were out of breath anyway. They filled the copper tub with water from the stream. Josefina knelt next to the tub. She took the root of a yucca plant out of the little leather pouch she wore at her waist and then pounded it between two rocks. The shredded yucca root made a nice lather of soapy bubbles in the water. Josefina put a dirty shirt in the tub and scrubbed it all over. Then she swooshed it around in the stream to rinse out the soap.

The sun was hot on her head and her back, and the water was cool on her arms and hands. Josefina liked to think about how the water started out as snow on the mountaintops. It melted and flowed all the way down to this little pool in the stream without ever losing its cool freshness. She knew that it was water that brought life to the rancho. Water from the stream was channeled into ditches so that it would flow through the fields. Without water, nothing would grow.

Josefina twisted the shirt to wring it out, and watched drops of water fall back into the stream and go on their way. Then she carefully spread the shirt on top of a bush.

"The sun and the breeze will dry the clothes quickly today," she said as she washed some socks.

"Yes," agreed Ana. "Mamá would have said, 'You see, girls? God has sent us a good drying day. Monday is laundry day even in heaven.'"

"And then Mamá would have said, 'Pull your *rebozos* up to shade your faces, girls. You don't want your skin to look like old leather!'" added Francisca as she adjusted her shawl on her head. Francisca was always careful of her skin.

The sisters laughed softly together and then grew quiet. Speaking of their mamá always made them thoughtful. Mamá had died the year before. The sorrow of her death was always in their hearts.

Josefina looked at the stream flowing past and listened to its low, rushing sound. Since Mamá died she had learned a truth that was both bitter and sweet. She had learned that love does not end. Josefina would always love Mamá, and so she would always miss her.

Josefina knew her sisters were also thinking about Mamá because Francisca said, "Look. See those yellow flowers across the stream?" She pointed with a soapy hand. "Aren't they evening primroses? They're in the shade, so they haven't wilted yet this morning. Mamá used to love those flowers."

"Yes, she did," said Clara, agreeing with Francisca for once. "Why don't you pick some, Josefina? You could dry them and put them in your memory box."

"All right," said Josefina. Papá had given her a little wooden box of Mamá's. Josefina called it her memory box because in it she kept small things that reminded her of Mamá, such as a piece of Mamá's favorite lavender-scented soap. The box had been made by Josefina's great-great-grandfather. On its top there was a carving of the sun coming up over the highest mountain and shining on the rancho just the way Josefina saw it rise every morning.

The quickest, driest way to the primroses was to walk across a fallen log that made a narrow bridge over the stream. Josefina climbed up onto the log. She held her arms out for balance and began to walk across.

"Oh, do be careful," warned Ana. Because she was

the oldest sister, Ana had become a motherly worrier since Mamá died.

Josefina did not think of herself as a brave person at all. She was afraid of snakes and lightning and guns, and shy of people she didn't know. But she wasn't afraid of crossing the log, which wasn't very high above the stream anyway. She walked across, picked the primroses, and tucked the stems in her pouch. She let the yellow flowers stick out so that they wouldn't be crushed. On the way back, she decided to tease Ana to make her laugh. She pretended to lose her balance. She waved her arms wildly up and down and wobbled more and more with each step.

"Josefina Montoya!" said Ana, who saw that she was fooling. "How can you be so shy and sweet in company when you're so playful with your sisters? You tease the life out of me. You'll make me old before my time!"

"You sound just like our grandfather," said Josefina as she jumped to the ground.

She pretended to talk like Abuelito. "Yes, yes, yes, my beautiful granddaughters! This was the finest trip I've ever made! Oh, the adventures, the adventures!

But this was my last trip. Oh, how these trips age me! They make me—"

"—old before my time!" all the sisters sang out together. Abuelito said the same thing after every journey.

Abuelito was their mamá's father. He was a trader, and once each year he organized a huge caravan. The caravan was made up of many carts pulled by oxen and many mules carrying packs. The carts and the mules were loaded with wool, hides, and blankets in New Mexico. Then the caravan traveled more than a thousand miles south to Mexico City. The trail the caravans used was called the *Camino Real*.

When Abuelito got to Mexico City, he traded the goods he'd brought from New Mexico for things from all over the world. He traded for silk and cotton goods and lace, for iron tools, paper, ink, books, fine dishes, coffee, and sugar. Then the caravan would load up and start the long trip back to New Mexico.

Abuelito had been gone more than six months. Josefina and her sisters were excited because they expected Abuelito's caravan to return any day now. Their rancho was always the caravan's last stop before the town of Santa Fe, where Abuelito lived.

"I can't wait until Abuelito comes!" said Josefina. She thought that the arrival of the caravan was the most exciting thing that happened on the rancho. The wagons were full of treasures to be traded in Santa Fe. But the most important treasure the caravan brought was Abuelito himself, safe and sound and full of wonderful stories. Sometimes the caravan went through sandstorms that were so bad they blocked out the sun. Sometimes robbers or wild animals attacked the caravan. Sometimes the caravan had to cross flooded rivers or waterless deserts. Abuelito loved to tell about his adventures, and the sisters loved to listen.

"I am going to go on the caravan with Abuelito someday," said Francisca, dreamily swirling a shirt in the stream. "I'll see everything there is to see, and then I'll settle down and live in Mexico City with Mamá's sister, our Tía Dolores. I am sure she lives in a grand house and knows all the most elegant people."

Clara rolled her eyes and scrubbed hard with her soap. "That's ridiculous," she said. "We hardly know Tía Dolores. We haven't seen her for the whole ten years she's been living in Mexico City."

Francisca smiled a superior smile. "I am older than you are, Clara," she said. "I was nearly six when Tía Dolores left. I remember her."

"Well," said Clara tartly. "If *she* remembers *you*, I am sure she won't want you to live with her!"

Francisca made a face and was about to say something sharp when Josefina piped up.

"Ana," said Josefina, trying to keep the peace. "What do you hope Abuelito will bring on the caravan?"

"Shoes for Juan and Antonio," Ana answered. She and her husband, Tomás, had two little boys—Josefina's beloved nephews.

"I hope he brings that plow Papá needs," said Clara. She was always practical.

"How dull!" said Francisca. "*I'm* hoping for some new lace."

"You think too much of how you look," said Clara.

Francisca smirked. "Perhaps you ought—" she began.

But Josefina interrupted again. "Well, I know one thing we *all* hope Abuelito will bring," she said cheerfully. "Chocolate!"

"Lots!" said Francisca and Clara. They spoke at exactly the same moment, which made them laugh at each other.

"You haven't said what you're wishing for," Ana said to Josefina. She was squeezing water out of a petticoat. "Perhaps you're hoping for a surprise."

"Perhaps," said Josefina, smiling.

The truth was, she didn't know how to name what she wished for. What she wanted most was for her sisters to be at peace with one another. She wanted the household to be running smoothly, and Papá to be happy and laughing and making music again. She longed for life to be the way it was when Mamá was alive.

Right after Mamá died, Josefina had felt that the world should end. How could life go on for the rest of them without Mamá? It had seemed wrong, even cruel somehow, that nothing stopped. The sun rose and set. Seasons passed from one to another. There were still chores to be done every day. There were clothes to be washed, weeds to pull, animals to be fed, socks to be mended.

But as time went by, Josefina began to see that the

steady rhythm of life on the rancho was her best comfort. Mamá seemed close by when Josefina and her sisters were together doing the laundry or mending or cooking or cleaning. The sisters tried hard to do the chores the way that Mamá had taught them. Every day, they tried to remember their prayers and their manners and how to do things right. But it was not easy without Mamá's loving guidance.

Josefina looked at the primroses in her pouch and thought of Mamá. Mamá had such faith in them all! She brought out the best in them. Now that she was gone, they struggled. Francisca and Clara squabbled. Ana worried. Josefina often felt lost and unsure. And Papá was very quiet. He had given his violin away, so he never filled the house with music anymore. Josefina sighed. She didn't see how the caravan could bring anything to help them.

"Here comes a surprise," said Clara. "But not one you will like, Josefina."

Josefina looked up. "Oh, no," she said.

It was a small herd of goats. They were coming down the hill to drink from the stream. Josefina disliked all goats and one goat in particular. The biggest, oldest, meanest goat was named Florecita. Florecita was a sneaky, nasty bully. She bit, she rammed, and she'd eat anything. Josefina was afraid of her. She frowned when she spotted Florecita at the edge of the herd.

"Now, Josefina," said Ana when she saw her frowning. "You mustn't dislike *these* goats. This is *our* herd."

Most of the rancho's sheep and goats were still in the summer pastures up in the mountains. But this herd was kept close to the rancho to provide milk to drink and to make into cheese. It was a small herd that had belonged to Mamá. She left the herd to Josefina and her sisters when she died. Josefina wished she hadn't. Mamá had always protected Josefina from things she feared and disliked, and Mamá had protected Josefina from the goats. "The goats are everything you are not, Josefina," Mamá used to say. "They are bold and loud and disagreeable and mean. It's no wonder you dislike them!" Josefina was sure that Mamá never intended her to have anything to do with the goats, so she avoided them as much as possible.

But right now, Josefina saw Florecita headed straight for her.

"She wants the flowers in your pouch!" warned Francisca.

Josefina put one hand over the flowers. She did not want Florecita to have them. They might be the last primroses of the year!

"Shoo!" she said to Florecita feebly, waving her free hand. "Go away!"

"Shoo! Shoo! Shoo!" cried her sisters with more force.

Florecita didn't even slow down. She kept walking steadily toward Josefina. Her yellow eyes were fixed on the primroses in Josefina's pouch.

"Wave a stick at her," suggested Francisca.

"Splash her," suggested Ana.

"Throw a pebble at her," suggested Clara.

But Josefina backed away. She had been poked by Florecita's sharp horns before, and she had no wish to be poked again. She scrambled up and stood on the log over the stream. Still Florecita did not stop coming. Josefina took one backward step, then another, then *SPLASH!* She missed her footing and fell off the log into the stream. It was very shallow, so she landed hard on the bottom.

"Oh, no!" she wailed. She saw that all but one sprig of the primroses had fallen out of her pouch. The flowers were floating on the water. Florecita snatched them up in her mean-looking teeth. She chewed them, looking satisfied. Then the goat turned and sauntered off to rejoin the herd.

"Are you all right?" Ana asked kindly. She helped Josefina to her feet. "You really must not let Florecita bully you like that!"

Josefina wrung out her skirt and smiled. "I tried to stand up to Florecita," she joked, "but I ended up sitting down, didn't I?"

She laughed along with her sisters, but she was annoyed with Florecita. She was even more annoyed with herself for letting Florecita scare her. As she looked at the one sprig of primroses left in her pouch, she thought of another thing she wanted that the caravan could not possibly bring her—the courage to stand up to Florecita!

Abuelito's Surprise

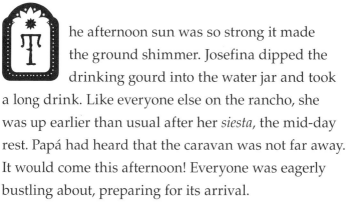

The afternoon sun was so strong it made the ground shimmer. Josefina dipped the drinking gourd into the water jar and took a long drink. Like everyone else on the rancho, she was up earlier than usual after her *siesta*, the mid-day rest. Papá had heard that the caravan was not far away. It would come this afternoon! Everyone was eagerly bustling about, preparing for its arrival.

Josefina poured some water into her cupped hand and held it to her face, cooling first one cheek and then the other. Then she opened her hand and let the water fall on a small cluster of flowers below. Mamá had planted these flowers, which grew in a protected corner of the back courtyard. Josefina's house was built around two square courtyards. The front courtyard was surrounded by rooms where Josefina and her family lived. The back courtyard was surrounded by workrooms, storerooms, and rooms for the servants. The two courtyards were connected by a narrow passageway.

Mamá, with Josefina at her side, had tended her flowers in the back courtyard with great devotion. She started them from seeds sent to her from Mexico City by her sister, Tía Dolores. Josefina remembered how pleased Mamá had always been when the caravan brought her some seeds from Tía Dolores. It had always seemed like a miracle to Josefina that the small brown seeds could, with water and Mamá's care, grow into beautiful, colorful flowers. Since Mamá died, Josefina had cared for the flowers by herself as best she could. Just now she sprinkled the rest of the water in the drinking gourd on them.

"I'm glad you remember to water your mamá's flowers, Josefina." Josefina turned and saw Papá. He was so tall, she had to lift her chin to look at his face. "Things grew well for your mamá, didn't they?" Papá added.

"Yes, Papá," Josefina answered. "Mamá loved her flowers."

"So she did," said Papá, dipping the drinking gourd into the water jar. "And I hear Florecita likes flowers, too."

Josefina blushed.

"Don't worry," said Papá. "You'll stand up to Florecita when you're ready."

Josefina grinned a little bashfully. She watched Papá drink his water. Papá's eyebrows were so thick, he looked fierce until you saw the kindness in his eyes. All the sisters were respectful and rather shy of Papá. He had always been saving of his words, but since Mamá died he'd become especially quiet. Josefina knew his silence didn't come from sternness or anger. It came from sadness. She knew because she often felt the same way.

Mamá used to say that Josefina and Papá were alike. They were both quiet, except with their family, but full of ideas inside! Papá didn't have Mamá's easy manner with people. It had always been Mamá who remembered the names of everyone in the village, from the oldest person to the newest baby. She remembered to ask if an illness was better, or how the chickens were laying. She gave advice on everything from growing squash to dyeing wool. Mamá was well loved and well respected. She was Papá's partner. She ran the household while he ran the rancho. Josefina knew that Papá missed Mamá with all his heart.

Papá tipped the gourd so that the last drops of water fell on the flowers. He smiled at Josefina, and then strode off out the gate toward the fields.

Josefina carried the water jar to the kitchen.

"Oh, there you are, Josefina," said Ana. Her hands were covered with flour, so she had to use the back of her wrist to brush the sweat off her forehead. The heat of the cooking fires was making her face red and her hair stick out. Pots full of delicious-smelling concoctions sizzled, steamed, and burbled over the fires.

There was always a big party with music and dancing, called a *fandango,* in the evening after the caravan arrived. Neighbors from the little town nearby, friends from the Indian *pueblo* village, and all the people traveling with the caravan were invited. They came to Josefina's family's house to eat and drink and sing and dance and celebrate the caravan's safe return. Mamá had always known just what to do to prepare for the fandango. But this was the first time Ana was in charge. Josefina could see that Ana was overwhelmed even though Carmen, the cook, was helping her. Two other servants were making *tortillas* as quickly as they could. Francisca and Clara were helping, too. They were peeling, chopping, and stirring as fast as their hands could move.

"Thank you for the water," said Ana. She handed Josefina a large basket. "Now please go to the kitchen garden and get me some onions."

"I'll come, too," Francisca said. "We need tomatoes."

The kitchen garden was just outside the back court-yard. Josefina always thought the garden looked like a blanket spread on the ground. The neat rows of fruits and vegetables and herbs made colorful stripes. The squash made a yellow stripe. The chiles made a red stripe. The pumpkins were orange, the melons were light green, and the beans were dark green. In between the rows, the earth was a dark reddish-brown, thanks to the water the girls carried up from the stream every day. A stick fence like a blanket's fringe surrounded the garden to keep hungry animals out. The sisters were all proud of the garden.

Josefina had gathered a basketful of onions when

suddenly she stood up. Francisca stood up, too, and the girls looked at each other.

"Is it . . . ?" Francisca began.

"Shhh . . ." said Josefina, holding her finger to her lips. She tilted her head and listened hard. Yes! There it was. She could hear the rumble and squeak of wooden wheels that meant only one thing. The caravan was coming!

Francisca heard, too. The girls smiled at each other, grabbed their baskets, and ran as fast as they could back through the gate. "The caravan! It's coming!" they shouted. "Ana! Clara! It's coming!" They dropped their baskets outside the kitchen door as Clara rushed out to join them.

The three girls dashed across the front courtyard and flew up the steps of the tower in the south wall. The window in the tower was narrow, so Josefina knelt and looked out the lower part. Francisca and Clara stood behind her and looked over her head.

At first, all they saw was a cloud of dust stirring on the road from the village. Then the sound of the wheels grew louder and louder. Soon they heard the jingle of harnesses, dogs barking, people shouting,

and the village church bell ringing. Next they saw
soldiers coming over the hill with the sun glinting on
their buttons and guns. Then came mule after mule. It
looked like a hundred or more to Josefina. The mules
were carrying heavy packs strapped to their backs.
She counted thirty carts pulled by plodding oxen.
The carts lumbered along on their two big wooden
wheels. There were four-wheeled wagons as well. And
so many people! Too many to count! There were cart
drivers, traders, and whole families of travelers. There
were herders driving sheep, goats, and cattle. People
from town and Indians from the nearby pueblo village
walked along with the caravan to welcome it.

Francisca stood on tiptoe to see better. She put
her hands on Josefina's shoulders. "Don't you love to
think about all the places the caravan has been?" she
asked. "And all places the things it brings come
from, too?"

"Yes," said Josefina. "They come from all over the
world, up the Camino Real, right to *our* door!"

Most of the caravan stopped and set up camp midway between the town and the rancho. But many of the
cart drivers camped closer to the house, in a shady area

next to the stream. Josefina saw Papá ride his horse up to one of the big, four-wheeled wagons. He waved to its driver.

"That's Abuelito!" Josefina cried. She pointed to the driver of the four-wheeled wagon. "Look! Papá is greeting him. See? There he is!"

Francisca leaned forward. "Who's that tall woman sitting next to Abuelito?" she wondered aloud. "She's greeting Papá as if she knows him."

But Josefina and Clara had already turned away from the window. They hurried down from the tower. Josefina ran to the kitchen and stuck her head in the door. "Come on," she said to Ana. "Papá and Abuelito are on their way up to the house."

"Oh dear, oh dear," fussed Ana as she wiped her hands and smoothed her hair. "There's still so much to do. I'll never be ready for the fandango."

When Papá led Abuelito's big wagon up to the front gate, Josefina was the first to run out and greet it. Francisca, Clara, and Ana were close behind. Josefina thought she'd never seen a sight as wonderful as Abuelito's happy face. He handed the reins to the woman next to him and climbed down.

"My beautiful granddaughters!" said Abuelito. He kissed them as he named them. "Ana, and Francisca! Clara, and my little Josefina! Oh, God bless you! God bless you! It is good to see you! This was the finest trip I've ever made! Oh, the adventures, the adventures! But I am getting too old for these trips. They make me old before my time. This is my last trip. My last."

"Oh, Abuelito!" said Francisca, taking his arm and laughing. "You say that every time!"

Abuelito threw back his head and laughed, too. "Ah, but this time I mean it," he said. "I've brought a surprise for you." He turned and held out his hand to the tall woman on the wagon. "Here she is, your Tía Dolores. She has come back to live with her mamá and me in Santa Fe. Now I have no reason to go to Mexico City ever again!"

Josefina and her sisters looked so surprised, Papá and Abuelito laughed at them. Tía Dolores took Abuelito's hand and gracefully swung herself down from the wagon seat.

Papá smiled at her. "You see, Dolores? You have surprised my daughters as much as you surprised me," he said. "Welcome to our home."

"Gracias," Tía Dolores answered. She smiled at Papá and then she turned to the sisters. "I've looked forward to this moment for a long time!" she said to them. "I've wanted to see all of you! My dear sister's children!"

She spoke to each one in turn. "You're very like your mamá, Ana," she said. "And Francisca, you've grown so tall and so beautiful! Dear Clara, you were barely three years old when I left. Do you remember?"

Tía Dolores took Josefina's hand in both of her own. She bent forward so that she could look closely at Josefina's face. "At last I meet you, Josefina," she said. "You weren't even born when I left. And look! Here you are! Already a lovely young girl!" Tía Dolores straightened again. Her eyes were bright as she looked at all the sisters. "I'm so happy to see you all. It's good to be back."

The girls were still too surprised to say much, but they smiled shyly at Tía Dolores. Ana was the first to collect herself. "Please, Abuelito and Tía Dolores. Come inside and have a cool drink. I'm sure you're tired and thirsty." She led Tía Dolores inside the gate. "You must excuse us, Tía Dolores," she said. "We haven't prepared any place for you to sleep."

"Goodness, Ana!" said Tía Dolores. "You didn't know I was coming. I didn't know myself, really, until the last minute. I've been caring for my dear aunt in Mexico City all these years. Bless her soul! She died this past spring. It was just before Abuelito's caravan arrived. I had no reason to stay. So, I joined the caravan to come home."

"Yes," Abuelito said to the girls. "Your grandmother will be so pleased! Wait till Dolores and I get to Santa Fe the day after tomorrow! What a surprise, eh?"

Josefina could not take her eyes off Tía Dolores as everyone sat down together in the family *sala*. The room's thick walls and small windows kept it cool even in the heat of the afternoon.

Francisca whispered, "Isn't Tía Dolores's dress beautiful? Her sleeves must be the latest style from Europe."

But Josefina hadn't noticed Tía Dolores's sleeves, or anything else about her clothes. *This is Tía Dolores,* she kept thinking. *This is Mamá's sister.*

Josefina studied Tía Dolores to see if she looked like Mamá. Mamá had been the older of the two sisters, but Tía Dolores was much taller. She didn't have Mamá's soft, rounded beauty, Josefina decided, nor her pale skin or dark, smooth hair. Everything about Tía Dolores was sharper somehow. Her hands were bigger. Her face was more narrow. She had gray eyes and dark red hair that was springy. Her voice didn't sound like Mamá's, either. Mamá's voice was high and breathy, like notes from a flute. Tía Dolores's voice had a graceful sound. It was as low and clear as notes from a harp string. But when Tía Dolores laughed, Josefina was startled. Her laugh sounded so much like Mamá's! If Josefina closed her eyes, it might be Mamá laughing.

There was a great deal of laughter in the family sala that afternoon as Abuelito told the story of his trip. Josefina sat next to Abuelito, her arms wrapped around her knees. She was happy. It reminded her of the old days to sit with her family this way and listen to Abuelito tell about his adventures.

"This was the most remarkable trip I've ever had," said Abuelito. "Oh, the trip to Mexico City was dull enough. But on the way home! Bless my soul! What an adventure! We were in terrible danger. Terrible! Terrible! And your Tía Dolores saved us."

"Oh, but I didn't—" Tía Dolores began.

"No, no, no, my dear daughter! You *did* save us,"

said Abuelito. He turned to Papá and the girls. "You see," he said, "I was so glad that Dolores was going to come home with me. I finished all my business in Mexico City as quickly as I could. All went well until the day I came to Dolores's house to load up her belongings. Then the trouble began." He lowered his voice, pretending he did not want Tía Dolores to hear. "I had forgotten how stubborn your Tía Dolores is. She is perhaps the most stubborn woman in the world. What did she insist that we bring? You'll never guess! Her piano!"

Amazed, the girls all repeated, "Her *piano*?"

"Yes!" said Abuelito. He was pleased to have astonished them all. "Such fuss and trouble! I told her it was too heavy and too big! But she said she'd sooner leave all her other belongings than her piano. So I grumbled, but I allowed the piano to be packed and loaded onto one of my wagons. We left Mexico City, and I complained about the piano every mile of the way." He shook his head. "Your Tía Dolores never said a word. She just let me go on and on, complaining. Well, then we came to Dead Man's Canyon. And do you know what happened?"

"What?" asked the girls.

"Thieves!" cried Abuelito in a voice so loud the girls jumped. "Thieves attacked the caravan! Oh, you've never seen such a fight! Shouting, swordfights, gunshots! The wagon with the piano was just behind ours. We saw two thieves climb up on it and push the driver onto the ground. Then six or seven of our men rushed over and wrestled with the two thieves, trying to pull them off the wagon. With all the yelling and fighting, the oxen harnessed to that wagon were scared. They bumbled into each other trying to get away. The wagon lurched forward, right to the edge of a deep gully. And then *crash*! Over it fell! Into the gully!"

The girls gasped.

Abuelito put his hand on his heart. "God bless us and save us all! What a sound that piano made when it fell!" he said. "A thud, and then a hollow *BOOM* that rumbled like musical thunder! It sounded like a giant had strummed all the keys in one stroke. The terrible sound bounced off the walls of Dead Man's Canyon. It seemed to grow louder with every echo. The thieves were terrified! They'd never heard such a sound in all their lives. Well! Didn't they take off as if they were on fire? All of them ran away as fast as their thieving legs could carry them! I'll bet they are still running!"

Everyone laughed. Abuelito laughed most of all, remembering with pleasure how frightened the thieves were. When he stopped laughing he said, "After that, I put the piano in my own wagon. I never complained again. And so you see! Dolores did save us all, by insisting that we bring her piano."

"Well done, Dolores!" said Papá.

"But Abuelito," said Josefina. "Was the piano badly hurt?"

Tía Dolores answered. "No, child," she said. "One leg is splintered, and the top is scratched. But I think it will sound fine."

"Oh," Josefina blurted, "may we see it?"

"No, no, no," said Abuelito. "We had to rebuild the crate. It's too much trouble to open it up. You'll just have to come to Santa Fe sometime to hear your aunt play."

Papá cleared his throat. "The girls and I have never seen or heard a piano," he said. "May I open the crate? I'll close it up afterward."

Tía Dolores turned to Abuelito. "Please," she said. "I'd like the girls to hear the piano."

Abuelito laughed and shrugged. "Of course, my dear, of course!" he said. "How can I say no to you after you saved my caravan?"

Tía Dolores kissed him. Then she and Papá led the girls outside to the wagon. The piano was in a big wooden crate. Papá pried a few boards off the crate. Tía Dolores climbed into the wagon. She reached into the crate and pushed back the lid that protected the piano's keys. She couldn't stand up straight, and she didn't have much room to move her hands, but she played a chord. And then, as Papá and the four girls listened, she played a spirited tune.

Josefina felt the music thrum through her whole body. It made her shiver with delight. The notes were muffled because the piano was in the wooden crate, but to Josefina, the notes sounded as beautiful as bells all chiming together in harmony. She had never heard music like the piano's music before. The notes were so full, so perfect and delicate, that Josefina imagined she could almost see them as they filled the air.

Josefina listened. She realized that, through the

music, Tía Dolores was telling them how happy she
was. The music expressed her happiness better than
words ever could, because it made all of them hearing it happy, too. Josefina stood still, barely breathing,
listening hard until Tía Dolores stopped.

"Oh, dear," said Tía Dolores. "I'm afraid the piano's
a little out of tune and I'm a little out of practice."
Gently, she closed the lid over the keys.

Josefina wanted very much to touch the piano keys.
She wanted to make the wonderful music happen herself. But she was too shy to ask Tía Dolores, so she said
nothing.

"Gracias, Dolores," said Papá as he helped her climb
down from the wagon.

"Oh, yes, gracias," said Ana, Francisca, and Clara.

"You must all come to see me in Santa Fe," said Tía
Dolores, smiling. "I'll play for you, and show you how
to play the piano yourselves."

The three oldest sisters followed Tía Dolores back
inside the house. But Josefina stood next to the wagon
until Papá had finished closing the crate. She wanted
to stay near the piano as long as she could. She knew
she would never forget the way Tía Dolores's music

had sounded, or the way it had made her feel.

When Papá was finished, he saw Josefina. "You liked the piano music, didn't you?" he asked.

"Oh, yes, Papá," answered Josefina. "I didn't want Tía Dolores to stop."

Papá smiled. "I didn't either," he said. "It made me miss playing my violin. Well, there will be plenty of fiddle music at the fandango tonight. You'd better go in now and get ready. The guests will be coming soon."

"Yes, Papá," Josefina answered. She took one last look at the piano crate, then started back inside. As she walked, she thought, *I wish there were some way I could let Tía Dolores know how much I loved the piano music. I wish I could give her something in return. But what?*

Later, when Josefina walked into the back court-yard, she knew the answer to her question. She thought of a fine gift to give Tía Dolores. *I'll give it to her during the fandango tonight*, she decided. She was pleased with her idea. She thought Tía Dolores would be pleased, too.

A Gift for Tía Dolores

tand still, Josefina," said Francisca. She was slowly and carefully brushing Josefina's hair with a brush made of stiff grasses. Abuelito had brought all four sisters beautiful blue silk hair ribbons. Francisca had put herself in charge of tying them for Josefina and Clara. Josefina fidgeted. She was grateful to Francisca, but she wished she'd *hurry up*. Josefina wanted to be ready for the fandango early, so that she could prepare her gift for Tía Dolores.

Clara tied her sash neatly, then undid it and tied it all over again. Francisca had already brushed Clara's hair and put the blue hair ribbon in it. "Do you think I look all right?" Clara asked.

Josefina and Francisca were surprised. It wasn't like Clara to worry about her appearance. Josefina was afraid Francisca might say something unkind. She was glad when Francisca looked at Clara for a moment and then said seriously, "You look very pretty. The blue suits you."

Clara beamed. She reached up to touch her hair ribbon.

It made Josefina happy to see her sisters getting along. *It's because Tía Dolores is here,* she thought. Francisca and Clara were in complete agreement about Tía Dolores. They both admired her very much. Josefina smiled to herself. Francisca and Clara would be pleased when *they* saw her gift for Tía Dolores, too.

"Finished!" said Francisca. She gave Josefina's ribbon one last adjustment. "You look fine. Use your wings and fly away now, Josefina. I can tell you're anxious to go."

"Gracias, Francisca," Josefina called back over her shoulder as she hurried from the room.

The sun had set. Cool evening air slid down from the mountains, bringing darkness with it. Small bonfires were lit in the front courtyard for light and for warmth. As she crossed the courtyard, Josefina could hear Ana and Carmen thanking some neighbor women who had come early with dishes of food for the fandango. No one noticed Josefina slip into the kitchen. She took a small water jar and slipped out again.

In the back courtyard, Josefina knelt in front of Mamá's flowers. One by one, she picked all the freshest and brightest-colored flowers. She put them in the water jar. Josefina was careful to break the flowers off near the ground so that the stems were long, but she didn't disturb the roots. There were not very many flowers, so Josefina had to pick almost all of them in order to have a bouquet anywhere near big enough and beautiful enough to give to Tía Dolores.

The corner looked bare when she was through. *It's all right,* she told herself. *Mamá would approve. After all, Tía Dolores was the one who sent Mamá the seeds, so Tía Dolores should be the one to enjoy the flowers. They* **should** *be a gift for her.*

Josefina straightened the flowers in the water jar. The bouquet looked scrawny somehow. So Josefina slipped the blue ribbon out of her hair and tied it around the flowers in a big bow. *There!* she thought with satisfaction. *That looks much better.* She wanted the bouquet to be a surprise for everyone, so she looked around for a place to hide it. She had just entered the narrow passageway between the front and back court-yards when she bumped into Papá.

"What's this you've got here?" asked Papá, peering at Josefina over the tops of the flowers.

"It's . . . they're a gift for Tía Dolores," explained Josefina. "I wanted to give her something to thank her for the music."

It was too dark to see Papá's face clearly, but Josefina could tell by his voice that he was smiling. "I think that is a very fine idea," he said. "I'll tell you what. I am going to make a formal introduction of Tía Dolores to all our friends and neighbors at the fandango tonight. After I do, perhaps you will give Tía Dolores the bouquet."

"Yes, I will!" said Josefina happily.

"Very well," said Papá. "It will be our secret until then."

"Gracias, Papá," said Josefina. After Papá left, Josefina put the jar of flowers under the bench in the passageway. No one would see it there, and she would be able to fetch it quickly when it was time to give it to Tía Dolores.

More guests arrived every moment. They called
out a chorus of greetings to each other as they
crossed the front courtyard to the *gran sala*, the
family's finest room. Because this was a very special
night, the gran sala was lit with candles. Their wavering light made the guests' shadows swoop and dance
on the walls.

Soon the musicians struck up a lively tune on
their fiddles and the real dancing began. It seemed to
Josefina that the dancers flew around the room with
as much ease as their shadows had. Their feet hardly
seemed to touch the floor at all as they whirled by in
a blur of bright colors.

No one whirled faster than Francisca. No one
looked happier or more beautiful. In the candlelight,
her dark curly hair seemed to shine like a black stone
in the stream. And Josefina was glad to see that Ana
had put her responsibilities aside for a while and was
dancing with her husband, Tomás. All around the
sides of the gran sala, older ladies sat holding babies
on their laps so that the babies' young mothers could

dance. The old ladies clapped the babies' hands in time to the music.

Josefina and Clara were still too young to be allowed to dance, so they stood outside in the courtyard and leaned on the windowsill, looking in at the dancers. Josefina's feet danced along to the music. It was impossible to be still! The music seemed to twist and turn in the air, wind its way around all the dancers, and find its way outside to tickle Josefina's feet so that they just had to move.

Every once in a while, over the music and conversation, Josefina and Clara could hear Abuelito's voice. He'd be saying, "*BOOM!* What a sound! Those thieves ran off and I'll bet they're running still." Clara and Josefina grinned at each other. Abuelito was telling the story about Tía Dolores's piano over and over again. The girls noticed that the number of thieves grew larger every time Abuelito told the story!

The person both girls liked best to watch was Tía Dolores. She was easy to pick out of the crowd because she was so tall, and because no one else had hair of quite such a rich, dark red.

"She dances well, doesn't she?" said Clara as

Tía Dolores swept by.

"Yes," said Josefina. "She's as graceful as . . . as the music."

Soon Papá came by the window and nodded to Josefina. Josefina nodded back.

"What's that all about?" asked Clara.

"It's a surprise," said Josefina, excited and smiling. "Stay here and you'll see."

She scurried across the courtyard to the passage-way where she'd left the bouquet. It was very dark. Josefina bent down and felt under the bench for the water jar with the bouquet in it. It wasn't there. *That's odd*, she thought.

Josefina stood up, perplexed. And then she saw the jar. It was lying on its side near one wall. It was empty. *Where is the bouquet?* Josefina wondered anxiously.

She looked all around the passageway. The bouquet was nowhere to be seen, but an odd white shape looming in the back courtyard caught her eye. She walked toward it and gasped. Oh, no! The white shape was Florecita! The goat must have broken out of her pen and found her way into the back courtyard.

Josefina did *not* want to put Florecita back in her pen.

When she turned away to get help, she stepped on something. She stooped down and picked it up. At first she didn't know what it was. And then she saw. It was a few green stems held together by a trampled, mud-stained blue ribbon. Suddenly, Josefina realized what had happened. *Florecita had eaten the bouquet!* This was all that was left of the flowers Josefina had picked for Tía Dolores.

But that was not the worst of it. At that instant, Josefina saw what Florecita was doing. Calm as could be, Florecita was standing smack in the middle of what used to be Mamá's flowers. She was chewing a mouthful of stems. One hollyhock, root and all, dangled from her mouth. Josefina could see that no other flowers were left. All that remained were some scraggly, chewed, crushed, and broken stems and a scattering of leaves and petals on the ground.

Florecita turned her nasty yellow eyes on Josefina. The goat looked very satisfied with herself.

Josefina was furious. "Florecita!" she hissed in a ferocious whisper. "You awful, awful animal! You've ruined *everything.*"

Josefina was so angry she forgot to be afraid of Florecita. She marched right up to the goat and yanked the hollyhock out of her mouth. Florecita looked surprised. She looked even more surprised when Josefina swatted her on the back with the stems, saying, "How could you? You ate the bouquet and you killed Mamá's flowers. Oh, I *hate* you, Florecita!"

Josefina shoved Florecita hard. Then she took hold of one of Florecita's fearsome horns and pulled with all her strength. "Come with me," she said. Josefina dragged Florecita to her pen. She slammed the gate shut. "I hate you, Florecita," she said again. "I'll hate you forever!"

Josefina ran all the way back to the bench in the passageway and slumped down on it. There was nothing to be done. She looked at the dirty blue ribbon and the chewed stems wilting in her hand and fought back tears of disappointment.

"Josefina?" a voice said. "What are you doing here in the darkness?"

Josefina looked up. She saw Tía Dolores coming toward her. Josefina could hardly talk. She showed the sad-looking stems to Tía Dolores. "This was a bouquet for you," she said in a shaky voice. "But our goat Florecita found it and ate it. And she killed Mamá's flowers, too."

"Ah," said Tía Dolores. She sat next to Josefina on the bench.

Slowly, Josefina explained. "I wanted to give you a gift to thank you for the piano music," she said. "So I picked all the best flowers. I tied my new hair ribbon around them. The flowers were so pretty. They grew from the seeds you sent Mamá. I've been watering them since Mamá died, because I know she loved them. Now there are none left. There will never be any more. The flowers are dead."

Tía Dolores was a good listener. She sat still and gave Josefina her full attention. Neither one of them noticed the noise and laughter coming from the gran sala. The fandango seemed far away. When Josefina was finished explaining, Tía Dolores said, "Show me your mamá's flowers."

Josefina led Tía Dolores to the corner of the back courtyard. "You see," she said. "There is nothing left."

Tía Dolores knelt down. She looked at what was left of the flowers. She scooped up a handful of soil and rubbed it between her fingers. Gently, she touched the short, bitten-off stems.

Then she smiled at Josefina. "Don't worry," she said. "Your mamá planted these flowers well. The roots are deep and strong. You've kept them healthy by watering the soil. They'll live, I promise." She stood and brushed the soil off her hands. "Do you like caring for flowers?" she asked.

Josefina nodded. "I used to help Mamá," she said.

"I brought some seeds with me when I left Mexico City," said Tía Dolores. "Perhaps you and I can plant them tomorrow."

"Oh, could we?" said Josefina.

"Yes," said Tía Dolores. "We'll wash your hair ribbon, too. Now we had better go back to the gran sala."

Papá met them at the door. "Josefina," he said. "Where have you been? I introduced Tía Dolores, but then I couldn't find you."

"Oh, Papá," said Josefina. "Florecita ate the bouquet! And then she almost ruined all the rest of Mamá's flowers."

"Ah, that's too bad," said Papá sadly. He looked

around the courtyard. "Is Florecita loose?"

"No," said Josefina. "I dragged her back to her pen and shut the gate."

"You did?" asked Papá. "But I thought you were afraid of Florecita."

"I am," said Josefina. "I mean, I was. I guess just now I was so angry at Florecita I forgot!"

Papá laughed. "Well, we never know where our courage is going to come from!" he said. "I am sorry about the flowers, though."

"Tía Dolores says the flowers will be all right," said Josefina. "She's going to help me plant new seeds tomorrow."

"Is she?" said Papá. He turned and smiled at Tía Dolores. "Well, then, Dolores," he said, "that means you'll have to come back often. You'll have to visit us to see how the flowers are coming along."

"I will," said Tía Dolores. "God willing."

"Come inside and have something to eat now," said Papá. "Ana would never forgive us if we didn't enjoy the food she's prepared."

Josefina followed Papá and Tía Dolores into the gran sala. She grinned to herself. *I guess the caravan didn't need to bring me the courage to stand up to Florecita after all,* she thought. *It turns out I already had it. But I might never have found out if I hadn't picked a bouquet for Tía Dolores.*

An idea danced through Josefina's head just then. As quick as the flicker of starlight on water, the idea appeared and disappeared. But it was an idea that would come again and again all the rest of the night and through the next day, until it grew from an idea into a heartfelt hope.

Josefina's Idea

ever had Josefina been more eager to begin a day. The next morning she was up even earlier than usual. Quietly, so that she wouldn't waken Francisca or Clara, Josefina rolled up the sheepskins and blankets that were her bed. She dressed and slipped outside. The moon hung low in the sky. It cast such a strong, pure light that everything was bathed in silver or shadow.

Josefina went to the kitchen. Early as it was, Carmen was already there grinding corn for the morning meal. Her husband, Miguel, was starting the kitchen fire. Carmen nodded good morning to Josefina and handed her a water jar to fill at the stream, just as she did every morning. But this morning was different for Josefina. This was the morning of the day Tía Dolores was going to spend with her and her sisters.

The huge front gate was closed, so Josefina stepped through the small door cut into the gate. She closed the door behind her and ran across the moon-washed ground to Abuelito's wagon. Standing on tiptoe, she looked in. There was the big crate with Tía Dolores's piano inside. Josefina poked her finger through a crack in the crate and touched the polished wood of the piano. She smiled when she remembered the pleasure its music had given her. Then she skipped down to the stream, thinking of the melody Tía Dolores had played.

The tune stayed in her head as she did her early-morning chores. She gathered eggs singing it. She swept the courtyards dancing to it. She piled wood next to the fireplaces in time to its rhythm. When the village church bell rang its call to prayers at seven o'clock, it seemed to ring along with the tune. And when the family said morning prayers together in front of the small altar in the family sala, dedicating their day's work to God, their voices seemed to rise and fall just as the piano notes had.

The music seemed to be everywhere Josefina went. Tía Dolores did, too! Tía Dolores was interested in everything. At breakfast she said, "I want to see as much of the rancho as I can today."

So after breakfast Josefina led Tía Dolores through the orchard, past the cornfields, and to the stream. They filled water jars and carried them up to water the kitchen garden. Then they picked some fat pumpkins for Tía Dolores to take home with her to Santa Fe the next day. "I am sure my mother has no pumpkins as big as these in her garden!" said Tía Dolores.

Wherever she went, Tía Dolores found something to praise. Josefina led Tía Dolores to the weaving room. There Clara showed her the sheep's wool she had carded, spun, and dyed. Tía Dolores admired the colors. "There are no colors finer than these in all of Mexico," she said.

Tía Dolores was a good teacher. She showed Clara a faster way to knit the heel on a sock. She showed Francisca how to sew a patch over a hole so that it hardly showed at all.

Josefina was in the back courtyard clearing away the dead stems Florecita had trampled when Tía Dolores joined her.

"I've brought you some seeds to plant," she said

to Josefina as she handed her a small package.

"Gracias!" said Josefina.

"I'll help you for a while. Then I promised Ana I would make bread with her," said Tía Dolores. She began to dig holes in the soil for the seeds. "Ana has lots of responsibilities, doesn't she?"

"Yes," agreed Josefina. "It's hard for Ana. Mamá ran the household so smoothly. But Ana doesn't always know what to do, and Mamá is not here to teach her."

"Ana is young," said Tía Dolores as she covered some seeds with soil. "It's a good thing she has you and Francisca and Clara to help her."

Josefina nodded slowly. "We try," she said. "But sometimes . . ." She stopped.

Tía Dolores gave her a questioning look.

Josefina sighed. She dug a little hole in the soil. "You see," she said, "Francisca and Clara fight a lot. They are so different! Clara is careful and practical, and Francisca is so quick and fiery. When Mamá was alive, she put a stop to their arguments before they began. But now . . . Well, Ana tries, but she is too soft-hearted and they won't mind her. I try to joke them out of fighting. Sometimes it works. But sometimes it doesn't."

"'Blessed are the peacemakers,'" said Tía Dolores softly, "'for they will be called the children of God.'" She smiled at Josefina. "You know," she said, "it's perfectly natural for sisters to disagree. You should have heard your mamá and me sometimes! She was quite a few years older than I was. I am sure she thought I was a miserable pest. I wanted to be like her. Once I wore her best sash without her permission, and I lost it. Your mamá was very angry. She wouldn't speak to me for days. But she finally forgave me."

Josefina realized suddenly, *Tía Dolores misses her sister. She misses Mamá, too, just as much as we do.* She said, "I wish you could be here to protect these flowers from Florecita when they bloom."

"I'd love to see the flowers," said Tía Dolores. "But *you* can protect them from Florecita. You aren't afraid of her anymore. You don't need me. You will make your mamá's flowers bloom again and keep them safe, Josefina. I know you will."

"Oh, Tía Dolores! It's beautiful!" said Ana. She draped a silk rebozo over her shoulders. Its colors were as bright as flowers. "Gracias!"

It was early afternoon, just after the mid-day meal. Ana, Francisca, Clara, and Josefina were gathered in the family sala. Tía Dolores had called them together. She had presents for them all.

"Francisca," said Tía Dolores. "This is a sewing diary I made for you." She gave Francisca a little hand-made book. "There are sketches of dresses in it, and samples of material, and notes about how to make the dresses."

"Gracias!" said Francisca. Eagerly, she looked at the sewing diary. "The dresses are so elegant, Tía Dolores!" she said. "I wish you could be here to help us make them." She looked up and joked, "I'm afraid I will sew a sleeve on upside down!"

"The notes and directions will help you," said Tía Dolores.

Francisca looked doubtful. "But I can't read," she said. "None of us can."

"Oh!" said Tía Dolores. "Well, then! Just use your good sense. I am sure if you and your sisters help each other, you will do very well."

For Clara, Tía Dolores had brought a fine pair of

scissors and some sewing needles. Clara was very pleased, because her gift was beautiful *and* useful.

"And this is for you, Josefina," said Tía Dolores. She handed Josefina a necklace. A small, dark red stone surrounded by gold hung from a delicate chain.

Josefina smiled. The necklace was lovely. "Gracias, Tía Dolores," she said. Her hands were shaky with excitement as she put the necklace on.

"My!" said Francisca. "Isn't that necklace quite grown-up?"

"Yes, indeed it is," said Tía Dolores firmly. "And isn't Josefina quite grown-up, too?"

Francisca said no more.

"Tía Dolores," said Ana. "How did you know what would be the perfect gift for each one of us?"

Tía Dolores smiled. "All the years I lived in Mexico City, I looked forward to the caravans coming," she said. "I knew Abuelito would bring stories about all of you and your life here on the rancho. Sometimes he would bring a letter dictated by your mamá. I felt as if I were watching you grow up even though I was far away. When I decided to come home, I enjoyed think-ing about what present to bring each of you."

"Well," said Ana. "I'm sorry we didn't know that you were coming. We have nothing to give you in return for your gifts."

"Oh," laughed Tía Dolores. "This day with you is all the gift I want."

When the afternoon had cooled into early evening, Tía Dolores and Abuelito walked to the village. They wanted to say a prayer at Mamá's grave. They were also going to visit Papá's oldest sister, who lived in the village.

Josefina and her sisters sat in a corner of the front courtyard that was still warm from the heat of the day's sun. Every now and then they could hear Ana's little boys laughing with Carmen in the kitchen nearby. The sisters were peeling back the husks from roasted ears of corn. They were going to braid the husks together to make a long string of ears so that the corn could be hung out to dry.

Josefina said, "Hasn't it been nice today, having Tía Dolores here?"

"Yes!" said Ana. "She was such a help to me! And she was so kind to my little boys."

"Tía Dolores is a very sensible, hardworking

person," said Clara. That was her highest praise.

"Oh, Clara!" protested Francisca. "You make her sound as dull as these ears of corn! I found her to be elegant and graceful."

Josefina decided the time had come to tell her sisters her idea. She picked up an ear of corn and peeled the husk slowly. "What if," she said quietly, "we asked Tía Dolores to stay?"

No one said anything. They were all too surprised.

Josefina went on. "She could help us and teach us, the way she did today."

"She wouldn't stay," said Francisca. "She's used to life in Mexico City, where there are lots of grand people and grand houses. She doesn't want to live on a rancho."

"But she said she always loved to hear about the rancho when Abuelito came to visit her, remember?" said Josefina. "And she doesn't act fancy or put on airs. She likes it here. She was interested in everything."

"Yes," said Ana. "But I think perhaps she has come home hoping to get married and start a family of her own. She's not too old for that, you know."

"She wouldn't have to stay here forever," said Josefina. "Just for a few months. And anyway, she is our aunt. We *are* her family."

Clara picked up several ears of corn and put them in her lap. "Well," she said in her flat, no-nonsense manner. "Even if Tía Dolores would be willing to stay, it wouldn't be proper for us to ask her. Papá would have to approve of the idea. He would have to be the one to ask her to stay."

Josefina's heart sank. She hadn't thought of that. She knew Clara was right.

"Who wants to be the one to present the idea to Papá?" Clara asked. "I certainly don't." She turned to Josefina. "It's your idea," she said. "Do you want to talk to Papá about it?"

Josefina looked down at the ear of corn in her hands. "No," she said in a small voice.

"Will you go to him, Ana?" Clara asked. "You are the oldest."

"Oh, I couldn't!" said Ana. "Papá might think I was complaining. If I say that I need Tía Dolores's help, he might think I don't want to do what it is my responsibility to do."

"Oh!" exclaimed Francisca. She stood up and brushed off her skirt. "*I'm* not afraid to talk to Papá.

I'll just march right up to him and say, 'Papá! You must ask Tía Dolores to stay!'"

Ana, Clara, and Josefina looked at each other. They knew that was not at all the right way to speak to Papá! It wasn't that Papá was stern or cold. But he was the *patrón*, the head of the rancho and the head of their family. The girls had never presented such an important idea to him before. It would have to be done politely and with respect.

"Wait, Francisca!" said Josefina. She stood up, too. "I think all of us should speak to Papá. We should go together. That way Papá will see that all four of us would like Tía Dolores to stay."

Ana and Clara didn't move.

"Come on," said Josefina. She grinned. "Don't worry. I'll do the talking if you don't want to. Last night I had the courage to stand up to Florecita. Papá is much, much kinder than *she* is!"

The sisters found Papá near the animal pens. He was tightening the latch on the gate.

He smiled when he saw Josefina. "The latch is stronger now," he said. "We shouldn't have any more goats in Mamá's flowers."

"That's good!" said Josefina. She swallowed. Francisca gave her a little shove forward. "Papá," Josefina said. "May we ask you something?"

Papá looked at the four girls. "Yes?" he said.

"Do you think," Josefina said carefully, "that you could ask Tía Dolores to stay here with us for a while?"

"Ask her to stay?" repeated Papá.

"Yes," said Josefina. "Not forever, just for a while. She could help us. And she could teach us, the way . . . the way Mamá did. Please, would you ask her?"

Josefina saw a look of sadness cross Papá's face. He turned away. "I'll consider it," he said.

"But Papá," Francisca blurted. "You must—"

Josefina tugged on Francisca's sleeve and frowned at her to make her stop talking.

"Gracias, Papá," said Josefina. She hesitated, and then she added, "We need Tía Dolores."

Then she and her sisters left.

"What do you think Papá will do?" Francisca whispered. She and Clara and Josefina were in their sleeping sala, getting ready for bed. "Do you think he will speak to Tía Dolores?"

"I don't know," said Josefina. "I hope so."

"And if he does ask her, what do you think she will say?" Francisca wondered aloud.

Josefina sighed. "I don't know," she said again.

"I think you're silly to wonder about it," Clara said. "We'll find out tomorrow. Abuelito and the caravan will leave first thing in the morning. Tía Dolores will either leave with him or not. We'll just have to wait and see."

"Oh! I hate waiting!" said Francisca.

The three sisters smiled at each other. They all hated to wait! On that they certainly agreed!

The next morning, they were up early. Even Francisca, who was usually slow getting dressed, was ready and waiting with Ana, Clara, and Josefina next to Abuelito's wagon. They watched the servants load Abuelito's small trunk onto the wagon.

Then, with sinking hearts, the sisters saw Tía Dolores's trunk loaded onto the wagon as well.

"Papá didn't ask her!" Francisca groaned.

"Or maybe he did, and she said no," said Ana.

"She doesn't want to stay," Clara added.

Josefina was so disappointed she couldn't talk. A lump rose in her throat when she heard Papá and Tía Dolores and Abuelito coming. Suddenly, Josefina didn't want to stand there by the wagon one second longer. She couldn't bear to kiss Tía Dolores and Abuelito good-bye.

Without a murmur, she slipped away, back inside the house. She went to the gran sala because it was the only room that was sure to be empty. As she walked into the cool darkness of the gran sala, she remembered how it had looked the night of the fandango, full of life and music. Now there was nothing but shadows.

Just then, in a corner of the room, Josefina saw a large, dark shape. She caught her breath when she saw what it was.

It was Tía Dolores's piano. Instantly, Josefina knew what that meant. Tía Dolores would never have left her piano, unless . . .

Josefina flew across the courtyard and out the front gate so fast it seemed as if she had wings on her feet. Tía Dolores caught her in her arms.

"There you are, Josefina!" Tía Dolores said. "I wanted to say good-bye to you."

Josefina pulled back and looked at Tía Dolores's face. "I'm going to Santa Fe," Tía Dolores said. "I'm going to see my dear mamá, whom I have not seen for ten years. But then I'll come back."

"When?" asked Josefina.

Tía Dolores laughed. "Soon," she said. "And when I come back, I'll stay as long as you need me."

Josefina hugged Tía Dolores hard. Then Tía Dolores swung herself up onto the wagon.

"Well, well, well," said Abuelito. He pretended to be cross. "Now it seems that if I want to see Dolores, I'm going to have to come here and see all of you girls, too. What a bother! What a bother!" He sighed. "At least I don't have to carry that piano with me today. Though if we meet up with any thieves, I'll just have to frighten them off with my singing, I suppose!"

Then he kissed Josefina and her sisters good-bye and gave them his blessing.

"*Adiós*, Abuelito!" called all the girls as the wagon pulled away. "Adiós, Tía Dolores."

"Come back soon!" Josefina sang out as she waved good-bye.

As soon as the wagon was out of sight, Josefina

hurried back inside. She went to the kitchen to get a jar. She wanted to fill the jar with water to sprinkle on Mamá's flowers.

Tía Dolores will be back soon, she thought. *I want the flowers to be beautiful when she returns!*

Josefina set off for the stream, whistling Tía Dolores's tune.

Light and Shadow

he month that Tía Dolores was away felt very long to Josefina. She missed her aunt every minute that she was gone. But Tía Dolores had kept her promise, and after visiting her parents in Santa Fe, she returned to the rancho with her servant Teresita in time to help with the harvest. Tía Dolores had been back for two weeks now, and Josefina was glad.

"María Josefina Montoya!" Tía Dolores said happily. It was a rainy night in October, and Josefina and her sisters were sewing in front of the fire in the family sala. "How beautiful you look!"

Josefina blushed and smiled at her aunt. "Gracias," she said. She smoothed the long skirt of her new dress with both hands. The cotton material felt soft and light. Josefina rose up on her toes and spun, just for the sheer pleasure of it. She was very proud of her dress, which she had just finished hemming. She had never had a dress made in this elegant new high-waisted style before. Tía Dolores had given Josefina and each of her sisters some material. Josefina's material was a pretty yellow, with narrow stripes and tiny berries on it. She had cut her material carefully, the way Mamá had taught her. Then, stitch by tiny stitch, she had sewn her dress together all by herself. Now, as she spun around, the hearth fire cast a pattern of light and shadow swooping across the dress like a flock of fluttering birds.

Josefina stopped spinning and sighed with peaceful contentment. She was grateful for the fire's warmth as well as its cheerful brightness. A steady, heavy rain was falling outside, but inside it was cozy. The thick, white-washed *adobe* walls kept out the cold and took on a rosy glow from the firelight.

Tía Dolores sat next to Clara. "Don't use such a long thread in your needle," she advised Clara gently. "It might tangle."

Josefina grinned. "Remember, Clara?" she said. "Mamá used to say, 'If you make your thread too long, the devil will catch on to the end of it!'"

All the sisters smiled and nodded, and Tía Dolores said, "I remember your mamá saying that to me when we were young girls learning to sew!"

Tía Dolores was smiling. But Josefina saw that her eyes were sad, and she knew that Tía Dolores was missing Mamá.

Josefina and her sisters thought of Mamá every day, with longing and love. Every day, the girls tried to do their chores the way Mamá had taught them to. They tried to be as respectful, hardworking, and obedient as she would have wished them to be. Every day, they recalled her wise and funny sayings and songs. And every day, they remembered her in their prayers.

As Clara shortened her thread, she looked at Josefina's dress. "You'll get a lot of good wear out of that dress," she said, sounding sensible as usual. "It was a good idea to make it too long. That way you can grow into it."

"Oh, dear!" said Josefina, looking at her hem. "Is my dress too long?"

"Not at all. It's perfect," said Ana in her tender-hearted way. "You've done a fine job, Josefina. And you are the first one of us to finish." Ana had not even begun her dress yet. She had decided to make vests for her two little boys first.

Francisca sighed a huge sigh. "I'm far from finishing my dress," she said. "I've still so much to do."

"You shouldn't have chosen such a fancy dress pattern," said Clara, pricking her material with the sharp needle. The sewing diary that Tía Dolores had given Francisca showed all the latest styles from Mexico City, and the girls had each chosen a dress pattern to follow. Clara was making a dress that was plain and simple. She prided herself on being practical and often felt called upon to point it out when someone else wasn't. That someone was usually Francisca.

Francisca had chosen an elaborate pattern from the sewing diary. She'd begun enthusiastically. She cut into the material boldly, talking all the while about how splendid her dress would be. But the long, slow work of sewing the pieces together bored Francisca. She complained with every stitch. "I'll never finish my dress," she said now, "unless someone helps me with this endless stitching." She glanced sideways at Tía Dolores.

Josefina saw the sideways look. She knew that

Francisca wanted Tía Dolores to sew for her. But Tía Dolores calmly continued her own sewing. She said nothing, even when Francisca sighed loudly again. Josefina was not surprised. In the last two weeks, she had learned that Tía Dolores was always willing to give help and advice. But she would not do the girls' work for them.

A few days ago, Josefina and Tía Dolores had worked together in the corner of the back courtyard where Mamá's flowers grew. Tía Dolores showed Josefina how to prepare the flowers for the winter. She explained how to cut back the dead stems and cover the earth with leaves to protect it from ice and snow. She watched with care to be sure Josefina was doing everything correctly. Tía Dolores helped, but she made it clear that the flowers were Josefina's responsibility. "I want you to know how to care for them by yourself after I leave," she'd said. "I know you can do it. I have faith in you."

Tía Dolores worked hard teaching, and she expected the girls to work hard learning. "Our energies and abilities are gifts from God," she often said. "He means for us to put them to good use." Sometimes

Josefina thought that perhaps Tía Dolores had a little too *much* faith in her abilities! As soon as she'd returned to the rancho, Tía Dolores had had her piano moved into the family sala. The piano had come all the way from Mexico City, and Josefina was eager to learn how to play it. So Tía Dolores gave Josefina lessons. Right away, Josefina had learned that making music on the piano was much harder than it looked. But Tía Dolores was generous with her encouragement. She never gave up, no matter how Josefina fumbled at the keys.

Now Francisca frowned and rustled her material. She made a great show of holding it up to the fire and squinting as she stitched. Clara glanced at the hem Francisca was sewing. "Just look at the size of your stitches!" she said. "They're much too big."

Francisca shrugged. "They'll hold the dress together," she said.

"That's not the point," said Clara. "They *look* bad."

"Oh, Clara!" said Francisca crossly. "The stitches are on the inside! No one will see them."

"Yes, they will!" said Josefina, who didn't like to hear her sisters squabble. "No one's dress swirls more than yours at a dance, Francisca. And no one is more admired!" Josefina whirled around the room, pretending to be Francisca dancing. "See my hem stitches?" she asked. She sang a dancing song that had been one of Mamá's favorites.

Tía Dolores knew the song, too. She went straight to the piano and began to play it. Ana and Clara sang along and clapped in time to the music. Francisca tried not to smile. But when Josefina danced over to her, holding out both hands, Francisca happily thrust her sewing aside and sprang to her feet. Josefina and Francisca danced around the room, weaving in and out of the light of the fire. Soon Ana and Clara were dancing with each other, too. Tía Dolores played away merrily. Her rebozo slipped down from her shoulders. Her dark, shiny hair had a reddish luster in the firelight.

Tía Dolores was playing so loudly and they were all singing and laughing so much that none of them heard the door open. But it must have, because the next thing Josefina knew, Papá was there, tapping his foot in time to Tía Dolores's music. He watched the girls dance until the song was over. When they stopped, he folded his arms across his chest and pretended to scold.

"Dancing instead of sewing?" he asked. He tried to look stern, but his eyes were full of fun. "Who started that fandango?"

"I did, Papá!" said Josefina, flushed and breathless. "I was celebrating. I've finished my dress!"

"Good!" said Papá. "And a fine dress it is, too."

"Gracias, Papá," said Josefina. She held out the sides of her dress. "The material comes from very far away. Tía Dolores gave it to us."

"How thoughtful of her," said Papá. He turned to Tía Dolores. "You are very kind to my daughters. Gracias."

Tía Dolores looked pleased. "My father bought the material this summer from traders who came to Santa Fe from the United States. The traders brought all sorts of things to trade—tools and clothes, paper and ink—"

"And pretty material!" Josefina added happily.

"*Sí*," said Papá. "I know about the *americanos* and the trail they follow. They first came to Santa Fe three years ago. Before that, it was illegal for them to come to New Mexico." He looked thoughtful. "I hope that trading with the americanos will be a good thing. I've heard that the traders need pack mules, so I'm raising some to take to Santa Fe next summer. I'll sell or swap the mules to get tools and other things we need on the rancho. It should be a profitable business."

"Oh, Papá," Josefina asked, "may we go to Santa Fe with you next summer?"

"Perhaps," said Papá, smiling at her eagerness. "But right now, I think all of you girls had better go to bed. I'm going to the village."

"In this storm?" asked Ana.

"It's because of the storm that I'm going," said Papá as he put on his hat. "I want to be sure Magdalena is all right." Tía Magdalena was Papá's sister. She was much older than he was, and she lived alone in the village about a mile from the rancho. "Her roof is not as strong as it should be, and her house is near the stream. I'm worried about flooding. Most of the time, nothing is more welcome than rain. But it's unusual for it to rain so late in the year, and such a hard rain can mean trouble."

Josefina listened. They'd been making so much noise, they hadn't noticed that the wind had an angry sound to it now, and the rain was coming down harder and harder. She watched Papá as he pulled on his woolen *sarape* that covered his chest and his back. Even that wouldn't keep him dry tonight. Josefina turned a worried face up to Papá.

"Now, now. There's no need for you to worry, my Josefina," Papá said in his deep, comforting voice. "Our house is high above the stream. God will keep you safe, and your Tía Dolores is here to look after you."

"Sí, Papá," said Josefina. "But if the stream floods—"

"Our harvest is safely in," said Papá. "We'll move the animals to higher ground if we need to. Now come and say good night to me before I go."

The girls knelt before Papá, the palms and fingers of their hands pressed together as for prayer. Papá gave each girl his blessing and kissed her praying hands. His smile was loving as he looked down on his daughters' upturned faces. "Go to bed," he said. "The sky will be blue tomorrow."

Tía Dolores opened the door for Papá. "God go with you," she said softly.

Papá nodded. Then he went out into the windy, rainy night.

Papá had told Josefina not to worry, but she could not obey. The sheepskins that were her bed were warm and soft and comforting, but they could not soothe away the worry that kept her awake. She lay on her stomach with her chin on her clenched hands and listened. Moment by moment the wind grew wilder. It shrieked and howled and hurled the rain against the roof and the walls as if it were trying to destroy the house with its anger. Josefina shivered at the sound of the storm's rage. *Please let Papá be safe,* she prayed. *Please.* She was glad she couldn't sleep. She hoped her prayers would protect Papá.

And so, when the church bell rang in the night, Josefina was already awake. The bell's fast *clang, clang, clang* came through the storm's uneven gusts. It was faint but steady. Josefina knew the church bell was an alarm. Its clangs meant *danger, danger, danger!*

"Francisca! Clara!" said Josefina urgently. "Wake up!" She stood and began to put on her clothes.

Francisca groaned and pulled her blankets over her head, but Clara sat up straight. "What's the matter?" she asked Josefina.

"The church bell is ringing," said Josefina. "Hurry!

Get dressed. Papá may need our help."

The sisters dressed as fast as they could. Just as they were finishing, Tía Dolores came to fetch them. She was carrying a small candle. Her voice was calm and very serious. She spoke against the sounds of the storm with the same steady determination as the ringing church bell. "Your papá is still down in the village. I fear the church bell means the flooding is bad there. I've wakened all the workers in the house. Some will herd the animals to higher ground. Others will try to build up the stream's banks so that the stream won't flood the fields. I've told Ana she must stay with her boys. But I want you girls to come with me. We must save as much as we can from the kitchen garden."

Josefina, Clara, and Francisca followed Tía Dolores. They were still under the cover of the roof when suddenly the sky was slashed in two by a jagged dagger of lightning. Its brilliant flash of light made everything white for a second. Then the light disappeared and the night seemed even darker than before. BOOM! A huge clap of thunder crashed so loudly it shook the house. Josefina stepped back, trembling.

"What's the matter?" Tía Dolores asked.

"It's the lightning," Francisca answered. "Josefina's afraid of it."

CRACK! Lightning split the sky again. Josefina couldn't move. All her life she had feared lightning. Mamá had understood. She would hug Josefina to her and wrap her rebozo around both of them. She'd cover Josefina's eyes with her hand so that Josefina wouldn't have to see the wicked flash of light or the plunge into darkness that followed. She'd hold Josefina so close that the beating of her heart almost blocked out the sound of the thunder. *Mamá!* thought Josefina now, bracing herself for another flash. *Help me!*

Just then, Josefina felt Tía Dolores put a strong arm around her shoulders. Tía Dolores's little candle sputtered wildly in the wind, but it didn't go out. By its feeble light, Josefina saw Tía Dolores's gentle face. "Come with me, Josefina," she said.

Josefina took a shaky breath. She leaned close to Tía Dolores. Together, they stepped forward. Clara and Francisca followed behind. The rain put the little candle out. But Tía Dolores's step was sure, even in the darkness. She led the girls across the front court-yard, through the passageway, and into the back courtyard. As they passed Mamá's flowers, Josefina remembered what Tía Dolores had said when they'd worked together: *I know you can do it. I have faith in you.* Lightning sliced the sky and thunder boomed, again and again. Josefina shuddered, but Tía Dolores's arm gave her courage. She stayed within its safe hold as they went out the back gate to the kitchen garden.

Carmen, the cook, and her husband, Miguel, were already there filling big baskets with squash, beans, chiles, and pumpkins. The kitchen garden was awash in mud. It made Josefina sad to see it. She and her sisters had worked so hard all spring and summer tending the garden! She was sorry to pick the squash that were not perfectly ripe yet, but she knew it was better than letting them be washed away or rot from lying in water.

And there was so *much* water! A river of it rushed through the center of the garden, and the rain was still falling in torrents. Mud pulled at Josefina's moccasins and splashed up onto her legs. Soon she was soaked to the skin. Her hands were numb with cold and caked with dirt. Her arms were tired from lifting mud-streaked pumpkins, and her back hurt from carrying her heavy basket. Lightning flashed all around her and thunder rumbled. But Josefina bent to her work, trying to ignore the force and fury of the storm.

Tía Dolores has faith in me, Josefina said to herself. *I can't let her down.*

Turning Blankets into Sheep

 ust as Papá had promised, the sky was a clean, clear blue the next morning. Only a few gray clouds remained, and they scuttled across the horizon as if they were ashamed, shoving against each other in their hurry to get away. Below, the ground was so wet it was shiny, reflecting the new blue sky. It was crisscrossed everywhere with thin little rivers no bigger than trickles, trying to find their way down the hill back to the stream.

Papá had come home from the village at dawn, just in time for morning prayers. As she'd knelt in front of the altar in the family sala, Josefina had thanked God for Papá's safe return.

Now the family was gathered in the kitchen for breakfast. Josefina was helping Clara and Carmen cook tortillas. Ana was rocking her younger boy,

Antonio, in a cradle that swung gently from the ceiling. Francisca was grinding corn. She would put a handful of dried corn on the flat *metate* stone and rub back and forth with the smaller *mano* stone until the corn was ground into coarse flour. As the cradle swung back and forth, it made a comforting *creak, creak, creak* sound, which the soft, regular *thud, thud, thud* of the mano matched in rhythm.

Papá looked tired. Tía Dolores gave him some mint tea. He sat down and took a long, grateful sip before he spoke.

"You all did a fine job of saving as much as you could from the garden," he said. "I'm afraid the news from the village is not as good. I was in time to save Magdalena's roof, but one whole corner of the church collapsed. Some of the villagers had not harvested yet, so their crops are lost. They were swept away by the stream when it rose over its banks."

"What a blessing it is that you brought our harvest in early!" said Ana. "We'll be able to share it with the villagers who lost their crops. No one will go hungry this winter."

"Sí," said Papá. "That is a blessing." He paused as

if he didn't want to say what he had to say next. At last
he said sadly, "But we've suffered another loss. I was
told about it late last night. It seems that the shepherds
were moving our sheep from their summer grazing
lands in the mountains down to the winter pastures
closer to the rancho. When the storm began, the shepherds took a shortcut to save time. Just as they were
crossing the bottom of a deep *arroyo*, a flash flood
came gushing through it. All of a sudden, the arroyo
was full of a raging torrent of water. The water came
so hard and so fast that the sheep couldn't get out of
its way. The shepherds risked their lives to save as
many sheep as they could. But hundreds of our sheep
were drowned." As if he needed to hear it again to
believe it, Papá repeated, "Hundreds of our sheep were
drowned."

Ana lifted Antonio out of the cradle and held him
close. Everyone else was still. They looked at Papá,
their faces full of concern. Then Josefina went to stand
by Papá's side. She put her hand on his arm and he
patted it while he stared into the fire. So many sheep
killed! Josefina knew that this was a terrible disaster.
How cruel the storm had been! The rancho could not

survive without sheep. They provided meat, and wool for weaving and for trading. What would Papá do?

Papá's voice was heavy with discouragement. "The sheep were very valuable," he said. "My father and grandfather built up the flocks over many years. It will take a long, long time for us to recover from this loss." He sighed. "We'll just have to start over. I'll have to trade the mules I was raising. I have nothing else to trade. I'll have to use the mules to get new sheep so that we can increase our flocks again."

"Perhaps not," said Tía Dolores. She'd been so quiet, they'd almost forgotten she was there. Now she spoke to Papá, respectfully but firmly. "Forgive me for speaking, but perhaps it won't be necessary to trade the mules. Perhaps you could use the old sheep to get new sheep."

They all stared at her. "Please go on," said Papá.

Tía Dolores explained. "The old sheep provided you with sacks and sacks of wool when they were sheared last spring," she said. "Your storerooms are full of their fleece. What if we used that wool to weave as many blankets as we can? We'll keep as few as possible for our own use, and trade most of the blankets to the villagers for new sheep. We can trade with the Indians at the pueblo, too."

"But they all weave their own blankets," said Papá. "Why would they want more?"

"To trade to the americanos," answered Tía Dolores. "My father told me that the americanos are glad to trade their goods for blankets. They value the blankets for their warmth and strength and beauty."

"I don't understand," said Francisca. "Who will do all of this weaving you talk about?"

Tía Dolores smiled. "We will," she said. "You and your sisters and I. The household servants will weave, and any workers on the rancho who are able."

Josefina saw that Francisca wasn't pleased with this answer, and Clara and Ana looked unsure. But Papá seemed to be giving the idea grave consideration. "Trading blankets for sheep," he said thoughtfully. "Perhaps it would be good for both sides. Our neighbors would help us by giving us the sheep we need. And *we* would help *them* by weaving blankets they can trade for goods that they need."

"Sí," said Tía Dolores simply.

Ana nudged Josefina with her elbow and raised her

eyebrows. None of the sisters had ever heard Papá discuss business with a woman before. He was the patrón, the head of the rancho and the head of their family. He had never discussed business with Mamá. But Papá didn't seem to be offended by Tía Dolores's forwardness. Still, Josefina was not sure it was proper for Tía Dolores to have such a conversation with him. Josefina knew she and her sisters should sit quietly. They all knew it wasn't their place to speak.

All except Francisca, of course. "But Tía Dolores!" Francisca protested. "I don't see how we can weave any more than we already do! We hardly have time to do all our household chores as it is."

"We'll get up earlier," said Tía Dolores briskly. "If all four of you help—"

"Josefina can't help," said Francisca. "She doesn't know how to weave."

Ana nodded, and even Clara agreed with Francisca for once. "That's true," Clara said. "Mamá never taught her, because Josefina was too small. She's *still* too small to work the big loom."

"My servant, Teresita, weaves on a smaller loom that hangs from the ceiling," said Tía Dolores. "I'm sure she'd be willing to teach Josefina to weave on one like it. And I'm sure Josefina is big enough to do it. Josefina can help."

Josefina saw Papá looking at her. His smile said that he loved her even if he wasn't sure she could be of help with the weaving. With all her heart, Josefina wanted to please Papá. She could tell that Tía Dolores's idea had caught his interest and given him a little hope. She didn't want her sisters' doubts to discourage Papá—or Tía Dolores. And so she spoke up with spirit.

"I'd like to learn to use the small loom," she said. "And anyway, I can help wash and card and spin wool for the big loom. I know where to find the plants we use to make dye to color the wool, and . . . and Mamá always used to say that I was good at untangling knots."

Papá laughed out loud. His laugh was a sudden, unexpected, wonderful sound. "Well," he said to Tía Dolores. "If all of your weavers are as eager as my little Josefina, you'll turn the wool into blankets and the blankets into sheep in no time! I think we should give your plan a try."

Tía Dolores was very pleased. "We will pray for God's help," she said, "as we put His gifts to good use. Won't we, girls?"

Her smile was so happy, so full of energy and encouragement, that all the sisters had to smile back and say "Sí!" Even Francisca!

That very afternoon, Tía Dolores brought Josefina to Teresita. "Will you teach Josefina to weave?" she asked.

Teresita was working at a loom that hung near one wall and stretched from ceiling to floor. She looked at Josefina, and then she smiled. Teresita's smile seemed to use her whole face, because her eyes were surrounded by wrinkles of good humor. "Sí," she said.

"Gracias," said Tía Dolores. "You might as well begin right now. As I always say, 'The saints cry over lost time.'"

She left, and Teresita watched her go with a twinkle in her eye. Josefina could tell that she and Teresita were thinking the same thing—that Tía Dolores gave the saints very little reason to cry! She never wasted time!

Josefina sat down next to Teresita and watched her weave. After a little while Josefina asked, "How did you learn to weave?"

Teresita's voice was unhurried as she answered. "Before I came here with your Tía Dolores, I was a servant in your Abuelito's house in Santa Fe," she said. "But when I was a little girl, I lived with my people, the Navajos. My mamá taught me to weave on a loom like this. I've never forgotten, even though I was captured by enemies of the Navajos when I was about your age and taken from my family."

Josefina knew that the Navajo Indians lived in the mountains and deserts far to the west. "Did you ever see your mamá again?" she asked Teresita.

"No," said Teresita.

"Did you miss her?" asked Josefina.

"Sí," said Teresita. Her dark eyes met Josefina's. "You and I are alike in that way, aren't we?" she said. "We both lost our mamás at a young age."

Josefina nodded.

"I am sure you remember the things your mamá taught you," said Teresita.

Josefina nodded again. "Oh, sí!" she said. "My

sisters and I try very hard to remember her lessons and stories and songs."

"Good," said Teresita. She was quiet for a long moment. With a light touch, she ran her hand across the loom. Then she said, "Here is a story my mamá told me. When the world was new, Spider Woman taught the Navajos to weave on a loom like this one. The upper crosspiece is the sky bar. The lower cross-piece is the earth bar, and this stick, which goes between the strands of yarn, is a sunbeam. I'll show you how it works."

Josefina watched. The loom looked like a tall harp. Long, taut strands of wool yarn connected the sky bar to the earth bar. The sunbeam stick held the strands apart. It made space between the strands so that Teresita could weave another piece of wool through them. When she had woven the wool through all the long strands, Teresita pulled the wool gently, pushed it down into place, then turned it and wove it back in the other direction. Teresita's hands made it look easy. Josefina could not wait to try. "May I do it?" she asked.

Teresita handed her the wool. "Remember," she said, "the earth, the sky, and the sun have already worked hard to provide us with this wool by growing grass for the sheep to eat. They didn't hurry their work, and neither should you."

Josefina worked very slowly indeed, but even so, the row she wove was loose and bumpy. Teresita helped her take it out and do it over again.

Josefina was weaving a straight row that was a pale gray color. But the part of the blanket that Teresita had woven had a lovely pattern of stripes and zigzagging lines and diamond shapes and triangles on it. The dark blue zigzags reminded Josefina of the mountains that surrounded the rancho, and the creamy white zigzags just above them looked like the snow that capped the mountains. Floating below the zigzag mountains were dark V's that looked just like the graceful wild geese Josefina saw flying across the autumn sky. And below them, Teresita had woven pale golden shapes that reminded Josefina of the cottonwood leaves that fell all around her when she went to the stream every morning. Most of the colors of the blanket were soft—deep browns, many gentle shades of gray and blue, and delicate gold and yellow. But every few rows, Teresita had woven in a yarn that was the fiery orange-red of the harvest moon. "The pattern is so pretty," said Josefina. "It reminds me of our rancho."

"Yes," said Teresita, wrinkling up her eyes in a smile. "A blanket should be as beautiful as the place it comes from." She was thoughtful for a while before she said, "Maybe this blanket will travel all the way to the United States. Maybe some little girl there will look at it, and then she will know how beautiful it is here in New Mexico."

Josefina liked that idea. "She'll probably like the red strands the best," she said, "just as I do. They stand out from all the rest."

"They do," said Teresita. "But every strand, dull or bright, is part of the pattern. Every strand adds to the strength and beauty of the whole blanket."

"Sí," agreed Josefina. "But the red wool seems to change everything around it somehow. It makes all the colors look better."

That first day, Josefina had to do her row of weaving over and over again before it was smooth and even. But Teresita was very patient, and slowly, slowly, Josefina's hands became accustomed to the feeling of the wool. When Josefina came for her next weaving

lesson, Teresita had set up a loom for her to use by
herself.

Josefina enjoyed her weaving lessons with Teresita.
It was a pleasure to weave the wool through the
strands, and to push the newly woven row down so
that it fit snugly next to the row below it. Part of the
pleasure was knowing that with each row, Josefina
was adding to a blanket that would help Papá replace
the sheep he'd lost. Josefina was pleased and proud to
be of help to her family. And as the days went by and
she learned to be a better weaver, she was pleased and
proud of herself for learning something new. *I may be
the youngest and the smallest, but I can help, just like my
sisters,* she thought. *I can help turn blankets into sheep!
Tía Dolores was right.*

Sometimes as she was weaving, Josefina smiled to
herself, thinking of Tía Dolores. It seemed to Josefina
that Tía Dolores was like the beautiful bright red wool.
She changed everything around her and made it better.

Rabbit Brush

F ollow me!" Josefina shouted happily. She ran up the hill as swift and light as a bird skimming over a stream. The air at the top smelled of spicy juniper and piney *piñón*. It was pure and cool and thin and sweet. Josefina turned around and called back to her sisters, "Wait till you see! There's *lots* of rabbit brush up here!"

Josefina and her sisters were on an expedition to gather wildflowers, herbs, roots, barks, berries, and leaves. They'd use them to make dyes to color the wool for weaving. Teresita had told Josefina that the Navajos used rabbit brush blossoms to make many shades of yellow. Ana, Francisca, and Clara were not far behind Josefina on the path. Josefina was glad it was almost time for the mid-day meal. She knew that Carmen had packed tortillas, onions, squash, goat cheese, and plums for them to eat. The canteen was full of cold water to drink. Miguel, Carmen's husband, was carrying the food and the canteen. He had come along to be sure the girls were safe.

"Oh!" said Ana when she reached the top of the hill. "Isn't it pretty up here!" Josefina thought Ana looked very pretty herself! She was a little breathless, and her cheeks were reddened by the climb and the wind.

All the sisters seemed to be in high spirits. They set to work gathering rabbit brush, delighted to be out in the bracing air and bright sunshine. Clara, who usually liked to keep her feet firmly on the ground, seemed to have a bounce in her step today. And Francisca, who was usually so careful of her appearance, didn't seem to care that her hair was windblown and tousled and had a yellow leaf caught in it.

"Look," said Josefina. She took the leaf out of Francisca's hair and twirled it on its stem. The leaf was such a sunny yellow, Josefina thought about saving it to put in her memory box along with the pretty swallow's feather she'd found earlier. She kept things that reminded her of Mamá in her memory box. Mamá had loved swallows, and she had loved autumn, too, when the bright yellow leaves stood out against the dark green of the mountainsides and shimmered against the deep blue sky. But Josefina knew that the little leaf would soon turn brown and crumble, so she let it go. She watched the breeze catch it and send it swooping and flying as if it were a tiny yellow bird.

Josefina loved autumn as much as Mamá had. It was a busy time on the rancho. All the harvested crops had to be stored properly to preserve them for the winter. The storeroom was full of garlic, onions, beans, corn, squash, pumpkins, cheeses, and meats. The adobe bins in the *granero* were full of grain to be ground into flour. Josefina and her sisters had made strings of squash slices, apple slices, red chiles, and herbs. The strings would hang near the hearth where they would dry and be handy for use in cooking throughout the winter. Josefina always enjoyed the cheerful bustle in the kitchen at harvest time, but it was a treat to be out and away today, high up on this golden hillside with her sisters.

The morning had flown by. Now it was mid-day and the sisters gathered around the food Carmen had packed for them. Miguel found a sunny spot nearby and took his afternoon rest while the girls ate.

Josefina bit into a plum that was warm from the sunshine. The breeze lifted her hair off her back and cooled her face. "I wish Tía Dolores had been able to come with us today," she said. "She'd enjoy this." Tía Dolores had gone to the village. She was bringing food to some of the villagers who had lost their crops in the flood.

"Sí!" agreed Ana and Clara. Francisca had a mouthful of tortilla.

Josefina grinned. She took a sprig of rabbit brush out of her basket and pretended to be Tía Dolores. "We'll put these flowers to good use, won't we, girls?" she said, imitating Tía Dolores's energetic manner. Ana and Clara laughed, especially when Josefina put the flowers to good use tickling them!

But Francisca grabbed the flowers away. "Whenever Tía Dolores talks about putting things to good use, it always ends up meaning more work for us," she grumbled. "All this weaving, for example."

Josefina smiled. "I *like* the weaving," she said.

"Well," said Francisca. "It's new to you. But I find it very dull." She collapsed back on the grass and fanned herself with the sprig of flowers. "I'm worn out from it!"

"Now, Francisca," Ana scolded in her kindly, motherly way. "You have plenty of energy for things you enjoy, like dancing. Pretend you're dancing while you work at the loom. Dance on the treadles!"

"I can't dance very well with the loom!" said Francisca shortly.

"You don't weave very well with the loom, either," said Clara. "Weaving is just the sort of slow, patient work you're not good at, Francisca."

Francisca made a face. "Work!" she said. "I thought that when Tía Dolores came, there would be *less* work for us, not *more*."

"She doesn't ask us to do any more than she does herself," said Clara.

"You're right," said Francisca, sitting up. "Tía Dolores is always at work. She's always trying to fix things and improve things and change things— especially *us*!" Francisca poked and prodded Clara's arm with the sprig of rabbit brush as she continued to complain. "Tía Dolores is always trying to poke and prod us into being different than we are. She's never satisfied. She always thinks we can be better."

"Tía Dolores came to teach us," said Ana. "She's not a servant."

"She certainly is not," agreed Francisca. "She seems to think she is the *patrona*! Look at how she's put herself in charge of the weaving business." Tía Dolores had also taken on the responsibility of keeping track of the number of blankets the rancho was producing.

"As Papá said, we must replace the sheep," Ana said calmly. She collected the remains of the food, and the girls started back down the hill with Miguel. Ana walked next to Francisca. "We should be grateful to Tía Dolores for her good idea and her hard work. She is helping us, and that is *exactly* what we asked her to do."

Francisca frowned. "Tía Dolores's help is not *exactly* what I expected it to be," she said. "Tía Dolores isn't, either. She seems different than she was when she came here the first time."

"Yes!" said Josefina. She turned around and walked backwards a few steps so that she could face her sisters. "Tía Dolores seems happier."

"I think she is," said Ana. "She even looks happier,

and prettier, too. She's not so thin and pale as she was."

"She's letting her skin get rough and red," said Francisca, who was vain about her own complexion.

Josefina did not like to hear Francisca criticize Tía Dolores. "Why are you speaking this way about Tía Dolores?" she asked Francisca. "You were the one who used to say that she was elegant and that her clothes were beautiful."

"She never wears those beautiful clothes anymore," said Francisca, "just everyday work clothes." She shook her head and said mournfully, "Soon, I expect none of us will have anything *but* worn-out, workaday clothes."

Clara snorted. "You'd have a fancy new dress if you'd ever settle down and finish it!" she said.

Francisca ignored her. "Tía Dolores is determined to weave all our wool into blankets," she said. "I'm sure she won't spare even enough for new sashes for us. Not that it matters how we look. We don't have time to do anything but work these days! We're up long before dawn—"

"Ah, that's it!" said Ana. "You are out of sorts because you have to get up so early!" Ana, Clara, and Josefina glanced at each other and hid their smiles.

Francisca was well known for being slow to rise in the morning. Ana went on, "Mamá always said no one has a sweeter temper than you do, Francisca—as long as you have plenty of sleep!"

Josefina noticed that when Ana mentioned Mamá, a strange look crossed Francisca's face. Francisca started to say something, but then she seemed to change her mind. She said nothing.

Josefina took hold of Francisca's hand and swung it as they walked together. "Remember the morning song Mamá used to sing to you to help you wake up?" she asked Francisca.

Ever so briefly, the strange look crossed Francisca's face again. Then she began to sing, "Arise in the morning . . ." She stopped. "How did it go?" she asked. "I've forgotten. Sing it for me, Josefina."

Josefina began to sing:

> *Here comes the dawn,*
> *now it gives us the light of day.*
> *Arise in the morning*
> *and see that day has dawned.*

Josefina sang the song in her clear, sweet voice as the girls made their way down the hill. Tía Dolores met them as they passed the orchard. She was carrying a basket full of apples, walking with her usual purposeful stride. Wisps of her ruddy auburn hair curled out from under her rebozo, and her skirt flapped in the wind.

"Josefina," she said, "I do love to hear you sing!" She smiled. "Perhaps you'll sing a special song for all the village to hear as part of the Christmas celebration this year."

Josefina could feel her own smile sink right off her face. "Oh, no, Tía Dolores!" she said quickly, too surprised to be polite. She spoke again, this time with more respect. "I mean, I beg your pardon, but no, thank you."

"Why not?" asked Tía Dolores. "A lovely voice like yours is a gift from God. I am sure God means you to use it to delight others, especially if you do so to celebrate Him."

Josefina thought of how it would feel to have everyone looking at her, everyone listening to her singing all alone. She shivered. It was scarier than lightning.

"I'm . . . sorry," she said, stumbling over the words. "I just *couldn't*."

Tía Dolores looked Josefina straight in the eye. "You mean you don't *want* to," she said. "But perhaps one day you will."

Josefina felt something jab her arm. It was the sprig of rabbit brush, and Francisca was poking her with it. Francisca raised one eyebrow and gave Josefina a look that said, *You see? Remember what I said about Tía Dolores poking and prodding us to be different than we are? Wasn't I right?*

The First Love

 few nights later, Josefina sat on a stool close to the fire in the family sala. The evening air had a sharpness that warned of the wintry cold to come. Josefina curled up her toes inside her warm knitted socks. She and Clara were spinning wool into yarn. They were using long spindles called *malacates* to twist tufts of wool into one long strand of yarn as the wool spun around. Ana was putting her boys to bed. Francisca sat nearby sewing her fancy dress, which, as Clara had pointed out, she still had not finished.

Tía Dolores was at her writing desk, bent close to her work. *Scritch, scratch, scritch, scratch.* Josefina loved the sound Tía Dolores's quill pen made as she wrote in the ledger she used to keep track of the weaving business. Paper and ink were precious, so Tía Dolores made

her numbers small and filled every inch of every page.
Papá sat nearby at the table, quietly watching her write.

Josefina looked around the family sala. *A piano,
a writing desk, paper, pen, ink, and a ledger!* she thought.
*Tía Dolores has brought so many new things to this room,
Mamá wouldn't recognize it!* But Tía Dolores's things
were not the only changes. Papá looked different, too.
His face looked less tired, as if he were not so weighed
down with sorrow as he had been, and sometimes he
even whistled again, as he used to.

"There!" said Tía Dolores. She put her pen down
with a pleased expression. "Would you do me the
honor of looking at the figures?" she asked Papá.

"Sí," said Papá. Tía Dolores brought the ledger to
the table, and she and Papá looked at it together.

"This shows how many sacks of wool we have,"
explained Tía Dolores as she pointed to a column of
figures in the ledger. "And this shows how many blankets I think we can weave. And this shows how many
sheep we'll get when we trade the blankets."

Papá nodded. "Excellent," he said. "The weaving
business should do very well, God willing. I am grateful to you, Dolores."

"Your daughters have worked hard," she said.

"Sí," said Papá. "They weave. But you have taken care of all this." He patted the ledger. "It is fortunate that you can read and write."

"My aunt taught me when I lived with her in Mexico City," said Tía Dolores. She thought for a moment, and then she said, "And now, with your permission, I'll teach your daughters to read and write. Then they will be able to continue the weaving business after I have left."

Francisca gasped. Josefina knew that meant she was not happy at the thought of yet another new thing to do. Now they would have lessons in reading and writing on top of everything else!

Tía Dolores must have heard and understood the gasp, too, because she said, "The lessons won't add any time to the day. I have a little speller I brought with me from Mexico City. We'll use it when we sit by the fire at night. We will be putting our evenings to *very* good use."

Francisca spoke up boldly. "I don't see the need for learning to read and write," she said. "I have no time to read books, and no one ever sends letters that have anything to do with *me*."

Tía Dolores smiled. "Ah, but soon they will, Francisca!" she said. "Soon your papá will be receiving letters from young men who want to marry you."

Francisca sniffed. "Hmph!" she said. "I won't read them! And I'll reply to any marriage proposal by handing the young man the squash."

"That's true," stated Clara. "She's already done it!" In fact, a young man had already proposed to Francisca. She had indeed followed the old custom of giving him a squash to let him know she was not interested in marrying him.

"Letters proposing marriage can be very persuasive," said Tía Dolores. "Your papá won your mamá's heart with his letters!"

Francisca's dark eyes were flinty. "Mamá could not read," she said.

"No," said Tía Dolores. "But she always said that she loved the way your papá signed his name with such fancy flourishes."

Papá laughed. "I was young and foolish," he said. "It was the custom to make flourishes to show what an important person you were, and to make your signature different from anyone else's. I don't bother with flourishes anymore."

"Please won't you show us how you used to do it, Papá?" asked Josefina.

Papá smiled but shook his head. "No, no. It's a waste of paper," he said.

"Not at all," said Tía Dolores. She handed him the pen and the green glass inkwell.

"Very well," said Papá agreeably. Josefina stood next to him and Clara peered over his shoulder. As they watched, Papá wrote his name in handsome, upright letters. Then, under his name, Papá made graceful swirls and curving spirals that looked like a long, lovely curl of ribbon.

"Oh, Papá, it's beautiful!" said Josefina. She turned to Tía Dolores. "Will we really learn to write like that?" she asked.

"Sí!" said Tía Dolores. "We'll begin tomorrow."

Josefina stared at Papá's beautiful writing. Then she looked up to smile at Francisca. Surely Francisca would enjoy learning to do something as fancy and elegant-looking as this!

But Francisca was gone. She had slipped out

quietly, without saying good night or waiting for
Papá's blessing.

Something woke Josefina in the middle of the night.
It was a sound, just a small sound, but one that made
Josefina sit up and tilt her head and listen hard. As
her eyes adjusted to the darkness, Josefina saw that
Francisca was not in her bed. Quietly, so as not to wake
Clara, Josefina pulled on her moccasins and wrapped
herself in her blanket. She crept outside. Francisca
was sitting in the courtyard. She was wrapped in her
blanket, too. There was no moon, but the stars were so
big and bright Josefina could see Francisca's face. It was
streaked with tears.

Josefina was surprised. She had not seen Francisca
cry since Mamá died. "Francisca!" Josefina whispered
as she came near. "What's the matter?"

"Go away," said Francisca fiercely.

Josefina knelt down next to her sister. "Are you
hurt?" she asked. "Are you ill? Shall I fetch Tía
Dolores?"

"No!" said Francisca. She spoke with such force

Josefina was startled. Her voice sounded hard as she said, "I've had quite enough of Tía Dolores!"

"What do you mean?" asked Josefina.

Francisca wiped the tears off her cheeks with an impatient hand. "Don't you see what's happening?" she asked. "Has Tía Dolores's praise for your sewing and weaving made you blind? Has she made you feel like such an important person that you don't care how she's changing everything? Nothing is the same as it was when Mamá was alive." Suddenly the bitterness left Francisca's voice. It was replaced by sadness. "Every change makes Mamá seem farther and farther away," she said. "Every change makes me feel as if I'm losing Mamá again. And oh, Josefina! I miss Mamá so!"

"So do I," said Josefina passionately. Her heart ached with sympathy for Francisca. Now she saw why Francisca had complained about Tía Dolores. Josefina tried to make Francisca feel better. "I miss Mamá, too," she said. "But Tía Dolores is good and kind! She is only trying to help us."

"By changing us!" said Francisca. "Now she's going to make us learn to read and write. Mamá didn't read or write. Mamá didn't ask anyone to teach us to read or write. Reading and writing will be one more way Tía Dolores will pull us away from Mamá. It'll be just one more way she'll fill our heads and our hearts so that we'll have no room left for Mamá. We'll start to forget her. We've already started."

"Oh, Francisca!" said Josefina. "That's not true!" But a dark fear stole into Josefina's mind. Was Francisca right? It was true that Tía Dolores had changed their lives. Josefina herself had changed. Hadn't she braved the lightning? Hadn't she learned to weave? But did Tía Dolores's new ideas and new ways mean there was no room for the old ways? Was Tía Dolores making them forget Mamá?

Francisca straightened her shoulders. "I am not going to do it," she said firmly. "I won't learn to read and write." She stood up and looked down at Josefina. "You'll have to make your own choice," she said. "Decide for yourself." Then she left.

Josefina stayed alone in the courtyard. She looked up at the huge, endless black sky and felt as if she were adrift in it. The stars seemed to be all around her— above her and below her and surrounding her on every side. Josefina felt lost. Francisca made it sound as if learning to read would be disloyal to Mamá. She made it seem as if Josefina had to choose between Mamá and Tía Dolores, between the old and the new.

What should I do, Mamá? Josefina asked. But she knew there would be no answer. The stars were as silent as stones.

Usually Josefina skipped and sang all the way to the stream on laundry day. But today she walked joylessly, thinking about the conversation she'd had with Francisca the night before.

Tía Dolores was waiting for Josefina by the stream. "There you are, Josefina!" she said cheerfully. "You're as quiet as a little shadow this morning. And where are your sisters?"

"They're helping Carmen in the kitchen," Josefina answered.

"Good!" said Tía Dolores. "Then after we do the laundry, you will have your first reading lesson by yourself!"

Josefina tried to smile.

❦ The First Love ❧

If Tía Dolores noticed that Josefina was not paying much attention to the clothes she was washing, she was too kind to say anything about it. They worked in an unusual silence. Tía Dolores spread a freshly washed white cloth on a bush to dry. There were already three other white cloths on the bush. "Look, Josefina!" said Tía Dolores with laughter in her voice. "They're four white doves perched on a rosemary bush!"

Josefina's face lit up for the first time that day. "Oh!" she said. "Mamá used to say that poem some-times!" She tried to recite the whole poem. "'Behold four little white doves, perched on a rosemary bush. They were . . . they were . . .'" Josefina faltered. "I can't remember the rest," she said sadly.

Tía Dolores nodded. "Don't let it trouble you," she said. She draped another cloth on the bush.

Josefina sighed so deeply and so unhappily that Tía Dolores gave her a questioning look. "Oh, Tía Dolores," Josefina said, full of misery. "It *does* worry me. I can keep things that remind me of Mamá in my memory box, but I can't keep her words anywhere, and I'm beginning to forget them. It makes me afraid that I'm beginning to forget Mamá herself."

Tía Dolores's eyes were gentle as she listened. When Josefina stopped talking, Tía Dolores dried her hands on her skirt and said, "Come with me, Josefina."

Josefina almost had to run to keep up with Tía Dolores's long strides. Tía Dolores led Josefina back to the house and into the family sala. Her writing desk was still there on its stand. Without saying a word, Tía Dolores opened the lid of the writing desk and pulled out a drawer. From a secret compartment in the drawer she took a little book bound in soft brown leather. She handed it to Josefina.

Very, very carefully, Josefina turned the pages of the book. She couldn't read the words, but on many pages there were little sketches. Josefina stopped when she came to a drawing of four white birds perched on a bush.

Tía Dolores read the words on the page aloud:

> *Behold four little white doves*
> *perched on a rosemary bush.*
> *They were saying to each other,*
> *"There's no love like the first love."*

As she listened, Josefina remembered hearing Mamá's own dear voice, low and lilting and full of love, saying those very words.

"Your mamá didn't read or write," said Tía Dolores. "She learned this poem by hearing our papá read it aloud to us when we were little girls. When I was in Mexico City, I made this book. In it I wrote prayers, poems, songs, stories, even funny sayings your mamá and I both loved when we were girls. It helped me feel close to her, even though I was far away." She smiled at Josefina. "When you learn to read and write, you can look in this book any time you like and read your mamá's words. In it you can write things you remember her saying. This book will be a place to keep her words safe, so that you'll never lose them."

Josefina smiled with tremendous relief and gladness. She felt as if she had received an answer from Mamá herself about what she should do. It was as if Mamá were encouraging her to learn to read and write. Francisca was wrong. Reading and writing wouldn't pull them away from Mamá—it would help them remember her. "Oh, please will you teach me to read this book?" Josefina asked Tía Dolores.

"This book and any other you like!" said Tía Dolores. "Reading is a way to hold on to the past, to travel to places you've never been, and to learn about worlds beyond your own time or experience. You'll find there are many grander books than this one! Would you like to keep this little book with your memory box to be your very own?"

"No, gracias," said Josefina. She smiled a little smile. "That wouldn't be putting it to good use! I think you ought to keep it and read to all of us from it sometimes."

"Very well," said Tía Dolores.

"But may I borrow it for a moment?" Josefina asked. "I'll be careful."

"Sí, of course!" said Tía Dolores.

"Gracias!" said Josefina.

With a light heart and light feet, Josefina ran to find Francisca. She was sweeping in the kitchen.

"Look, Francisca!" said Josefina breathlessly. She opened Tía Dolores's little book to the drawing of the four doves. "The words on this page are Mamá's poem about the four doves," she said. "Do you remember it?"

Francisca thought. "Just the last line," she said.

"I think it ends, 'There's no love like the first love.'"

"Sí!" said Josefina. "This whole book is filled with prayers and poems and sayings of Mamá's. Tía Dolores made it. Don't you see, Francisca? When we can read this book, it will be like hearing Mamá's voice. And when we can write, we can add things we remember her saying. This book will be a place to keep her words safe forever." Josefina put the book into Francisca's hands.

Francisca looked at the book and smiled. She didn't say anything, but her eyes were shining.

Josefina smiled back. "Come with me," she said. "Perhaps Tía Dolores will read more to us."

The two sisters hurried to the family sala. "Tía Dolores," said Josefina. "Francisca would like to hear you read something of Mamá's from your book. Would you read to us?"

"With pleasure," answered Tía Dolores. "But first, I would like to write your names in the book."

Francisca and Josefina watched eagerly while Tía Dolores dipped her pen in the ink. "This is your name, Francisca," she said.

Scritch, scratch, the pen moved across the page in the

small book. "And now I'll write your name, Josefina."

"Be sure to add lots of flourishes," said Francisca, "to show what an important person she is!"

"I will!" said Tía Dolores. She wrote:

María Josefina Montoya

Christmas
Is Coming

CHAPTER 9

The wind was playing with Josefina. First it
made her skirt billow out behind her and the
ends of her rebozo fly up like wings. Then it
swirled around and pushed against her back, hurrying
her along like a helpful but impatient hand. Josefina
smiled. She could see that the wind was playing with
her sisters and Tía Dolores, too. They looked like birds
with ruffled feathers as they were blown along the road
on this blustery morning.

Josefina, her three sisters, and Tía Dolores were on
their way to the village about a mile from their rancho.
The road ran between the stream and the fields and
under tall cottonwood trees. The trees were bare now.
The windswept fields were a wintry, stubbly brown.
It was December. Christmas was coming, and today
everyone was gathering to clean the church so that it

would be ready to decorate. Josefina's papá had gone ahead with a burro loaded with wood for Christmas bonfires. The sisters and Tía Dolores would join him and their friends and neighbors at the church.

"Oh!" exclaimed Francisca, exasperated. The wind was blowing her hair so that it curled wildly around her face. Francisca was always careful about how she looked, especially when she was going to the village. She pulled her rebozo up over her head and tried to hold it in place with one hand as she struggled to carry a basket in her other hand.

Josefina didn't care if her hair was windblown. She slipped her arm under Francisca's basket. "I'll carry this," she said.

"Gracias," said Francisca. She let go of the basket and held her rebozo tightly under her chin with both hands.

Josefina glanced at the bright red chiles in the basket. "Why are you bringing these?" she asked Francisca.

"They're for Señora Sánchez," said Francisca.

"Don't you remember, Josefina?" asked Ana. "Mamá always gave Señora Sánchez some of our chiles at this time of year. Señora Sánchez claimed she couldn't make her traditional stew without them."

"Oh, that's right," said Josefina. "I remember."

Tía Dolores smiled at Josefina. "I'm eager to taste Señora Sánchez's famous stew," she said. "I'm glad Christmas is coming soon."

Josefina could only manage a very small smile in return. She saw that Clara was frowning. Ana and Francisca didn't look very enthusiastic, either.

Tía Dolores looked at the sisters' faces. "What's the matter?" she asked.

Ana answered. "When Mamá was alive, Christmas was always happy," she said. "But last Christmas was the first one after Mamá died. All we could think of was how much we missed her."

Tía Dolores spoke quietly. "It must have been very hard," she said.

Josefina slid her hand into Tía Dolores's. She knew that last Christmas must have been hard for her, too. Tía Dolores had been far away in Mexico City when Mamá, her sister, died. How sad and lonely she must have been!

"Last year, Christmas was very quiet," said

Francisca. "There were no parties or dances, out of respect for Mamá. No one felt like celebrating anyway."

For a while the sisters and Tía Dolores walked without talking. They were all remembering last year and wondering what this Christmas would be like. Josefina listened to the stream as it splashed over rocks and around curves. The stream flowed steadily and cheerfully. Josefina wished she could be as carefree about the holiday that lay ahead.

She asked Tía Dolores about one thing that was worrying her. "Would it be wrong to be happy this Christmas?" she asked. "Would it be disrespectful to Mamá?"

"No, I don't think so," said Tía Dolores. "The time of mourning has passed. Christmas is a blessed time. I'm sure God means for us to be happy, and to celebrate the birth of His son, Jesús." She looked down at Josefina. "And I'm sure your mamá would want you to be happy. She'd want you to pray and sing and celebrate with your friends and neighbors."

"Sí," Ana agreed. "Mamá would want us to follow all the Christmas traditions."

"I think so, too," said Francisca.

"Well," Clara said flatly. "We may follow the traditions, but they won't be the same without Mamá."

Somewhere inside Josefina a knot tightened. *Clara is right*, she thought.

"Mamá loved Christmas traditions," Josefina said to Tía Dolores. "She even started a new one in our family. Every Christmas, she'd make a doll dress for—"

"Oh, Josefina!" exclaimed Ana, interrupting. "You're talking about Niña, aren't you? Niña should have been given to you last Christmas."

"But she never was," said Josefina.

Tía Dolores looked puzzled. "Who's Niña?" she asked.

Ana explained, "When I was eight, Mamá made a doll for me. She named the doll Niña. Every Christmas, Mamá made a new dress for Niña. Then, the year Francisca was eight, I gave Niña to her."

"Sí," said Francisca. "And the Christmas when Clara was eight, I gave Niña to *her*."

"Of course, last year Mamá was not here to make a dress for Niña," said Ana sadly. She turned to Clara.

"But you could have given Niña to Josefina anyway, Clara. What happened?"

Josefina was curious to hear Clara's answer.

But Clara only shrugged and said, "I guess I forgot."

"Never mind, Clara," said Tía Dolores. "You can give the doll to Josefina this Christmas. I'll help you make a new dress for her. Where is Niña? I've never seen her."

"I haven't seen her in a long time, either," said Francisca.

"Neither have I," said Josefina, looking at Clara.

"Oh, she's around somewhere," said Clara. Her voice sounded unworried, but just for a second, a troubled look clouded her eyes. The look came and went so quickly, Josefina thought she must have imagined it.

Francisca, who was messy, liked to tease Clara, who was neat. "Heavens!" she said. "Do you mean to say that you've *lost* Niña?"

"She's not lost," said Clara crossly, kicking a pebble with her shoe. "I told you. She's around somewhere. I'll look for her when I have time."

"Would you like me to help you look?" Josefina

asked. She didn't want to make Clara more cross, but she really did want Niña. "Christmas is coming soon, and—"

"I know!" said Clara sharply. "I don't need any help! I'll find her!"

"Of course you will, Clara," said Tía Dolores.

Tía Dolores sounded so sure that Clara would find Niña. Josefina wished *she* could be as sure. How could Clara possibly have misplaced something as precious as Niña? Where could the doll be?

At that moment, Josefina made up her mind. She was going to look for Niña herself, no matter what Clara said. After all, Niña was *supposed* to be hers. Josefina's decision to look for Niña cheered her. She couldn't help feeling a little hopeful, just as she couldn't help feeling a little excited because she heard music. Josefina quickened her steps. The music was faint but clear, floating up from the village.

"Listen!" said Tía Dolores.

They all lifted their faces and listened. The music grew louder and stronger. It seemed to urge them, *Come along! Come along!* Soon they were all walking so fast they were practically dancing. Josefina's thick

braid bounced against her back, and even sensible
Clara skipped a little bit. The sound of the music
mixed in the air with the spicy scent of burning
piñón wood. As they came to the village, they saw
smoke rising up from chimneys into the cloudless
blue sky.

It was a small village. Josefina knew everyone in
all of the twelve families who lived there. She knew
their houses, too, which were built close together and
seemed to lean toward each other like old friends. The
houses were made of earth-colored adobe. They were
surrounded by hard-packed dirt, fenced pens for the
animals, and vegetable gardens now sleeping under
bumpy winter blankets of brown dirt. Most of the
houses faced the clean-swept *plaza* at the center of the
village. The biggest and most important building in
the village was the church. It was one story tall except
for the front, where the bell was hung high above
the doors.

Today, the doors of the church were wide open.
People scurried in and out carrying brooms and
brushes, tools, and scrubbing rags. They hauled big,
sloshing tubs of water up from the stream.

"*Buenos días!* It's good to see you! How are you today?" everyone called out when they saw Tía Dolores and the sisters.

"Buenos días! We're very well, thank you," they called back over the sound of the music and the noise of dogs barking and hammers pounding. People were talking, and every once in a while Josefina would hear swoops of laughter from the little children as they chased one another.

Clara, Francisca, and Ana went inside the church to start working. But Tía Dolores and Josefina lingered outside next to the musicians. One man was playing a guitar, and two others were playing violins. As Josefina and Tía Dolores listened, the music changed. The men began to play a slow, sweet song. All the noise and conversation seemed to fade away for Josefina. All she could hear was the music.

"I haven't heard this lullaby since I was a child," said Tía Dolores. She hummed along with the music for a moment, and then she asked Josefina, "Please, will you sing it for me?"

Josefina nodded. Very softly, she began to sing:

Sleep, my beautiful baby,
Sleep, my grain of gold.
The night is very cold,
The night is . . .

Josefina's throat tightened, and she couldn't finish the song. She turned her head away and looked down at the basket of chiles she was carrying so that Tía Dolores wouldn't see that her eyes had filled with tears.

But Tía Dolores had seen them already. She put her hand under Josefina's chin and gently turned Josefina's face toward her.

"Mamá used to sing that lullaby to me when I was little," said Josefina. "Papá played it on his violin. And we always sang it together at church on Christmas Eve to baby Jesús."

Tía Dolores used the soft edge of her sleeve to dry Josefina's cheek. Then she asked, "Does everyone sing it?"

"Everyone sings the end," said Josefina. "But not the first part. That's sung alone by the girl who is María in *Las Posadas*."

"You know," said Tía Dolores. "You're old enough to be María."

"Oh, I couldn't!" said Josefina. Her heart pounded faster at the very thought! Las Posadas was one of the most important and holy Christmas traditions. For nine nights in a row, everyone in the village acted out the story of the first Christmas Eve, when María and José were searching for shelter before baby Jesús was born. A girl took the role of María, riding a burro just as Jesús's mother did, and a man took the role of José. María and José and their followers went from house to house asking for shelter. Again and again they were turned away, until finally they were welcomed into the last house. On Christmas Eve, the final night of Las Posadas, everyone was welcomed into the church instead of a house, and then Midnight Mass began.

"Sometimes," said Tía Dolores thoughtfully, "a girl wants to be María because she wants to pray for something special. I wonder what your prayer would be, Josefina, if you were María?"

Josefina did not have to wonder. She knew what her prayer would be. "I'd pray that this will be a happy

Christmas," said Josefina, "for us and for Mamá in heaven."

Tía Dolores smiled. "That's a good prayer," she said. "Are you sure you don't want to be María?"

Josefina listened to the last notes of the lullaby. Part of her wanted to be María, but part of her knew she couldn't do it. "Last year, I could hardly sing the songs in Las Posadas," she said. "They made me so sad, because they reminded me that Mamá was gone. I'm afraid it'll be the same this year." She shook her head. "I couldn't possibly be María."

"I understand," said Tía Dolores. "It's still too soon for you." She tucked a strand of Josefina's hair behind her ear. "Let's go in now."

Josefina nodded, and walked into the church with Tía Dolores.

The church was usually a quiet, solemn place, and dim because the windows were very small and set deep in the thick walls. But today it was busy and noisy. Light poured in from the open doors and peeked through gaps in the roof where it had been damaged in a storm that fall.

Everywhere Josefina looked, she saw friends and

neighbors and workers from Papá's rancho who'd put aside their usual chores to come and clean the church. Señora Sánchez, Señora López, and several other women chatted together as they swept. Josefina saw Papá's sister, Tía Magdalena, with a group of women who were polishing candlesticks. Ana, Francisca, and Clara were in a group of girls who were dusting. Boys, who were supposed to be scattering water over the floor to settle the dust, were splashing each other. Most of the men of the village stood together, their arms crossed over their chests, looking up at the roof and discussing the damage caused by the storm in the fall.

Josefina saw Papá standing with the men. Then Papá excused himself. "There you are!" he said to Josefina and Tía Dolores. "I was looking for you."

"We stopped outside to listen to the music," Tía Dolores explained.

"I might have known!" Papá said. His eyes twinkled. "You two are the musicians in our family."

Josefina could tell that Papá's compliment pleased Tía Dolores because she blushed a little. "Well," she said, "we're ready to work now!"

"Good," said Papá. He caught the eye of Señor García, who came over.

Señor García was the *mayordomo*. It was his job to assign tasks, because he and his wife took care of the church. Señor García was an old man, thin and stooped, with very white hair. He had a husky voice and stately manners. Everyone respected him for his knowledge and liked him for his kindness.

"God bless you!" Señor García said to Tía Dolores and Josefina. "I'm glad to see you. We need good willing hands like yours to help! I'm afraid the storm has made our work harder than usual. The roof caused terrible damage when it fell in. We have a lot to do before the priest comes on Christmas Eve. Will you two help with the sweeping?"

"We'd be glad to," said Tía Dolores.

"Gracias," said Señor García. Then he turned to Papá. "May I ask your family to wash and iron the altar cloth, as you have done for many years?"

"Of course," said Papá.

"I remember when your dear wife gave that cloth to the church," said Señor García. "She'll be in our prayers this Christmas, I'm sure."

"Sí," said Papá quietly.

Señor García turned to Josefina again. "Josefina," he said. "I was wondering if you would like to be María in Las Posadas this Christmas, perhaps to offer a special prayer for your mamá?"

Josefina froze. Papá looked at her, waiting to hear her answer.

Tía Dolores put her arm around Josefina's shoulders. "It's very kind of you to ask, Señor García," she said. "But I think not this year."

"Ah, I see, I see," said Señor García gently. "Perhaps next year . . . Well, well, Margarita Sánchez can be María this Christmas."

Josefina didn't say anything. Just for a moment she leaned into Tía Dolores's arm, grateful for her understanding. Then she went to find Señora Sánchez to give her the basket of chiles.

The morning flew by so fast that Josefina was surprised when Señor García called everyone together for the closing prayer. "May God accept our work here today as a prayer of thanks for His merciful love," he said.

"Amen," said everyone together.

Josefina said her good-byes and walked out into the sunshine with her family. She had enjoyed sweeping and listening to the singsong of the women's voices as they gossiped and chattered around her. It had been nice to be part of the friendly group all scrubbing and sweeping and dusting together. Because of their work, the church shone. But now Josefina headed home with eager steps. She was determined to begin looking for Niña that very afternoon.

Where Is Niña?

osefina closed her eyes and tried to picture Niña. The last time Josefina had seen her, Niña was wearing a pale blue skirt. Her arms and legs were flat because some of her stuffing had fallen out, and her black yarn hair was tangled. Josefina clearly remembered Niña's lively black eyes and smiling pink mouth, and she was pretty sure she remembered a green sash tied around Niña's waist. *I'll just keep my eyes sharp for any bit of green or black or pale blue,* Josefina thought. *Niña has to be somewhere.*

The first place Josefina looked was in the room she shared with Clara and Francisca. Standing on tiptoe, Josefina ran her hand along all the high shelves built into the walls. She looked in corners, under blankets, and behind the trunk that Clara and Francisca kept their clothes in. No Niña.

Josefina opened the trunk to search inside. Clara's clothes were folded neatly and stacked in precise piles. Josefina looked between them and under them but saw nothing. Francisca's clothes were loosely folded and piled in the trunk in such a haphazard way that Josefina had to dig through them. She did find a missing stocking, a broken button, and a hair ribbon that Francisca had loudly complained about losing. But she didn't find Niña.

Josefina sat back on her heels and sighed. *Where is Niña?* she wondered.

It was a question she asked herself hundreds of times a day as Christmas came nearer. No matter where she was or what else she was doing, Josefina was looking for Niña. She'd start searching early in the morning when the snow on the mountains still had its cool blue glow, and she wouldn't stop until late in the afternoon when sunset made the snow look rosy.

Josefina's eyes searched the sala when she knelt there first thing in the morning for prayers with her family. Every time she walked to the stream to fetch water for the day, she looked around, hoping to see Niña hiding behind a rock or nestled at the foot of a tree. She explored every nook and cranny of the storerooms, the stables, and the chicken coops as she did her daily chores. She looked in the kitchen while she made *bizcochito* cookies and in the courtyard while she waited for bread to bake. She looked in the cradle when she rocked Ana's baby son, Antonio, to sleep. She looked in the weaving room behind the looms, in the stacks of finished blankets, and in baskets full of wool waiting to be carded and spun. Still no Niña.

In desperation, Josefina even searched the goats' pen. "You haven't eaten Niña, have you?" she asked her old enemy, Florecita. The yellow-eyed goat looked at Josefina, blinked once, and turned away.

Josefina tried hard not to be discouraged, even though she soon felt as if she'd searched every inch of the rancho. Then one day, Josefina and her sisters and Tía Dolores were invited to Señora Sánchez's house. Josefina was glad to go. She knew that Clara and Margarita Sánchez used to play dolls together. Maybe *that's* where Niña was. At least it was a new place to look!

"Buenos días! Please come in!" said Señora Sánchez as she welcomed everyone to her house. Almost all of the women and children from the village were there. The women had brought with them scraps of cloth and paper. They were using them to make flowers called *ramilletes* to decorate the church on Christmas Eve. Tía Dolores had brought some yellow material that was left over from the new dress Josefina had made for herself.

Señora Sánchez was a stout, good-hearted woman who was well known for being generous and neighborly. She'd been a special friend of Mamá's. They used to visit back and forth to share food and news and advice. Señora Sánchez always had time to sit and talk. And yet she seemed always to have something delicious cooking on the hearth, and her house was as neat as a pin. Mamá used to say she didn't know how Señora Sánchez did it!

But Señora Sánchez's house wasn't neat today. The women were gathered in the kitchen around the bright jumble of colored scraps. Josefina searched the kitchen with her eyes, hoping to see Niña. There was no doll to be seen, but Josefina couldn't help smiling at the pile of finished ramilletes. It looked as if a flower garden were blooming right there in the middle of Señora Sánchez's kitchen! Josefina turned to Tía Dolores. "The ramilletes remind me of the flowers Mamá planted in our court-yard," she said.

"Josefina, your mamá would be pleased with the way you've cared for the flowers she planted," said Tía Magdalena, who was Josefina's godmother.

All the women murmured in agreement.

"Things grew well for your mamá," said Señora López.

"Of course they did!" said Señora Sánchez. "And no wonder! She used to say to me, 'You must treat flowers like people!'"

The women nodded, and Señor García's wife said, "Well, she certainly treated people kindly. Look how beautifully her daughters are growing." Señora García turned to Tía Dolores. "And you've done well to teach the girls to read and write, and to encourage them to weave."

Tía Dolores smiled. "They've worked very hard," she said.

Josefina felt a warmth that came from more than the fire and the hot, sweet mint tea Señora Sánchez served. She had known these women all her life, as far back as she could remember. They'd helped her when she was a fat-legged toddler always underfoot and falling down just like the toddlers there today. They'd known her when she tagged along watching Clara and Margarita play dolls, back before Niña disappeared. When Mamá died, all of these women had lost a dear friend. Josefina knew they'd never forget Mamá, any more than she herself would.

"Look!" said Francisca. She held a cloth flower behind one ear. It was made of the yellow material that Tía Dolores had brought. Francisca twitched her skirts and swirled around gracefully as if she were dancing.

Everyone laughed. Ana said, "The flower looks pretty in your hair, Francisca. But it'll look just as pretty in the church on Christmas Eve!"

"We'll put the ramilletes in an arch over the altar," said Señora García to the girls. "And we'll put the cloth your mamá made on the altar."

"Didn't she have a fine hand for *colcha* embroidery?" said Tía Magdalena. "No village in New Mexico has a lovelier Christmas altar cloth."

Señora Sánchez turned to her daughter Margarita, who was going to be María in Las Posadas this year. "Sing for us, Margarita," she said. "Sing the lullaby we always sing on Christmas Eve."

Josefina held her breath while Margarita sang:

> *Sleep, my beautiful baby,*
> *Sleep, my grain of gold.*

And everyone but Josefina joined in:

> *The night is very cold,*
> *The night is very cold.*

This time, the lullaby didn't make Josefina cry. Instead, as she listened, Josefina thought, *A song like this must go straight up to God like a prayer.*

With all her heart, Josefina wished she had the courage to be María in Las Posadas this Christmas. But with all her heart she was sure that she did not.

The December afternoon was short. The weak winter sun slid down behind the mountains early, and it was nearly dusk when Papá came to walk home with

Tía Dolores and the sisters. He had been to the church to get the trunk that had the Christmas altar cloth in it.

Señora Sánchez beckoned to Josefina. "Come with me," she said. "I have something for you and your sisters, to thank you for the chiles."

Josefina followed Señora Sánchez outside. She was very surprised when Señora Sánchez handed her a little cage made out of bent wood. Inside the cage there was the plumpest, prettiest black-and-white hen Josefina had ever seen. "Oh, Señora Sánchez!" Josefina exclaimed. "Gracias!"

Señora Sánchez beamed a generous smile. "She's a vain little hen, very proud of herself, I'm afraid!" she said. "But she has reason to be proud. She lays very fine eggs. I thought you and your sisters could raise her chicks to increase your flock. I know you'll take good care of her."

Josefina thanked Señora Sánchez again. She held up the cage to look at the hen, who puffed herself up and met Josefina's gaze with her beady black eyes. Then Papá strapped the hen's cage onto the burro, next to the trunk from the church. He and Tía Dolores and the sisters began the long walk home.

"Adiós!" the women called out after them. "God keep you well!"

Josefina turned and waved. "Adiós!" she called.

It had been a long, full day and Josefina was tired. As she walked along next to Clara she said happily, "The ramilletes we made will look beautiful in the church, won't they?"

"I suppose so," said Clara, rather sourly. "Of course, no one will know how to arrange them as nicely as Mamá used to." She sighed. "Oh, well, at least the altar cloth will look all right. *It* will be the way it used to be."

When they were home at the rancho, Papá carried the trunk into the kitchen and set it down near the fire. "Wait till you see Mamá's altar cloth," Josefina said to Tía Dolores. "The birds that Mamá embroidered on it look so real you expect them to sing!"

Tía Dolores smiled. She knelt next to the trunk. Papá and all the sisters crowded around, peering over her shoulders as she lifted the lid. Tía Dolores lifted the altar cloth out of the trunk and they all looked at it. For a moment, no one said anything. Then Papá pulled his breath in sharply, as if something had hurt him. Without a word, he turned and left the room.

Josefina was confused. What was this torn, bedraggled cloth in Tía Dolores's hands? This cloth looked like a rag. It was chewed by mice. It smelled of mildew. It was water-stained and dirty. It couldn't be Mamá's beautiful embroidered altar cloth. But it was.

"Oh, no," said Ana, sounding miserable. "Water from the flood must have rotted the leather of the trunk so that mice and dampness got in. Just look at the damage that's been done."

"It's *ruined*!" Clara cried out. "It's ruined, just like Christmas!" She rushed from the room.

The door slammed behind her, and the whole room and everyone in it was shaken. It wasn't like Clara to act like that. Her words echoed in Josefina's head: *It's ruined, just like Christmas* . . . The knot inside Josefina tightened again. Just when Josefina had begun to hope that this Christmas might be happy, *this* had to happen. The beautiful altar cloth Mamá had made so lovingly was destroyed. It hurt Josefina to look at it on Tía Dolores's lap.

Tía Dolores unfolded the altar cloth slowly,

never minding the dirt and mildew that soiled her skirt. The more she unfolded it, the more damage Josefina saw.

Francisca lifted one corner, using just the tips of her fingers. "Just look!" she said. "It's in shreds!"

Ana sighed. "I'm glad Mamá is not here to see this," she said. "It would break her heart."

Tía Dolores didn't say anything. She examined the cloth carefully, running her hands over it. Then she said, "I think we can repair this."

Ana, Francisca, and Josefina looked at each other. "But how?" asked Francisca.

"First, we'll wash it," said Tía Dolores. "Then we'll iron it. We'll mend the embroidery wherever we can."

"But what about the embroidery that the mice chewed away?" asked Ana.

"We'll replace it with new embroidery," said Tía Dolores.

Francisca looked doubtful. "We'll need Clara for that," she said. "Mamá taught us all colcha embroidery, but Clara's the best. She's the only one who's even close to doing colcha as well as Mamá."

"Very well," said Tía Dolores. "Josefina, please

go to Clara and ask her to come back so that I may speak to her."

Josefina nodded. Quickly, she crossed the courtyard to the room she shared with Francisca and Clara. The door was partly open, and through it Josefina heard the sound of Clara crying. Josefina stood still, not sure what to do. As she hesitated, she looked into the room. It was dark, but Josefina saw Clara open the clothes trunk and take out an old skirt that was neatly folded into a thick bundle. Clara unfolded the skirt. Josefina saw a bit of something pale blue, a flash of green, *and there was Niña*!

Josefina gasped in surprise and bewilderment. Clara had Niña! The doll had been hidden in Clara's trunk all this time! Josefina took one step into the room, then stopped short when she saw Clara bury her face in Niña and sob. Clara cried as if her heart were broken, and she held on to Niña as if the doll were her only comfort in the world. Josefina turned away quietly so that Clara wouldn't hear her.

When Josefina got back to the kitchen, Ana and Francisca were gone. Tía Dolores was alone, still holding the altar cloth.

"Is Clara coming?" asked Tía Dolores.

"I . . . I don't know," stammered Josefina.

Tía Dolores looked confused. She asked, "Didn't you speak to her?"

"No," said Josefina. Suddenly, she burst out, "Tía Dolores, Clara has Niña! I saw her! The door was open a little and when I looked in, I saw Clara holding the doll!" Josefina spoke as if she could hardly believe what she had seen. "Clara has known where Niña is all along. She's been keeping her for herself!"

Tía Dolores put the altar cloth down and took both Josefina's hands in her own. "I'm not sure I understand it," she said slowly. "But I think Clara misses your mamá very, very much. Your mamá made Niña, and she made a new dress for her every Christmas. So Niña is a way for Clara to feel close to your mamá. She's a comfort. Clara needs her."

"But why did she pretend she didn't know where Niña was?" asked Josefina indignantly. "That wasn't *true*."

"Do you remember the other day when you told me how you're not ready to be María in Las Posadas?" Tía Dolores asked.

Josefina nodded.

"Well, Clara is not ready to give you Niña. That's why she's hiding her," said Tía Dolores. She looked at Josefina's long face and tried to cheer her. "At least we know that Niña isn't lost. She's safe. That's good, isn't it?"

"I guess so," Josefina admitted grudgingly. "But when will Clara give her to me? Will Niña ever be mine?"

Tía Dolores sighed. "I don't know," she said. "No one knows, probably not even Clara. It may take a long time." She put Josefina's hands aside and picked up the altar cloth again. "Just as it will take time to repair this altar cloth. But we'll do it. The sooner we begin, the better." Tía Dolores tried to tease a smile out of Josefina. "What do I always say?" she asked.

Josefina had to smile just a little bit, in spite of Clara, in spite of Niña, and in spite of herself. "You always say, 'The saints cry over lost time.'"

"Precisely!" said Tía Dolores briskly. "We'll start tomorrow!"

The Silver Thimble

And they did start repairing the altar cloth the very next day—everyone except Clara. Josefina helped Tía Dolores wash the altar cloth in warm, soapy water and rinse it in clear, cool water. Gently, Tía Dolores wrung out the cloth. Then she and Josefina spread it to dry in a sunny corner of the back courtyard. When the cloth was dry, Ana ironed it smooth, being careful not to scorch it with the hot irons heated by the fire. Francisca helped Josefina mend some of the holes the mice had chewed, and Tía Dolores cut off the end where the holes were too big to mend. She attached a new piece of material in its place.

At last the time came to begin the colcha embroidery. Tía Dolores and the four sisters gathered in front of the fire as they did every evening. Tía Dolores spread out the altar cloth. "What shall we embroider?" she asked, looking at the sisters.

Josefina looked at the altar cloth. Firelight brightened the colors of the designs that Mamá had stitched. Josefina had an idea. "Wait," she said. Very quickly, she went to her room and found her memory box, the little box in which she kept things that reminded her of Mamá. She brought the box back to the fireside. "Mamá made the altar cloth," she said. "I think we should embroider things on it that she loved. Maybe the things in my box will give us ideas."

Josefina opened her memory box, and Francisca took a swallow's feather out of it. "Mamá loved swallows," Francisca said. "I'll embroider swallows and other birds on the altar cloth."

Ana took a bit of lavender-scented soap out of the box. She smelled it. "I'll stitch sprigs of lavender," she said. "Mamá loved its scent."

"And I'll embroider leaves and flowers," said Josefina as she took a dried primrose out of her memory box. "Because Mamá loved them."

"And what will you embroider, Clara?" Tía Dolores asked.

Clara was only halfway in the firelight. She looked at the altar cloth with critical eyes. "It doesn't matter," she said. "We can't make that cloth look right again without Mamá anyway."

"We can," said Tía Dolores firmly. "It'll take time, but we can repair it. And if we all work together, I think we'll even enjoy doing it."

Clara drew back out of the light, but Josefina saw her face. It looked as sad as it did in the moment Josefina had seen Clara holding Niña and crying. Suddenly, Josefina felt sorry for Clara. "Doing the colcha embroidery makes me miss Mamá, too, Clara," Josefina said. "It makes her seem very far away, doesn't it?"

Clara didn't answer.

"Perhaps this will help," said Tía Dolores. She reached in her pocket and took out a silver thimble. "Your mamá gave this to me a long time ago when we were girls. She was trying to teach me how to do colcha. I didn't like it because I kept pricking myself with the needle and it hurt. She gave me the thimble to protect my finger. Now all of you may use it to protect *your* fingers."

Clara leaned forward on her stool. She looked at the thimble and then at Tía Dolores. "If Mamá gave something like that to me, I'd keep it forever," she said. "I wouldn't dream of giving it away!"

Just like Niña, thought Josefina with a heavy heart.

"But it makes me happy to share the thimble," said Tía Dolores. "When we use it, we'll think of your mamá with every stitch we make. Perhaps it will make her seem closer, not farther away."

"Oh, please, may I use it?" Josefina asked.

Tía Dolores handed the silver thimble to Josefina and she put it on her finger. It looked shiny in the light of the fire. As she began stitching, Josefina used the thimble to help push the needle through the cloth. She knew Clara was watching her. When Josefina started to tie a knot at the end of the wool she was using, Clara moved next to her.

"Don't," said Clara. "Have you forgotten? Mamá said never to knot the wool. Use your second stitch to hold your first stitch in place. Here, let me show you. I'll stitch the stem of that flower for you."

Clara spread the cloth over her knees and took the needle from Josefina. She began to stitch. Francisca nudged Ana, and Ana raised her eyebrows at Josefina as if to say, *This is a surprise!*

Josefina took the thimble off her finger. "Use this," she said.

Clara stopped for a moment and looked at the thimble. Then, slowly, she took it from Josefina and slipped it on her own finger. "Gracias," she said, but so quietly only Josefina could hear her.

Josefina gave herself the job of untangling knots in the wool Tía Dolores was using. When she looked up a little while later, Josefina saw that Clara had finished stitching the stem and was embroidering a yellow blossom on the end of it. Josefina saw that Clara's stitches were smooth and sure and secure.

She also saw that Clara hadn't taken the silver thimble off her finger.

On a still, cold evening a few days later, Tía Dolores and the sisters were working on the altar cloth in front of the fire. "Francisca," said Josefina. "That chicken you're stitching looks just like the pretty little hen that Señora Sánchez gave us."

Francisca groaned and pretended to be annoyed. "It's not supposed to be a chicken," she said. "It's supposed to be a sparrow!" She held the altar cloth up so that Tía Dolores, Ana, and Clara could see it, too. "What do you think?" she asked. "Can we pretend that it's a very fat sparrow?"

"One that clucks instead of singing?" teased Josefina.

They all laughed, and Clara said, "I can fix it for you. It just needs its feathers smoothed a bit."

"Gracias!" said Francisca. She let Clara take her needle with relief.

Ana had been wearing the silver thimble, but now she handed it to Clara. "You'll need this," she joked. "Francisca's chicken might peck at you!"

Tía Dolores was right, thought Josefina as they all laughed again. *We are enjoying working together to repair Mamá's altar cloth.*

"I remember when Mamá taught me to do colcha," said Clara. "She told me, 'You'll like colcha. You have hands that need to be busy.'" Tía Dolores and the sisters smiled at Clara's memory. Josefina watched Clara stitch and admired, as she always did, the way the silver thimble shone in the firelight.

The four sisters and Tía Dolores worked on the cloth almost every evening, and it was a time Josefina looked forward to. They took turns wearing the silver thimble. Francisca made a game out of it. She said that whoever wore the thimble had to share a memory about Mamá. Sometimes the memories would make Josefina sad. But sometimes they made her laugh because they reminded her of happy times. Just as the thimble protected Josefina and her sisters from the pain of being pricked by the needle, it seemed also to protect them from the pain that memories of Mamá used to bring.

Repairing the altar cloth was slow work. But as the days went by, stitch by stitch the cloth became beautiful again. And as the days went by, bit by bit Josefina began to feel better about all the things this Christmas might bring—even though she was now quite sure Niña was *not* going to be one of them.

Before they knew it, Christmas was only nine days away, and it was time for Las Posadas to begin. On the

first night of Las Posadas, it was snowing lightly when
Josefina and her family walked to the village. Papá led
the way, holding a lantern high to light the road. When
they came into the plaza, Josefina could see hot orange
sparks from the bonfires rising up to meet the cold
white snowflakes. The biggest bonfire was in front of
the church. Almost all their friends and neighbors and
all the workers from Papá's rancho had gathered around
it. Everyone greeted the Montoyas when they joined
the circle, and their breath puffed clouds into the sharp
air. As Josefina watched Margarita Sánchez climb onto
the burro and settle her skirts around her, she thought
Margarita would be a very fine María. Because it was
the village tradition, Margarita's papá was being José.
He led the burro to the first house and everyone followed. He knocked on the door, and they all sang:

In heaven's name, we ask for shelter.

And the people inside sang back:

This is not an inn! Be on your way!

At first, Josefina didn't even try to join the singing. She hung back, expecting to feel the same heavy, ice-cold weight of sorrow she'd felt last year. Back then, she had missed the sound of Mamá's voice so much that the music had been painful to hear. Papá must have felt the same way, because he gave away his violin. But tonight, the music wasn't painful. It sounded gentle and familiar. Josefina listened very hard. It seemed to her that the music helped her remember the sound of Mamá's voice, and so she was glad to hear it. Josefina looked at the faces that surrounded her. She saw Señor García's thin, kindly old face and Margarita Sánchez's young, round face. She saw Ana, Francisca, and Clara with snow-flakes clinging to their hair. She heard Papá's voice, so low she could feel it inside her, and Tía Dolores's voice, strong and clear. It was a comfort to be surrounded by these good people who had loved Mamá too. *Oh, Mamá,* Josefina thought. *We all miss you so much!* Somehow, the thought made missing Mamá easier to bear.

Josefina shivered. But it was the beautiful music that made her shiver, not cold or sorrow. As she listened, Josefina thought about how people had been singing these same songs at Las Posadas for hundreds of years.

They sang to honor God and to remember the first Christmas when Jesús was born. Josefina thought back to when Mamá taught *her* the songs so that she could join in the tradition. She remembered all the Christmases when she and Mamá had taken part in Las Posadas together, and the memories were both sad and sweet.

Tonight, the last house the procession went to was the Sánchez family's house. This time, after the people outside asked for shelter, the people inside opened the door wide. Josefina saw Señora Sánchez's good-natured face in the doorway and heard her sing louder than anyone else:

Come in, weary travelers. You are welcome!

Josefina grinned. No one could doubt that Señora Sánchez truly meant the welcoming words from her heart! And Josefina meant it, too, when she and the others sang their thanks in return:

God bless you for your kindness,
And may heaven fill you with peace and joy!

Then everyone crowded inside for prayers and more singing before the party began. In the Sánchez family's house, the air was spicy with the delicious aroma of meat pies and tamales and, of course, Señora Sánchez's famous stew. Josefina saw Clara and Margarita warming themselves by the fire. They were looking at the ramilletes, and Clara was holding up a scrap of yellow cloth as if she were planning to make more flowers. Her face looked happy and eager.

Josefina thought that Clara must be feeling the same way she was—as if a heavy burden had started to slip away.

La Noche Buena

very day was colder than the one before, and Christmas Eve day was bone-chilling. The sky was dark as stone from dawn till dusk, and sleet fell without stopping. Josefina's hands were stiff as she and Clara put the final stitches in the altar cloth late that afternoon.

At last the cloth was finished. Tía Dolores held one end and Ana held the other so that they could fold it carefully. One of the flowers Clara had embroidered ended up on top. Tía Dolores stroked the flower gently. "Clara," she said. "You have your mamá's gift for embroidery. Truly you do."

"I can't tell Clara's flowers from those Mamá made," agreed Ana.

A quick, pleased smile lit Clara's face. She took the silver thimble off her finger and held it out to

Tía Dolores. "Thank you for sharing this with us," she said.

Tía Dolores didn't take the thimble. Instead she said, "Perhaps Josefina will let us keep it in her memory box. It'll be handy there."

"Sí," said Josefina. "Go ahead, Clara. You can put the thimble in the box. It's on the shelf in our room."

But Clara put the thimble in the palm of Josefina's hand and then curled Josefina's fingers around it so that it was held tight in her fist. "No," Clara said. "I think you should go and put it in your memory box, Josefina."

"Sí, put it safely away," said Tía Dolores. "And Clara, you'd better go, too. It's time for you girls to change your clothes." She smiled. "It's Christmas Eve!"

Josefina and Clara hurried across the courtyard to their room. Francisca, who shared the room with them, had finished dressing. She'd left a small candle in the room to give Clara and Josefina light to dress by. But as they came in, it seemed to Josefina that the room was illuminated by more than one single candle. Josefina smiled when she saw why. Someone had laid out Josefina's best black lace *mantilla*, her comb, and her new dress on top of the trunk. The pretty yellow dress brightened the whole room. Josefina walked toward it, then stopped, stared, and gasped in surprise. For there, sitting on top of her yellow dress, was Niña!

Josefina lifted Niña up. She saw that Niña's face looked just as she remembered it. The eyes Mamá had sewn out of black thread still looked lively, and the mouth Mamá had sewn out of pink thread still smiled sweetly. Niña's yarn hair was smooth and untangled. Her arms and legs were plump with new stuffing. Best of all, Niña had a new yellow dress that exactly matched Josefina's. It had a long skirt and long sleeves gathered in puffs up near the shoulders. Niña even had a tiny new mantilla like Josefina's, and pantalettes and a petticoat. Josefina hugged Niña and kissed her soft cheeks.

"She's yours," said Clara.

"Oh, Clara!" Josefina whispered. "Gracias!" She hugged Niña closer. "I thought she never would be."

"Why not?" asked Clara.

"I . . . I knew that you had her," Josefina admitted, "and I—"

"You knew?" interrupted Clara.

"Sí," answered Josefina.

"Why didn't you say anything?" Clara asked.

"Well," said Josefina, "Tía Dolores told me that you needed her."

Very slowly, Clara nodded. "I did need her," she said. "I thought she was all I had left from Mamá. But now I know that I have Mamá's gift for embroidery, and I'll never lose that."

Josefina touched the smooth ribbon around the high waist of Niña's dress. "Did you make this dress for Niña?" Josefina asked.

"Sí," said Clara. "I wanted to carry on the tradition that Mamá started."

Josefina smiled broadly at Clara. "Niña's dress is beautiful," she said. "I think maybe you have Mamá's gift for making doll dresses, too!"

Clara smiled back. Then she looked lovingly at Niña. "I went to Niña for comfort because I thought I had nowhere else to go," she said. "But now I know that there's comfort all around me if I need it."

"Sí," said Josefina. "I'm finding that out also." She opened her fist, and the silver thimble shone in the candlelight. "I'll put the thimble in my memory box so that we can share it," Josefina said to Clara. "And we'll share Niña, too. She'll sleep between us from now on."

Christmas Eve was called *la Noche buena*—the good night. And this Christmas Eve felt like a very good night to Josefina. Niña was hers to love and care for at last. The weather was still sleety and cold, so Josefina wore a rebozo crisscrossed over her chest and tied behind her waist under the outer blanket she wore for warmth. She tucked Niña inside her rebozo and held her tight as she and her family walked to the village. It was later than usual, because tonight Las Posadas would end at the church and the priest, Padre Simón, would begin Mass at the stroke of midnight. After Mass, everyone would stream out of the church into the frosty blackness and wish each other *feliz Navidad*— happy Christmas. Then there was going to be a party at the Garcías' house. Josefina knew there would be music and dancing and a wonderful feast. Ana was bringing a silver tray piled high with sweet bizcochito cookies like Mamá used to make. Josefina hugged Niña in happy anticipation of it all.

A big bonfire glowed gold in the darkness in front of the church. Josefina was glad to see it. She was glad to go inside the church, too, where it was dry. Sleet had beaded her blanket as if it were covered with thousands of tiny pearls. Josefina took the blanket off and shook it just inside the door of the church. She checked to be sure that Niña was held safe in her rebozo, then hurried to catch up with Papá and Tía Dolores and her sisters. They were near the altar with Señor García and other friends and neighbors who had come to decorate the church.

Tía Dolores gave the altar cloth to Señor García.

"Gracias, gracias!" said Señor García to Tía Dolores and the sisters. "I am told that all of you had to work hard to repair this. God bless you!"

"Everyone is grateful," added Señora López. "Now our altar will be as beautiful as it has been in years past."

"Padre Simón is on his way," said Señor García. "Some men from the village have gone to greet him and lead him to the church. Perhaps we had better begin to decorate. Soon it will be time to start Las Posadas."

Only a few candles were lit. Most were being saved for when Padre Simón would say Mass. The church was shadowy, and Josefina felt as if she and the others who quietly set about decorating were preparing a lovely surprise. Josefina helped Papá and Señor López arrange pine branches around the little wooden stable that was part of the Nativity scene. The branches smelled fresh with the tang of mountain air. Then Josefina helped put the carved wooden figures from the Nativity scene in their places. She helped spread the cloth on the altar and smooth out any wrinkles. Ana and Francisca and a group of girls had just finished arranging the colorful ramilletes in an arch over the altar when Señora Sánchez hurried into the church. She looked distressed.

"Pardon me, Señor García," she said breathlessly. "I'm afraid I have bad news. My daughter Margarita is ill. She must have caught a cold from being outside on these bitter nights. She is too ill to be María tonight. She can't stir from her bed!"

"Poor Margarita!" said Señor García.

Everyone dropped what they were doing and gathered around Señora Sánchez and Señor García. They shook their heads and murmured, "Oh, the poor child! Bless her soul!"

Josefina's heart beat fast. She asked herself a question, and thought hard about the answer. Slipping one hand inside her rebozo so that it was touching Niña, Josefina used the other hand to tug gently on Señor García's sleeve.

Señor García turned to her. Josefina's voice was small but steady as she looked up at him and said, "Please, Señor García, may I be María?" Everyone looked at Josefina as she went on, "I'd like to pray that this will be a happy Christmas for us and for my mamá in heaven."

Señor García's thin old face was solemn. Slowly, he nodded. "Sí, my child," he said to Josefina. "You may be María."

Josefina turned to Papá. "Will you be José?" she asked him.

"I will," said Papá gravely. He didn't smile, but he looked at Josefina with pride and love.

Tía Dolores did, too.

When it was time, Josefina handed Niña to Clara
for safekeeping. "Please hold her for me," Josefina said.
"Keep her warm."

Clara took the doll. "I will," she promised.

They all went outside. The wind was blowing hard,
driving the sleet so that it stung Josefina's face. Papá
lifted Josefina up onto the burro's back. She knew
Señor Sánchez's burro was gentle. But still, she felt very
high off the ground. Josefina was glad Papá would
be walking at her side leading the burro. She took the
reins and held on tight.

A gust of wind made the skirt of her dress flutter.
Papá was wearing an extra blanket over his sarape. He
took it off now and said, "You'd better wear this over
your own blanket. It'll keep you warm."

"Gracias," said Josefina as Papá wrapped her in
the blanket. It covered her from head to foot.

As the villagers gathered to begin the procession,
many people stopped to speak to Papá and Josefina.
Gently, they touched Papá's shoulder or Josefina's
foot or the end of the blanket Papá had wrapped

around her. "May God grant you a good and long life," they said.

Josefina tried to sit up as straight as she could on the burro's back. Then, with a slow *clop clop* of the burro's hooves on the frozen ground, they moved to the first house. Papá knocked on the door, and they all sang:

In heaven's name, we ask for shelter.

And the people inside sang back:

This is not an inn! Be on your way!

Josefina's voice was unsteady at first. She felt nervous and stiff because she was self-conscious. But, as they had on every other night, the lovely music and words soon made Josefina forget all about herself and her shyness. After a while, Josefina was singing the Las Posadas songs in a voice that was full of all the hope and happiness of Christmas.

Papá led the burro from house to house. At each house, he and Josefina and everyone with them sang, asking for shelter. And at each house, the people inside sang back, telling them to go away. Then everyone inside the house came out to join the group behind Papá. After the last house, Papá turned back to the church. By that time, everyone in the whole village and all the workers from the rancho were in the crowd. Josefina felt as if everyone she knew and loved in the world were there behind her.

When they got to the church, Papá knocked on the doors. *Boom! Boom! Boom!* The sound echoed inside. Then everyone sang:

> *María, Queen of Heaven, begs for shelter*
> *For just one night, kind sir!*

Padre Simón opened one of the church doors just a bit. He looked out and sang:

> *Come in, weary travelers. You are welcome!*

Then Padre Simón flung both doors open wide. Golden candlelight flooded out. The church bell rang. And everyone sang:

God bless you for your kindness,
And may heaven fill you with peace and joy!

Papá lifted Josefina down off the burro. She was glad for his strong arms, because her legs felt wobbly and numb from the cold. The big blanket Papá had wrapped around her was weighted down with a coating of sleet, but when she took it off, her own blanket underneath it was dry.

"Josefina," she heard someone whisper. It was Clara, who handed Niña to her. Josefina tucked Niña safe inside her rebozo again. Then Tía Dolores took Josefina by one hand and Papá took the other, and they walked into the church behind Padre Simón. Ana, Francisca, Clara, and everyone else followed.

Josefina could hardly breathe. The church was so beautiful, she felt as if she were walking into a dream. All the candles were lit. Their brightness made the candlesticks shine and the polished wood glow. The candles cast a warm light on the Nativity scene in its nest of pine branches and on the delicate ramilletes arched gracefully above the altar.

But to Josefina, the most beautiful thing by far

was Mamá's altar cloth. Perhaps it was because she knew and loved every stitch of it after working on it for so long with Tía Dolores and her sisters. In the wavering candlelight, the soft, flowing leaves and flowers seemed to be floating in a gentle breeze, and the colors were rich and true. Josefina looked at the newly embroidered flowers with pride. *Mamá would be pleased,* she thought.

By now the church was full of people, and Padre Simón began the Mass. When it was time for her to sing the beginning of the lullaby, Josefina stood up, closed her eyes, and sang:

> *Sleep, my beautiful baby,*
> *Sleep, my grain of gold.*

Her voice was the only sound in the church, like a bird singing all alone on a mountaintop. Then Josefina opened her eyes, and everyone sang with her:

> *The night is very cold,*
> *The night is very cold.*

Josefina listened to all the voices soaring up around her, and she felt as safe and as loved as she used to feel when Mamá sang the lullaby to her.

Josefina hugged Niña close, sure that her prayer for a happy Christmas had been answered.

INSIDE Josefina's World

Today, New Mexico is part of the United States. But in 1824, when Josefina was a girl, it belonged to Mexico, and before that to Spain. In fact, Spain once ruled huge areas that are now part of the United States. Spanish and Mexican settlers first arrived in New Mexico more than 400 years ago, in 1598—even before the Pilgrims landed in America.

New Mexican settlers built homes in the mountains and valleys along the Rio Grande river. Santa Fe was the capital, but most settlers lived in villages and on ranchos. Drought was a constant worry, and so were sudden floods caused by heavy rainstorms. Lightning, grizzly bears, mountain lions, and rattlesnakes killed farm animals and sometimes people. To survive, everyone worked hard.

The settlers spoke Spanish, kept their Catholic faith, and enjoyed music and dances from Spain and Mexico. They grew familiar crops such as wheat, onions, and apples. They built irrigation ditches called *acequias* much like the ones used in Spain. But they also learned from their Pueblo Indian neighbors to use native foods like corn, squash, and pine nuts, and to make clothing such as moccasins.

Only a few villages had schools, but whether or not children learned to read and write, they received many kinds of education as they grew up. From their mothers, aunts, and grandmothers, girls learned the skills they needed to run a home of their own. A nine-year-old like Josefina would already know a great deal about sewing, knitting, spinning, weaving, cooking, gardening, and preserving food for the winter.

When winter came to the mountains of New Mexico, everyone began to look forward to Christmas, or *Navidad*. The Christmas season lasted nearly a month. It was a time for people to celebrate their faith and to enjoy evenings filled with delicious food, music, dancing, and the company of friends and relatives.

The *Camino Real*, or Royal Road, was the trail that connected Santa Fe with towns and cities hundreds of miles south. There, New Mexican goods such as wool blankets, animal hides, and pine nuts were traded for needed items like iron tools and luxuries like chocolate, Chinese silks and spices, and European lace, fabrics, and fine jewelry.

A caravan like Abuelito's took four or five months to reach Mexico City. There were deserts, canyons, mountains, and rivers to cross, and there was always the danger of attack. For more than 200 years the Camino Real was New Mexico's only link to the rest of the world. Then, in 1821, American traders began leading wagon trains from the state of Missouri to New Mexico. They made an important new trade route, which became known as the Santa Fe Trail. For the first time, people and goods from the United States began flowing into New Mexico.

Josefina's world was about to change.

GLOSSARY of Spanish Words

Abuelito *(ah-bweh-LEE-toh)*—Grandpa

acequia *(ah-SEH-kee-ah)*—a ditch made to carry water to a farmer's fields

adiós *(ah-dee-OHS)*—good-bye

adobe *(ah-DOH-beh)*—a building material made of earth mixed with straw and water

americano *(ah-meh-ree-KAH-no)*—a man from the United States

arroyo *(ah-RO-yo)*—a gully or dry riverbed with steep sides

bizcochito *(bees-ko-CHEE-toh)*—a kind of sugar cookie flavored with anise

buenos días *(BWEH-nohs DEE-ahs)*—good morning

Camino Real *(kah-MEE-no rey-AHL)*—the main road or trail that ran from Mexico City to New Mexico. Its name means "Royal Road."

colcha *(KOHL-chah)*—a kind of embroidery made with long, flat stitches

fandango *(fahn-DAHNG-go)*—a big celebration or party that includes a lively dance

feliz Navidad *(feh-LEES nah-vee-DAHD)*—Merry Christmas

gracias *(GRAH-see-ahs)*—thank you

gran sala *(grahn SAH-lah)*—the biggest room in the house, used for special events and formal occasions

granero *(grah-NEH-ro)*—a room used for storing grain, such as wheat and corn

la Noche buena *(lah NO-cheh BWEH-nah)*—Christmas Eve.

Las Posadas *(lahs po-SAH-dahs)*—a religious drama that acts out the story of the first Christmas Eve. Its name means "The Inns."

malacate *(mah-lah-KAH-teh)*—a long, thin spindle used to spin wool into yarn. New Mexicans used malacates instead of spinning wheels.

mano *(MAH-no)*—a stone that is held in the hand and used to grind corn. Dried corn is put on a large flat stone called a *metate*, and then the mano is rubbed back and forth over the corn to break it down into flour.

mantilla *(mahn-TEE-yah)*—a lacy scarf that girls and women wear over their head and shoulders

mayordomo *(mah-yor-DOH-mo)*—a man who is elected to take charge of town or church affairs

metate *(meh-TAH-teh)*—a large flat stone used with a *mano* to grind corn

Navidad *(nah-vee-DAHD)*—Christmas

Padre *(PAH-dreh)*—the title for a priest. It means "Father."

patrón *(pah-TROHN)*—a man who has earned respect because he owns land and manages it well, and is a good leader of his family and his workers

patrona *(pah-TROH-nah)*—a woman who has the responsibilities of a *patrón*

piñón *(pee-NYOHN)*—a kind of short, scrubby pine that produces delicious nuts

plaza *(PLAH-sah)*—an open square in a village or town

pueblo *(PWEH-blo)*—a village of Pueblo Indians

ramillete *(rah-mee-YEH-teh)*—a branch or bouquet of flowers used for decoration

rancho *(RAHN-cho)*—a farm or ranch where crops are grown and animals are raised

rebozo *(reh-BO-so)*—a long shawl worn by girls and women

sala *(SAH-lah)*—a room in a house

Santa Fe *(SAHN-tah FEH)*—the capital city of New Mexico. Its name means "Holy Faith."

sarape *(sah-RAH-peh)*—a warm blanket that is wrapped around the shoulders or worn as a poncho

Señor *(seh-NYOR)*—Mr.

Señora *(seh-NYO-rah)*—Mrs.

sí *(SEE)*—yes

siesta *(see-ES-tah)*—a rest or nap taken in the afternoon

tía *(TEE-ah)*—aunt

tortilla *(tor-TEE-yah)*—a kind of flat, round bread made of corn or wheat

Read more of JOSEFINA'S stories,

available from booksellers and at *americangirl.com*

 *Classics*

Josefina's classic series, now in two volumes:

Volume 1:
Sunlight and Shadows

Josefina and her sisters are
excited when Tía Dolores
comes to their *rancho*, bringing
new ideas, new fashions, and
new challenges. Can Josefina
open her heart to change
and still hold on to precious
memories of Mamá?

Volume 2:
Second Chances

Josefina makes a wonderful
discovery: She has a gift for
healing. Can she find the
courage and creativity to mend
her family's broken trust in an
americano trader and to keep her
family whole and happy when
Tía Dolores plans to leave?

 *Mystery*

A thrilling adventure with Josefina!

Secrets in the Hills

Josefina has heard tales of treasure buried in the hills, and of
a ghostly Weeping Woman who roams at night. But she never
imagined the stories might be true—until a mysterious stranger
arrives at her rancho.

Second Chances

A Josefina Classic
Volume 2

Josefina's adventures continue in the
second volume of her classic stories.

osefina opened one sleepy eye. Could she be dreaming? It was not quite dawn, and yet she seemed to hear music. Suddenly, Josefina grinned to herself. She remembered what day it was: the feast day of San José and her birthday.

Very slowly, the door to her room opened. In the pearly morning light she saw Papá, Tía Dolores, Ana and her husband Tomás, Francisca, Clara, Carmen the cook, and her husband Miguel. They began to sing:

> *On the day you were born*
> *All the beautiful flowers were born,*
> *The sun and moon were born,*
> *And all the stars.*

In the middle of the song, the little goat Sombrita poked her head around the corner of the door and bleated as if she were singing, too. Everyone laughed, and Tía Dolores said, "We wanted to surprise you with a lovely morning song, but I think someone forgot the words!"

Josefina picked up Sombrita and gave her a hug.

"Gracias," she said to everyone, feeling a little shy at all the attention. "I liked it."

The morning song was only the first surprise in a day full of them. Ana made cookies called *bizcochitos* for everyone to eat before breakfast. At morning prayers, Francisca showed Josefina how she'd decorated the family altar with garlands of mint and willow leaves and how she'd surrounded the statue of San José, the saint Josefina was named for, with white wild lilies and little yellow celery flowers. Clara, who liked to be practical, surprised Josefina by helping with her chores.

But when it was time to dress for the party, Clara had an impractical surprise for Josefina. It was a dainty pair of turquoise blue slippers. "It's about time I handed these down to you," said Clara. "I hardly ever wear them."

"Oh, Clara!" said Josefina, very pleased. She put the slippers on. They were only a *little* too big for her.

"If you're going to be so elegant," said Francisca, "you'd better carry Mamá's fan."

"And wear Mamá's shawl!" said Ana.

The four sisters shared Mamá's fan and shawl

and brought them out only on very special occasions. Josefina swirled the shawl around her shoulders and looked behind her to see the brilliant embroidered flowers and the slippery, shimmery fringe on the back. She fluttered the fan and felt very elegant indeed.

The party table looked elegant, too. There was a beautiful cloth on it, and the family's best plates and glasses and silverware. Tía Dolores had made a special fancy loaf of bread. There were meat turnovers, and fruit tarts, and candied fruit that looked like jewels. But best of all, in the center of the table there was a red jar with one small branch of apricot blossoms in it. Josefina smiled when she saw the perfect blossoms. She knew that Tía Dolores had cut the branch from *her* tree—the tree she liked to climb. Josefina remembered the day Tía Dolores had comforted her next to that apricot tree. "We're all given second chances," Tía Dolores had said. "We just have to be brave enough to take them."

About the Author

VALERIE TRIPP says that she became a writer because of the kind of person she is. She says she's curious, and writing requires you to be interested in everything. Talking is her favorite sport, and writing is a way of talking on paper. She's a daydreamer, which helps her come up with her ideas. And she loves words. She even loves the struggle to come up with just the right words as she writes and rewrites. Ms. Tripp lives in Maryland with her husband.

About the Advisory Board

American Girl extends its deepest appreciation
to the advisory board that authenticated Josefina's stories.

Rosalinda B. Barrera, Professor of Curriculum &
Instruction, New Mexico State University, Las Cruces

Juan R. García, Professor of History and Associate Dean
of the College of Social & Behavioral Sciences,
University of Arizona, Tucson

Sandra Jaramillo, Director, Archives & Historical Services,
New Mexico Records Center & Archives, Santa Fe

Skip Keith Miller, Co-director/Curator,
Kit Carson Historic Museums, Taos, NM

Felipe R. Mirabal, former Curator of Collections,
El Rancho de las Golondrinas Living Museum, Santa Fe

Tey Diana Rebolledo, Professor of Spanish,
University of New Mexico, Albuquerque

Orlando Romero, Senior Research Librarian,
Palace of the Governors, Santa Fe

Marc Simmons, Historian, Cerrillos, NM

Second Chances

A Josefina Classic
Volume 2

by Valerie Tripp

★ American Girl®

Published by American Girl Publishing
Copyright © 1998, 2000, 2014 American Girl

Questions or comments? Call 1-800-845-0005,
visit **americangirl.com**, or write to Customer Service,
American Girl, 8400 Fairway Place, Middleton, WI 53562.

Printed in China
15 16 17 18 19 20 21 LEO 11 10 9 8 7 6 5 4 3

All American Girl marks, BeForever™, Josefina®,
and Josefina Montoya® are trademarks of American Girl.

Grateful acknowledgment is made to Enrique R. Lamadrid for permission
to reprint the verse on p. 49, adapted from "*Versos a la madre* / Verses to Mother"
in *Tesoros del Espíritu: A portrait in sound of Hispanic New Mexico,* University of
New Mexico, University of New Mexico Press, © 1994 Enrique R. Lamadrid.

This book is a work of fiction. Any similarity to real persons, living or dead,
is coincidental and not intended by American Girl. References to real events,
people, or places are used fictitiously. Other names, characters, places, and
incidents are the products of imagination.

Cover image by Michael Dwornik and Juliana Kolesova

Cataloging-in-Publication Data available from the Library of Congress

To Peggy Jackson,
with thanks

To Kathy Borkowski,
Val Hodgson, Peg Ross,
Jane Varda, and Judy Woodburn,
with thanks

To Rosalinda Barrera, Juan García,
Sandra Jaramillo, Skip Keith Miller,
Felipe Mirabal, Tey Diana Rebolledo,
Orlando Romero, and Marc Simmons,
with thanks

Beforever™

The adventurous characters you'll meet in
the BeForever books will spark your curiosity
about the past, inspire you to find your voice
in the present, and excite you about your future.
You'll make friends with these girls as you share
their fun and their challenges. Like you, they are
bright and brave, imaginative and energetic,
creative and kind. Just as you are, they are
discovering what really matters: Helping others.
Being a true friend. Protecting the earth.
Standing up for what's right. Read their stories,
explore their worlds, join their adventures.
Your friendship with them will BeForever.

TABLE *of* CONTENTS

1 Spring Sprouts..1

2 Tía Magdalena..16

3 Second Chances..30

4 Rattlesnake..43

5 The Bird-Shaped Flute..................................54

6 Heart's Desire...67

7 A Charm from the Sky.................................77

8 Shining Like Hope..91

9 Gifts and Blessings.....................................105

10 Sleet...119

11 Josefina's Plan..136

12 Heart and Hope...147

Inside Josefina's World...................................156

Glossary of Spanish Words............................158

Josefina and her family speak Spanish, so you'll
see some Spanish words in this book. You'll find
the meanings and pronunciations of these words
in the glossary on page 158.

Remember that in Spanish, "j" is pronounced
like "h." That means Josefina's name is
pronounced "ho-seh-FEE-nah."

Spring Sprouts

osefina loved spring. She loved the way it came swooping in like a bird on a breeze. She loved the way it woke the earth up from its deep winter sleep and made the *rancho* a busy, lively place. Baby animals were born in the spring. The sun stayed longer in the sky, and there were small green surprises here and there where things were beginning to grow.

Just now, Josefina had a surprise to share. She swung open the door to the weaving room and poked her head inside. "Tía Dolores!" she said eagerly. "Please, come with me. I have something wonderful to show you."

Tía Dolores looked up. The wind through the open door fluttered the pages of her ledger book, which was on her lap. Josefina saw that Papá was in the weaving room, too. He was counting finished woven blankets, and Tía Dolores was writing the numbers in her ledger with her quill pen.

"Oh! Forgive me for interrupting, Papá," said Josefina.

"Well," said Papá cheerfully. "I'd like to see something wonderful, too. I suppose our counting can wait, don't you, Dolores?"

"Of course!" said Tía Dolores, putting down her pen.

Papá made a little bow from the waist and held out his hand toward the door. Tía Dolores swept by him, and they both followed Josefina as she walked quickly across the courtyard to the back corner.

"Just look!" said Josefina. She knelt down and lifted a handful of dead leaves. Underneath, skinny yellow-green sprouts were sticking up out of the soil. Josefina lifted another handful of leaves, and then another, and every time there were green shoots underneath. "Sprouts everywhere!" she said. "More than ever before! Pretty soon the whole corner will be full of flowers."

"*Sí*, it will," agreed Papá. He sounded pleased. He put his hand on Josefina's head and smoothed her hair.

Tía Dolores knelt down, too. Josefina loved the way her aunt never minded getting dirt on her skirt or her hands. The sun shone on Tía Dolores's dark red hair as she bent over the sprouts. Josefina knew Tía Dolores was pleased, too. These sprouts were a promise kept.

Josefina's mamá had planted the flowers in this corner. During the year after Mamá died, Josefina had cared for the flowers as well as she could. Then last fall, Florecita, the meanest goat on the rancho, had torn up the flowers and eaten every last one. Josefina had thought Mamá's flowers would never grow again. But Tía Dolores had promised that they'd be all right. Now she turned and smiled at Josefina. "Didn't I tell you?" she said. "Flowers with roots as deep as these can survive a lot—even a visit from Florecita!"

Josefina grinned. "I'm still going to keep Florecita away from them!" she said.

"Don't worry," said Papá. "Florecita will be too busy to bother your flowers this spring. She's going to have a baby very soon."

"Oh, no!" said Josefina, pretending to groan. "I hope Florecita's baby isn't like her. I don't think I could stand two horrible goats trying to bully me!" Josefina laughed along with Papá and Tía Dolores. She used to be afraid of Florecita. She wasn't the least little bit afraid of the goat anymore, but she didn't like her the least little bit, either.

It was cool that night. Josefina was glad she had left a blanket of dead leaves spread over the sprouts to protect them. And she was glad she had a blanket of woven wool spread over her lap, though the family *sala* was warm.

Josefina and her sisters, Ana, Francisca, and Clara, were sewing blankets. Woven material came off the loom in narrow strips, which had to be sewn together to make one wide blanket. Josefina made her stitches strong and straight. All the sisters were good at sewing blankets. They'd sewn many since the fall.

Tía Dolores was adding numbers in her ledger. After a while, she paused and asked, "Josefina, your birthday is coming soon, isn't it?"

"Sí," said Josefina. "I was born on March nine-teenth, the feast of San José."

"When Mamá was alive, we always had a

celebration," said Francisca. She was Josefina's second oldest sister, and she loved parties.

"Well, I think we should have one this year, too," said Tía Dolores.

The sisters looked up, delighted.

"After all, we'll have several things to celebrate," Tía Dolores went on. "It's the feast of San José. Josefina will be ten. Spring will be here. And . . ." Tía Dolores smiled as she said, "God willing, we should have quite a lot of new sheep by then. I've added the figures. We've made sixty blankets. That's enough to trade for ninety sheep—forty-five ewes and forty-five lambs."

"That *is* good news!" exclaimed Josefina. She and Francisca both put their sewing aside and went to look over Tía Dolores's shoulder at her ledger. Ana, the oldest sister, murmured a prayer of thanks. Clara, who was next to Josefina in age, calmly continued to sew.

"It's good," said Clara. "But it doesn't mean we can stop making blankets. We'll need them to trade for *more* sheep."

"Oh, baa, baa, baa," Francisca bleated at Clara. "Don't be so tiresome! We all know that ninety sheep aren't enough to replace the hundreds that Papá lost in the flood last fall. But it's a good start! I think we should be very proud of ourselves. Sixty blankets is a lot. I know I worked hard on them."

Ana, Clara, and Josefina glanced at each other and then burst out laughing. Francisca complained more than anyone else about working on the blankets. Now she made it sound as if she'd been responsible for them all!

At first, Francisca scowled at her sisters' laughter. But in a moment she was laughing at herself along with them. "All right, all right," she admitted grudgingly. "The rest of you worked hard, too."

"We might not have *any* blankets to trade if it weren't for Tía Dolores," said Josefina. "It was her idea to turn blankets into sheep."

All the sisters nodded and looked at their aunt with fondness. After the terrible loss of the sheep, Tía Dolores had suggested that she and the sisters and other workers on the rancho weave the wool they already had into blankets and trade them for sheep. Now, just when spring lambs were being born, they had sixty blankets to turn into sheep!

"Papá will be pleased," said Ana.

"When do you think he'll go to the *pueblo* village to trade the blankets for Esteban Durán's sheep?" asked Josefina. Esteban, Papá's great friend, was a Pueblo Indian.

"Soon," said Tía Dolores. She smiled over her shoulder at Josefina. "Maybe you'd like to go with him." Tía Dolores knew that Josefina loved to go to the pueblo and see her friend Mariana, who was Esteban's granddaughter.

"May I find Papá right now and ask him?" Josefina said.

"Sí," said Tía Dolores, who always understood Josefina's eagerness. "Go. Wrap your *rebozo* around you. It's chilly."

"*Gracias!*" said Josefina. She gave Tía Dolores a quick hug and pulled her rebozo up over her head. She was just about to hurry out the door when an idea stopped her. "Tía Dolores," she said. "Won't you come with me? You should be the one to tell Papá about the blankets and the sheep."

Tía Dolores started to say no, but Ana and Francisca chimed together, saying, "Go on. It *is* your news to tell."

"Very well," laughed Tía Dolores. She put her sewing aside and took Josefina's hand, and together they went out into the cool spring night.

They found Papá in the goats' pen. He was sitting next to one of the goats with a lantern at his side. He glanced up when they came in, but he didn't say anything.

"Papá," Josefina began excitedly. "Tía Dolores has good news for . . ." Josefina stopped. She realized that the goat next to Papá was Florecita. But she had never seen Florecita like this. The goat was lying on her side, hardly breathing. Her eyes were shut. "Papá," asked Josefina, "what's wrong?"

"Florecita had her baby tonight," said Papá. "But she's too weak to nurse it. I don't think she'll live."

Josefina looked down at her old enemy, Florecita. Living on a rancho, Josefina had seen many animals die. She knew better than to think of the animals as anything more than useful and valuable property. Still, as she looked at Florecita—the goat who had bullied her and poked her and torn up Mamá's flowers— somehow she just couldn't help feeling sorry. "Can't we do anything?" she asked Papá.

"I don't think so," said Papá.

Josefina let go of Tía Dolores's hand and knelt next to Papá. She stroked Florecita's side, but the goat didn't move or open her eyes. Her breathing grew slower and slower until at last it stopped. Florecita was dead.

Josefina sighed. "Poor Florecita," she said softly. Then she remembered something important. She turned to Papá. "Where is Florecita's baby?" she asked.

Papá lifted the front corner of his *sarape.* Cradled in his arm was a tiny goat.

"Oh!" gasped Josefina, pulling in her breath. Tía Dolores gasped, too, and sank down on her knees behind Josefina.

Very gently, Josefina reached out and touched the goat's silky little ear. The goat turned her head and nuzzled the palm of Josefina's hand. "Oh," Josefina said again. The goat opened her eyes and Josefina had to smile, because her yellow eyes looked just like Florecita's, but without the evil glint. Suddenly, Josefina knew what she must do. "Please, Papá," she asked. "May I take care of Florecita's baby?"

Papá's kind face was full of concern. "The baby is

very weak, Josefina," he said. "It isn't easy to care for an animal this needy. I think you might be too young for the responsibility."

"I'm almost ten!" said Josefina. "Please let me try."

Still Papá hesitated. "You must realize . . ." he began. Then he stopped.

Tía Dolores put her arm around Josefina's shoulder. Then, in a gesture so swift Josefina thought she must have imagined it, Tía Dolores touched Papá's hand. Papá looked up at Tía Dolores, and Josefina saw that his eyes had a question in them. Tía Dolores nodded. She seemed to know what Papá had started to say, and she was encouraging him to say it.

Papá spoke slowly. "You must realize that there's a good chance the baby won't live, even if you do care for her," he said to Josefina. "Think how you'll feel if you become fond of the little goat and then she dies."

Josefina understood. Papá was afraid her heart would be broken as it had been when Mamá died. And for a moment, Josefina was afraid, too. But then she looked at the little goat and all her doubts fell away. "I have to try to save Florecita's baby, Papá," she said. "When any of God's creatures is sick or weak we have to try to make it better, don't we?" She held out her arms for the goat. "Please, Papá," she said.

Papá sighed. Carefully, he put the baby goat into Josefina's arms. She held the soft warm body nestled close to her chest and rubbed her cheek against the goat's fur. The baby goat gave one small bleat, closed her eyes, and went to sleep as if Josefina's arms were the safest place in the world.

"Take her back to the house," said Papá, "and keep her next to the fire. I'll bring some milk. She's too weak to nurse from one of the other goats. You'll have to teach her to drink." He stood up and looked at Josefina holding the helpless, sleeping goat. "She's yours to care for now."

"I'll take good care of her," said Josefina. "I promise."

"That's *Florecita's* baby?" Francisca asked. "She's such a sweet little thing!"

"*Very* little," said Clara. "Puny, really. It's going to be a lot of work and worry to make *that* goat healthy and strong."

"The poor motherless baby!" said Ana tenderly.

Josefina's sisters were gathered around her, staring at the baby goat, which was now awake in her arms. Tía Dolores poured the milk Papá brought into a bowl and placed it on the hearth. But when Josefina put the goat next to the milk, the little animal didn't seem to know what to do.

"Here," said Josefina. She dipped her fingers in the milk and then held them up to the goat's mouth. At first, the goat seemed too weak even to open her mouth. But then she sucked the milk off Josefina's fingers. "That's it," said Josefina. "That's the way."

Patiently, Josefina dipped her fingers in the milk again and again, feeding the little goat almost drop by drop. Josefina liked the tickling feeling of the goat's rough tongue on her fingers. She was sorry when the goat fell asleep again, before the milk bowl was empty.

"Clara's right. Taking care of that goat will be hard," said Francisca. "But I hope she grows up to be as big as Florecita, just not as mean."

"So do I," said Josefina, hugging the goat. "So do I."

That night, Josefina and the baby goat slept on a

wide bunk above the kitchen hearth called the shepherd's bed. Shepherds sometimes brought orphaned lambs there to sleep because it was heated by the hearth fire through the night. The little goat slept curved like a cat, her legs tucked under her body, her bony head resting on Josefina's hand. Josefina woke up often during the night. She wanted to be sure she could feel the little goat's heart beating and the warmth of its soft breath on her hand.

The little goat made it through the night. Before dawn the next morning, Papá brought Josefina a pouch filled with goat's milk. He attached a rag to the end of the pouch. Josefina held it to the baby goat's mouth. After licking it once or twice, the goat sucked on the rag and hungrily drank the milk out of the pouch.

"Look, Papá!" said Josefina. "Isn't she clever?"

"Sí," said Papá. He stroked the goat's head with the back of his finger.

Josefina thought the goat was *very* clever to have figured out how to drink from the pouch. In fact, Josefina believed that Florecita's baby was a superior animal in every way—even if she *was* rather small.

The baby goat grew stronger as each bright spring day passed. She seemed to thrive on warm sunshine, warm milk, and Josefina's warm affection. It was not long before the goat was following Josefina around everywhere on her quick, sturdy little legs.

"She's just like your shadow!" joked Tía Dolores. And so they all began to call the goat Sombrita, which means "little shadow."

Soon everyone was used to seeing Josefina and Sombrita together all over the rancho. Sombrita trip-trotted down to the stream every morning when Josefina went to fetch water for the household. Sombrita tagged along while Josefina fed the chickens, which made the chickens cluck and fuss. The little goat chased Josefina's broom as if it were a toy and sweeping were a game she and Josefina played with it. She dozed peacefully while Josefina worked at the loom, and bleated noisily while Josefina had a piano lesson with Tía Dolores. Josefina loved to look down and see Sombrita's cheerful face raised toward her hoping for a quick pat, a hug, or a scratch behind one floppy ear.

As Sombrita grew more frisky, Josefina had to keep an eye on her all the time. The rancho was a dangerous place for such a small creature. She might be kicked by a mule or stepped on by an ox. Josefina especially worried about snakes. Snakes were just awakening from their winter hibernation, so they were hungry. In the spring, a rattlesnake was quite likely to strike a baby animal like Sombrita and kill her. Josefina kept Sombrita close by, safe from harm. She had promised to take good care of the little goat, and it was a promise she intended to keep.

Tía Magdalena

One warm day, Tía Dolores, Josefina, and the sisters were planting seeds in the garden. Josefina used a sharp stick to make a hole in the earth. She dropped a seed in the hole, covered it with dirt, then patted the dirt in place. Josefina always liked to give the dirt an extra little pat, to encourage the seed to grow. Josefina and her sisters tended their garden with care. During the summer they'd carry water up from the stream every day to keep the earth moist. They'd pull weeds and shoo away pests. Then in the fall they'd harvest squash, beans, chiles, pumpkins, and melons.

"Oh, I'd love a big slice of melon right now!" said Francisca.

"Me, too," agreed Josefina. She sat back on her heels for a rest. The earth was cool beneath her knees, but the sun was hot on her shoulders.

"You'll have to wait until the end of the summer," said Clara. "We ate all our melons months ago."

"We were lucky to save as many as we did," said Ana. The same storm that had killed Papá's sheep had flooded the kitchen garden.

"We'll harvest all we plant today, God willing!" said Tía Dolores. She nodded toward Sombrita, who was bleating at the birds flying low near the garden. "Fierce Sombrita is scaring away all the birds trying to steal the seeds."

The sisters laughed, because the bold birds weren't the least bit frightened by Sombrita. The goat saw that she was the center of attention. She began to show off by kicking up her heels and bleating even louder.

"Who is that noisy animal?" someone asked. It was Tía Magdalena, walking through the gate. She was Papá's older sister, who lived in the village.

The girls and Tía Dolores greeted her politely. Then Tía Dolores answered her question. "That's Sombrita," she said. Her voice was full of fondness and pride as she went on to say, "Josefina has cared for her since she was born. The mother died."

"We all thought Sombrita would die, too," said Clara, who was always matter-of-fact. "She was so weak and pitiful."

Tía Magdalena looked interested. She bent down and scooped up Sombrita. She stroked the little goat gently, and Sombrita settled calmly in her arms. Then Tía Magdalena looked at Josefina. Her soft brown eyes were warm. "Why did you decide to take care of Sombrita?" she asked.

Josefina didn't know what to say. "I . . . I didn't stop to think about it," she said honestly. "I just . . . I had to, that's all."

"Has it been hard work?" asked Tía Magdalena.

"Oh, no!" said Josefina. "I love taking care of Sombrita!"

"You have done a good job of it," said Tía Magdalena. She handed Sombrita to Josefina. "Sombrita is a fine, healthy goat."

"Gracias, Tía Magdalena," said Josefina. She was pleased to be praised by her aunt. Tía Magdalena was an important person in her family, especially to Josefina, because she was Josefina's godmother. She was an important, respected person in the village, too.

Tía Magdalena was the healer, or *curandera*. She knew more about healing than anyone else. People who were injured or ill went to her for care, and she always knew just what to do.

Now Tía Magdalena turned to Tía Dolores. "Here are the mustard leaves you asked for," she said. "Tell your cook Carmen to brew tea from them and give it to her husband Miguel to drink if his stomach ache comes back."

"Gracias," said Tía Dolores, taking the leaves.

"Please tell her not to use it all at once," said Tía Magdalena. "I haven't many leaves left. Tansy mustard is usually blooming everywhere by now, but I haven't been able to find any yet this year."

"I've seen some growing by the stream," Josefina piped up.

"Your young eyes are better than my old ones!" said Tía Magdalena. "Perhaps you'll gather some leaves for me." Tía Magdalena tilted her head and looked at Josefina as if she were considering something. "And perhaps when you bring the leaves, you can stay for a while and help me. My storeroom needs a spring cleaning."

"Oh, I'd like that very much!" said Josefina.

"Good!" said Tía Magdalena. She smiled, and Josefina blushed with pride and pleasure. How nice to have pleased Tía Magdalena!

The very next day Josefina skipped along the road to the village under a clean blue sky. She had a bunch of tansy mustard leaves in her hand for Tía Magdalena. Papá, Tía Dolores, and the sisters were going to the village, too. Josefina had left Sombrita behind under Carmen's watchful eye. Josefina missed Sombrita, but she knew the little goat would only be in the way today. In the morning, the men and boys were going to clean out the water ditches, called *acequias,* while the women and girls replastered the church. And in the afternoon, Josefina would be too busy to keep an eye on Sombrita when she went to help Tía Magdalena.

Most of the villagers had already gathered in the *plaza* at the center of the village when Papá and his family arrived. They called out greetings. *"Buenos días!"* they said.

"Buenos días," Papá replied. "It's a fine day to work, by God's grace."

"It is," said Señor Sánchez, who was in charge of the water ditches. "Let's begin." He and Papá and the other men shouldered their tools and set off to work. Clearing the acequias was a very important springtime job. Later in the spring, when the snow on the mountaintops melted, the acequias had to be clear of leaves and sticks and weeds so that the water could flow to the fields. Without water, nothing planted that spring would grow.

"We'd better begin our work, too," said Señora Sánchez. The women and girls agreed. They took off their shoes, rolled up their sleeves, covered their hair, and tucked up their skirts. Replastering the church was another important chore. It was normally done later in the spring. But the weather had been so unusually warm the past few weeks, the women were replastering much earlier this year. Josefina was glad. As she scooped up a handful of gritty mud plaster, she decided replastering was a chore that was fun.

"Watch out!" Josefina shouted at Clara, who stood between her and the church. Clara ducked down, and

Josefina flung her handful of mud plaster at the wall of the church, where it stuck—*splat*—in a glob.

Clara laughed, saying, "You'll splatter mud all over if you do it that way." Clara was neat. She *pressed* her handful of mud plaster against the wall.

But even Clara was easygoing today, thought Josefina as she spread the glob of mud over the *adobe* bricks so that it was smooth and even. The women and girls gossiped and chattered as they worked. The very oldest ladies sat in the shade, keeping an eye on the babies. They called out jokes and encouragement to the others. Every once in a while someone would start a song and everyone would join in. Voices high and low, in tune and out of tune, rose up from all around the church.

Josefina liked making the church walls whole again. Later, she and some other children climbed up onto the roof to spread a new layer of mud plaster on it as well. Josefina loved the feeling of the mud oozing between her bare toes. It was exhilarating to be up high, closer to the huge white clouds and the brilliant blue sky. Josefina and the others shrieked with joy as they slipped and slid on the slick mud to tamp it flat.

"Josefina!" Clara called out. She was standing below on the ground, looking up, shading her eyes with her hand. "Tuck your skirt up higher in the back or you'll get mud on it and look messy at Tía Magdalena's this afternoon."

"And pull up your rebozo so that it shades your face," Francisca added. "Your nose is getting as red as a tomato."

Josefina looked down at tidy, sensible Clara and at beautiful Francisca, who was fussy about her skin. She knew that right now her sisters envied her. *They* were too old to be on the roof.

Almost ten is a wonderful age to be, thought Josefina, exuberantly slooshing her feet through the mud. *I'm not too old to slip and slide on the roof, and yet I am old enough to take care of Sombrita and old enough to help Tía Magdalena!* She waved to her sisters and cheerfully ignored their advice.

"Bless you, child!" said Tía Magdalena that afternoon when she saw Josefina at her door with the bouquet of mustard leaves. "Come in!"

"Gracias," said Josefina. She stepped inside and took a deep breath. Nowhere else on earth smelled quite the way Tía Magdalena's house smelled. It reminded Josefina of the way the corner of the back courtyard smelled when the sun shone strong on Mamá's flowers. But mixed in with the scent of flowers was the sharp, nose-tickling scent of spices and the musty, earthy tang of the herbs that hung upside down in bunches from the beams.

Tía Magdalena smiled when she saw Josefina looking up at the herbs. "You'd like to know how to use them, wouldn't you?" she asked.

Josefina nodded, wondering how Tía Magdalena had known.

"The mint leaves ease stomach aches. The pennyroyal brings a fever down. I use the *manzanilla* flowers to make a tea to cure a baby's colic," Tía Magdalena said, pointing to each herb as she named it. "And speaking of babies, how is your sweet Sombrita today?"

"She's *very* well, thank you," answered Josefina, grinning.

"She's *very* fortunate to have you caring for her!" said Tía Magdalena. Her face looked merry. Tía

Magdalena was much older than Papá. Her gray hair was streaked with white. But when she smiled as she did now, her expression was lively. And when she moved, her step was quick and light. "Now, we must do some work," she said. "Come with me."

Tía Magdalena led Josefina to the small storeroom at the back of her house. The ceiling was low and there was only one narrow window. But the room looked bright because the walls were whitewashed a snowy white and the wooden table and door frames were polished until the wood was a shiny yellow. More herbs hung from the beams in this room. Along one wall there were shelves lined with jars of all shapes and sizes.

Tía Magdalena tilted her head toward the jars. "Here's where I need your help," she said to Josefina. Her eyes sparkled. "Why don't we make a game of it? You lift a jar down from the shelf, look inside, and see if you can guess what's in it. I'll dust the jar, you dust the shelf, and then you can put the jar back. All right?"

"Sí!" said Josefina. She reached for the biggest, most important-looking jar of all. It was blue-and-white china.

"Oh, not that jar!" said Tía Magdalena. "It's empty."

"It looks very old," said Josefina.

"Indeed it is," said Tía Magdalena. "It's probably the oldest thing in this house. It's even older than I am!" she joked. "It's an apothecary jar. I don't know how it came to be in our village, but I know that it's been here for more than a hundred years. The woman who was curandera before I was gave it to me. She got it from the woman who was curandera before her. Long ago, I believe, there was a whole set of jars like it. That's the only one left." Tía Magdalena pointed to a smaller jar next to the blue-and-white one. "Let's start with that jar instead," she said.

Josefina took the smaller jar off the shelf and looked inside. "It looks like pumpkin stems," she said. "Could it be?"

"Sí," said Tía Magdalena. "You're sharp to recognize them." She dusted the jar as Josefina dusted the shelf. "There's nothing in the world better for a sore throat," she said. "You toast the pumpkin stem, grind it to a powder, mix it with fat and salt, and rub it on the throat inside and out."

Josefina wrinkled her nose when she smelled the

inside of the next jar. "I think it's bear grease," she said.

"Right again," said Tía Magdalena. "You mix it with onions and rub it on a person's chest to ease congestion."

The next jar Josefina opened made her sneeze. "Oh, that must be *inmortal*," said Tía Magdalena, chuckling. "It makes you sneeze and sneeze and sneeze. The more you sneeze, the sooner your cold is gone."

Josefina enjoyed helping Tía Magdalena. Every jar had a story in it, because every jar held something that Tía Magdalena used as a remedy. There was dried deer blood to be mixed with water and drunk for strength. There was vinegar that was so strong it made Josefina's eyes water. It was used as a soak to stop infections. In another jar there was a terrible-smelling herb that was used to soothe achy joints. Josefina guessed what was in most of the jars. But once she came to something she didn't recognize.

"I don't know what this is," she told Tía Magdalena.

"That's the root of a globe mallow plant," said Tía Magdalena. "I crush it and make a paste to put on a rattlesnake bite to draw out the poisonous venom."

She handed one of the roots to Josefina. "Put that in your pouch and take it home with you," she said with a mischievous look. "And someday, ask your papá if he recognizes it."

"Papá?" asked Josefina.

"Sí," said Tía Magdalena. "Once, when he was a boy just about your age, he was guarding the sheep. He tried to scare away a rattlesnake by hitting it with a pebble from his sling. He missed. The snake got mad and bit him. Your papá killed the snake with a rock before he came to me for help. That was very brave, but very foolish of him! If you don't get the venom out right away, it can kill you." She shook her head. "I'll never forget the sight of him coming toward me, so proud of his own courage, and with that dead snake slung over his shoulders!"

Josefina put the root in her pouch and shuddered. She hated even *hearing* about snakes! But she liked to hear Tía Magdalena tell stories about Papá when he was a boy.

"Your papá was always too fearless and too stubborn for his own good," Tía Magdalena said as she dusted a jar. "And too quiet. But that didn't matter when your mamá was alive. She knew what he was thinking anyway."

Josefina was surprised at how easy it was to talk to Tía Magdalena about Mamá as they worked. "Sometimes it seems so long ago that Mamá died," Josefina said. "Sometimes it seems like it just happened. And sometimes I'll see Mamá in a dream, and it seems as if she's still with us."

"Sí," said Tía Magdalena. Her old brown eyes seemed to see right into Josefina's heart. "That is how it is always going to be for you."

"Sí," said Josefina, running her cloth over a shelf to dust it. "And for Papá, too, I think. He's not quite so quiet and sad as he was just after Mamá died. It has been better for us all since Tía Dolores came. We needed her."

"Well," said Tía Magdalena, handing a jar to Josefina. "Perhaps *she* needed *you*, too."

Josefina wondered what Tía Magdalena meant. But just then, Tía Magdalena said, "I think it's time for a cup of tea, don't you?" And so Josefina didn't have a chance to ask.

Second Chances

hen they were seated with their tea and some sweet cookies, Tía Magdalena said, "You've done well today."

"Gracias," said Josefina. "I was glad to help." She sipped her hot mint tea and gathered her courage to say what she was thinking. "I've really enjoyed all of this afternoon," she said. "And I was thinking . . . I was thinking that I'd like to be a curandera when I am older."

Tía Magdalena studied Josefina's face as she listened.

Josefina was encouraged. "Do you think you could teach me?" she asked. "When I'm old enough, I mean. I know I'm too young now."

Tía Magdalena thought for a while. When she answered, her voice was kind. "You can't simply choose to be a curandera," she said. "You have to know which herbs cure which ills, and you have to be obser-vant and careful. But more than all that, you must be a healer."

"A healer," repeated Josefina. "How will I know if I'm a healer or not?"

"You'll know," said Tía Magdalena. "You'll know. It will be clear to you and to everyone else if you are."

Josefina sighed. "I hope I am," she said.

"You'll find out," said Tía Magdalena. "In time."

While Tía Magdalena cleared up after their tea, Josefina went back to the storeroom to finish dust-ing. All the while, she was remembering what Tía Magdalena had said. How she wished there were some way to prove to Tía Magdalena that she was the right kind of person to be a curandera!

Josefina looked at the big blue-and-white jar on the shelf and thought about how it had been handed down from curandera to curandera. The jar was dusty. Surely Tía Magdalena would be pleased if she dusted it as a surprise for her. Josefina stood on her tiptoes to take the jar off the shelf. She could reach it with only one hand. She tapped the jar to move it to the edge of the shelf so that she could lift it off with both hands and . . . CRASH!

The jar fell to the floor and smashed into a thousand pieces. Josefina's heart stopped beating. For a terrible moment she stood still, staring in horror at what she had done. Then, without thinking, Josefina ran from the room. She flew past Tía Magdalena, out the door, and ran away as fast as she could.

Shame, shame, shame! The word pounded in Josefina's head with every step she took. Josefina ran without thinking about where she was going. Faster and faster she ran, out of the village, up the road to the rancho, toward the house, until she came to the orchard. She climbed up into her favorite apricot tree. Its branches were thickening with buds, but there were no blossoms to hide Josefina. *How could I have been so clumsy?* she thought. *Tía Magdalena treasured the blue-and-white jar, and I destroyed it. Then I ran away! What a stupid, childish thing to do! Not like a girl who's nearly ten. I'll never be able to face Tía Magdalena again!*

Josefina clung to the trunk, and hot tears ran down her cheeks. She had been sitting that way a while when she heard someone say, "Josefina?"

Josefina looked down through the branches and saw Tía Dolores's face lifted toward her. Josefina felt as if all her bones had melted. She slid down from the tree right into Tía Dolores's arms and buried her face in Tía Dolores's shoulder. Then she cried and cried. Tía Dolores rubbed her back and let her cry. When at last her sobs stopped, Tía Dolores put a cool hand on Josefina's cheek and looked at her with sympathetic eyes.

"Your papá went to Tía Magdalena's house to walk home with you," said Tía Dolores. "She told him what happened, and he told me."

"Is Tía Magdalena angry?" asked Josefina. "And Papá, too?"

Tía Dolores smoothed Josefina's hair and said, "They're sad and . . ."

"And disappointed," Josefina finished for her. Roughly, Josefina wiped the tears off her cheeks. "I broke Tía Magdalena's most precious jar. Then I made it worse by running away. I ruined everything."

"Everything?" asked Tía Dolores.

Josefina was so ashamed and miserable she could hardly speak. "I was hoping Tía Magdalena would

teach me to be a curandera when I am old enough,"
Josefina said. "Now she won't want to."

"Ah, I see," said Tía Dolores. "Can you tell me why
you want to be a curandera?"

"It's hard to explain," said Josefina. She put her
hand on her pouch and felt the root Tía Magdalena
had given her. "I like helping people feel better. And
I've . . . I've always wondered if there's a reason why
Mamá chose Tía Magdalena to be my godmother.
Maybe Mamá hoped I'd be a curandera."

"You mean, maybe she had the same hope for
you that you have for yourself," said Tía Dolores. She
hugged Josefina and said, "You know what you must
do right now, don't you?"

"Sí," said Josefina. "Sweep up the mess I made,
and apologize to Tía Magdalena."

"And you must ask her to give you a second
chance," said Tía Dolores.

Josefina sighed hopelessly.

Tía Dolores bent down so that her eyes were
level with Josefina's. "Spring is the season for second
chances," she said. "Didn't your mamá's flowers sprout
again? Didn't Sombrita get another chance to live when

you promised to take care of her?" Tía Dolores smiled. "We're all given second chances. We just have to be brave enough to take them."

Josefina hugged Tía Dolores. She hoped Tía Dolores was right. Oh, if Tía Magdalena would give her a second chance, she would be so grateful!

Tía Magdalena had only one thing to say after Josefina apologized. "The jar cannot be repaired," she said. "But perhaps your hopes can."

Whenever Josefina made up her mind to do something, it cheered her. She felt awful about what she had done at Tía Magdalena's. But she wasn't going to let her mistake kill her hopes. She still wanted to be a healer. Tía Magdalena had said that it would be clear to her and to everyone else if she was. She was determined to find out. Josefina kept the root Tía Magdalena had given her in her pouch as a reminder to herself.

It was cold and rainy. It seemed as if winter had returned. But finally, just the day before Josefina's birthday, the clouds brightened from gray to white and the sun shone. On that spring morning full of promise, Josefina set out with Papá and his servant Miguel to go to the pueblo.

Papá and Miguel were leading mules that were loaded down with blankets. The mules kicked up a lot of mud, so the blankets were wrapped in cloths to protect them. The path to the pueblo wound its way next to the stream. The banks were dotted with wildflowers. In the trees above, birds sang loudly, trying to outdo one another. Josefina couldn't help feeling proud when she looked at the blankets. She had made some of them, and now Papá was going to trade them to his friend Esteban.

Josefina had another reason to be happy. She was going to see *her* friend Mariana, Esteban's granddaughter. Josefina had tucked her doll, Niña, into her sash because Mariana liked to play dolls. And of course she'd brought along her faithful little shadow, Sombrita, to meet Mariana.

The pueblo was five long miles downstream from the rancho, and after the first mile Sombrita lagged. Josefina had to pick her up and carry her. Josefina was relieved when the stream widened and the pueblo seemed to appear all of a sudden. It rose up between the stream and the mountains. The pueblo was made of adobe just as Josefina's house was. But it was much taller than Josefina's house because several stories were built one on top of the other. Ladders led from level to level.

When Papá, Josefina, and Miguel arrived at the pueblo, they entered its big, clean-swept center plaza. There they were greeted by small children and curious dogs. Sombrita was timid. She hid her face in the crook of Josefina's elbow.

Esteban met them at his doorway. "Welcome," he said to Papá.

"Gracias, my friend," answered Papá. "May God bless you."

Miguel began to unload the blankets from the mules. Sombrita stayed with Miguel as Esteban led Papá and Josefina inside. They sat down by the fire, and almost immediately Mariana and her grandmother appeared with bowls of food. There were little pies with fruit inside and cups of hot tea. Mariana didn't say anything, but she smiled shyly at Josefina and her eyes had a welcome in them. Josefina smiled back. Both girls knew they shouldn't speak unless one of the grown-ups asked them a question. It wouldn't be good manners.

As they ate, Papá and Esteban talked about the weather, their crops, and their animals. Papá told Esteban about the meeting the village men had held to hear how much water each one would be allowed to use from the acequias. Esteban told Papá how much wool the spring sheepshearing had brought. Even though both men knew Papá had come to trade, they didn't talk about it. To begin by talking about business would be rude. Sometimes the two men just sat together in a comfortable silence. They seemed to have all the time in the world.

But Josefina was impatient. She couldn't wait to show Sombrita to Mariana. Josefina tried to sit as still as her friend did but it was hard. At last Papá and Esteban finished their food. As Mariana and her grandmother removed their bowls, Josefina admired the way Mariana moved so gracefully in her soft deerskin moccasins. Mariana wore a beautiful blanket draped over one shoulder and belted with a woven sash. Her bangs fell to her eyebrows, and her dark hair framed her face.

"My friend," said Esteban. "Thank you for bringing the blankets."

"Thank you for accepting them," said Papá. "I've brought sixty."

"Good," said Esteban. "When the sheep are old enough, I'll drive them to your rancho."

Papá nodded. This was the way he and Esteban had always traded. Nothing was written. Esteban's spoken promise was enough. Papá said that his family and Esteban's family had always respected each other and traded with each other fairly.

Josefina knew that this summer both Papá and Esteban were going to trade for the first time with the *americanos* who came to Santa Fe from the United States. Papá planned to trade mules, and Esteban would trade the blankets that Josefina and Papá had brought to him today.

"I hope trading with the americanos will be a good thing," Papá said.

Esteban nodded to show that he shared Papá's hope. Then Mariana caught her grandfather's eye and he smiled. Both Josefina and Mariana knew that was a sign that they could go. They stood up eagerly and hurried outside into the sunshine. Josefina picked up Sombrita and held her to face Mariana. "This is my Sombrita," she said. "We call her that because she follows me like a shadow wherever I go."

"Oh!" sighed Mariana. Her eyes were wide with delight. She scratched Sombrita behind her ear, just where the little goat liked it best. "Will Sombrita follow us to the stream?" Mariana asked.

"Of course!" said Josefina. "Watch!"

As Josefina and Mariana walked toward the stream, they peeked over their shoulders from time to time and shared a giggle at the sight of Sombrita following right on their heels. When they reached the stream, the girls found a sunny spot to play. Sombrita curled up in the warm grass and went to sleep. Josefina took her doll, Niña, out of her sash. Mariana had a doll too, made out of cornhusks. The girls pretended that their dolls were sisters. They made necklaces for them out of tiny wildflowers, and boats from curves of bark.

They had just launched their boats in the stream when suddenly Josefina stood up. "Where is

Sombrita?" she asked Mariana. "I don't see her."

Mariana stood up, too. The girls shaded their eyes and looked all around. But the little black-and-white goat was nowhere to be seen. "We'll have to look for her," said Josefina. "She can't have gone very far." She tucked Niña into her sash and Mariana picked up her doll, and they walked along the narrow footpath that led downstream. Josefina hoped they were going in the right direction. She could still see the pueblo behind them, but it seemed to shrink smaller with every step they took. Both girls knew they should not be so far from the pueblo, but they *had* to find little Sombrita. They couldn't stop. The farther they went, the faster they walked, and the more worried they both became.

Neither girl said anything for a long while. Then Josefina spoke as if she were thinking aloud. "Sombrita's not lost," she said, trying not to sound shaky. "She's not lost until we stop trying to find her."

With anxious steps, the girls kept going. Just after they'd rounded the next bend in the path, Josefina squinted. She thought she saw something black and white in the grass ahead. Could it be? It was! Josefina's heart lifted. "Oh, Sombrita," she cried as she ran forward.

Sombrita didn't look at her. The goat was staring at something else with friendly curiosity, as if it might be a delightful new plaything.

When Josefina saw what it was, she stopped short. All her relief turned to horror. Between her and the little goat was a huge rattlesnake.

Josefina swallowed hard. She felt sweat on her forehead and an odd trembling in her stomach. The snake was coiled and ready to strike. Josefina heard its eerie rattle. She saw its scary, skinny tongue darting in and out of its mouth. She saw the snake's beady black eyes in their sunken sockets. Josefina bit her lip. The snake's cruel stare was fixed on Sombrita.

Rattlesnake

osefina," said Mariana in a low voice. She saw the snake, too.

Josefina signaled Mariana to stay back. She had only one thought. *She had to save Sombrita!* Ever so slowly, Josefina sank down and picked up a rock. She held it out behind her to Mariana. Mariana understood and silently stretched out her hand to take it.

When their hands touched, Josefina whispered, "I'm going to get Sombrita. Don't throw the rock unless the snake moves, because if you miss . . ."

Mariana squeezed Josefina's hand, then she took the rock.

Very, very slowly, Josefina edged forward. She made a wide arc around the snake. Inch by anxious inch she moved next to Sombrita who, for once, stood still. Josefina stooped, gathered Sombrita in her arms, and straightened. Then everything happened so fast it was a blur. The snake gave a menacing rattle. Mariana threw the rock at it and missed. The snake whipped its head around, shot forward, and struck Mariana on the arm with its fangs.

"Mariana!" cried Josefina as she saw her friend grab her arm and stumble back. Suddenly furious, Josefina put Sombrita down and snatched up a rock. She threw with all her might. The rock hit the snake in its middle. With one last sickening hiss, the snake slithered away so fast it seemed to simply disappear.

Mariana moaned, sinking to her knees as if all the strength had gone out of her. She didn't cry, but her breath was ragged. Her eyes were shut tight.

Josefina bent over her friend. "Let me see your arm," she said. Gently, Josefina took Mariana's arm in her hands. She couldn't help gasping when she saw two tiny holes where the snake's fangs had sunk in. The wound was an ugly purplish color, and it was already beginning to swell. In her mind, Josefina heard Tía Magdalena's voice saying, *If you don't get the venom out right away, it can kill you*. Josefina spoke with urgency to Mariana. "We've got to get back to the pueblo," she said. "We need help."

Mariana tried to stand but dropped back on her knees. "I can't . . . I can't go that far," she said in a hoarse whisper.

Josefina's heart twisted with fear. She knelt down and something hard in her pouch thunked against her. It was the globe mallow root Tía Magdalena had given her. Without hesitating, Josefina took it out. She crushed the root between two rocks and spit on it to make it pasty. Then she pressed it against Mariana's arm where the snake had struck. She squeezed Mariana's arm gently to bring the venom up. Mariana whimpered, but she didn't pull her arm away.

Again and again, Josefina pressed the crushed root against the wound. Again and again, she pressed Mariana's arm. Again and again and again . . . Josefina knew she had to stay calm, but she had to fight against a rising feeling of panic. The globe mallow didn't seem to be working! Mariana's arm was still swollen and bruised-looking. Oh, how long would it take? What if she was using the root the wrong way? Perhaps she had misunderstood. What would happen to Mariana if the venom poisoned her blood? If only someone would come to help!

But no one came. The minutes felt like hours. Josefina was just about to give up and run for help when—oh, at last!—she heard Mariana take a deep, shuddery breath. Mariana opened her eyes, and color came back to her face.

Josefina said a quick, silent prayer of thanks. Then she asked Mariana, "Do you think you can walk if I help you?"

Mariana nodded.

Carefully, Josefina helped Mariana stand. Mariana looped her good arm over Josefina's shoulder, and Josefina put her own arm behind Mariana's back to support her. "Lean on me," Josefina said. Then she turned and looked down at Sombrita. "Listen," she said to the little goat. "Now you must really be my *sombrita,* my little shadow. Stay right behind me. Do you understand?"

Sombrita seemed to. She stayed close to Josefina and Mariana every step of the weary walk back. Slowly, the two girls trudged along the path next to the stream. Slowly, they trudged up the long incline to the pueblo. Josefina knew they had been gone a long time, and Papá and Esteban would be worried. But she and Mariana could not move fast. Their tired feet dragged. Their tired shoulders drooped. They were only halfway between the stream and the pueblo when Josefina saw Papá and Esteban coming toward them. She had never been so glad to see anyone in her life!

Papá and Esteban rushed to the girls, and Josefina saw that their faces were tight with worry. Mariana said quickly, "A rattlesnake bit me, but Josefina knew what to do." She smiled weakly at Josefina. "Tell them," she said.

Papá and Esteban stared at Josefina, but she was too worn out to explain. Instead she held out her hand to show them the crushed root. "It draws the venom out," she said. "I had it in my pouch."

Esteban's expression did not change. His voice was very deep when he said, "Gracias, Josefina. Gracias." He lifted Mariana up. Papá, Josefina, and Sombrita followed them the rest of the way back to the pueblo.

Later, as they were walking home to the rancho, Papá asked Josefina to tell him the whole story of what had happened. So Josefina did. She didn't leave out anything, even though she was out of breath because she had to take two steps for every one of Papá's. They hadn't gone very far before Papá lifted both Josefina and Sombrita up onto a mule's back. After that Josefina couldn't see Papá's face, but somehow she knew that he was still listening hard to every word she said.

Josefina opened one sleepy eye. Could she be dreaming? It was not quite dawn, and yet she seemed to hear music. She sat up. Her sisters Francisca and Clara were gone from the room that they shared with her. Suddenly, Josefina grinned to herself. She remembered what day it was: the feast day of San José and her birthday.

Very slowly, the door to her room opened. In the pearly morning light she saw Papá, Tía Dolores, Ana and her husband Tomás, Francisca, Clara, Carmen the cook, and her husband Miguel. They began to sing:

On the day you were born
All the beautiful flowers were born,
The sun and moon were born,
And all the stars.

In the middle of the song, Sombrita poked her head around the corner of the door and bleated as if she were singing, too. Everyone laughed, and Tía Dolores said, "We wanted to surprise you with a lovely morning song, but I think someone forgot the words!"

Josefina picked up Sombrita and gave her a hug. "Gracias," she said to everyone, feeling a little shy at all the attention. "I liked it."

The morning song was only the first surprise in a day full of them. Ana made cookies called *bizcochitos* for everyone to eat before breakfast. At morning prayers, Francisca showed Josefina how she'd decorated the family altar with garlands of mint and willow leaves and how she'd surrounded the statue of San José, the saint Josefina was named for, with white wild lilies and little yellow celery flowers. Clara, who liked to be practical, surprised Josefina by helping with her chores.

But when it was time to dress for the party, Clara had an impractical surprise for Josefina. It was a dainty pair of turquoise blue slippers. "It's about time I handed these down to you," said Clara. "I hardly ever wear them."

"Oh, Clara!" said Josefina, very pleased. She put the slippers on. They were only a *little* too big for her.

"If you're going to be so elegant," said Francisca, "you'd better carry Mamá's fan."

"And wear Mamá's shawl!" said Ana.

The four sisters shared Mamá's fan and shawl and brought them out only on very special occasions. Josefina swirled the shawl around her shoulders and looked behind her to see the brilliant embroidered flowers and the slippery, shimmery fringe on the back. She fluttered the fan and felt very elegant indeed.

The party table looked elegant, too. There was a beautiful cloth on it, and the family's best plates and glasses and silverware. Tía Dolores had made a special fancy loaf of bread. There were meat turnovers, and fruit tarts, and candied fruit that looked like jewels. But best of all, in the center of the table there was a red jar with one small branch of apricot blossoms in it. Josefina smiled when she saw the perfect blossoms. She knew that Tía Dolores had cut the branch from *her* tree—the tree she liked to climb. Josefina remembered the day Tía Dolores had comforted her next to that apricot tree. "We're all given second chances," Tía Dolores had said. "We just have to be brave enough to take them."

Soon music and laughter and happy voices swirled around the beautiful table. Friends and neighbors and workers from the rancho arrived bringing small gifts of dried fruit or nuts, sweets, or chocolate for Josefina. Esteban and Mariana brought a wonderful gift. It was a melon that had been buried in sand since last fall's harvest to keep it fresh.

When Josefina thanked her, Mariana said, "It's not much, but my heart goes with it."

Papá quieted everyone. "Today is the feast of San José," he said, "and today my daughter Josefina is ten years old. I'm going to tell you a story about her." Josefina felt Mariana's hand slip into her own. They both stood still, eyes shyly cast down, while Papá told the story of the rattlesnake. Papá began at the beginning and told everything that had happened. He described the snake in such a scary way it made everyone shiver. When the story was finished, Papá called Josefina to him. He handed her something that looked sort of like a shell. It was rattles from a rattlesnake. "I've saved these since I was a boy just your age," said Papá to Josefina, "to remind me of something I was proud of. Now I am giving them to you, because I am proud of you."

Everyone clapped, and Papá leaned down to kiss Josefina's cheek. Josefina thought she had never in her life felt so happy or so proud.

Suddenly, Tía Magdalena was by her side. "Dear child," she said.

Josefina smiled. She held out her hand to show Tía Magdalena the snake's rattles. "I'm going to put these in my memory box," she said. "They'll remind me of the moment when I found out something important about myself. I found out that I am a healer."

Tía Magdalena smiled deep into Josefina's eyes. "Sí," she said simply. "You are."

Later that evening, when the party was over, Josefina and Papá walked to the goats' pen together.

Rattlesnake

They wanted to check on Sombrita, who had not been invited to the party. Sombrita was fast asleep.

"It's unusual to see her so still, isn't it?" said Josefina. She and Papá smiled, looking at the peaceful goat.

"She's healthy and lively," said Papá. "She might not have been, if you hadn't kept your promise to take care of her after Florecita died. You gave her a second chance at life."

Papá and Josefina walked back to the house. On the hillside, the flowering fruit trees in the orchard were lit by the moon, as if a pale cloud had settled on them. The night air was cool, but softened by the scent of blossoms. Josefina took a deep breath. She thought the air smelled like apricots.

"Papá," she said. "We're all given second chances. We just have to be brave enough to take them. That's what Tía Dolores says."

"Does she?" asked Papá. "Does she indeed?"

The Bird-Shaped Flute

igh up on a breezy hilltop, Josefina sat playing her clay flute. The flute was shaped like a bird and sounded like one, too. When Josefina played it, a clear, fine tune just like a bird's whistle looped through the air into the blue, blue sky.

The soft days of spring had flown by swiftly, and now it was July. Josefina and her family were visiting her grandfather's rancho, which was about a mile from the center of Santa Fe. Josefina loved this hilltop behind Abuelito's house. From here she could see the flat rooftops of buildings in Santa Fe and the narrow streets that zigzagged between them. She could see the slender silvery ribbon that was the Santa Fe River, and the long road that led home to Papá's rancho fifteen miles away.

A few days ago, Josefina, her papá, two of her

sisters, and Tía Dolores, had traveled on that road to come to Abuelito's rancho. The trip was hot and dusty, but Josefina had been too excited to mind. She and her family had worked, planned, and looked forward to the trip for almost a year.

They were traveling for a very important reason. They needed to be in Santa Fe when the wagon train from the United States arrived. Papá had brought mules and blankets with him to trade with the americanos. Josefina understood how much depended on this trade. If the americanos paid well for the mules and the blankets, Papá would be able to replace his sheep that had been killed in a terrible flood last fall. If Papá could not replace the sheep, it would be a hard, hungry winter for everyone on the rancho. They needed sheep for food and for wool to weave. Josefina had prayed and prayed that Papá's trading with the americanos would go well.

Josefina and her sisters couldn't wait to see the fine and fancy things the americanos would bring. There'd be toys and shoes and material for dresses that had come hundreds of miles on the Santa Fe Trail, all the way from the United States! The wagon train was

expected to arrive any day now, and Josefina was keeping a lookout for it. As soon as she'd finished her chores
this morning, she'd climbed up here to her favorite
hilltop to look at the southeast horizon. She was hoping
to see a cloud of dust stirred up by the wagon train, but
the horizon looked the same as always.

Just now, though, Josefina *heard* something new.
It sounded as if a real bird were singing along with her
clay flute. Josefina stopped playing and tilted her head
to listen. Then she grinned. It wasn't a real bird at all.
It was a person whistling.

"Buenos días!" Josefina called out. She turned,
expecting to see that the whistler was one of her sisters who'd come to watch for the wagon train, too.
But it wasn't. The whistler was a young man Josefina
had never seen before. Josefina scrambled to her feet
so quickly she almost dropped her flute. The young
man was a stranger. And not just any stranger, either.
Josefina immediately folded her hands, bowed her
head, and looked down at the ground, which was the
polite way for a child to stand before an adult. But she
could tell just by looking at the tips of the stranger's
boots that they came from the United States. She knew

because Abuelito had a pair of boots like them that he'd bought last summer from the americanos.

"Buenos días," said the young man. He spoke in Spanish, but with an accent Josefina had never heard before.

Josefina had a sudden, excited thought. The young man must be an americano who'd come ahead of the wagon train! Josefina was usually shy around strangers, but right now her curiosity was stronger than her shyness. If the young man was an americano, he'd be the first she'd ever met face to face. She raised her eyes and sneaked a peek. He had a very *nice* face, Josefina decided. He had blue eyes, a sunburned nose, and a friendly smile.

"Forgive me for surprising you," the stranger went on. "I thought you were a bird."

I thought you were a bird, too! Josefina almost said. She wanted to ask, *Please, señor, who* are *you?* But of course she didn't. It wasn't good manners for a child to ask a grown-up questions. In fact, Josefina wasn't sure whether it was proper for her to talk to the stranger at all. Perhaps she should *act* like a bird and fly away! But that didn't seem very polite.

While Josefina stood wondering what she should do, the young man did something astonishing. He took a case off his back, opened it, took out a violin, and began to play. Josefina smiled when she realized that he was playing the same notes that she had played on her bird-shaped flute. The young man wound the notes together into a tune that danced in the air. When he finished, he swept his hat off his head and bowed. "I'm Patrick O'Toole, from Missouri," he said. "What is your name?"

"By God's grace," Josefina answered, "I am Josefina Montoya."

"Josefina Montoya," Patrick repeated slowly. "I'm glad to meet you. I'm looking for the home of Señor Felipe Romero. Do you know him?"

"Sí," answered Josefina politely. "He's my grand-father." She pointed to Abuelito's house nearby. "He lives right there."

"Well, then, Señorita Josefina," said Patrick as he put his violin away. "Will you lead me to your grand-father's house?"

"I will," answered Josefina. "Please, follow me." She slipped the string of her clay flute around her neck and led Patrick down the hill. She couldn't help smiling a secret smile when she thought how surprised her family would be!

Abuelito's house was built around a center court-yard. The doors to the kitchen, the sleeping rooms, the weaving room, and the family sala opened onto it. Josefina led Patrick across the courtyard. She stopped outside the family sala, where her family was gathering for the mid-day meal. Abuelito had come to the door and was staring out at her.

"Abuelito," Josefina said respectfully. "Please permit me to introduce Señor Patrick O'Toole, from"—Josefina pronounced the English word carefully—"Missouri."

Abuelito was used to having unexpected guests, but this was the first time one of his granddaughters had brought a complete stranger to visit. And the stranger was an americano, too! But Abuelito was always a gracious host. *"Bienvenido,"* he said to Patrick. "You are welcome in my house, young man. Please come in."

"Thank you, sir," said Patrick. Josefina tapped her head to warn him to duck down so that he'd fit under the low doorway, and they both stepped inside. "I know you were expecting my father, who did business with you last summer, but—"

"Oh!" said Abuelito as he realized who Patrick was. "You're the son of my friend, Señor O'Toole." Abuelito shook Patrick's hand. "Your father is a fine man. I hope he's in good health?"

"I believe so," said Patrick. "You see, he's farther south in Mexico, so he asked me to conduct his business here in—"

"Fine, fine," interrupted Abuelito. "There will be time for us to talk about business later, plenty of time."

Josefina could see that Patrick didn't understand. Abuelito would consider it very poor manners to discuss business matters right away, especially with someone he did not know. It was the custom in New Mexico to have a friendly conversation first, *then* talk about business.

Patrick tried again. "Well, sir," he began. No one saw Josefina tug on his sleeve. When Patrick glanced at her, she frowned and shook her head just the smallest bit to tell him no. Patrick looked confused for a moment, but then he seemed to understand. "As you say, sir," he said to Abuelito. "We can talk about business later."

"Good!" said Abuelito. "Allow me to introduce you to my family." He introduced Patrick to Papá, and

then to Abuelita, Josefina's grandmother, and then to
Tía Dolores.

"We're so glad Dolores is home for a visit," Abuelito
said. "She's been away, staying on my son-in-law's
rancho for almost a year now, helping him take care
of his daughters since his own dear wife died. You've
already met his youngest daughter, Josefina. His eldest,
Ana, stayed home to help her husband look after the
rancho. These are his daughters Francisca and Clara."

The sisters stood with their heads bowed. But
Josefina saw Francisca studying Patrick from under her
long, dark eyelashes.

"Please sit and have something to eat, señor," said
Abuelita generously. "Honor us by joining us."

"Gracias," said Patrick.

Josefina sat between Francisca and Clara. Both sisters poked her and looked at her with raised eyebrows
that said silently in sister language, *Oh, we can't wait
to find out how you met the americano!* Josefina grinned
back, pleased to have made her sisters curious.

During the meal, Abuelito kept the conversation
away from business. He spoke to Patrick about the
beautiful summer weather they were having and asked

Patrick about weather in Missouri. Abuelita said nothing, but her sharp eyes never left Patrick's face. Papá
didn't say anything either. But Josefina could tell that
he was listening carefully to everything Patrick said.

I hope Papá likes Señor Patrick, Josefina thought. *I hope
everyone does.* She was glad when Tía Dolores said to
Patrick, "You speak Spanish well. How did you learn?"

"My father taught me," said Patrick. "I can't read
or write Spanish at all, and I'm afraid I don't always
remember the right words to say."

"You are doing fine," said Abuelito kindly.

In fact, Josefina thought Patrick was doing beautifully. He stumbled over his words only once, and
that was when Francisca poured him some tea.
Patrick looked up at her and seemed to forget how
to say thank you—or anything else. But Josefina had
seen *that* happen to men who spoke perfect Spanish.
Francisca was very beautiful.

Finally everyone had finished eating and the servants had cleared the table. Abuelito turned to Patrick.
"Now," he said. "Tell us. When will the wagon train
arrive?"

"Tomorrow morning, sir," said Patrick.

"That's good news!" said Abuelito. "But how is it that you are here before the rest of the wagon train?"

"I'm one of the scouts," explained Patrick. "Scouts ride ahead of the wagon train. We find the safest places to cross rivers, the easiest passes through the mountains, and the best places to set up camp along the way."

"I'm sure you've had lots of adventures," said Abuelito.

"Not as many as you have, sir," said Patrick. "My father told me that you've been a trader on the *Camino Real* for many years. He said you've had adventures enough for twenty men!"

Abuelito was pleased. "I'll tell you about my adventures on the Camino Real sometime," he said.

"I'd like that," said Patrick. "You see, I'll be here in Santa Fe for about a week. I have to be ready to leave at a moment's notice. As soon as the captain of the wagon train gives me the word, I'll be heading down the Camino Real. Many of the americano traders are continuing farther south into Mexico when they leave Santa Fe, so the scouts have to go ahead of them and explore the route. Anything you can tell me would be a great help, Señor Romero."

"It will be a pleasure," said Abuelito.

"Thank you, sir," said Patrick. "Maybe you can help me in another way, too. The traders are going to need fresh mules for their trip down the Camino Real. They asked me to find some. Do you know anyone who has mules to sell or trade?"

Abuelito didn't answer right away. He glanced at Papá.

Josefina knew that Abuelito and Papá were being careful. Before they decided to do business with Patrick, they'd want to be sure he was honest and trustworthy. Papá had been watching Patrick as if he were trying to decide what sort of person the young man was.

Now Papá spoke slowly. "I have mules to trade," he said.

"Oh!" said Patrick. "May I see them, Señor Montoya?"

Papá nodded. "You may see them," he said. "Come with me." He stood and gestured toward the door.

Abuelito went outside and Patrick started to follow. But before he left, Patrick thanked Abuelita for her hospitality. Then he turned and smiled at Josefina. "I certainly am glad I heard that bird whistling on the hilltop," he said. "I hope I'll hear it again soon!"

Josefina smiled back.

After the men had left, Josefina and her sisters helped Abuelita and Tía Dolores tidy the room.

"So!" said Francisca to Josefina. "Where did you find the americano?"

"Well, I guess he found me," said Josefina. "I was on the hilltop looking for the wagon train and he surprised me."

"And *you* surprised *me,* Josefina," said Tía Dolores. She put her hands on her hips and smiled at Josefina. "I've always believed that you were shy of strangers. Not anymore, I see!"

"You and the americano seem to have become acquainted very quickly," said Clara.

"Too quickly," said Abuelita, frowning. "We don't really know this americano at all. How do we know he is truly Señor O'Toole's son? How do we know he is honest?" She shook her head. "All we know for certain is that he's very young. I hope your papá will be careful. I don't think it's wise to trust a stranger, especially when the business is so important!"

"Nothing is decided yet," said Tía Dolores quietly.

Abuelita went on. "If this young man isn't reliable, it'll be a terrible mistake to do business with him," she said.

Abuelita sighed and Josefina's shoulders drooped. She had been so proud to be the one who brought Patrick to her family! Would Papá be wrong to trust Patrick? Was *she* wrong to like Patrick?

Tía Dolores moved closer to Josefina. "How *did* you get acquainted with Señor Patrick so quickly?" she asked.

Josefina held up the little bird-shaped flute. "I was playing this clay flute that you gave me," she said. "Then Señor Patrick played the same song on his violin." She smiled, remembering. "The music sounded so friendly."

Tía Dolores laughed. "Music *can* sound friendly," she said. "Sometimes music can say things better than words can. Don't you think so, Josefina?"

"Sí!" said Josefina, cheered by Tía Dolores's understanding. She hurried to finish helping so that she could go outside. She wanted to play Patrick's song on her bird-shaped flute.

Heart's Desire

his is a day I'll remember as long as I live, thought Josefina. She was holding Tía Dolores's hand, and she gave it a squeeze. Tía Dolores smiled down at Josefina's glowing, upturned face. "Any minute now," Tía Dolores said. They were standing in a crowd that had gathered in front of the Palace of the Governors in Santa Fe. Everyone was waiting, waiting, *waiting* for the wagon train to pull into town. *Any minute now,* thought Josefina with a delighted shiver. *Any minute!*

Soon after dawn while the air was still cool, Josefina and her family and one of Abuelita's servants had walked into Santa Fe. Abuelita had stayed home because she didn't like crowds. But everyone else was eager to join the people gathering to see the wagon train. All along the road, they saw tents that had sprung up overnight. Indians had come with pottery and blankets and horses to trade. Fur trappers had come down from the mountains. Soldiers had come from their fort up on the hill. People had come from villages and ranchos for miles around. They all gathered in the plaza that was in the center of Santa Fe. Even the long, low adobe buildings built around all four sides of the plaza seemed to lean forward expectantly, looking for the wagon train.

Josefina had never seen so many people! Words in different languages swirled around her in a confused jumble, until suddenly she heard one shout above the others.

"The wagons! The americanos! The wagon train is here!" someone called out. Then many voices rose up together in a roar. Church bells rang. Josefina's heart was pounding. She called out with the others, "The wagon train is here!"

Around Josefina, many people were clapping, cheering, and waving as the americanos' wagons lumbered into view. But other people were not so enthusiastic. They stood quietly, arms crossed over their chests, watching the wagons with questioning looks, as if they were not convinced that the arrival of the americanos was a good thing. Josefina stood on tiptoe to see the wagons better. But she didn't let go of Tía Dolores's hand, and she was glad to be safely wedged between Tía Dolores and Papá. The wagons were so heavy they rumbled like the thunder of an oncoming storm and made the earth shake under Josefina's feet.

The americanos driving the wagons whooped and hooted and whistled and threw their hats into the air. They circled their whips and then snapped them so that they made a *pop!* as loud as a gunshot. Wagon after wagon rolled into the plaza. Josefina counted more than twenty. Some were pulled by plodding oxen that seemed half asleep in spite of all the noise. But most of the wagons were pulled by mules that pricked up their ears and looked pleased at all the attention.

"Tía Dolores," said Josefina. "Look how big the wagons are!"

The wagons *were* enormous. Their wheels stood higher than Josefina's head! Some of the wagons were flying a flag different from the Mexican flag Josefina was used to. This flag was red, white, and blue. The flag's stripes and stars looked snappy and clean in the bright sunshine. Josefina thought the americanos looked cleaned up, too, as if that morning they'd scrubbed their faces, slicked down their hair, put on their Sunday-best clothes, and polished the dust of hundreds of miles off their boots. Some of the men looked rough, while others looked quiet and well mannered. But to Josefina's eyes, *all* the americanos looked glad to be in Santa Fe and at the end of the trail at last.

Papá bent his head toward Tía Dolores so she could hear him above the hubbub. "Your father and I are going to look for Señor Patrick at the customs house," he said. "The americanos have to go there to make a list of their goods and to pay taxes. The servant will stay with you and the girls."

Tía Dolores nodded. "Very well," she said. "Go ahead."

But Papá didn't go. His eyes had a twinkle in them as he looked at Tía Dolores. "Have you told the girls?" he asked her.

"Not yet," answered Tía Dolores.

"Told us what?" asked Francisca immediately.

Papá laughed. "Tell them," he said to Tía Dolores. "After all, it was your idea. We wouldn't have as much to trade today if it were not for you." His voice was full of gratitude and affection. Tía Dolores smiled, and then Papá went off with Abuelito to find Patrick.

"Please, Tía Dolores! Tell us what Papá meant!" begged the sisters.

Tía Dolores's eyes were shining. "Your papá and I think that you girls deserve something for all the hard work you've done weaving," she said. "We've decided that you may each choose one of the blankets you wove, and you may sell it or trade it for anything you wish."

"*Oh!*" gasped Francisca and Clara. "How wonderful!"

Josefina didn't say anything. Instead, she hugged Tía Dolores. Josefina and her sisters had never expected to use the blankets they'd woven to get anything for themselves. *It's just like Tía Dolores to think of something so generous,* thought Josefina.

"Well!" said Francisca. She had an eager gleam in her eyes. "We'd better look around and decide what we'll get with our blankets."

There was certainly much to see! Tía Dolores and the sisters walked slowly around the plaza to watch the americanos unload their wagons. Some of the americanos had rented small stores to display their wares. Others had wooden stalls or spaces on the street where they set out their goods. Never in her life had Josefina imagined such a variety of things. She saw bolts of brightly colored cottons, wools, and silks. There were veils, shawls, sashes, and ribbons. There were shoes and hats, boots and stockings, combs, brushes, toothbrushes, and even silver toothpicks!

Clara stood for a long time studying pots and pans until Francisca dragged her away to look at buttons and jewelry she saw sparkling ahead. Clara stopped halfway there to gaze at knitting needles. Tía Dolores was distracted by some books, and the girls were fascinated by the mirrors that reflected their delighted faces. Many people were crowded around the watches and clocks, and even more were crowded around the tools. A few people were paying for the americanos' goods with silver coins, but most people were trading or swapping. Josefina saw a man from the pueblo swap a beautiful pottery jar he'd made for an americano's glass bottle. A fur trapper traded a bear skin for a hunting knife.

There were so many things, Josefina didn't know how she'd ever choose something for herself. Then Tía Dolores and the girls stopped in front of a trader who had toys among his goods. One toy in particular caught Josefina's eye. It was a little toy farm carved out of wood.

"Oh, look!" said Josefina as she knelt in front of it. There was a tiny cow, a horse pulling a cart, a goat, and a funny pink pig standing in front of a white stable. Two green trees shaded a painted house with a white fence behind it.

"You can almost hear the cow moo, can't you?" someone joked. It was Patrick. He and Papá and Abuelito had finished their business and had come to find Tía Dolores and the girls. "That reminds me of how the farms look back home in Missouri."

Josefina imagined what it would be like to sit in the shade of the two green trees or climb on the white fence. "I wish I could magically shrink," she said to Patrick. "I'd like to go inside the house. I've never seen a house that's so straight up and down, with such a steep roof and so many big windows!"

"It's different, isn't it?" said Patrick. "Here in New Mexico your houses are low. They look like they grew right up out of the ground because they're made out of earth, and they don't have any sharp corners. Where I come from the buildings seem to want to stick up and call attention to themselves. Sort of like the people, I guess!"

"I think the farm is very pretty," said Josefina. "I like it."

Clara looked over Josefina's shoulder. "But it's just a toy, Josefina," she said. "You shouldn't waste your blanket on *that*!"

Josefina sighed. Clara was being sensible, as usual. But Josefina couldn't help wanting the farm. She was sure it would be fun to play with the pink pig! And knowing that the little farm reminded Patrick of his home made Josefina like it even more.

Papá looped his finger around one of Josefina's braids and moved the braid behind her ear. Then he stooped and spoke softly so that only Josefina could hear. "We'll come back," he said kindly. "And you can look at the toy farm again." Josefina looked into his understanding brown eyes. "If that's what you want, then that's what you should get," Papá said. "Don't let anyone talk you out of your heart's desire."

Papá took Josefina's hand and stood up straight. Then in a louder voice he said to Tía Dolores, "I have good news. Señor Patrick has found traders who want to buy all of our mules."

"Oh?" said Tía Dolores. Her eyes had a question in them.

"Sí," answered Papá. His voice was serious and sure. "I have decided to let Señor Patrick trade the mules for us. He knows the americano traders. He can speak English to them. And he has promised to get me a good price."

"My friends will be glad to get the mules," said Patrick quickly. "Mules are sturdy. They do better than oxen on the wagon trails. Oxen are fussy eaters. They have delicate feet, and they get sunburned." Patrick pointed to his own red nose and joked, "Just like me!" Everyone laughed, and Patrick went on. "I can get you silver for the mules," he said.

Silver! This was lucky indeed. Normally, Papá would have traded the mules for goods from the americanos. Then he would trade the goods for sheep. Josefina knew Papá must be pleased. It would be much easier to buy the sheep they needed with silver.

"Señor Montoya, may I come by later today to get the mules?" Patrick asked Papá. "I can bring some of your silver today, and the rest at the end of the week after I've sold all the mules."

"Very well," said Papá. "I know I can trust you to keep your word." He and Patrick shook hands to seal their agreement. Josefina saw that Papá's grasp was firm. *Oh, I am so glad Papá has decided to trust Señor Patrick,* thought Josefina.

Abuelito seemed glad, too. "When you come for the mules, you must stay for dinner," he said to Patrick. "We'll celebrate!"

"And please remember to bring your violin," said Tía Dolores. "We can't celebrate without music!"

"I'll remember," said Patrick. He said *adiós* to everyone. Then he strolled away, cheerfully whistling Josefina's bird song.

A Charm from the Sky

ater that afternoon, Patrick came to Abuelito's rancho to get Papá's mules. He was going to take them back to Santa Fe after dinner. Josefina had climbed to her hilltop to meet him and lead him to the house.

Before they started down the hill, Patrick tilted his head back and said, "I've never seen a sky so blue."

"Mamá used to say the sky is that blue because it's the bottom of heaven," said Josefina.

Patrick smiled. He pulled a small brass telescope out of his coat pocket. As Josefina watched, he focused the telescope on a point to the southeast. "Look through there," he said as he handed her the telescope.

Josefina focused the telescope for herself. "I see San Miguel Chapel," she said. She recognized the church easily even though it was far away. It came clearly into view through the telescope, as if someone had painted a perfect picture of it in a tiny round frame.

"Well," said Patrick, "yesterday I climbed up to the bell of San Miguel Chapel. While I was up there a little bit of the sky fell off, right into my hand. See?"

Josefina giggled when she looked. Patrick held a small chunk of turquoise in his hand. The turquoise *was* the same glorious blue as the sky.

Patrick tossed the chunk of turquoise up in the air, caught it with the same hand, and put it in his pocket. "Now I'll have a little bit of New Mexican sky with me even when I go back home," he said, patting his pocket as if he had a treasure in it. Then he pretended to frown. "What's this?" he asked. He pulled a sheet of paper out of the same pocket, unfolded it, and then handed it to Josefina with a grin. "I believe this is for you, Señorita Josefina."

"Gracias!" said Josefina. The paper was sheet music. It had the notes and the words to a song printed on it. Josefina couldn't read the words because they were in English. She didn't know how to read the notes, either, which were lined up like orderly black birds on straight black branches. But she had seen sheet music before. Tía Dolores had some. "Perhaps when we go home, Tía Dolores will teach me to play this song on the piano," Josefina said to Patrick. "She knows how to read music. I think Papá does, too, unless he's forgotten." Josefina hesitated, then said, "Papá used to play the violin."

"Did he?" asked Patrick.

"Sí," said Josefina. She looked down at the sheet music and said quietly, "He used to play when Mamá was alive. But when . . . when she died, he gave his violin away. I think he was just too sad to play it anymore. We were all too sad for music for a long, long time." Josefina looked up at Patrick. "It's been better since Tía Dolores came to stay with us. We've all been happier, especially Papá. And Tía Dolores loves music. She even brought her piano with her when she came up the Camino Real from Mexico City with Abuelito's caravan. You should hear Abuelito tell *that* story!"

"He promised to tell me some of his adventures," said Patrick as they headed down the hill to the house. "If I ask, do you think he'll tell me the piano story this evening?"

"With pleasure!" answered Josefina. She knew there was nothing in the world Abuelito liked better than telling a story!

It was with *great* pleasure that Abuelito told the piano story and many other stories about the Camino Real during dinner. Then Patrick told stories about the Santa Fe Trail. He talked about herds of buffalo so endless they made the plains look black, and rivers so wide you could not see across them.

After dinner, Patrick took out his violin. He played such lively tunes that he soon had everyone clapping their hands and tapping their feet. The sun set and the fire was lit, but the moon poured so much silvery light into the room that they didn't need to light candles. Patrick's music was merry and lighthearted, full of fancy, funny twists and turns. Abuelito kept time slapping his leg, and Abuelita's dangling earrings swung and sparkled as she nodded her head to the rhythm of the music.

Patrick played and played. He was right in the middle of a song when, in one smooth movement, before anyone realized what he was doing, he handed his violin to Papá, saying, "Now it's your turn, Señor Montoya."

Suddenly, the room was completely quiet.

What is Señor Patrick doing? worried Josefina. *I told him Papá didn't play anymore!*

But Papá did not frown. Slowly, as if he were both eager and reluctant at the same time, Papá tucked Patrick's violin under his chin. He held the slender neck of the violin in his broad hand and delicately ran the bow over the strings. Chills ran up and down Josefina's spine.

"What shall I play?" Papá asked.

No one answered.

Josefina hopped up and put the sheet music Patrick had given her in front of Papá. "Play this, Papá," she said.

Papá began to play. He played softly at first, but every note became surer. Then Patrick began to sing the words. His voice was husky and low. Though Josefina could not understand the English words he was singing, she understood the wistful feeling of the song. Patrick sang:

'Mid pleasures and palaces though we may roam,
Be it ever so humble there's no place like home;
A charm from the skies seems to hallow us there,
Which seek through the world, is ne'er met with
elsewhere.

Patrick stopped singing. But Papá continued to play, making up a song that blended Patrick's song with an old Spanish song. Josefina sat still, listening intently, with her eyes fixed on Papá's face. Josefina knew that Papá's song was telling a story full of longing and hope.

Josefina wished the music would never end. Tía Dolores must have felt the same way. As the last note faded, she sighed a sigh that seemed to come straight from her heart. "Oh," she said to Papá. "That was lovely!"

Papá handed the violin back to Patrick, then smiled at Tía Dolores.

In that moment, Josefina knew what she wanted to trade for her blanket. She knew without a doubt what her heart's desire was.

She wanted Patrick's violin for Papá.

"No."

It was much later. Patrick had left, taking Papá's mules with him.

"No," said Clara again. She and Josefina and Francisca were in the sleeping sala they shared. All three were sitting on the bed Josefina and Clara slept in. But the sisters weren't even close to sleeping. They were having an argument. "I won't," said Clara flatly. "It's just not sensible."

Josefina and Francisca shared an exasperated look.

"But Clara," pleaded Francisca, who had agreed with Josefina's plan right away. "We need your blanket, too. It will work only if we all do it. Patrick's violin is worth at *least* three blankets."

"How about Ana's blanket?" asked Clara.

"We couldn't use it without asking her," said Josefina. "Anyway, Tía Dolores is going to trade it for boots for Ana's little boys."

"I want to trade my blanket for something practical, too!" said Clara. "It's different for you. You want that silly toy farm, and Francisca wants a mirror, which is just a luxury. I want useful things like knitting needles."

"Clara," coaxed Francisca. "When we go home, I will give you all of my knitting needles. I promise. They're good as new."

"Because you never use them!" said Clara. "Besides, I could get lots more than knitting needles. The americanos pay well for woven blankets."

Francisca started to say something sharp, but Josefina spoke first. "Didn't you see how happy Papá looked while he was playing Señor Patrick's violin?" Josefina asked Clara. "We have to get it for him. We just have to."

"Señor Patrick will probably say no anyway," said Clara stubbornly.

But Josefina could be stubborn, too. "We've got to at least *ask* him," she said. She looked straight into Clara's eyes and said something she *knew* would convince her to cooperate. "The truth is, it isn't only Papá's happiness I'm thinking of. You must have seen how much Tía Dolores loved it when Papá played. She's been so kind to us. Don't you think we owe it to her to please her if we can? Think how happy she would be at home if Papá played the violin while she played her piano."

Clara groaned and flopped facedown on the bed. But Josefina knew that by now she was only pretending to be cross. "Oh, all right!" Clara said, her voice muffled. "I'll do it! May God forgive me for being so foolish!"

Josefina and Francisca smiled at each other in triumph. They knew Clara couldn't refuse a chance to make Papá *and* Tía Dolores happy.

The next afternoon, the sun shone down straight and strong. It baked out the spicy scent of the *piñón* trees as the sisters and Tía Dolores walked to the plaza. A servant was with them because it wasn't safe while the traders were in town for ladies to go there without a man to protect them. The servant stayed with the sisters while Tía Dolores stepped inside a shop to trade Ana's blanket for boots for Juan and Antonio.

Patrick soon came up to the sisters to say hello. Even though it was very hot, Clara had been clutching her blanket tightly to her chest. But she handed it over without a murmur when Josefina and Francisca gave their blankets to Patrick.

"These are beautiful," said Patrick. "And they are

worth a great deal. Why are you giving them to me?"

Josefina took a deep breath. "We were wondering if you would consider taking them in trade for your— for your violin," she said all in a rush. That's what she said aloud. Inside she was praying, *Please let Señor Patrick say yes.*

Patrick looked surprised. "But I thought you wanted the little farm," he said to Josefina. "And you told me you wanted a mirror, Señorita Francisca. And you wanted knitting needles, Señorita Clara. You could get those things and more with these blankets."

"We *all* want the violin more than anything else," Josefina said firmly. "We want it for Papá."

"Ah!" said Patrick. He looked at the blankets and ran his hand over them. At last he said, "Your papá is very lucky to have daughters who love him so much. I'd be honored to trade my violin for blankets made by such good-hearted girls as you."

"Oh, gracias, Señor Patrick!" said Josefina with a huge smile.

"It's I who must thank you for these soft blankets," Patrick said. Then he added with a chuckle, "That violin isn't very comfortable to sleep on!"

Josefina laughed and Patrick went on to say, "Meet me here tomorrow afternoon at this same time. I'll give you the violin then."

"We'll be here!" promised Josefina and Francisca.

As Patrick walked away with their blankets, Clara shook her head. "I hope we can trust him," she said.

"Of course we can!" said Francisca stoutly. "Papá trusted him with the mules, didn't he?"

But Clara couldn't answer because Tía Dolores had returned. "Why, girls," she asked, "where are your blankets?"

"I hope you don't mind," said Francisca. "We traded them already."

Tía Dolores smiled. "What did you get?"

"Well," said Josefina. "We . . . it's . . ." Finally she gave up and grinned at her aunt. "We really can't say," she explained. "But you'll see tomorrow."

Tía Dolores laughed. "How nice!" she said. "You'll surprise me!"

"We certainly will," said Clara with a sigh.

But Josefina knew Clara was as excited about their surprise as she and Francisca were. Josefina was having a hard time hiding her own excitement. Her thoughts raced ahead to the next day. She couldn't *wait* to get the violin for Papá. She hoped the hours would fly by until it was time to meet Patrick!

Though it was raining hard the next afternoon, the three sisters went to the plaza with a servant to meet Patrick. They stood exactly where he had told them to be. They pulled their rebozos over their heads and hunched their shoulders against the rain. Hour after hour after hour the girls waited. By the time the bell in San Miguel Chapel rang for six o'clock prayers, their skirts were drenched and their shoes were sopping. It was clear that the servant was sorry he had come and was eager to go home where it was warm and dry. Josefina couldn't blame him. A gust of wind drove rain into her face so that it was as wet as if she had been crying.

"What shall we do?" asked Francisca. A strand of her hair was stuck flat against her cheek.

Clara shivered. "Let's go *home*," she said. "We've waited three hours. Señor Patrick is not coming. That's all. He's just not going to come."

"Maybe he forgot," said Josefina. "Maybe we misunderstood. Maybe we were supposed to come tomorrow."

"Maybe!" exclaimed Clara. "You can *maybe* all you want, but I'm going home right now! Abuelita will be worried sick about us."

"Wait!" said Josefina. She saw a man she knew was a friend of Patrick's. She gathered up all her courage and hurried to him. Clara and Francisca followed close behind. "Excuse me, señor," Josefina said. "Do you know where Señor Patrick O'Toole is?"

"Patrick O'Toole?" said the man. "He's gone."

Josefina's heart dropped. "But . . . but he was supposed to meet us here," she said. "There must be some mistake."

The man shrugged. "O'Toole's a scout," he said. "Last night, the captain of the wagon train told the scouts to head out for the Camino Real. By now they're long gone." The man nodded a brisk good-bye, then rushed off in the rain.

Gone! The word echoed inside Josefina's head. She felt as if she were in a cold, cruel nightmare. She stood numbly, too confused and miserable to talk.

Francisca was silent, too. But Clara had a lot to say. "I knew we shouldn't have trusted that Señor Patrick," she said furiously. "You know what this means, don't you? Señor Patrick has cheated us, so I'm sure he's cheated Papá, too! We've lost our blankets, but Papá has probably lost all the mules! We've got to get home to tell him."

"That's enough, Clara," said Francisca, her voice tired. She slid her arm around Josefina's shoulders. "Let's go."

Homeward the girls trudged. The wind swirled the rain around them. Josefina hardly noticed. She could think only of Patrick. With all her heart, she wanted to hold on to her trust in him. But it certainly seemed that Clara was right and that Patrick had lied to them all.

As they passed the toy trader, Josefina peered out from under her dripping rebozo and saw that the toy farm was gone. *Not that it matters,* Josefina thought sadly. *Now I have nothing to trade for it anyway.* But that was only a tiny disappointment compared to what Patrick seemed to have done. *Oh, Señor Patrick,* thought Josefina. *How could you betray us like this?*

Shining Like Hope

 apá and Abuelito had gone to trade blankets for tools and did not come home until it was time for dinner. As soon as they walked in the door, Clara rushed to Papá. "Something terrible has happened," Clara said. "Señor Patrick is gone!"

"Gone?" gasped Abuelito. "But he hasn't paid your papá the rest of the silver he owes him. He promised—"

"Señor O'Toole's promises are lies," said Clara. "Yesterday Francisca, Josefina, and I gave him our blankets. He was supposed to meet us today to give us something in return for them. But he took our blankets and left! He stole them!" Clara looked at Papá and said, "He cheated us, so I'm certain he's cheated you, too."

"I knew it was a mistake to trust that americano!" said Abuelita. "He used his jokes and flattery and music to trick us into liking him! We didn't really know him at all!" She turned to Papá. "If you go to town right now, perhaps you can find your mules and get them back," she said.

Papá's face looked hard as stone.

Tía Dolores spoke carefully. "It's still possible that this is just a misunderstanding," she said. "If you reclaim your mules, you'll be saying that Señor Patrick is dishonest. If you're wrong, you'll shame him and yourself. You'll ruin his good name and your own as well."

"Sí," said Abuelito. "The other americanos won't want to trade with you, and you'll get nothing for your mules this year. You'd better be sure—"

"Sure?" interrupted Abuelita. "How much more sure could anyone be?" She spoke to Papá with urgency. "Señor O'Toole stole from your daughters. If he'd stoop to that, you can be sure he stole from you, too! Go now, get your mules back before the rest of the americanos leave, before it's too late!"

Papá was a wise man who did not act hastily. He thought for a long moment. Then he spoke in a sad, tired voice. "It seems I have been wrong to trust young

Señor O'Toole," he said. "I don't want to ruin my chances of trading with the other americanos, but I can't risk losing twenty good mules. I must do what I can to get them back."

"Sí!" began Abuelita. "Go—"

But Papá held up his hand. "It's useless to go now," he said. "It will be impossible to find the mules in the dark. I'll go tomorrow, at first light."

Abuelita pressed her lips into a thin, worried line and said no more. No one had any more to say. Soon after dinner, they all went to bed.

But Josefina was too miserable to sleep. For hours she lay awake, staring out of the narrow window. Finally she gave up. She rose, dressed, slipped outside, and climbed the hilltop behind the house.

The rain had washed the air clean, and the full moon was bright, shining like hope in the sky. Suddenly, out of the corner of her eye, Josefina saw a shadow move. "Señor Patrick?" she whispered, thinking wildly that he had come to find her.

But no. It was only an old tortoise making its way patiently across the sandy ground. Josefina sighed, and watched the tortoise stop under a piñon tree. Oddly, the ground looked white there. Josefina looked again. The ground wasn't white. Someone had left a piece of paper under the tree. Josefina bent down to look at the paper and gasped. *On top of the paper she saw Patrick's chunk of turquoise!*

With trembling hands, Josefina picked up the turquoise and the paper. She unfolded the paper carefully, knowing that Patrick must have left it for her. It was soggy from being in the rain. The ink had run so much that the drawing was blurry. When Josefina held it up so that the moon shone on it, she could see that it was a drawing of a church. But which church? There were five in Santa Fe.

Was this one of Patrick's jokes? Josefina looked at the chunk of turquoise and remembered how Patrick had joked that it was a piece of the sky that fell into his hand when he climbed to the top of . . . Oh! Josefina pulled in her breath. San Miguel Chapel! That was it! Patrick had left the chunk of turquoise on top of the paper so that she would know that the drawing was San Miguel Chapel. Josefina's heart skipped a beat. That was where the violin was! Josefina squeezed her fist shut around the piece of turquoise.

Oh, Señor Patrick! she thought. *Forgive me for thinking that you lied.*

Josefina slipped and slid down the rain-slick hill, tripping over her own feet in her hurry. She crossed the courtyard and burst into the room she shared with Francisca and Clara. "Wake up!" she hissed, shaking her sisters' shoulders. When they opened their eyes, Josefina waved the drawing at them and said, "Señor Patrick didn't lie! He left this to tell me where the violin is." She swallowed to catch her breath. "He left the violin in San Miguel Chapel."

"Let me see that," said Francisca. She lit a candle and took the drawing.

Clara looked bewildered. "But why . . ." she began.

"Señor Patrick put the violin in San Miguel Chapel because he knew it would be safe there," explained Josefina. "He had to leave Santa Fe in the middle of the night. He couldn't bring the violin here and wake up the whole household. He couldn't leave it up on the hilltop where it would be ruined by rain. He couldn't write a note to tell us where it was because we can't read English and he can't write Spanish. So he left me the drawing and his chunk of turquoise. He trusted me to figure it out." Josefina took the paper back from Francisca. "I'll show this to Papá, and it will prove to him that Señor Patrick is honest. Papá won't have to break off the trade!"

"Don't bother Papá with that! It's just a piece of paper," said Clara. "It doesn't prove anything. Only the violin would prove that Señor Patrick didn't cheat us— and Papá, too."

"Then I'll have to *get* the violin, won't I?" said Josefina. "I'll go now."

Clara was horrified. "Josefina!" she sputtered. "You can't go into Santa Fe by yourself in the middle of the night! It's dangerous. The traders drink too much. They gamble and fight and shoot off their guns." She shuddered. "You can't go."

"Not by yourself," said Francisca. She stood up and began to pull on her clothes. "I'll go with you."

"Oh, gracias, Francisca!" said Josefina. "We'll have to hurry. It'll be sunrise in a few hours. We've got to get the violin before Papá goes to town to take his mules back." She looked at Clara. "You must promise you won't tell anyone that we've gone."

"I promise," said Clara. "But *you* must promise to

be careful. I'll pray for you." She sighed. "If only I'd traded my blanket for those knitting needles!"

Josefina and Francisca crept from their room, tip-toed across the courtyard, and slid out the front gate. They sidled along the outside wall of the house. Then they darted to the kitchen garden and crouched behind its stick fence to catch their breath.

In a moment, Francisca touched Josefina's shoulder and then pointed toward the road. Josefina nodded. Both girls sprang forward, dashed to the road, and ran down it as fast as they could. With every step, the lantern she'd brought banged against Josefina's leg. Soon her arm ached from carrying it. Her stomach was in a knot, and her chest was burning because she was out of breath. But she kept on. Francisca was right by her side.

Soon light shining from windows and doorways spilled across the road. The girls heard bursts of music and clapping and the thunder of dancing feet coming from *fandangos* and parties. "We'll have to stay away from the plaza," whispered Josefina as she and

Francisca skittered down a narrow lane. "Too many people."

Francisca nodded. "Let's—" she began.

But just at that moment, the girls heard voices. A group of men swayed toward them, singing and laughing and all talking at once.

Quickly, Josefina and Francisca shrank into a door-way, pushing themselves flat against the door, holding their breath. Josefina's heart was pounding so loudly, she felt sure the men would hear it! But the rowdy men lurched by the girls' hiding place. Their voices filled the lane and then faded as they moved farther away. When she thought the men were gone, Josefina lifted her lantern and cautiously looked out to see if anyone else was coming. When she didn't see anyone, she sig-naled to Francisca to follow her.

But the moment the girls stepped out of the door-way, a rough voice frightened them. "What have we here?" said the voice. It belonged to a tall man who loomed toward them out of the darkness. "Two señoritas!" growled the man. He stepped forward, but Josefina tripped him, and he fell with a heavy thud. Josefina took hold of Francisca's hand and the two girls ran for all they were worth, not caring where they went as long as it was *away*.

Like birds of the night, Josefina and Francisca darted from shadow to shadow, skirting the center of town and never stopping. Just when Josefina thought she could not run another step, the moon-washed front of San Miguel Chapel rose up before them into the dark night sky. Up the steps they flew. Josefina grasped the handle of one of the huge doors with both hands and pulled it with all her strength. Slowly, the door creaked open and the two breathless girls ran inside.

Trembling, the girls walked forward. It was cold inside the church, and at first it seemed darker than outside. Josefina's lantern made only a small circle of light around her feet. But as her eyes adjusted, Josefina saw candles placed in a cluster on the floor in front of the altar where people had lit them and left them as a kind of prayer. The candles shone like stars fallen from the sky. With careful steps, Josefina and Francisca walked toward them.

Suddenly, Josefina's heart soared up with happiness. For there, safely placed against the wall by a small altar, was Patrick's violin in its case. *God bless you, Señor Patrick!* Josefina thought. She grabbed Francisca's hand and pulled her over to the violin. "Look!" she breathed. Patrick had even tied a ribbon around the violin case. Josefina knelt down and grinned. "I think Señor Patrick knew that you would come with me," she said to Francisca. Because next to the violin was the mirror that Francisca had wanted to get with her blanket.

Francisca smiled her beautiful smile. "He left something for you, too," she said. She picked up a small box and handed it to Josefina.

Josefina looked inside, and the first thing she saw was the funny pink pig. It was the little farm! All of the pieces fit together neatly in the small box. Josefina touched the farmhouse. *Gracias, Señor Patrick*, she thought. *I promise I will remember you every time I play with the little farm.*

"We'd better go," said Francisca.

The girls stood. When Josefina picked up the violin, something poked her hand. Josefina looked. Patrick had used the ribbon to tie knitting needles for Clara to the back of the violin case!

Josefina and Francisca glanced at each other and smiled. But there was no time to lose. When the girls walked outside the church, a thin streak of gray above the mountains was already hinting that the sun would soon rise. Josefina knew that meant Papá was probably awake and getting ready to come into town. She and Francisca had to get home fast. They had to stop him!

Though they were tired, Josefina and Francisca pushed themselves homeward as fast as they could go. The road home had never been so long.

As they ran toward Abuelito's house, they saw that they were just in time. Papá and Tía Dolores were standing together. Papá's horse was saddled, and he was just about to mount up to ride into town.

Josefina didn't hesitate. She ran straight to Papá and held out the violin. "Look, Papá," she said, all out of breath. "This is Señor Patrick's violin. This is what we traded our blankets for. He didn't lie to us. He left the violin for us in the church. Please don't go into town! Please don't take back your mules. Señor Patrick is honest. The violin proves it!" She thrust the violin into Papá's hands. "If he kept his promise to us, then surely he'll keep his promise to you."

Papá was astounded. He looked at the violin and then at his two daughters.

Tía Dolores was the first to speak. "Do you mean to say that you two—" She broke off, as if the rest of her question were too unbelievable to ask. "You two went into Santa Fe by yourselves in the middle of the night to get this violin?"

Josefina and Francisca nodded. "We're sorry," said Josefina.

"But we had to prove to Papá that Señor Patrick is honest," Francisca added.

They all looked at Papá. "You stopped me from making a serious mistake, and I am grateful," he said in his deep and deliberate voice. "Now I am sure that somehow Señor Patrick will get me the money he owes me for the mules." He paused, then said, "Go inside. Your abuelita will have some sharp words to say to you when she finds out what you have done, and I . . ."

The girls hung their heads. They knew they deserved the scolding they expected. But all Papá said was, "I must ask a servant to unsaddle my horse. It seems I won't be going to town this morning after all."

Francisca and Josefina glanced at each other. Wasn't

Papá going to scold them any more than that? They didn't wait to see, but turned to go inside.

"Wait!" said Papá. He held the violin out to Josefina. "Take your violin."

"Oh!" said Josefina. "The violin isn't for us. It's for you, Papá."

"For me?" Papá asked. "Why?"

"Because," said Josefina, "it made you and Tía Dolores happy."

Papá looked at Tía Dolores, and Josefina saw something that *might* have been a smile pass between them.

That evening, a friend of Patrick's brought the rest of the silver to Papá. Josefina and Francisca had only a peek at the man as he was leaving after dinner. They'd had to spend the day in their room as punishment for sneaking into town. Abuelita said that they should pray for God's forgiveness and everyone else's as well. But then she hugged both sisters, so Josefina thought she wasn't *too* angry. Clara was so delighted with her new knitting needles that she kept Josefina and Francisca company and knit all day. Francisca amused them by using her mirror to make reflected sunlight dance on the walls and flit across their skirts like tiny gold birds. Josefina spent the time quietly playing with her toy farm. And so the day passed peacefully. Josefina was tired after her adventure. She went to bed early and fell into a dreamless sleep.

Something woke her in the middle of the night. It wasn't the moon, because the sky was cloudy. Josefina got out of bed and opened the door to feel the cool night breeze on her cheeks. A sound nearly too soft to be heard drifted on the breeze. Josefina had to hold her breath to hear it. She almost wasn't sure what the sound was. When she realized, she smiled. Papá was gently, very gently, playing an old Spanish song on his violin.

The breeze blew the clouds away, and suddenly the courtyard was full of moonlight. Josefina saw that she was not the only one awake and listening to Papá. Standing in the doorway to her room, humming Papá's song, was Tía Dolores.

Gifts and Blessings

 CHAPTER 9

osefina and her family returned to their
rancho, and soon summer turned into fall.
Then winter came, and all of Josefina's
world was dusted with white, glittering snow and
full of the excitement of the holiday season.

Early on the morning of January sixth, a whisper
tickled Josefina's ear. "Josefina," it said. "Wake up."

Josefina was as cozy as a bird in its winter nest.
But she pushed back her blanket and opened her
sleepy eyes. She saw her little nephews, Juan and
Antonio, crouched next to her. They were so close
that she could feel their warm breath on her cheek
and she could see, even in the darkness, that their
faces were bright with excitement.

"Look!" whispered Juan. He and Antonio held
up their shoes to show Josefina. "The three kings

were here! They put treats in our shoes!"

"Yours, too, Josefina!" said Antonio, with a mouth full of sweets.

"Oh!" breathed Josefina. She sat up quickly and Antonio handed her one of her own shoes. In it, wrapped up in a scrap of clean cloth, there were pieces of candied fruits, slices of dried apples and apricots, and a small cone of sugar. Far down in the toe of her shoe there was a tiny goat carved out of wood that looked just like her pet, Sombrita.

January sixth was *La Fiesta de los Reyes Magos,* the Feast of the Three Kings. The night before, the children had followed an old tradition. They'd filled their shoes with hay and left them outside. The story was that the three kings would pass by on their way home from bringing gifts to the Christ Child in Bethlehem. The kings' camels would eat the hay, and the kings would leave sweets and gifts in the children's shoes to say thank you.

"The three kings were very generous to us," said Josefina as she nibbled a piece of candied melon.

Antonio sighed and Josefina saw that his shoe was already nearly empty. "My shoe's too small," he said, forgetting to speak softly.

"Shh!" shushed Juan. Josefina shared her sleeping sala with Clara and Francisca. Everyone knew that Francisca was grouchy all day if awakened too early. "Antonio, you had lots of sweets," whispered Juan, who was five. "You ate them too fast!"

Antonio hung his head. Josefina felt sorry for him. After all, he was only three. This was the first year he'd put his shoe out. Josefina remembered very, very well how it felt to be the youngest and to have the smallest shoe and to be so excited that she ate up her sweets instead of saving them the way her older sisters did. All that had changed. Francisca and Clara considered themselves too grown up, so now Josefina was the oldest child in the family to put out her shoe. "You can have some of my sweets," she said to Antonio. "I need my shoe, anyway. I can't hop to the stream on one foot."

"Gracias," said Antonio. He popped one of Josefina's sweets in his mouth and hopped around the room, first on one foot and then on the other.

Josefina watched him as she neatly rolled up her sheepskin and blankets and propped her doll, Niña, on top. "You boys had better hop back to your room and get dressed," she said quietly. "There's lots to do to get ready for the *fiesta* tonight." There was always a big fiesta, or party, to celebrate the Feast of the Three Kings, which was the last day of the Christmas season.

Clara was awake by now. She opened the door and a blast of cold air as sharp as an icicle came through. Francisca groaned and pulled her blanket over her head. "It snowed in the night," Clara said. "If it starts again, there might not be any fiesta."

Antonio stopped hopping and Juan asked, "No fiesta?"

"Don't worry," said Josefina. Now that she was almost eleven, she didn't let Clara's unhappy predictions discourage her. "It's early yet. As soon as the sun comes up, the sky will be blue. I'm sure of it. Now go!" She shooed the boys back to the room they shared with their parents, Ana and Tomás. Then she pulled on an extra petticoat, warm socks, and her warmest sarape and headed to the stream.

Josefina fetched water for the household first thing every morning. She enjoyed going to the stream even on wintry days like this one because each day was different. Today fresh new snow squeaked under her feet. The noisy stream greeted her, rushing around rocks capped with snow, then curving away out of sight. Josefina knew that the old saying *El agua es la vida* was true. Water was life to the rancho. Nothing could grow without it. The stream flowed along as steadily as time and blessed the rancho as it passed.

Josefina filled her water jar with the stinging-cold water. She put a ring of braided yucca leaves on her head and then balanced the jar on top of it. She walked back up the path thinking about all the delicious foods for the fiesta that this water would be used to make. There would be bizcochito cookies, spicy chile stew, and warm turnovers stuffed with fruit. Best of all, there would be dark, sweet hot chocolate. Josefina's feet moved faster at the thought of it.

Papá met her halfway up the path. "Oh, it's my Josefina," Papá said as he fell into step alongside her. "I thought you were a sparrow flying up the hill toward me. You're in a hurry this morning."

"Sí, Papá," said Josefina, "because of the fiesta tonight."

"Ah!" said Papá. "Tía Dolores tells me that you're

going to play the piano at the fiesta. She says you have a gift for music."

Josefina blushed. "Tía Dolores is very kind," she said.

"Sí," agreed Papá. "She is." They walked a few steps and then he said, "I can remember when you'd have been much too shy to play music at a fiesta."

"I am worried about it," Josefina admitted. "I don't think I could do it at all if it weren't for Tía Dolores. She taught me the piece of music I'm going to play and we've practiced it a lot. It's a waltz. I'm hoping everyone will be so happy dancing that they won't notice my mistakes! I especially hope Tía Dolores will be dancing. No matter how flustered I get, if I can look up and see her dancing, I'll be fine. I'll pretend I'm playing only for her."

"I'll tell you what," said Papá. "I'll ask Tía Dolores to dance the waltz with me. Then you need not worry."

"Oh, will you, Papá?" asked Josefina.

"I promise," he answered.

When Josefina and Papá came to the house, they saw that everyone was up and beginning the day's work. Juan and Antonio were energetically sweeping the snow out of the center courtyard. Or at least Josefina guessed that's what they were *supposed* to be doing. Actually, they were using their straw brooms to swoop the snow up into the air. Then they stood with their heads tilted back so that they could catch snowflakes on their tongues.

"I suppose we should stop them," said Papá with a grin.

Josefina didn't want to. The swirling snow was pretty. It glittered as it caught the early morning sun.

"Oh, please don't," said Tía Dolores, smiling as she came from the kitchen. She had a bundle of twigs, which she added to the fire already burning in the outdoor oven called the *horno*. "Ana has everything running smoothly in the kitchen. But we were tripping over those boys. They would not stop pestering us for tastes of food. They must have asked for cookies twenty times! Ana sent them out here, and the longer they're not in the way, the better."

Papá laughed and Josefina's heart lifted, as it always did, to hear him. Josefina remembered how it was just after Mamá died. Back then Papá seldom laughed or smiled. She and her sisters had been crushed by sorrow, too.

Then Tía Dolores had come to stay with them. Josefina looked at her aunt laughing along with Papá and thought about the wonderful changes Tía Dolores had made. She'd taught Josefina and her sisters to read and write. She'd helped them weave blankets to sell and trade. She'd brought her piano to the rancho and taught Josefina to play. Many evenings Papá played his violin while Tía Dolores played her piano. The rancho was a different place because of Tía Dolores. Josefina thought the best change of all was that Tía Dolores had helped their family to be happy again— especially Papá.

"Come along, Josefina," Tía Dolores said now in her brisk way. "Ana needs that water in the kitchen."

"Sí," said Josefina, smiling to herself. One thing Tía Dolores had taught *everyone* on the rancho was her favorite saying: *The saints cry over lost time.*

No time was being lost in the kitchen! It was humming with activity. Ana, who was in charge, was making turnovers. Carmen, busy cooking as usual, was stirring a big copper pot full of stew. Tía Dolores helped Carmen set the pot on an iron trivet over hot coals from the fire. Francisca's sleeves were rolled up and she was kneading bread dough.

"Bless you, Josefina," said Ana. She took the water jar. "Please help Francisca. I want the dough to rise while we're at morning prayers. The horno should be hot enough to bake the bread after prayers."

Clara was kneeling on the floor, using the *mano* and *metate*. She put a handful of dried corn on the flat metate stone and crushed it with the mano stone, rubbing back and forth until the corn was ground into coarse flour.

"Clara," Josefina said as she took off her sarape, "it's sunny. There's not one snow cloud in the sky."

Clara shrugged. "Not yet," she said, crushing another handful of corn. Then Clara surprised Josefina by smiling. "It's not that I want to be discouraging," she explained. "I just think it's foolish to get your hopes up the way you always do, Josefina. You're bound to be disappointed."

"I can't help it," said Josefina. "My hopes seem to go up whether I want them to or not."

"Like this bread dough," joked Francisca. She

pressed her fists into the dough and pushed down. "No matter how I flatten it, it rises up again."

"Hope is a blessing," said Tía Dolores.

"Sí," agreed Ana as she put some turnovers on a plate. "I think it's good to keep trying and never give up."

Just then, Juan and Antonio stuck their heads in the door. "Please," Juan asked for the twenty-first time, "can we have some cookies now?"

"What was that you said about never giving up?" Josefina asked Ana. And suddenly the kitchen was full of laughter.

After morning prayers and breakfast, Josefina and Tía Dolores carried the fat loaves of bread dough outside. Josefina took the wooden door off the horno, and smoke from the fire inside rose up into the blue sky. Josefina and Tía Dolores shoveled out the hot coals and swabbed the inside of the horno clean. When they finished, Tía Dolores put a tuft of sheep's wool on a wooden paddle.

"Oh, Tía Dolores, may I do it?" asked Josefina.

"Certainly," said Tía Dolores.

She gave Josefina the paddle, and Josefina put it into the horno. When the sheep's wool turned a toasty brown, Josefina knew the horno was just the right temperature to bake the bread. Josefina used her finger to press the shape of a cross on the tops of the loaves as a reminder that all the earth's bounty was a gift from God. Then, as Tía Dolores watched, she carefully put the loaves into the horno and wedged shut the heavy wooden door.

"Well done!" said Tía Dolores.

"I can take them out at the right time, too," said Josefina, boasting a bit.

"Good for you!" said Tía Dolores. "You don't need my help with the bread at all anymore, do you? But maybe I *can* help you practice the music you're playing tonight."

"Oh, yes, please," said Josefina. They walked together toward the *gran sala*, where the piano had been moved for the fiesta. "I'll practice playing the waltz, and perhaps you'd like to practice dancing it."

"Gracias," said Tía Dolores, laughing. "But that won't be necessary. I plan to be sitting right next to you at the piano while you play."

Josefina stopped and looked at her aunt. "Oh, but Tía Dolores," she said seriously. "Papá is hoping you'll dance the waltz with him. He told me so. You wouldn't want to disappoint him, would you?"

Tía Dolores slipped her arm around Josefina's shoulders. "No," she answered just as seriously. "I would never want to disappoint your papá."

Josefina was sure there had never been a more beautiful night for a fiesta. The huge, cold, black sky was sprinkled with stars, and the ground was silvery because of the moonlight shining on the snow. In the center courtyard of the house, a line of little fires lit the way to the gran sala, the biggest and grandest room, which was used only for special times like this.

Inside the gran sala, candlelight caught the bright colors of the ladies' best dresses and glinted off the men's buttons. Josefina and Clara were too young to dance, but they were allowed to sit on the floor and watch. Francisca swung by with her partner, and Ana waved gaily as she danced past with Tomás. Josefina saw stout Señora Sánchez and kindly Señora López both dancing with their husbands, and stately, white-haired Señor García dancing with his wife. The guests were friends from the village or from nearby ranchos, and Josefina had known them all her life. Somehow, though, their familiar faces looked different tonight. Perhaps it was the gentle glow of candlelight or just the magic of happiness that made the ladies look so lovely and the men look so handsome.

After a while, Clara nudged Josefina. "Time to play your waltz," she said.

Josefina stood, smoothed her skirt, and straightened her hair ribbon.

"You look fine," Clara said. Then she stood too and said kindly, "I'll go with you. Come on." The two sisters walked through the crowded room to the piano. Josefina was pleased to see that Francisca and Ana were waiting for her there. They smiled encouragingly as she sat down.

Josefina had never played music in front of a large group of people before. Her hands were trembling. Then, out of the corner of her eye, she saw Papá bow and hold out his hand to Tía Dolores. Josefina began to play, and Papá and Tía Dolores began to dance. Josefina had always liked the lilting rhythm of the waltz: *one-two-three, one-two-three, one-two-three.* And tonight the music seemed to spiral up, up, up in ever more graceful swoops and swirls as she played. She never took her eyes off Papá and Tía Dolores. It was as if all the other dancers had faded away. Around and around and around Papá and Tía Dolores whirled. Tía Dolores danced so lightly in Papá's arms it seemed as if the music were wind and she and Papá were birds carried on it.

Around and around and around they danced. *Papá and Tía Dolores belong together,* thought Josefina. *They love each other.* With her whole heart, she was sure of it. Ana, Francisca, and Clara were watching Papá and Tía Dolores, too. Josefina knew that her sisters were thinking the same thought she was. And she knew they were wishing, just as she was, that the dance would never end.

Sleet

he bad weather Clara had predicted came howling in the next day. The sky was hard, dark and gray, and sleet clattered and bounced on the roof of the gran sala. Tía Dolores and the sisters had gathered in the gran sala to dust and sweep so that the room could be closed up until the next fiesta. The day was dreary, but Josefina needed only to close her eyes to imagine the way the gran sala had glowed with candlelight the night before. She hummed the waltz to herself as she swept.

Papá came in with two servants. They were going to move the table and chairs back to their usual places and put Tía Dolores's piano back in the family sala.

"Wasn't it a lovely fiesta?" Josefina sighed, looking at the piano.

"You know, I used to think a fiesta was hardly

worthwhile," said Clara, sounding unusually cheery. "There's so much work to do to get ready and even more work afterward to clean up! But last night's fiesta was worth it."

"And just wait till you're old enough to dance," said Francisca, twirling around her broom. "Then you'll love fiestas as much as I do."

"Preparing for a fiesta used to overwhelm me," said Ana. "But Tía Dolores has taught me to enjoy it. Now I think it's a pleasure to cook food for our friends to share."

"You did a wonderful job," Tía Dolores said to Ana. "All of you did." She looked around at all the sisters. Josefina thought Tía Dolores's face looked pale, as if she had not slept well the night before. "I am proud of you."

Papá spoke up. "Tía Dolores is right," he said. "Thanks to your hard work, that was a fiesta we'll all remember with great pleasure."

"Gracias, Papá," said the sisters happily. Such praise from Papá and Tía Dolores was delightful indeed! They all went contentedly back to work.

Except for Tía Dolores. She asked, "Do you remember that when I first came here, I said I would stay as

long as you needed me?" The sisters stopped sweeping
and looked at her as she went on. "You've all learned
to do your sewing and weaving and household tasks
very well. And you all did so beautifully preparing for
the fiesta yesterday! I can see that you don't need me
the way that you used to. So . . . so I've written to my
parents and asked them to come here and take me back
to Santa Fe with them. I'm going home."

The room was completely silent. The sisters were
stunned still. Josefina felt as if a drop of freezing sleet
were running right down her spine. "But Tía Dolores,
this is your home," she burst out. "We thought you were
happy here with us!"

"I am," said Tía Dolores. Then she squared her
shoulders and spoke firmly, as if she'd made up her
mind after a long struggle with herself. "But it's time
for me to leave."

Josefina turned to Papá. He looked as shocked as
she felt. Surely he would say something to Tía Dolores!
But Papá only bowed his head for a moment. When he
looked up, his face was composed and grave. He left
the room without saying a word.

Tía Dolores watched him go. Then she picked up

her broom and went back to work. But Josefina and her sisters stared after Papá, as if he alone had the answer to a question that was desperately important to them all.

The more she thought about it, the angrier Josefina was with herself. Bragging about how she could make bread! Showing off playing the piano! *No wonder Tía Dolores doesn't feel needed!* Josefina thought. The sleet had stopped, but it was still very windy and cold as Josefina walked to the goat pen to see Sombrita. "But I know how to make things right," Josefina said to the little goat as it chewed on the fringe of her sarape. "I'll start tomorrow."

The odd thing was that her sisters seemed to have hit upon the same idea. The next morning, Francisca spilled tea at breakfast. Josefina was quite sure she did it on purpose. Francisca was wearing Clara's sash instead of her own, and the sash was badly stained. Francisca and Clara had sharp words about it, bickering just as they used to in the days before Tía Dolores had come and taught them to get along. Later that

morning, Clara, who seldom made mistakes, snarled
the wool, and four rows of weaving had to be disentan-
gled from the loom. Ana somehow forgot to put salt in
the sauce, so dinner tasted terrible. Josefina made mistakes all day long. She burned some *tortillas,* dropped
a basket in a puddle, forgot part of a prayer, sat on her
best hat, and was all thumbs at her piano lesson.

That evening Tía Dolores and the sisters gathered
in front of the fire in the family sala. Papá didn't join
them. His violin lay neglected on top of the piano.
Papá might as well give the violin back to Patrick O'Toole,
thought Josefina with a sigh. *He'll have no pleasure in
playing it if Tía Dolores leaves.*

No one had much to say. Then Clara dropped her
ball of knitting yarn. She and Ana leaned forward at
the same time to pick it up and knocked heads. Ana
pulled back so quickly she jarred Francisca's elbow, and
Francisca pricked her finger with her sewing needle.
Francisca yelped, which startled Josefina so that she
made an ink splotch on her paper.

Tía Dolores shook her head. "I see what you girls
are up to," she said. "You're deliberately bungling
things so that it'll seem as if you still need me. But it

won't work. And you'd better stop before one of you sets your skirts on fire!"

She laughed, and the sisters had to laugh at themselves, too.

"But Tía Dolores," said Clara, "we *do* need you." Sometimes Josefina was glad that Clara was so straightforward.

"Sí," agreed Francisca. "Not just as a teacher, but as part of our family."

"We were so unhappy and lost after Mamá died," said Ana softly. "And you made everything better."

"We need you because we love you," said Josefina.

"Bless you!" said Tía Dolores, not laughing anymore. "I love you, too. That will never change. But you girls have come a long way toward healing from the sorrow of your mamá's death, God rest her soul. Your papá has come a long way, too. It's time for him to marry again, to give his heart to someone. If I am here, I'm afraid I may be in the way. That's why it's time for me to go. That's why I *want* to go."

"Oh, but Tía Dolores!" said Josefina. "Papá—" But Ana squeezed Josefina's arm to stop her. They all knew it would be wrong for Josefina to finish her sentence and say to Tía Dolores, "Papá loves *you*." Children did not say such things to adults.

"Besides," said Tía Dolores with her usual briskness, "if I am going to start a whole new life for myself in Santa Fe, the sooner I begin, the better."

The sisters could not look at one another or at Tía Dolores. There was nothing more they could say to her.

There was, however, a great deal for Josefina, Francisca, and Clara to say to one another later when they were together in their sleeping sala.

"Maybe this cold, sleety weather will stop Tía Dolores's letter from getting to Santa Fe," said Josefina, listening to the wind whistling outside the door. "Then Abuelita and Abuelito won't come to take her away."

"Don't be silly," said Clara. "Sooner or later, Tía Dolores is going to leave. Didn't you hear her say that she *wants* to go?"

Things were always black and white for Clara, plain as a wintry landscape of bare trees and snow. But

Josefina saw glimpses of color even in the starkest view.

"I don't think it's that simple," Josefina said now. "I don't think Tía Dolores truly wants to leave. She loves us, and . . ." Josefina swallowed and went on boldly, "I think she loves Papá. He loves her, too, but she doesn't know it."

"That's right," said Francisca. She sighed dramatically. "How terrible to love someone and think he doesn't love you in return. No wonder Tía Dolores wants to leave. Her heart must ache every time she sees Papá."

"Heavens above!" groaned Clara. "What nonsense! Tía Dolores isn't so foolish."

Josefina spoke with great certainty. "I know that Tía Dolores would stay," she said, "if Papá—"

"Asked her to marry him," all three sisters finished together.

"Sí," said Josefina. "The truth is, I've hoped he would for a long time now."

"Well," said Clara calmly. "Papá and Tía Dolores would be a good, sensible match, and a practical one, too." All the girls knew it was not unusual for a man to marry his wife's sister after his wife died. The families already knew each other, and it kept their property together.

"If they do decide to marry, they shouldn't waste any more time about it," said Clara. "Neither one of them is getting any younger. Besides, it's always best to have a wedding in the winter so that it won't get in the way of planting or harvesting."

"Oh, Clara!" exclaimed Francisca. "How can you be so matter-of-fact? You're forgetting all the wonderful steps in courtship. First, Papá has to write a letter asking Abuelito for Tía Dolores's hand in marriage. Then Abuelito and Abuelita ask Tía Dolores if the proposal is acceptable to her. If it isn't, then to say no, Tía Dolores must give Papá a squash—"

"There'll be no squash in this case. I'm sure of it!" Josefina cut in.

"And don't forget the engagement fiesta," Francisca rattled on, "and the groom's gifts to the bride, and—"

"Stop!" interrupted Clara. "There's one thing you're both forgetting: There's nothing *we* can do about *any* of this."

Josefina refused to give up. "There must be *something*," she said.

"Children are not involved in such matters," said Clara flatly. "It would be absolutely improper for us to talk to Tía Dolores or Papá."

Clara was right, as usual. But that did not stop Josefina. She thought for a while, and then she said, "I know someone we could talk to."

"Who?" asked her sisters.

"Tía Magdalena," said Josefina. "After all, she is Papá's sister and oldest relative, and the most respected woman in the village."

"When?" asked Clara.

"I'm sure Tía Magdalena will come to see Abuelito and Abuelita while they're here," said Josefina. "We'll ask her to speak to Papá. Oh, now I'm *glad* Abuelito and Abuelita are coming! That will make it all happen faster."

Francisca and Clara threw back their heads and started laughing.

"What's so funny?" asked Josefina.

"You are!" said her sisters.

"You find the sweet in the sour," said Clara. "The warm in the cold."

"The soft in the hard," added Francisca. "And

the light in the dark."

"Every time!" Clara and Francisca ended together.

Josefina didn't mind her sisters' teasing. She could tell that now they too were eager for Abuelito and Abuelita to arrive.

They did not have to wait long. Abuelito and Abuelita arrived from Santa Fe only a few days later. And just as Josefina had expected, Tía Magdalena came up from the village to see them the very first afternoon.

Before, during, and after dinner, Josefina waited for a chance to speak to Tía Magdalena, but they were surrounded by family all the time. It was not polite for a child to draw an adult aside for private conversation. Josefina knew she'd just have to sit and watch and wait and listen and hope for a quiet moment. It was hard because she was bubbling over with secret excitement.

Juan and Antonio were excited, too. They loved to see their great-grandparents, Abuelito and Abuelita. The boys showed their happiness with their whole bodies, frisking and dancing about the family sala until Abuelita scooped up Antonio, held him on her lap, and sat Juan right beside her.

"These are the finest boys in New Mexico," Abuelita said to Ana. "I really think that they should be educated by the priests in Santa Fe. Juan is old enough, and Antonio will be soon."

"Sí," agreed Abuelito. "It's an exciting time we live in. It's important for the boys to be educated so they can keep up. The world changes so fast!"

"And not all the changes are good," said Abuelita. "So many americano traders are coming to New Mexico now, with their different manners and customs and language! Most of them don't even share our Catholic faith." She shook her head. "I fear our most precious beliefs will be lost if we don't do all we can to teach them to our children."

"Now, now," said Abuelito. "Not all the americanos are so bad." He turned to Papá. "Don't you agree?"

Papá nodded. "Señor Patrick O'Toole is an honest young man," he said. "I plan to continue trading mules and blankets to the americanos with his help. He's a good fellow. I look forward to seeing him soon when he passes by on his way home to Missouri."

Abuelito leaned forward. "Then you will be interested to hear my news," he said. "I've been invited to join Señor O'Toole's wagon train and travel with it to Missouri. And I've decided to go!"

Everyone gasped. Abuelito went on with a pleased expression on his face. "I'll travel with the wagon train over the Santa Fe Trail to Franklin, Missouri. Then I'll ride a steamboat to St. Louis! I'll bring goods to trade and arrange for goods to be sent back here. What an adventure it will be! I guess I'm not such an old man after all!"

"May God watch over you," said Tía Magdalena, who'd been listening silently.

Josefina was trying to imagine what a steamboat might look like when Abuelito said something that made her heart stop.

Abuelito smiled at Tía Dolores. "You know, my dear, I must thank you," he said. "I wasn't going to accept the invitation. I didn't want to leave your mother alone all the months I'd be away. But when we got your letter saying that you wanted to come home,

I knew I could say yes. Because you're coming home to Santa Fe, I can go to Missouri with the americanos!"

Oh, no! thought Josefina. *This is terrible.*

Then it got worse. "I was glad to get your letter, too, my daughter," said Abuelita to Tía Dolores. "Your father and I have waited a long time for you to come home to Santa Fe. It's such a comfort to know you'll be living with us as we grow old."

"I'm glad to be needed," said Tía Dolores softly.

Needed! Josefina felt a door slamming shut when she heard the word. She and Francisca and Clara exchanged agonized looks. How could Papá ask Tía Dolores to marry him *now*? It would seem selfish, and it would hurt Abuelito and Abuelita. Tía Dolores would never say yes if Papá *did* ask her. Her first duty was to her parents. It would be unthinkable for her to let them down.

Josefina could not bear to hear any more. Quietly, she slipped out of the family sala, ran across the cold courtyard, and went to her sleeping sala. It was dusk, and the room was full of shadows. Josefina sat on the floor, hugging her knees to her chest.

She was all alone for a few minutes. Then someone

came into the dark room and asked, "Josefina?"

It was Tía Magdalena.

Josefina jumped to her feet and stood, head bowed, in the respectful way children were supposed to stand in the presence of an adult.

Tía Magdalena sat on the *banco* and motioned Josefina to sit next to her on the bench. "All afternoon I've had the feeling that you wanted to ask me something," she said.

"Sí, Tía Magdalena," said Josefina. "I did. But . . . I beg your pardon, but I don't need to anymore."

"I see," said Tía Magdalena. But she didn't leave. Instead she said, "I've invited your Tía Dolores to stay with me for a few days before she goes to Santa Fe with her parents. I've grown so fond of her, and it'll be a long, long time before I see her again. Santa Fe's too far for me to travel anymore. Ah, well, we'll *all* miss your Tía Dolores very much when she leaves, won't we?"

Now the words spilled out of Josefina. "Oh, Tía Magdalena!" she said. "It will be terrible if Tía Dolores leaves. It will be the way it was just after Mamá died, when we were all so sad. We were . . ."

Josefina faltered. Gently, Tía Magdalena finished for her. "You were heartsick with sorrow," she said.

"Sí!" said Josefina. She spoke with conviction. "Tía Dolores mustn't leave! She belongs here! I was going to ask you to speak to Papá so that you could ask him to . . . to set it all straight." Josefina shook her head as she went on. "But now Abuelito and Abuelita need Tía Dolores in Santa Fe. She *has* to leave. There's nothing anyone can do."

"Dear child!" said Tía Magdalena. "I'm afraid you're right. Curanderas don't have medicine to heal such troubles."

Josefina sighed. There was one narrow window in the sleeping sala, and only a sliver of the twilight sky showed through. Josefina could see just one star, a tiny pinprick of light, shining very far away. "With all my heart," she said softly, "I want Tía Dolores to stay."

Tía Magdalena took Josefina's hand in hers. "Here," she said. She put something as smooth and cool as a raindrop into Josefina's palm.

It was so dark, Josefina had to lift her hand close to her eyes to see what Tía Magdalena had given her. It was a *milagro,* a little medal. Josefina knew that a

milagro was a symbol of a special hope or prayer.
When someone wanted to ask a saint for help, he'd
pin a milagro to that saint's statue. If he was praying
to find a lost sheep, he would choose a milagro in the
shape of a sheep. If he was praying for a hurt foot to
heal, he would choose a milagro in the shape of a foot.

"I want you to keep this milagro with you," said
Tía Magdalena. "It will remind you to pray for your
family's happiness, for your sorrow to be healed.
And perhaps it will help you not to lose hope in your
heart's desire."

"Gracias, Tía Magdalena," said Josefina. She looked
closer. The milagro Tía Magdalena had given her was
in the shape of a heart.

Josefina's Plan

arly the next morning, Tía Dolores left Papá's rancho and went to Tía Magdalena's house in the village, which was about a mile away. It was a bleak day. The tree branches were coated with hard, new ice, and they clinked when the wind knocked them together.

All that day, Josefina thought that the rancho seemed to be under a terrible spell, frozen in gloom, even though everything ran smoothly enough. No one spilled tea or ruined weaving or burned tortillas. Dinner was well cooked and served on time. Josefina did not make one single mistake when she practiced playing the piano. And yet somehow, the music was all wrong. It was just noisy, clanging sound. There was no joy in it. Since the piano would soon be gone with Tía Dolores, there didn't seem to be much point in practicing anyway. There didn't seem to be much point in anything at all.

This is what it will be like forever after Tía Dolores leaves, thought Josefina sadly. She was wearing the heart milagro on a thread around her neck. Every time she moved, she felt the cool little heart touch her chest. She was grateful for its comfort. It was like a gentle voice saying, *Perhaps there's still hope. Perhaps there's a way Tía Dolores can stay. Perhaps tomorrow you'll think of something. . . .*

But the next day came and Josefina felt as dull as the weather. Fat gray clouds hung so low over the mountains that the snowy peaks poked through. Everyone seemed unhappy, except for Abuelita and Abuelito. Abuelito talked to Ana's husband, Tomás, about the new plow Tomás had bought from the americano traders and the new system of ditches Tomás and Papá had dug on the rancho to bring water to the fields.

"That Tomás is a clever fellow," Abuelito said to Abuelita. "He's not afraid of change. He did a fine job managing the rancho last summer while the rest of the family was in Santa Fe. I wish I had a manager who'd do as well for me while I'm away."

Josefina and Abuelita were in the family sala
playing clapping games with Juan and Antonio.
Abuelita looked at Abuelito and smiled. "Cleverness
runs in the family," she said. "Ana manages this
household as smoothly as any I've ever seen. And
I've never known two brighter boys than little Juan
and Antonio." She sighed and hugged the boys.
"Bless their dear hearts," she said. "How I shall miss
them when we leave! I wish I could watch them grow
and change!"

Josefina's brain seemed to wake up at that moment.
An idea started to take shape. She thought about it all
day, then presented her plan to Clara and Francisca
that night as they were getting ready for bed. They
sighed and shook their heads doubtfully when they
heard Josefina's idea.

But Josefina was determined. "We've got to *try*,"
she said.

So the next morning, Francisca, Clara, and
Josefina presented the plan to Ana. She spoke to
her husband, Tomás, and then all four sisters went
together to Papá.

Papá was in the family sala. He had a pen in his

hand and Tía Dolores's ledger book lying open in front of him, but he was staring into the fire when the girls came into the room.

The four sisters stood with their hands folded and their heads bowed, waiting for Papá to acknowledge them.

He turned and said, "Sí?"

"With your permission," said Ana, "we'd like to speak to you, Papá."

"Sí," Papá said again.

Ana looked at Josefina, Clara, and Francisca. They nodded to urge her to begin.

"Papá," said Ana respectfully. "Would you honor us by considering an idea we have?" She paused. "Do you think it might be possible for Tomás and our sons and me to go to Santa Fe with Abuelito and Abuelita?"

Papá looked at the fire again as Ana went on. "Tomás could manage Abuelito's rancho while Abuelito is away on his trip to Missouri," she said. "I could keep Abuelita company and help her run her household. Juan could go to school and be educated by the priests. And Antonio, well, he will be happy to be with his dear great-grandmother who loves him so."

"Is this plan your idea?" Papá asked Ana.

"No," said Ana.

"It was Josefina's idea," said Clara.

Papá folded his arms across his chest and looked at Josefina. Then he asked Ana, "Is this what you and Tomás want?"

"Sí," answered Ana. "We'll be sad to leave here. But this would be a step forward for Tomás and our little family. I think it would be a good thing for Abuelito and Abuelita, as well. It would be good for you, too, Papá, and my sisters because—"

"Because then Tía Dolores would stay here!" Josefina ended.

Papá's face softened. His voice was gentle when he spoke. "I think this idea would be a wonderful thing for almost everyone," he said. "But I'm afraid that there is a problem with it. Tía Dolores has told us that she wants to leave our rancho and go to Santa Fe. If you go instead, Ana, she'll feel she's needed here to help run our household. It seems to me that all her life she's had to go where she was needed instead of where she wanted to go."

"But we don't believe that she really wants to go to

Santa Fe," Josefina blurted out. "It's just that she thinks she should. You could convince her to stay, Papá!" Josefina didn't come right out and say *If you asked her to marry you*, but that is what she meant.

"Dear child!" said Papá, smiling. "You have a great deal of faith in my ability to change Tía Dolores's mind!"

"Please, Papá," asked Ana. "May we ask you to think about our idea, and perhaps consider presenting it to Abuelito and Abuelita? They may have an opinion about it."

"I will consider it," said Papá. "You have my word."

"Gracias, Papá," said the sisters. Quickly, they left the room.

"I don't think that went very well," said Clara.

"He *said* he'd think about Josefina's plan," said Ana.

"But he has to do more than that," said Francisca. "He has to ask Abuelito and Abuelita for Tía Dolores's hand in marriage. She won't stay here if he doesn't."

"Well, he'd better do it soon," said Clara. "Tía Dolores will come back from Tía Magdalena's any day now. As soon as she does, she'll leave with Abuelita and Abuelito for Santa Fe."

"Oh, I hope Papá asks Tía Dolores to marry him," said Francisca.

"He will!" said Josefina. "I just know Papá will!"

Josefina's sisters couldn't help but smile at her.

"Josefina," said Ana in her gentle way. "Don't get your heart set on it."

"It's too late," Josefina said cheerfully. She patted the heart milagro. "My heart's been set on it for a long, long time already."

That very evening, when the family was gathered in front of the fire, Francisca jabbed Josefina to make her look up. Josefina tugged on Clara's skirt and Clara nudged Ana. All four sisters watched Papá hand Abuelito a folded piece of paper. They heard Papá ask Abuelito, "Would you do me the honor of reading this?"

"Of course!" said Abuelito. He and Papá and Abuelita left the room.

"Did you see that?" said Josefina joyfully. "Papá just gave Abuelito a letter asking for Tía Dolores's hand in marriage!"

"No, he didn't," said Clara. "The letter just presents the idea of Ana and Tomás and the boys going to Santa Fe."

Of course, there was no way of knowing who was right. But Josefina was sure she was, especially the next morning when she and Clara saw Abuelito and Abuelita setting out to walk to the village.

"Oh!" exclaimed Josefina, hugging Clara in her excitement. "Abuelita and Abuelito are going to ask Tía Dolores if she accepts Papá's marriage proposal!"

"No," said Clara. "They're just going to ask Tía Dolores how she feels about your plan. If she wants to go to Santa Fe, then Ana and Tomás won't go."

It was a blustery day and the whole sky was a pale, ghostly white, as if the clouds were full of snow waiting, waiting, waiting to fall. Josefina and her sisters were waiting, waiting, waiting, too, for Abuelita and Abuelito to come back from the village. Josefina came up with a hundred excuses to go outside and look down the road to see if she could spot them returning.

"What could they be doing?" she fussed to her sisters. They were in the kitchen preparing the mid-day meal. A stick hung crossways in front of the hearth with dried squash and garlic and chiles dangling from it. Josefina tapped the stick to make the vegetables jiggle, as if they felt the same jittery impatience that she did. "Why is this taking so long? All Tía Dolores has to do is say yes or no!"

"*If* they're talking about marriage," said Clara, "which they're not."

Ana tried to soothe things. "Abuelito and Abuelita have many friends in the village," she said. "Their friends have probably come to Tía Magdalena's house to visit with them. And I suppose that Abuelito has told them that he's going to Missouri with the americanos, so they all have a lot to say. I'm sure everyone is surprised."

"Oh!" exploded Josefina. "In another minute I'll run to the village myself to see what is going on!"

"Heavens!" said Clara rather primly. "You can't do that. Remember, this is none of our business. Children are not involved in such things."

Francisca rolled her eyes at Josefina and grinned. They knew that Clara was really every bit as curious as they were, though she liked to hide it.

It was late afternoon before Abuelito and Abuelita returned from the village, just in time for evening prayers. After prayers, as they all walked out into the courtyard, Abuelito turned to Papá.

"Well, Dolores surprised us," Abuelito said. The sisters were hardly breathing so that they could hear every word. "We discussed the idea of Ana and Tomás coming to Santa Fe instead of her."

Clara gave Josefina a look that said, *I told you so.*

Josefina's heart sank. So Clara had been right. Papá's letter had *not* been a proposal of marriage. *Oh, Papá!* thought Josefina, bitterly disappointed.

Disappointment turned to horror and disbelief when Abuelito went on to say, "Dolores thinks that Francisca and Clara and Josefina are perfectly capable of running this household without her help *or* Ana's! She says it's time for her to leave even if Ana leaves too. She's coming to Santa Fe no matter what Ana and Tomás do. So we'll pack up her belongings tomorrow, and we'll leave the day after."

"Very well," said Papá in a low, even voice.

No! Josefina wanted to shout out loud. *No!* Tía Dolores leaving *and* Ana leaving? That's not at all what was supposed to happen! Oh, how could her plan have turned out so badly? Hot tears filled Josefina's eyes. With a rough yank, she broke the thread with the heart milagro on it. She flung the milagro onto the slushy ground and walked away.

Heart and Hope

hen Mamá died, Josefina had thought that the world should stop. It had seemed wrong to carry on with everyday chores, as if nothing had changed. But over time, she had learned that work was a great comfort in hard times. It was a blessing to do simple tasks like cooking and washing and sweeping, tasks that had to do with hands, not hearts.

Josefina felt that way the next morning. She was glad to go out into the biting cold to fetch water from the stream. She was glad the water jar was heavy and the hill was steep as she trudged back to the house. She was glad her heart pounded in her chest from the hard work, else she'd think it had withered from sadness. When Mamá died, Josefina had thought she could never feel that sad ever again. Now she knew she'd been wrong.

Papá met Josefina halfway up the hill, just as he had on the morning of the fiesta. But this morning, they walked in silence. They'd almost reached the house when Papá stopped. He reached into his pocket. "Josefina," he asked, "I found this in the courtyard last night. Is it yours?"

Josefina put her water jar on the ground and looked. She saw something muddy dangling from Papá's hand. It was the heart milagro. Josefina frowned. "It was mine," she said. "But I don't want it."

Papá held the milagro in his hand and wiped the mud off it with his finger. "I suppose there's nothing harder to give someone than a heart she doesn't want," he said slowly. "Tell me why you don't want this one."

"Tía Magdalena gave it to me," Josefina explained. "She said it would remind me to pray for our family's happiness, for our sorrow to be healed. And . . ." Josefina sighed, remembering. "She said it would help me not to lose hope in my heart's desire."

"I see," said Papá. The day's very first ray of sun peeked over the mountaintop and between two clouds. Papá tilted his hand so that, just for a second, sunlight found the milagro and made it shine. When he spoke, Josefina knew that he was trying to comfort her. "I know what your heart's desire was, Josefina," he said. "When you and your sisters came to me with your plan, I knew what you were thinking. You wanted to make it possible for me to ask Tía Dolores to stay here as my wife. That would have made you happy. And it would have made me happy, too."

Josefina looked at Papá with a question in her eyes. But he was looking up at the mountains, so he didn't see.

"The simple truth is that we can't always have what we hope for in life," Papá said. "Tía Dolores told us that she wants to leave, and so we mustn't stop her. When we love someone, *especially* when we love someone, we must let her go if she wants to go. We must put her heart's desire before our own." Papá turned to Josefina. "Do you understand?" he asked gently. "We want Tía Dolores to be happy, don't we?"

"Oh, but Papá!" said Josefina desperately. "Tía Dolores doesn't want to leave. She thinks she should, for *your* happiness. She said that it's time for you to give your heart to someone, and she's in the way."

Then Josefina gathered up all her hope and courage and told the truth straight out. "Don't you see, Papá?" she said. "Tía Dolores loves you. That's why she *can't* stay. Because she thinks that you don't love her in return."

Papá shook his head and looked away from Josefina.

It's no use, thought Josefina. She lifted the water jar back onto her head and started to walk up the hill to the house.

"Josefina!" Papá called after her. "Do you want your milagro?"

Josefina turned. The heart milagro looked very, very small in Papá's hand. "No thank you, Papá," she said. "It's yours now."

Josefina did not see Papá again until the mid-day meal.

"Josefina," said Papá. "Your grandparents are walking to the village this afternoon. They're going to bring Tía Dolores back here. I want you to go along to help."

"Sí, Papá," said Josefina, even though there was no walk in the world she dreaded more. She had no desire to help Tía Dolores begin to leave them!

Josefina, Abuelito, and Abuelita set forth for the village under a winter sun so pale it didn't warm the air at all. Josefina's nose hurt and her mouth had the bitter taste of cold in it. A mean wind made her eyes water, so she bent her head forward and pulled down the brim of her hat.

"Brrr!" shivered Abuelito. "That wind cuts through me! My hands are frozen stiff." He glanced at Josefina. "My child," he said. "Put this paper in your pouch and carry it for me." Abuelito handed Josefina a folded paper and she put it in a leather pouch that hung from a string around her neck. "Gracias," said Abuelito. He rubbed his hands together to warm them. "Oh, how glad I'll be to get to your Tía Magdalena's house and stand in front of her fire!"

They were *all* glad to come into the warmth of Tía Magdalena's house. A cheerful fire crackled on the hearth, and steam rose in a cloud from a big kettle. Tía Dolores smiled at Josefina, and Tía Magdalena helped Abuelita sit next to the fire. "Come! Sit and be comfortable," Tía Magdalena said. "You must have a cup of tea."

"Gracias," said Abuelita. "You are very kind."

When they were settled, Abuelito said, "Josefina, please give me the paper." Josefina took the folded paper out of her pouch and handed it to Abuelito. He gave it to Tía Dolores, saying, "A letter for you, my dear."

As Tía Dolores unfolded the letter, something fell onto her lap. It was small and shiny and bright as a spark in the firelight. "Why, what's this?" asked Tía Dolores, holding the little object in her fingertips and looking at it curiously.

Josefina gasped. *It was the heart milagro!* Suddenly, Josefina knew. The letter was a proposal from Papá! She was so happy, she wanted to jump up and shout for joy. "It's a heart!" she exclaimed. "It's Papá's! He's giving it to you. Oh, please read the letter, Tía Dolores! Then you'll see."

Tía Dolores began to read the letter, and her eyes grew wide. "Oh!" she exclaimed softly. Then, "Oh," she said again.

Everyone sat perfectly still, watching Tía Dolores.

When she finished reading, Tía Dolores looked at Abuelito and Abuelita, and her face was lit with pure happiness. "Well," she said finally in a voice that trembled a little. "Josefina's papá has done me the honor of asking for my hand in marriage. Please tell him that my answer is yes."

"Bless you, my child!" exclaimed Abuelito. "We will."

Josefina jumped up and threw her arms around Tía Dolores's neck. She could feel Tía Dolores's happy tears on her own cheek.

On the day that Papá and Tía Dolores were to be married, the sun shone down on snow as white as new milk and dazzled the world with light. And yet the air carried a wisp of softness. Josefina took a deep breath as she walked up the hill from the stream. There was no mistaking the teasing hint of spring. She smiled to herself, thinking of the sprouts still sleeping under the snow, soon to be awakened by the spring sun.

This morning, both Papá and Tía Dolores met Josefina partway up the path to the house from the stream. They stood together, smiling, as they waited for Josefina to draw near.

"Josefina," said Papá. "Tía Dolores and I want you to do something."

Tía Dolores pulled Josefina's hand toward her and put the heart milagro in it. "This is rightly yours," she said, "because you never forgot your heart's desire."

"Will you keep the heart milagro safe for us?" asked Papá, smiling at Josefina with love.

"I will," said Josefina. "I promise."

Josefina remembered her promise later. She held the heart milagro in her hand as she stood outside the church after the wedding ceremony. Everyone she loved most dearly was gathered around her. Brave Abuelito, who was about to set forth on a new adventure. Dignified Abuelita, who held her chin up as if she were wearing a crown. Tía Magdalena, whose kindness and wisdom never failed her. Sweet Ana, her devoted Tomás, and their lively boys. Headstrong Francisca and sensible Clara. Josefina was sure that Mamá was there, too, in everyone's thoughts.

Villagers and neighbors, workers from the rancho, and friends from the pueblo cheered Papá and

Tía Dolores, who smiled and waved. Musicians struck up a lively tune, and the church bell rang out joyously. A flock of birds, startled by the sound, rose up with a great exuberant fluttering of wings. Josefina smiled. She knew just how those birds felt. Her heart rose up with them into the endless blue sky.

INSIDE Josefina's World

For more than 200 years, New Mexican settlers lived as the Montoyas did. But when Josefina was a girl, a time of great change was beginning for New Mexico.

The changes started in 1821, the year that Mexico won independence from Spain. Until then, foreigners were not allowed to do business in New Mexico. But after 1821, American traders began traveling to Santa Fe from Missouri. The wagon trail they took was called the Santa Fe Trail. Within just a few years, dozens of American wagon trains were coming to Santa Fe every summer.

The flood of American goods began to affect the way New Mexicans dressed, did their chores, and decorated their homes. By the time Josefina was a mother, she might have had glass windows, wallpaper, and some American-style furniture. By the time she was a grandmother, she might have given up practical New Mexican–style clothes and started to wear corsets, hoopskirts, and bonnets.

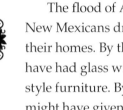

Many Americans of the time looked down on Mexican people or made fun of customs they did not understand. Still, people in the United States saw opportunity in the Mexican lands to the southwest, and they began to feel that these lands should belong to the U.S.

In December 1845, the U.S. government tried to buy Mexico's northern lands. When Mexico refused to sell, the U.S. declared war. American soldiers arrived in Santa Fe in August 1846 and established American rule there without any fighting. Some New Mexicans welcomed the change, but others feared that their way of life and most precious traditions would soon be lost.

The Mexican War was fought farther south and west until 1848. By then, the U.S. had taken almost all the land that is now New Mexico, Arizona, California, Nevada, Utah, and Colorado. Everyone living there, except Native Americans, was granted U.S. citizenship. Josefina would have become an American when she was 33 years old.

After the war, more and more Americans came from the East, including missionaries, cattle ranchers, miners, and outlaws. Some native New Mexicans suffered great losses as a result. Many families lost valuable land they had owned for 200 years or more, or lost precious rights to use water for irrigating their fields. The Apache and Navajo tribes were forced onto reservations.

In the 1880s, as railroads began bringing tourists and artists to the Southwest, Americans started to develop greater appreciation for New Mexico's landscape, climate, and cultures. New Mexico and Arizona were granted statehood in 1912.

New Mexicans learned to take part in American life. But they also worked to hold on to their cultures—their faith, language, beliefs, arts, foods, and other traditions. Today the Southwest is a vital and unique part of the United States that reflects the rich cultural traditions of all the people who call it home.

GLOSSARY of Spanish Words

Abuelita *(ah-bweh-LEE-tah)*—Grandma

Abuelito *(ah-bweh-LEE-toh)*—Grandpa

acequia *(ah-SEH-kee-ah)*—a ditch made to carry water to a farmer's fields

adiós *(ah-dee-OHS)*—good-bye

adobe *(ah-DOH-beh)*—a building material made of earth mixed with straw and water

americano *(ah-meh-ree-KAH-no)*—a man from the United States

banco *(BAHN-ko)*—a bench built into the wall of a room

bienvenido *(bee-en-veh-NEE-doh)*—welcome

bizcochito *(bees-ko-CHEE-toh)*—a kind of sugar cookie flavored with anise

buenos días *(BWEH-nohs DEE-ahs)*—good morning

Camino Real *(kah-MEE-no rey-AHL)*—the main road or trail that ran from Mexico City to New Mexico. Its name means "Royal Road."

curandera *(koo-rahn-DEH-rah)*—a woman who knows how to make medicines from plants and is skilled at healing people

doña *(DOH-nyah)*—a term of respect for an older woman

El agua es la vida. *(el AH-gwah es lah VEE-dah)*—a traditional New Mexican saying that means "Water is life." It shows how important water is to people living in a desert climate.

fandango *(fahn-DAHNG-go)*—a big celebration or party that includes a lively dance

fiesta *(fee-ES-tah)*—a party or celebration

gracias *(GRAH-see-ahs)*—thank you

gran sala *(grahn SAH-lah)*—the biggest room in the house, used for special events and formal occasions

horno *(OR-no)*—an outdoor oven made of *adobe*, or earth mixed with straw and water

inmortal *(een-mor-TAHL)*—a plant called "spider milkweed" in English. It can be used to make a medicine for colds.

La Fiesta de los Reyes Magos *(la fee-ES-tah deh lohs REY-es MAH-gohs)*—the Feast of the Three Kings. This is the Catholic feast day that celebrates the Bible story of the three wise men bringing gifts to the baby Jesus.

mano *(MAH-no)*—a stone that is held in the hand and used to grind corn. Dried corn is put on a large flat stone called a *metate*, and then the mano is rubbed back and forth over the corn to break it down into flour.

manzanilla *(mahn-sah-NEE-yah)*—a plant known as "chamomile" in English. It can be used to make a soothing tea.

metate *(meh-TAH-teh)*—a large flat stone used with a *mano* to grind corn

milagro *(mee-LAH-gro)*—a small medal that symbolizes a request that a person is praying for or a prayer that has been answered

piñón *(pee-NYOHN)*—a kind of short, scrubby pine that

produces delicious nuts

plaza *(PLAH-sah)*—an open square in a village or town

por favor *(por fah-VOR)*—please

pueblo *(PWEH-blo)*—a village of Pueblo Indians

rancho *(RAHN-cho)*—a farm or ranch where crops are grown and animals are raised

rebozo *(reh-BO-so)*—a long shawl worn by girls and women

sala *(SAH-lah)*—a room in a house

San Miguel *(sahn mee-GEHL)*—Saint Michael

Santa Fe *(SAHN-tah FEH)*—the capital city of New Mexico. Its name means "Holy Faith."

sarape *(sah-RAH-peh)*—a warm blanket that is wrapped around the shoulders or worn as a poncho

señor *(seh-NYOR)*—Mr. or sir

señora *(seh-NYO-rah)*—Mrs. or ma'am

señorita *(seh-nyo-REE-tah)*—Miss or young lady

sí *(SEE)*—yes

sombrita *(sohm-BREE-tah)*—little shadow, or an affectionate way to say "shadow." The Spanish word for "shadow" is *sombra.*

tía *(TEE-ah)*—aunt

tortilla *(tor-TEE-yah)*—a kind of flat, round bread made of corn or wheat

Read more of JOSEFINA'S stories,
available from booksellers and at *americangirl.com*

✿ *Classics* ✿
Josefina's classic series, now in two volumes:

Volume 1:
Sunlight and Shadows
Josefina and her sisters are excited when Tía Dolores comes to their *rancho*, bringing new ideas, new fashions, and new challenges. Can Josefina open her heart to change and still hold on to precious memories of Mamá?

Volume 2:
Second Chances
Josefina makes a wonderful discovery: She has a gift for healing. Can she find the courage and creativity to mend her family's broken trust in an *americano* trader and keep her family whole and happy when Tía Dolores plans to leave?

✿ *Mystery* ✿
Another thrilling adventure with Josefina!

Secrets in the Hills
Josefina has heard tales of treasure buried in the hills, and of a ghostly Weeping Woman who roams at night. But she never imagined the stories might be true—until a mysterious stranger arrives at her rancho.

❧ A Sneak Peek at ☙

Secrets
in the Hills

A Josefina Mystery

Josefina's adventures continue
in an exciting mystery.

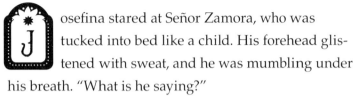osefina stared at Señor Zamora, who was tucked into bed like a child. His forehead glistened with sweat, and he was mumbling under his breath. "What is he saying?"

Tía Dolores shook her head. "He's not making sense. That can happen with high fevers. Will you fetch more water, please? I'll have his leg bandaged by the time you return."

Josefina saw Señor Zamora's face in her mind as she hurried to the stream with a water jar. She had been worried about tending Doña Felícitas in the village— and now a patient with more serious problems had appeared! Had the mysterious stranger been sent to test her skill and knowledge?

As Josefina returned to the sala, she heard Tía Dolores talking to Señor Zamora in a soothing tone. "Your things are safe here, señor."

"Is his mind clearer?" Josefina asked, putting the water jar by the bed.

Tía Dolores shook her head. "Not really. He seems to be worried about his clothes." She gestured to a pile by the door. "Miguel provided our guest with a clean shirt to wear."

"We should put a damp cloth on his forehead," Josefina said. "That will help bring his fever down."

"You go ahead," Tía Dolores said. "I need to make sure that dinner preparations are well in hand. I'll return in a moment."

Josefina poured water into a bowl, wrung out a cloth, folded it neatly, and draped it over her patient's forehead. His eyes opened for a moment, as if he was startled by the coolness. "Señorita?" he whispered.

"My name is Josefina."

Señor Zamora clutched her arm with unexpected strength. "*Por favor*—where is my sarape?"

"Right over there." Josefina waved her hand toward the pile of clothes. "Don't worry, señor. With God's help, you will soon be well."

His hand fell back to the blanket, and his eyes flickered closed. Josefina touched the damp cloth and found it already warm. She replaced the cloth with another, and Señor Zamora began to murmur again. "The search . . . I must continue my search . . ."

"No, señor," Josefina told him quietly. "Your search for the horse can wait."

His head turned from side to side. "The rock,"

he muttered. "I found the rock."

Josefina bit her lip. "Please, señor," she begged. "Try to rest."

Teresita entered the sala, her quiet calm as comforting as Tía Dolores's brisk efficiency. "Your aunt asked me to sit with him," she told Josefina. "How is he?"

"Not well," Josefina said, regarding their visitor.

Teresita gave Josefina a reassuring smile that lit her whole face. "Don't worry, Señorita Josefina. If God wills it, our guest will recover."

Josefina nodded. She'd done what she could for Señor Zamora.

As she left the sala, she carried his dirty sarape out to the courtyard. It was too late in the day to launder his filthy shirt and trousers, but she could at least shake the dust from his sarape. It had once been of good quality, woven well of yellow and blue and red wool, but Josefina had trouble seeing the pattern through the dirt.

She gripped the woven cloak by the edge and gave it a hard, snapping shake. A cloud of dust billowed into the air. And something white fluttered to the ground.

Josefina stooped to pick up the piece of paper. It

was thin, stained, and tattered. Three sides of the paper were cut straight. The fourth was ragged, as if this piece had come from a larger piece of paper that had been torn in two.

Squinting at the faded ink, Josefina made out an outline that looked familiar: a tall column supporting a flat surface. *That looks like Balancing Rock!* she thought. Was *that* the rock Señor Zamora had been speaking of? She tried to make out the other faint sketches: arrows, a turtle, curved lines that looked like a rainbow.

A burst of conversation from the kitchen interrupted Josefina's study, and her cheeks grew warm. This paper didn't belong to her! Taking a closer look at Señor Zamora's sarape, she found that he had stitched a small piece of thin hide to the inside of the cloak, making a hidden pocket. The map must have fallen from that pocket when she shook the sarape.

Clara appeared at the kitchen door. "Josefina? We're ready for the evening meal."

"Coming!" Josefina called. She slipped the fragile map carefully back into the sarape's hidden pocket, gently brushed what dust she could from the cloak, and folded it in such a way that the pocket—and the map it contained—lay flat. Then she returned the sarape to the sala. She would wash the other clothes tomorrow, and whenever Señor Zamora was ready to be on his way, he would find his map just where he had left it.

But tucking the map away couldn't erase it from Josefina's mind. She remembered their servant Miguel's reaction to the cross scratched into a cave wall: "If God wants me to find buried treasure, I hope He will send me a map!"

Señor Zamora had told Miguel that he'd been searching for a missing mare. Yet his map, old as it was, had surely not been drawn to show him where to look for a horse! He was searching for something else, she was sure of it. Something secret. So . . . what was he seeking?

About the Author

VALERIE TRIPP, the author of *Sunlight and Shadows* and *Second Chances*, says that she became a writer because of the kind of person she is. She says she's curious, and writing requires you to be interested in everything. Talking is her favorite sport, and writing is a way of talking on paper. She's a daydreamer, which helps her come up with her ideas. And she loves words. She even loves the struggle to come up with just the right words as she writes and rewrites. Ms. Tripp lives in Maryland with her husband.

About the Advisory Board

American Girl extends its deepest appreciation
to the advisory board that authenticated Josefina's stories.

Rosalinda B. Barrera, Professor of Curriculum &
Instruction, New Mexico State University, Las Cruces

Juan R. García, Professor of History and Associate Dean
of the College of Social & Behavioral Sciences,
University of Arizona, Tucson

Sandra Jaramillo, Director, Archives & Historical Services,
New Mexico Records Center & Archives, Santa Fe

Skip Keith Miller, Co-director/Curator,
Kit Carson Historic Museums, Taos, NM

Felipe R. Mirabal, former Curator of Collections,
El Rancho de las Golondrinas Living Museum, Santa Fe, NM

Tey Diana Rebolledo, Professor of Spanish,
University of New Mexico, Albuquerque

Orlando Romero, Senior Research Librarian,
Palace of the Governors, Santa Fe, NM

Marc Simmons, Historian, Cerillos, NM

Song of the Mockingbird

Mockingbird

My Journey with Josefina

by Emma Carlson Berne

★ American Girl®

Published by American Girl Publishing
Copyright © 2015 American Girl

Questions or comments? Call 1-800-845-0005, visit **americangirl.com**,
or write to Customer Service, American Girl,
8400 Fairway Place, Middleton, WI 53562.

Printed in China
15 16 17 18 19 20 21 LEO 10 9 8 7 6 5 4 3 2 1

All American Girl marks, BeForever™, Josefina®,
and Josefina Montoya® are trademarks of American Girl.

Special thanks to Sandra Jaramillo, former Director,
Archives & Historical Services, New Mexico Records Center & Archives

Cover image by Michael Dwornik and Juliana Kolesova
Piñón tree image by qingwa/iStock/Thinkstock

Cataloging-in-Publication Data available from the Library of Congress

For my dad—
with whom I've shared many adventures

Beforever™

The adventurous characters you'll meet in
the BeForever books will spark your curiosity
about the past, inspire you to find your voice
in the present, and excite you about your future.
You'll make friends with these girls as you share
their fun and their challenges. Like you, they are
bright and brave, imaginative and energetic,
creative and kind. Just as you are, they are
discovering what really matters: Helping others.
Being a true friend. Protecting the earth.
Standing up for what's right. Read their stories,
explore their worlds, join their adventures.
Your friendship with them will BeForever.

A Journey Begins

This book is about Josefina, but it's also about a girl like you who travels back in time to Josefina's world of 1824. You, the reader, get to decide what happens in the story. The choices you make will lead to different journeys and new discoveries.

When you reach a page in this book that asks you to make a decision, choose carefully. The decisions you make will lead to different endings. (Hint: Use a pencil to check off your choices. That way, you'll never read the same story twice.)

Want to try another ending? Go back to a choice point and find out what happens when you make different choices.

Before your journey ends, take a peek into the past, on page 184, to discover more about Josefina's time.

Josefina and her family speak Spanish, so you'll see some Spanish words in this book. You'll find the meanings and pronunciations of these words in the glossary on page 186. You'll find pronunciations of Spanish names on page 189.

Remember that in Spanish, "j" is pronounced like "h." That means Josefina's name is pronounced "ho-seh-FEE-nah."

The last bell chimes through the hallways, and I stack my notebooks and head for my locker. School is over for the day, and it has not been a success—again. Oh, on the surface things look fine. I'm talking to my teachers and smiling and playing kickball at recess. But underneath, here's the truth: I just don't want to be here. I want to be back at my old school—back in my old *life*.

I miss Chicago—the skyscrapers against the blue sky, traffic horns blaring, and cabs whizzing by on Michigan Avenue. The tall stone apartment buildings crowded together, the downtown lights sparkling on the lake. I miss rumbling above the streets on the screeching El on Saturday afternoons with Danielle to see shows. I miss my old school, with its huge gray stone front and twisty iron gates. I miss the halls crammed with kids, all talking and shouting to each other. I miss parties. I miss Drama Club—I was supposed to be the lead in *Annie*.

That was before my parents told me and my older brother, Henry, that we were moving. And where were we moving *to*?

The halls are almost empty now, and I wrench my

stuck locker door open. To Santa Fe, New Mexico, that's what they told us. I didn't even know where that was. I thought it was in actual Mexico.

We've been out here for two weeks now. It's so different here. Rocks, sand, cactus. Wind. Silence. And the buildings, a tan mud color, crouching low on the landscape under the sky that seems like a huge blue bowl turned upside down.

Our new house is made of mud too, like all of the houses out here—*adobe,* Dad calls it. He says that in the Southwest, houses have been built this way since ancient Indian times. The new house is out a ways from town, set alone on a little road. In our apartment in the city, I could look right into the windows of the family across the courtyard. They always looked so cozy in there, playing the piano or watching movies. Here, I look out at my new neighbors—big rocks. They *are* pretty—especially in the evenings when the sun turns them rosy red. But they sure aren't very cozy.

And at night, after the ruby-red sunset fades, there are no lights. No sounds either, except for this eerie noise that I thought at first was children scream-ing. Turns out it was only coyotes howling. I almost collapsed in relief when Dad told me.

Henry loves it out here, of course. He always likes anything new. And I'm *trying* to like it, too. After all, I've always loved adventures. But on our first day here, I went out with Daisy, my black German shepherd, for a walk. We took this winding little path that leads away from the house toward some kind of rocky hills. We were just wandering along, looking around, when we almost stepped on this strange little reptile right in our path. It looked like a cross between a toad and a lizard. Daisy barked at it and lunged toward it, and all of a sudden, it shot blood out of its *eyes* and splattered her right in the face. She yelped and I screamed and we both ran back toward the house as fast as we could. Mom said that thing is called a horny toad and it does that blood trick to ward off predators. After that, I managed to stop crying.

That was *not* the kind of adventure I had in mind. How will I ever feel at home in this place?

✸ *Turn to page 4.*

omeone's coming down the hall. It's Audrey again. She sits beside me in Mrs. McGlynn's class. I turn back to my locker quickly and bury myself in it, pretending to get out more books. I don't want to be mean, and actually I kind of like Audrey herself, but some little part of me keeps thinking that maybe if I'm miserable enough here, Mom and Dad will listen to me and let me move back to Chicago. I could live with Danielle!

"Hi," Audrey says. She's standing right beside me. I pull my head out of my locker.

"Oh! Hi," I say, as if I'm surprised to see her.

She smiles. "Want to walk over to La Plata Street? Some of my friends usually meet at the ice cream shop after school—you should come."

I know she's being really nice, but honestly, all I want to do is get home and Skype with Danielle. "No," I mumble. "I mean—no, I can't go today. I— um—have to catch the bus." Lame excuse.

Audrey's face falls slightly, but she shrugs. "Okay. Maybe tomorrow."

I just kind of nod, and Audrey trails along beside me down the echoing hallway. I slow to a stop at the school bulletin board, and together we gaze at a flyer posted in the middle. *Love Acting?* it says. *Join the Skit Club! Auditions on Tuesday! A Part for Everyone!* I stare at it. I've always loved singing and dancing—my parents used to call me "Mockingbird," because I would sing every song I heard. Now they shorten it to "Birdy." But ever since leaving Chicago, I feel like I left the music in my heart behind too.

I can't help sighing, and Audrey glances at me. "Are you going to try out?" she asks.

I shake my head no. "Are you?"

She laughs. "Only if someone holds my hand. I get stage fright. Once when I was six, my mom had to come onstage during a piano recital and lead me off. I was frozen and couldn't move. I think I've been scarred for life."

I giggle in spite of myself. "That doesn't sound too bad. I once fell off the stage in the middle of a song. Right into the brass section." I realize we've walked all the way down the hall to the front doors.

Audrey pauses. "Sure you don't want to go for ice cream?"

I feel the laughter draining out of me and the

now-familiar heaviness setting in. "No thanks. I'd better get home." The late bus is waiting at the end of the circular driveway. It's my last chance unless I want to call Dad for a ride.

Audrey studies me for a minute as if she's trying to figure something out. Then she shrugs. "Whatever." She walks down the pink-brick path without looking back.

"Audrey, wait..." I call, but if she hears me, she doesn't turn around.

When she's disappeared, I start down the path and trudge slowly toward the idling yellow bus. I've hurt her feelings and I feel bad, but how can I expect her to understand? I just want to go home—all the way home.

✳

"Is that you, hon?" Dad calls out from the kitchen as I'm easing the side door closed. I wince. I was hoping to sneak upstairs and do what I've done every day since we arrived: chat with Danielle while I browse through our old pictures. No chance now.

Daisy bounds over to me, toenails skritching on

the tile. She joyfully paws me, her tongue lapping at my hands.

"Yeah!" I call back, trying to make my voice cheery. I sling my backpack into the hall closet and kiss Daisy's head. In the tiled kitchen, I find Dad standing at the counter, mixing some kind of thick yellow dough in a bowl. There's cornmeal on the floor, cornmeal in the sink, and cornmeal on his glasses.

"How was school?" Dad asks, scraping the dough from the wooden mixing spoon with his fingertips. "I don't think it's supposed to stick like that," he mutters to himself.

"What're you making?" I stick my head into the fridge to peruse the contents.

"Masa." Dad starts laying out something that looks like damp leaves. I take a closer look. They *are* damp leaves. "Look, you spread this on these corn husks. Then you spoon in the filling—spiced shredded pork!"

I roll my eyes, though my face is still behind the fridge door. He and Mom have been seized with a passion for all things New Mexican since we've been out here. Yesterday they tried to give us scrambled eggs and green *chiles* wrapped in *tortillas* for breakfast.

"Remember Chicago hot dogs?" I ask Dad, digging a spoon into a jar of peanut butter. "Wouldn't you love one of those for dinner? With tomatoes and pickle relish and a poppy-seed bun?" My mouth waters just talking about it.

Dad nods and works two forks around in the pan of shredded pork. "Oh boy, I would. And next time we go back to visit, I'm eating one before we even get out of the airport. But meanwhile, how about homemade *tamales* for dinner?" He spoons pork into each of the corn husks and wraps them up like little packages.

I'm not too sure about food that comes wrapped up in leaves, like some kind of gourmet takeout for raccoons. "Sure." I can't muster much enthusiasm, and Dad smiles a little. I stick the spoon in the dishwasher and head for the stairs.

"Hey there." Dad's voice freezes me on the bottom step with one hand on the banister.

I peek back into the kitchen. "What?"

"Want to go for a walk?" He puts the *tamales* in a steamer basket waiting on the stove, then wipes his hands on a dishcloth and plucks his sunglasses from the hook by the door.

I open my mouth to respond and Dad holds up his hand. "Let me rephrase that. We're going for a walk. Daisy!" he calls.

Daisy capers around his feet, panting, and takes off the minute he opens the door.

Traitor, I tell her silently as we start off down the path toward the hills. *Don't you remember the horny toad?*

❋ *Turn to page 10.*

The late-afternoon sun is huge in the sky, which is so blue it almost hurts. The air is cool, but through it, I can feel the heat of the day coming off the rocks and sandy soil.

"Sage!" Dad says, pointing at a twiggy, silvery plant sprouting nearby. "And Indian paintbrush!" He bends to examine a small flower with a feathery, bright orange blossom. "Look at the orange color, honey."

"Yep." Dad *looooves* all of New Mexico's plants, animals, rock formations—you name it. "It's great."

Dad gives me a knowing look, but just nods. Daisy bounds ahead of us happily, barking at something only she can see. The deep green *piñón* trees line the base of the pinky-red rocks stacked against the horizon ahead of us. Suddenly, a mule deer bounds across the path right in front of us. I gasp and grab Dad's arm, and then, in a flash of white tail, it's gone, as if it never was.

"Wow!" I exclaim. "Did you see how fast it was?"

Dad grins at me. "Now there's something you wouldn't see on the Chicago streets."

I remember my bad mood and let my face lapse into a scowl again as we scuff our feet along the path.

"Birdy, Mom and I know how much you miss Chicago," Dad says quietly. "Bright lights, big city. Excitement. Adventure."

I steal a quick glance at him. He's picking his way around the rocks with his eyes on his boots.

"Yeah," I mumble.

"Believe it or not, we do too."

I can't help snorting in disbelief.

"We do." Dad raises his voice slightly for emphasis. "But we're trying to embrace our new home. We hope you will too. We hope you'll trust us that this will work out."

Don't count on it, I think, but I don't say anything. I just nod, which seems safest. We've reached the rocky hills at the end of the path. Daisy scrambles up on some bigger boulders and noses around the openings between them.

"That looks almost like a cave." I point out a larger opening, more to change the subject than anything else.

Dad climbs up on the rock beside Daisy and peers in. He looks around, his face excited. "It is! Here, come on. Let's peek in."

I grab his outstretched hand and haul myself up on

the rock too. We poke our heads and shoulders inside. It's cool and dark in there, and Dad clicks on the little pocket flashlight that always hangs from his key chain and holds it up. The ghostly white beam illuminates a rough rock floor and sloping walls that extend about ten feet back. Daisy slips inside and sniffs around the back of the cave.

"Want me to boost you in?" Dad offers. "It's stable—look up." He shines the flashlight up at the roof and we both laugh. It's more than stable—it's solid rock.

"Sure," I say, a little excitement bubbling up. I squeeze in and peer out at Dad from the opening. I can just stand up. Looking from the inside out makes me feel like I've entered a separate world—a little cold, dark, alien space. Outside, the high desert spreads big, hot, and blue-green-yellow. It seems miles away.

"See anything interesting?" Dad asks. He passes his flashlight in, and I scan the walls with it.

"Just rock—" I start to say, and then I see Daisy nosing under a pile of stones by the rear wall, digging with her front feet. She sticks her nose into the pile, sniffing deeply. She backs up and barks once, a sharp, excited bark.

"Daisy's found something in there," I say.

"Careful," Dad warns. "It might be a snake."

Moving slowly, I bend over and shine the flashlight into the little scattered pile of stones. There's no snake, but one of the rocks is shaped oddly. I move closer. It's not a rock at all, I realize. It's an object made of clay.

"Dad—it's some kind of..." I bend closer. It's a bird-shaped figure, made of gray clay and coated with dust.

I pick it up. It's about the size of my hand, and hollow. Traces of yellow paint glow in the dimness. As I turn it, I see there's a hole at the end of the bird's tail and another at its mouth, and a few small holes along its back. "It's a whistle. Or maybe a little flute." The clay is strangely warm and smooth.

I clutch the figure tightly and follow Daisy out through the opening.

❋ *Turn to page 14.*

I n the sunlight, Dad and I examine the flute.
He points out lines scored in the clay to represent the bird's wings and tail feathers. "This little flute is probably from the early nineteenth century."

Dad pushes his sunglasses up on his forehead and peers at the flute more closely. "Handmade, most likely for casual use." Dad is a professor of Southwestern art at the university, so he knows about stuff like this. "It's in great shape. It was probably hidden in those rocks for a long time—that's why it hasn't fallen apart from time and moisture." He claps me on the shoulder. "What an adventure! Let's go find Mom—she'll want to see our new treasure too."

We start back to the house, me cradling the bird flute in my hands and Daisy trotting beside us. But when we reach the yard, I slow down. Through the big picture windows, I can see Mom and Henry in the kitchen. They must have just gotten home. She picks up Henry at the high school on her way home from the health center—she's a social worker there.

I don't want to face the bustle inside, Mom asking questions, Henry raving *again* about how cool it is here and how he's going rock climbing or spelunking with

José or Dave or Simone or some other awesome friend he seems to have made instantly.

"Actually, I think I'm going to just chill out here for a while," I tell Dad. I hoist myself up on one of the bigger boulders that sits about ten yards from the back of the house. From here, I can see right into the house—but I'm still alone. "I need to relax."

He smiles and nods. "Okay. We'll show Mom and Henry the flute at dinner." He pauses for a moment with one hand on the door. "Why don't you keep that flute safe with you, Birdy? At least until we figure out if a museum should have it. For now, though—it's a little gift from Santa Fe to you." He disappears through the side door.

✸ *Turn to page 16.*

O nce Dad's gone, I draw my knees up to my chin and loop my arms around them. Daisy lies down beside me, licking at her side and flopping her tail. The rock underneath us is warm, like a heater, which feels good in the cool air. The first afternoon we were here, I was shocked when the temperature plunged twenty degrees as soon as the sun dipped behind the hills. Now I know that the high desert can be as chilly at night as it is hot during the day.

I rub the flute idly between my fingers and gaze out at the hills. Some have flattened tops; some are rounded. The dark dots of the pines stud their sides, like cloves stuck in an orange. Just in front of me, three hills, taller and thinner than the others, rise like rounded spires into the sky. *Almost like the Chicago skyline,* I think to myself. If I squint my eyes, I can practically see the tower of the John Hancock Center. The sun flashes between the spires for a moment, blinding me. I look down at the flute in my hand and turn it over.

I can see the faint indentations where the maker pressed his or her fingers while molding it. The delicate head of the bird flows into the rounded body, and the tail balances gracefully behind it. There is a tiny chip out of the very end of the tail.

Carefully, I raise the flute to my lips and blow. The delicate note drifts away on the breeze. I place my fingers over the holes and try a scale. The notes are clear and light. I stumble through "When the Saints Go Marching In," and Daisy raises her head and looks at me with her soulful dog eyes.

I lower the flute. "Do you like that, girl? Me too." And I do like it. I like it almost more than anything else I've heard since we moved.

My fingers brush a bit of roughness on the bottom of the flute, and I turn it over. There, carved in letters so small I didn't notice them before, is a word. I squint at it. *María.* This was María's flute, then. The maker must have carved her name in it when it was made so long ago. I trace the curves of the name with the tip of one finger. I can still feel the tiny ridges where the sharp point scored the wet clay. It's like reaching through time.

I lift the flute to my lips again, but before I can blow, the notes of a bird's song float over to me. I lower the flute. A mockingbird is sitting on the branch of a pine shrub only a few feet away. It sings again.

Trill-trillEE. Trill-trillEE. Its smooth gray chest swells with the song, and its bright black eye gleams.

I look down at the flute, and my heart gives a little jump. It's a mockingbird! The flute is modeled after a mockingbird—same plump breast, same long, balancing tail. The bird sings again. *Trill-trillEE. Trill-trillEE.*

I smile to myself. My parents didn't call *me* Mockingbird for nothing. I raise the flute to my lips and form the notes with my tongue and fingers: *Trill-trillEE. Trill-trillEE.* The mockingbird's song flows from my mockingbird flute.

But as soon as the notes are out, I feel myself topple suddenly, pitching forward, falling, clutching at nothing, aware only of the flute still squeezed in my hand. Darkness slams down over me like an iron door.

✸

I open my eyes. My cheek is lying in dirt, and my whole body aches. I push myself up onto my hands and look around.

I'm sprawled at the bottom of the boulder—I must have fallen and gotten knocked out. Daisy's gone. My temples are throbbing, and my hands are covered with dust and dirt. The bird flute is lying a few feet away. I push myself up a little more and reach for it. But something about the day seems different now, and for a moment I can't figure it out. Then I know—it's the light. The sun seems to have gotten higher. My heart gives a quick thump. *Higher?* That's weird.

I sit up and shake my head, and then I squint at the sun again. It *is* higher, and hotter. I'm sweating in my white blouse.

Wait. *My white blouse?* I was wearing a T-shirt! I look down at myself and freeze. I'm wearing different clothes. A puffy blouse, and a long flouncy skirt with a fringed sash around my waist. And moccasins. Moccasins! They look strangely like my bedroom slippers, and for a brief, insane moment I wonder if my mother came out here and dressed me in these clothes while I was knocked out. I should go ask her.

I turn toward the house, and my heart freezes in my chest like a galloping horse at the edge of a cliff.

The house is gone.

✸ *Turn to page 27.*

I open my eyes.

I'm outside. I'm lying on a big rock—the boulder outside my house. Daisy! Daisy is beside me. She's still licking her side. I'm wearing jeans again! A T-shirt! I sit up and twist around so fast, I almost fall off the rock. There's my house! I can see Mom and Henry inside, talking to Dad.

I look down at my hand. The whistle is clutched in it. My mouth is suddenly very dry. "Daisy," I whisper. She looks up at me and thumps her tail. "Something very strange is happening." She licks my hand and then rests her chin on her paws.

I prop my elbows on my knees and cover my eyes with my hands. *Okay. Think.* Aside from the fact that this is the freakiest thing that has ever happened to me in—oh, my entire life—these seem to be the facts: First, somehow, I am traveling back and forth through time. Second, playing the mockingbird song will send me into the past and then bring me back to my own time. Third, for whatever reason, maybe decided by the Time-Traveling Council of the Universe or something, no time in the present passes while I'm in the past. Go figure.

I stare down at the flute. The dot marking the bird's eye looks back at me. I could go back. *Why not?* I seem to hear the bird say. *Didn't that girl Josefina seem nice?*

Why not? I respond silently. Why not? Because it was scary, that's why! Cool, but scary. On the other hand, I *have* been looking for a little adventure, haven't I?

I take another look back at the house. Henry has taken a paper from his backpack and is showing it to Mom and Dad. I never thought our flat *adobe* house could look so much like home. Part of me longs to run inside to my family. But on the other hand . . . they'll never know I'm gone.

> ✺ *To stay in the present,*
>   *turn to page 45.*

> ✺ *To go back to Josefina's time,*
>   *turn to page 47.*

Let's visit Sombrita before we go back inside, María," Josefina says. "You haven't met her yet, and she will love you."

Sombrita must be another sister. Josefina didn't mention her before. Or perhaps she's a servant. "Sure," I agree.

Josefina leads me around the side of the house. "There's Sombrita," Josefina says. "Isn't she lovely?" She points under a tree near the house.

"Where?" I can't see anything but the goats that sniffed me when I first arrived.

"Right there." Josefina is pointing to one of the animals. "She's the little gray-and-white one."

"Sombrita is a goat?" I ask and burst out laughing.

"Well, yes!" Josefina looks a little confused. "I've had her since she was just a baby."

"I thought she was another sister!"

Josefina chortles. "Poor sister—with horns and yellow eyes!" Then we're both laughing so hard, we have to clutch each other to keep from falling over. I realize I'm having more fun than I've had since leaving Chicago. Being with Josefina is almost like being with Danielle.

The little goat bounces up to us like she's on springs. She sniffs my legs and nudges me with her hard head. I give her a tentative pat. Her fur is very soft, like a puppy's, and when I scratch her, I can feel the tiny buds of horns at the top of her head.

"Oh, Sombrita." I dissolve into giggles again. "We don't mean to make fun of you. Your yellow eyes are perfect for you." The goat gazes up at me as if she understands what I'm saying. Daisy would probably like her. They'd be friends, just like Josefina and me. "Where did you get her, Josefina?"

"Oh, it was special," my friend says. She kneels on the ground, and the little goat climbs into her lap like a dog. She reaches up and sniffs Josefina's face. "Her mother, Florecita, died right after Sombrita was born. Papá thought the baby wouldn't live, but I begged him to let me keep her." Sombrita stretches her front legs up on Josefina's shoulder.

"I fed her carefully, and she grew stronger and stronger." The little goat nimbly leaps right up on Josefina's shoulder, as if she's a ladder, and I squeal.

Josefina laughs and reaches up behind her to pull Sombrita back down off her shoulders. She holds the little goat up to her cheek and nuzzles her soft fur. "I promised I'd always take care of her. Now I can't imagine not having her as my friend."

I drop down on my knees next to Josefina and stroke Sombrita's back. She squirms around, and her little tongue laps out as if tasting my cheek.

Josefina hugs her tighter and then carefully sets her on her feet. "There, little one. Run and play." Sombrita obeys as if she can understand the words. With her little tail wagging constantly and her ears flopping, she rears up on her hind legs, then drops down and scampers over to a log lying under the tree. She jumps up on it as if she's on a trampoline and then runs up and down the length.

"Woo-hoo, Sombrita!" I shout, applauding.

Josefina looks over at me as if she's never heard anyone say that before—which, I realize, she probably never has—and echoes me. "Woo-hoo, Sombrita!" she calls.

We stand up slowly, dusting off our skirts, and just then, a bell bongs somewhere far away. I must look startled because Josefina says gently, "Do you remember how the church bells call us to prayer?" She bows her head, and it takes me a minute to realize that she's praying. She must be pretty religious.

Josefina opens her eyes as a sweaty man on a horse rides up and halts in front of us. I almost jump out of my skin.

"Miguel, you're back," she says, and Tía Dolores appears in the doorway, wiping her hands on her apron.

"There are no signs of enemies in our hills," Miguel says, leaning over the saddle pommel. "This *cautiva* must have wandered far from the place where she escaped."

Tía Dolores's face relaxes. "Ah. Good."

"Thank heaven," Josefina says. Then she turns businesslike. "Now, I'll help you remember how to do things. We'll work together, so you can learn again. Would you like to go collecting with me in the hills?" she asks. "If Tía Dolores says we may, of course." She looks over at her aunt, who nods. "Teresita has asked me to gather plants for dyes. Or we can gather squashes from the garden instead, if you are not feeling strong enough for an expedition. Then I'll show you how to string slices of squash to dry for the winter."

The hills still sound a little scary. What if enemies showed up while we were out there? I shiver as I think of being swept up onto an enemy's horse. But I know Miguel has just made sure we're safe, and it would be fun to hike with Josefina out in the wind and sunshine—more fun than with Dad, probably. Josefina seems like someone who's not afraid of adventures.

> ✻ *To collect squashes from the garden,*
>   *turn to page 31.*

> ✻ *To go on an expedition in the hills,*
>   *turn to page 36.*

nother kind of house is there instead. It's *adobe* too, but much, much bigger than ours, with only a few teeny windows and a giant wooden front door. It looks like a fortress. The driveway is gone too, and the cars, and the telephone lines. Instead, a few chickens are pecking near the door, and—I squint—are those *goats*? They can't be. Probably the neighbor's dogs have escaped again. I rub my eyes. No. They are goats.

Panic wells up in me, and I have a feeling like I'm drowning. Is this what it feels like to go crazy? Then instantly, the explanation occurs to me, and it's so simple, I almost laugh. I'm dreaming. That's the answer, of course. Why didn't I think of it before?

Just then, a girl comes out of a little door cut right into the big front door of the house-that-is-not-mine. She's about my age, ten, with a long, shiny, dark brown braid, and she's carrying a big empty basket. She stops when she sees me, and we stare at each other. Then she drops the basket and rushes over to me.

"Oh my goodness, are you lost?" She looks me up and down. "You're covered in dirt. Are you hurt?"

Whoa, I'm kind of freaking out again. The words coming out of her mouth aren't English—but I can understand her. Then I remind myself: *I'm dreaming. Weirdness is normal.* The sound of the girl's words is familiar too—Spanish! Just like in Spanish class back home. I don't know much, though—I only studied it for one year. I wonder if this girl knows English.

"I think I do need help," I say, but then I snap my mouth shut. I can feel my eyes bulging. That was Spanish that came out of my mouth. Very carefully, I try again. "I was just sitting on this rock—" Still Spanish. But I can understand what I'm saying! And the girl is nodding, like she can understand me too.

All right. Apparently, it's an all-Spanish-speaking dream. That's cool. I can go with it.

The girl is peppering me with questions, but I can't stop staring at her clothes. She's dressed just like me— long blouse, full, gathered skirt, a long sash, and moccasins. She has a little leather pouch tied to the sash at her waist. And the house and the chickens … This must be a dream taking place in old-fashioned days. But it's weirdly vivid. The most real dream I've ever had.

"I'm Josefina Montoya," the girl tells me. "What's your name? Where on earth did you come from? How did you arrive at our *rancho*?"

I look around. She must mean this place. It *is* like a ranch: Off in the distance, beyond a row of golden cottonwood trees, fields are spread out like blankets, and men in wide hats are working in them. As I watch, two men ride toward them on horses. A big herd of sheep is milling around bleating in a kind of enclosure made of sticks. But Josefina is still staring at me expectantly.

"Um, is that where I am—your *rancho*?" I ask. The Spanish words are starting to feel more natural.

Josefina's big dark eyes look concerned. She reaches out and fingers a long tear in my skirt, then touches my forehead. "You have a big streak of dirt here. Have you hit your head?" Her voice is gentle. "Here, let's go inside. Tía Dolores will help you."

Josefina leads me toward the huge wooden door. We pass the goats, which sniff me interestedly. The little door cut into the big door stands open. I catch my foot on the high threshold and stumble, but Josefina quickly catches my arm. "You're not well," she says.

I nod. That is certainly true. I *must* not be well, because whatever is happening feels more and more like reality and less and less like a dream. Perhaps I have sunstroke? Dust-stroke?

Josefina squeezes my hand. Her fingers are strong, and I feel comforted. "I'll make you chamomile tea. Tía Magdalena says that's the best for calming nerves."

I have no idea who Tía Magdalena is, but I'm going to do whatever Josefina says. I'm thirsty, dirty, and confused. I think of the chamomile tea that Mom always makes me when I'm sick. Tears well up unexpectedly at the thought, and I swipe my hand fast across my eyes.

"Oh dear!" Josefina clasps both of my hands tightly. "Don't worry. You're safe now, whatever's happened to you. We're going to take care of you."

I nod, not trusting my new Spanish-speaking voice, which I'm sure would be clogged with tears.

Just as Josefina leads me through the doorway, something makes me turn to the horizon. There, like Chicago's skyscrapers, are the three rounded spires, standing tall against the blue New Mexico sky.

❋ *Turn to page 39.*

I'd like to see your garden," I say.

Josefina smiles. "Of course. But first you'll need a *rebozo* to shade your face from the sun. You must have lost yours on the journey."

My what?

Josefina runs off through one of the doorways and is back in a moment with a large piece of cloth that I realize is a shawl. "Here you go." She has one too, I notice. It's been hanging around her shoulders, but now she pulls it up over her head. I copy her, which is hard since the slippery wool keeps sliding around on my hair. Then Josefina plucks two big empty baskets from the corner of the entryway. She hands one to me. "Come with me. The garden is behind the house."

I almost drop the big basket as I try to balance it on my hip as gracefully as Josefina. I might be an expert at traveling back and forth in time, but I can see I'm going to have a lot to learn in Josefina's world.

I follow Josefina out through the courtyard at the back of the house. We nod and smile at a servant carrying a huge earthen jug of water on her head. She steadies it with one hand, and there's a ring of cloth between her head and the bottom of the jug—that must help her balance it. It looks like a lot of work just for one jug of water. I picture the kitchen faucet at home—endless water, all the time. I bet Josefina's family would like that.

The doors in the walls are closed, but in one corner, a mass of flowers blazes like a rainbow fallen to earth. Josefina pushes open a small rear door and leads me to a high fence made of sticks. Sombrita bounces over to us and tumbles around our ankles as Josefina unlatches a gate to reveal a big garden. It reminds me of one of the blankets from the house—stripes of red, green, and yellow, with splashes of orange. "No, Sombrita, you know you're not allowed in! These vegetables are for eating this winter, not snacking on now," Josefina tells the goat, and pushes her gently away from the gate before she closes it behind us.

She walks carefully down a row of plants, and I follow. She kneels down beside the bushy green vines heavy with yellow squashes, and from the bottom of her basket produces two small, sharp knives. She hands one to me and begins busily cutting yellow squashes from their prickly, sprawling vines. I kneel beside her and clumsily follow her example. The late-afternoon sun is hot on our backs, and all around us is the rich, dank odor of the vegetables and the earth.

There are no sounds except the whisper of the wind, and far away, the cry of a hawk. I've never been in a place so quiet—even in our new house, you can still hear the hum of traffic from the highway or a phone ringing. "Do you have any neighbors?" I ask, trying not to slice my own thumb off as I struggle with the big woody squash stems.

"No, not near the *rancho*," Josefina answers cheerfully. "The nearest neighbors are in the village. It's not far. Only a half-hour walk," she tells me, expertly slicing through a small stem. "And Santa Fe, where Abuelito and Abuelita live, is only half a day's ride by wagon."

Wagons. This is sounding like Laura Ingalls Wilder.

"So you're all alone out here?" I say. "Isn't that scary?"

Josefina laughs as if I've made a clever joke. "I'm far from alone! There are my sisters, of course, and Papá, and Tía Dolores—she's my mamá's sister and came to live with us last year. And Ana's husband Tomás and their two little boys. And Teresita, and Carmen the cook, and her husband Miguel, and all the other servants and farmhands who live here."

"That *is* a lot of people," I agree, finally cutting through the tough squash stem and placing the vegetable in my basket. I shuffle forward on my knees and reach for another one. "And there's your mother too, right? I haven't seen her yet."

Josefina's hands stop moving, and her head bows.

"I'm sorry. What is it?" I reach over and put my hand on her back.

She looks up, and I see that her beautiful dark eyes are brimming with tears. "Mamá died almost two years ago." She swallows hard and takes a deep breath. "Tía Dolores has been staying here, to help care for us, and she has been a great comfort. But I miss Mamá still."

I feel my own eyes getting wet. "I'm sorry, Josefina." She nods, and we are both still, thinking our separate thoughts.

"You know what it is to miss something," Josefina says. "You had to leave your whole family and your home."

I know that Josefina is imaging a *cautiva*'s life, but her words still ring true for me. Our brownstone apartment building and the view down our old Chicago street suddenly float up in front of me, and my stomach twists with sadness. I almost gasp. "I do know what it is to miss something," I whisper. I mean for only the squashes to hear, but a tanned hand suddenly reaches over and covers mine. I look up into Josefina's face. Her eyes are still wet, but she is smiling.

"Destiny has brought us together as friends, María," she says. "We have lost precious things, but we have found each other."

Her words feel very true, and suddenly I feel happy again. "Yes," I say. "I've needed a friend."

"And here, you have one!" she tells me.

✸ *Turn to page 55.*

'm up for an expedition," I say, trying to be brave.

I follow Josefina back into the house through the now-deserted courtyard, washed with sun, and into another room. We step into the dim space, and I pause to let my eyes adjust. The doorway is a hot, bright rectangle, but in here, everything is cool and shadowy. It's like the cave where I found the flute, but it holds different treasures. A huge wooden structure I recognize as a loom takes up most of the room. White strands of yarn are taut across its top, fanning out as if spun by a tidy spider. Some blue strands are woven halfway across the web of white yarn. Big hanks of bright wool hang from pegs on the walls—yellow, blue, gray, black. My eyes are drawn to a red that glows like fire against the soft tan *adobe.* Against another wall, baskets of fluffy raw wool are lined up.

A whole room, just for weaving.

A soft rustle draws my eye to the corner. Teresita is kneeling there at what I guess is a loom hung on the wall. Two heavy beams are suspended horizontally a few inches from the ceiling. Another beam hangs near the floor, also horizontally. And a third, smaller beam is suspended about halfway down. More white yarn is strung tightly on the beams from the top to the bottom. I watch Teresita pass a small ball of gray yarn through the white strands and push it down on top of other strands of gray she's already woven. The blanket she's working on has a zigzag pattern in black and red.

Teresita looks over at us, but her hands never stop moving the gray yarn back and forth. "Are you ready to find rabbit brush?" she asks.

"Sí," Josefina says. "Rabbit-brush flowers make this yellow color, María." She gestures toward a blanket folded on a table in the corner. Sunny stripes alternate with black.

"There should be plenty in the hills," Teresita says.

"And we'll find it," Josefina assures her.

A short while later, I find myself striding from the house with a basket over my arm, just like Josefina. My flute is tucked into a leather pouch at my waist just like Josefina's. Josefina pulls the shawl that's been draped around her shoulders over her head in one fluid movement. She glances at me. The shawl she's just given me is still around my shoulders. The sisters wore theirs the same way in the house. "Don't you need to pull up your *rebozo*?" Josefina asks, with a hint of surprise in her voice.

"I'm good," I say, but then I catch the surprise on my friend's face. Oops. Wrong answer. I pull the silky wool shawl up onto my head. Another rule for girls, apparently. There seem to be a lot of them.

Sombrita has decided to accompany us and bounds ahead on her springlike legs. Behind us, Miguel is following with another basket over his arm.

"Josefina," I whisper, hurrying to keep up. "Does Miguel need some rabbit brush too?"

Josefina giggles. "No, he's going with us as our chaperone and guardian, of course."

I turn this over as we climb into the rising hills behind the house. I guess Josefina and her sisters don't go out without someone watching over them. That makes sense, though—after all, I was supposed to have been captured. And maybe that's why Josefina's house reminds me of a fortress.

I shiver. How dangerous *is* this world?

✻ *Turn to page 58.*

I follow Josefina into a large open courtyard with a floor of hard dirt and smooth stones. Walls surround the courtyard on all sides. I glimpse a walkway leading to another courtyard at the back of the house. The courtyard walls have many door openings, and I catch glimpses of rooms beyond. There is a round clay thing like a kiln in one corner of this courtyard, some more chickens pecking randomly about, and baskets of shiny red peppers sitting around.

Josefina leads me over to three girls and a woman sitting together in the middle of the courtyard. They're dressed just like her, but the older two girls and the woman wear their hair in low buns. The younger girl has a braid, like Josefina and me. "My aunt is staying here at the *rancho* with my sisters and me for a while, to help us," she tells me on the way.

"Tía Dolores," Josefina says to the woman, "I've found this girl wandering outside. She's lost, I think. May she rest here at our home?"

Josefina's voice sounds different—lower, respectful. The other girls stop what they're doing and stare at me, open-mouthed. I try not to stare too much back.

Tía Dolores jumps to her feet. She looks at my face,

touches my brow. "Where in heaven did you come from?" she murmurs. Then she stops herself. "But you must be tired. Questions can wait. Josefina is right— you must rest here."

Josefina introduces me. "This is Ana, my oldest sister. She's married and has two little boys. And these are my other sisters, Francisca and Clara." The girls all have piles of the red peppers in their laps. Josefina hasn't mentioned her mother—maybe she's somewhere in the house.

Ana smiles at me kindly. "Sit here by me. Josefina, I think our visitor might like a cool cloth for her face." I sink down next to Ana and squirm a little on the woolen blankets spread on the hard ground. The sisters look as comfortable as if they were sitting in armchairs.

"May I make our visitor some chamomile tea also?" Josefina asks Tía Dolores.

"Yes, please do," the aunt says. She has clear, understanding gray eyes, and her hair is a deep, deep auburn red.

Josefina disappears through one of the doorways that open onto the courtyard. I sit still beside Ana. This is all feeling very real. Very, very real, I have to say.

I claw my fingernails into my palm so hard, it hurts. Pain. Don't they say you can't feel pain in dreams?

Josefina appears with a steaming cup, which I almost grab at to distract my spinning mind. Josefina wipes my face with a cool, damp cloth, which feels wonderful against my dusty skin. I take a tentative sip of the tea, which is in a kind of pottery mug, like the ones Mom buys at art fairs.

The warmth spreads through me and I feel my muscles unclenching. I let out a deep breath and smile at the sisters, who are watching me anxiously. They smile back and return to sorting the red peppers piled in their laps, but I can sense that they're dying to ask me more questions.

"What's that in your hand?" Clara asks. Everyone looks, and I realize I'm still clutching the clay bird flute.

"It's my flute," I say, but even as the words leave my mouth, I realize that the flute looks different now—newer, not as dusty. The chip off the bird's tail is gone too. I swallow. The strange thoughts are pushing in further.

"May I see the flute?" Francisca asks.

I hand it to her, and she runs her fingers over the

markings, like Dad did. "This is beautifully made," she says. "It's so graceful." She turns the flute over. "María. Is that your name?"

They all look at me. I nod uncertainly. I don't know what else to do.

I'm having the increasingly certain feeling that this is not a dream—but if it's not, then what *is* happening? I have to get myself alone, to think for a minute.

"I—I'm feeling a bit dizzy," I say to Tía Dolores. "Is there a place I could lie down?"

"Did you hit your head outside?" Her brow creases in concern. "You must rest," she says. "Josefina, take María to your sleeping *sala*."

Who's María? Oh, right. That's me.

"Here, come this way." Josefina leads me through one of the doorways into a small room with plain *adobe* walls. Big rolls of soft material are stacked against one wall. A blue-and-white blanket hangs from a rod on the other wall. I lean in to examine it and draw in my breath.

"Josefina, this is beautiful!" I say. The fibers are woven so smoothly together, I can hardly see them. The blue stripes are the deep blue color of the Santa Fe sky.

Josefina looks down at her feet and smiles shyly. "Thank you. It's the first blanket I wove by myself."

"You *wove* this?" I look more closely. "Wow!" Mom just recently taught me to sew on a button. Weaving a whole blanket would be like me cooking Thanksgiving dinner for twenty. "I wish I could do that."

"You'll be comfortable here," Josefina says. At first, I don't know how that's possible, since there's no bed in sight, and then I realize that she is unrolling one of the big bundles. It's bedding—a sheepskin and some more of the amazing blankets. "Is this your bed?" I try not to sound too incredulous. I don't want to insult her or anything. They sleep on the floor?

Josefina gives me a strange look. "Of course. Clara's is there, and Francisca's is there. Ana and Tomás—that's Ana's husband—have their own room."

So not only does she sleep on the floor, she also shares with both her sisters. I flash on my own four-poster bed at home—in my own room.

Josefina helps me lie down and covers me with a woven blanket that has a pattern like diamonds. The sheepskins are surprisingly comfortable and smell vaguely like my favorite wool sweater. "Here, close your eyes," Josefina says, and I do.

But the moment she's gone, I sit up and try to think. This is not a dream. It's—something else. A mystery. How did I get here? The flute. The flute came here—wherever I am—with me. I was sitting on the rocks outside the house, and I played it, like this. I blow a tentative note. Actually, it wasn't exactly like that. I was listening to the mockingbird and then I played its song. I moisten my lips and place my fingers on the holes. *Trill-trillEE. Trill-trillEE.*

Then it happens again. I feel myself falling through space. Everything is dark. I try to breathe and can't, and then—*wham!*

✻ *Turn to page 20.*

ome is right in front of me, I think. *It's where my family is.* But maybe I had to lose them—temporarily—before I could realize how much they mean to me.

With my heart feeling lighter than it has in a long time, I climb off the rock, and Daisy bounds down after me. The afternoon sun touches the *adobe* of the house with a warm, golden light. I never thought this funny flat-roofed house could look so welcoming. But maybe that's because I didn't realize that it's actually what the house *contains* that matters.

I pull open the side door, and Daisy pushes in ahead of me. My family's faces turn toward me—familiar, smiling. "There you are, honey," Mom says. She comes over and gives me a little hug. "I want to hear about your day."

"Hey, sis," Henry says. "Looked for you after school—I thought you might want a ride. I guess we missed each other."

I lean against the counter, considering my brother's words. Dad moves over to the stove and checks the *tamales.* They smell delicious. "You know, Henry," I tell him, "I think you might be right. We *have* missed each other. Except that now I'm home. For good."

I smile at him and he smiles back, looking slightly confused. I reach into the cupboard by the sink and grab a stack of plates. The *tamales* are ready. And I'm starving.

❋ *The End* ❋

To read this story another way and see how different choices lead to a different ending, turn back to page 21.

ee you soon, Daisy-girl," I whisper. I raise the flute to my lips. *Trill-trillEE. Trill-trillEE.*

And just like that, I'm back in the plain little room. The diamond-patterned blanket is spread over me. I'm wearing the blouse and the skirt and—I peek under the blanket—the moccasins. My mind feels much clearer now that I know I'm not going crazy, and I throw back the blanket with new energy. I climb off the sheep-skin and clumsily roll it up against the wall again. It's heavier than it looks.

"María!" From the courtyard, Josefina spots me peering out of the doorway. She motions me over. "Come sit with us." The sisters have sorted the peppers, it seems, and two big baskets of perfect, shiny ones sit nearby. Josefina, Tía Dolores, and Clara are now sitting around a big pile of roasted ears of corn, pulling back the pale gold husks and removing the dark silk.

Josefina pats the ground beside her and I sink down, trying to tuck my bulky skirt underneath me like the others. They're watching me, which makes my cheeks hot. I grab an ear of corn and awkwardly wrestle with the leaves.

"Where is your family, María?" Tía Dolores asks.

Her hands move without stopping, smoothly stripping back the husk and revealing rows of yellow kernels. "We must return you to them—they must be very worried."

"I, um . . ." I look down at the half-husked ear in my lap. "I'm not sure exactly where they are." How could I even begin to explain?

"Do you mean you've gotten lost?" Clara asks, her eyebrows knitting together with concern.

"Something like that." *Lost in time,* I think—but how can I tell them I'm from the *future*? "I've had a really . . . strange experience that brought me here."

Everyone is quiet for a moment, and then from behind me, someone says, "We *cautivas* sometimes find it hard to talk about our experiences."

I turn around. In a corner of the courtyard sits an older woman I hadn't noticed before. Her face is deeply wrinkled and tanned. She wears her hair in a different style from Tía Dolores—a twist bound by colorful threads. She is rubbing a pot with something—sand, it looks like. She must be scrubbing it—Mom cleans pots like that when we're camping.

"Oh, a *cautiva*!" Josefina draws in her breath, and

her hand creeps over mine and squeezes my fingers.

Francisca and Clara murmur and shake their heads, looking distressed.

That word they keep saying—*captive.* They think I've been taken captive? Like kidnapped?

"My poor child!" Tía Dolores says, and I feel her draw my head briefly to her shoulder in a kind of hug.

"María, this is Teresita, our servant," Tía Dolores says. She pauses, as if unsure of something, and then looks at Teresita, who nods as if giving permission. "She was also a *cautiva.*"

Teresita's hand goes around and around in the pot. "I too was taken from my people, the Navajos, by enemies when I was a little girl. Just as enemies took you from your people, the Spanish."

Huh? Captive? Enemies of my people? The others must know what Teresita is talking about, though, because they are nodding sympathetically. It sounds like Teresita was sort of kidnapped when she was younger, and now everyone thinks that the same thing happened to me.

"How old were you when you were captured?" Francisca asks.

"I—" *How old was I?*

"Did the Indians treat you kindly?" Clara interrupts.

"I, um…" I stutter. *Indians?*

"Did you escape?" Josefina asks. "You must have wandered a long time, you were so dusty when I found you. Who gave you the Spanish clothes?"

The questions are coming fast, and I'm getting flustered. "I, um…" I don't want to lie. "I did have a… long journey." *Through time, that is.* "This is all strange to me." I indicate the pile of corn, the chickens, the tidy sisters sitting so gracefully on their blankets.

"Of course it is," Tía Dolores breaks in soothingly. She puts aside a husked ear of corn and brushes silk from her lap. "And you must have been captured very young. I have heard that *cautivas* taken from their families as children often remember little of their early life with their families."

"And besides, you hit your head," Josefina puts in. "That might be affecting your memory too."

The others nod agreement, their faces concerned.

Josefina tilts her head. "Can you remember which Indians captured you? The Apaches, perhaps? Or the Comanches? Did they live in tepees or—"

Suddenly, the pieces fit together. They think I was captured from my family, who would be Spanish, like them, and that I've been living as a captive with a group of Indians ever since. And Teresita—the same thing must have happened to her a long time ago, but in reverse. She was a Navajo Indian captured by the Spanish.

"We must tell Josefina's papá," Tía Dolores says firmly. "He will need to inform the officials in Santa Fe that we've found a *cautiva*. We will ask him also if María may stay here until we can find her relatives." She stands up. "Come, María."

Tía Dolores reminds me of my favorite teacher, Mrs. Burton from second grade. She had that same way of talking, take-charge but not bossy. She always knew just what to do—and I bet Tía Dolores is the same way.

Josefina bounces up also. "May I come too, Tía Dolores?"

"You may. I believe your papá is outside saddling his horse." Tía Dolores smiles at both of us and leads us out of the courtyard and through the big front gate.

A tall man is lifting a saddle onto a light tan horse

with a black mane and tail. He wears a hat with a wide brim, kind of like my grandfather used to wear when he was hiking. His face is lined and serious.

"Andres, may we speak a moment?" Tía Dolores says. Her voice is low and respectful.

"Yes?" Señor Montoya answers. "Do we have a visitor?"

"This girl's name is María," Tía Dolores says. "Josefina found her wandering outside." She quickly explains that I seem to be a *cautiva* who was taken so young that I don't remember much of my early life.

Señor Montoya studies me with grave eyes, and I look down. Out of the corner of my eye, I see Josefina standing beside me with her hands clasped in front of her and her head bent. I mimic her and say nothing. I have the feeling that I'm not supposed to speak unless someone asks me a question. I remember reading that in the old days, they would always say, "Children should be seen and not heard." It seems like Josefina's family follows that rule, too.

"You are welcome here, María," Señor Montoya says, and his voice is kind. "I will notify the Santa Fe officials and make inquiries to see if anyone knows of a family whose daughter was taken years ago."

My ears perk up at the words "Santa Fe." I *am* somewhere I know. Just not in the time I know.

Señor Montoya goes on. "I will send Miguel and some other men to check the hills. The *rancho* is not safe if enemies are nearby. In the meantime, you must stay here with us. We will find a home for you, if we cannot find your family."

"Oh! Um . . ." I stammer. This family I don't even know is going to all this trouble for me, and now they're going to be searching for an enemy that doesn't even exist. "Ah . . . my journey has been a long one." I choose my words carefully. "I'm very far from where I started. I don't think there are any enemies nearby."

Señor Montoya raises his brows and looks at me more closely. I hastily cast my eyes down.

"Nonetheless," he says, "the area must be checked."

Josefina gives me a sideways smile and reaches out to squeeze my hand.

Señor Montoya notices, and the corners of his mouth twitch up. "I see that my youngest daughter will take good care of you." He glances at Tía Dolores and she smiles back, her own eyes twinkling.

"Yes, Papá," Josefina says, her eyes still on the ground. "Thank you, Papá."

That's all she says, and as her papá swings up onto his horse and trots away, I think of how Dad and I talk and argue and laugh together at home. It's different here, but it seems like Josefina loves her father the same, even if she doesn't talk to him in the same way.

Josefina gives me a warm smile. "I'm so glad you'll be our guest, María! I've never had a girl my own age to stay before. It's like having another sister!"

❋ *Turn to page 22.*

he sun is low in the sky, and a hint of chill has flavored the air by the time we return to the courtyard. The delicious scent of frying wafts from the kitchen. After Josefina and I have hauled in our heavy baskets and dumped out the squashes, I sit on one of the blankets and help Josefina, Clara, and Francisca slice them into round disks. Then they show me how to string the slices with a needle and thread into a kind of really big squash necklace, which they call a *ristra.* Then they'll hang the *ristras* to dry—sort of like making dried apple slices, I guess.

"So much squash!" Josefina rejoices. She lifts one of the *ristras* high so that the end just touches the ground.

"So much water-carrying from the stream!" Francisca says. "My head aches just at the thought of it." She puts her hand delicately up to her forehead.

Why would her head ache from carrying water? I wonder. Maybe she thought about it too hard? Then I remember the servant with the water jug that we saw earlier.

"You'll be glad of these dried squashes this winter," Clara retorts. "We all will."

Tía Dolores appears in the kitchen doorway and

comes over to inspect our work. "My nieces are keeping their hands busy, as God intends," she says, smiling at us approvingly. "After all—"

"The saints cry over lost time!" Josefina interrupts, and she, Clara, and Francisca laugh. Their merriment is infectious, and I laugh too.

"I'm glad to see I've taught you well," Tía Dolores says with a twinkle in her eyes.

I sit quietly, thinking. At home we can get anything we want, all year round, just by driving to the supermarket. But it seems like Josefina's family wouldn't have enough to eat if they didn't grow and dry these vegetables. It must be hard work, hauling water in the heat of a desert summer, but they don't seem unhappy.

Francisca holds a small squash up behind her ear. "How do I look?" She tosses her glossy black hair. "Should I wear this to the harvest *fandango* tomorrow?"

A *fandango*—a party! My ears perk up. I do love parties.

Clara sighs and yanks the squash away. "Francisca, be serious. Squash *blossoms* in your hair, perhaps. But that's our food, not decoration."

"She's *wearing* the squash instead of *giving* the squash!" Josefina cries, and she and Francisca burst into laughter.

Josefina sees my confusion. "When a young lady wants to refuse a marriage proposal from a gentleman, her family sends his family a squash!" she tells me.

What a funny custom! I can't help laughing too, but seeing them all together, their heads almost touching as they murmur to one another, gives me a pang for Danielle. I want to whisper and laugh with my best friend.

As I pick up my *ristra* again and get back to work, Audrey's face swims up in front of me. *A new friend.* I push the image away.

❋ *Turn to page 63.*

We walk farther and farther from the house, skipping over tiny streams, skirting boulders, watching black ravens wheel and call to one another far above our heads. Sombrita bounds up a steep boulder. I stare up into the sparkling blue depths of the sky. Pine-scented air tingles my nose. Bright yellow cottonwoods cluster along the streams. My nervousness ebbs away. No enemies in sight. And I haven't spotted a single horny toad—yet.

"Mmm!" Josefina breathes in and closes her eyes. "*Piñón* is my favorite scent! Don't you love it, María?"

"It smells delicious," I agree, and together we close our eyes and inhale at the same time. "Mmm!" We open our eyes and giggle at each other.

"Sombrita! Stay close!" Josefina calls to the little goat, who is wandering into some bushes. She kneels down as Sombrita runs back to her. "You must stay near, little one," she says gently, looking into the goat's face. "There are dangers out here." She pats Sombrita firmly on the head and rises.

"I have to teach her," Josefina explains. "She's never had a mother to show her how to be a proper grown-up goat, so I try my best to do it."

"What happened to her mother?" I ask, struggling behind as Josefina strides up a rise. Small pebbles have collected in my moccasins, and the sun is hot now, baking the top of my head.

"She died giving birth to her." Josefina stops walking and rests with her hands on her waist. "Maybe that's why I feel so strongly that I have to help her. She doesn't have a mother . . . and neither do I."

I inhale. "Where—where is your mother?" I almost don't want to hear the answer.

"She died. Two years ago." Josefina looks toward the horizon, and I sense that she doesn't want me to say anything else. So I stay silent, but after a moment I reach out and squeeze her hand. She doesn't look at me, but squeezes back and swipes a wrist under her eyes.

We start walking again. After a few moments, I ask, "So . . . how did Sombrita survive after her mother died? Wouldn't she starve?"

Josefina smiles, though her eyes are still shiny. "Papá gave me a pouch of milk, and I taught her to suck it out through a rag in the top. That first night, I slept with her by the hearth. I kept her warm and fed until she was stronger."

I think of Fern feeding Wilbur the runty pig with a baby bottle in *Charlotte's Web.* "I've heard you can do that with baby animals. It must have been fun to take care of her."

We top the small rise and stop to look over the dry, brushy landscape. "It was," Josefina agrees. "But it was more than that, too. I just felt like I *had* to. And now Tía Magdalena—that's my godmother, Papá's older sister—is teaching me so that I can become a *curandera* like her, one day."

I must look confused because she clarifies, "A healer— Oh, here!" she breaks off. "I see rabbit brush over on the next rise." She points to a gentle slope where clusters of small shrubs are bursting with mustard-yellow flowers.

We hike over and set down our baskets. Josefina begins plucking the flowers and stems. A short distance away, Miguel gathers twigs and small sticks— I imagine for kindling—while Sombrita wanders through the low brush, munching leaves. Tentatively, I twist off a few flowers, trying not to mangle them, and drop them into my basket. "Mamá always loved autumn," Josefina says, her hands working quickly. The wind blows brown tendrils of her hair across her face. "It was her favorite season. She always said that the colors are giving us their last show before they go for their winter's rest." She holds up a rabbit-brush flower against the blue sky. "Look, María! Look at this yellow against the blue."

I gaze up at her strong, tanned hand. In the crystalline air, the yellow vibrates and glows against the jewel-like blue. It almost hurts, the colors are so brilliant. My breath catches. "It's beautiful." Then my eyes drop to Josefina's face, and I watch as she sweeps her gaze around the landscape. Her face is alight.

She loves this land, I think. *She loves it like I love Chicago.* This is her home. And I guess it's mine now too, sort of. Maybe someday I'll love it like Josefina does. But right now, the spiny stems of the rabbit brush have pricked my palm, and I bring my hand to my mouth to cool the sting.

Josefina notices my grimace. "Here, María, pick them lower down, to avoid the spines."

"Right." I watch her deftly pick a couple of flowers. "You know so much about all this—gathering the plants, how to find them. And how to weave, and how to make these into dyes for the yarn."

Josefina pauses, her face surprised. "I never thought of it that way. Gathering plants for dyes and weaving—that's nothing special. I'm not good at organizing the household, the way Ana and Tía Dolores are. And Francisca knows how to choose the most beautiful colors for weaving, and Clara always weaves so smooth and tight . . . I'm just learning, really, María."

I raise my eyebrows. "Well, it doesn't seem that way to me. You can be *my* teacher."

Josefina's round face crinkles into a smile, and she seems to grow a few inches taller.

❋ *Turn to page 67.*

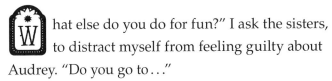 hat else do you do for fun?" I ask the sisters, to distract myself from feeling guilty about Audrey. "Do you go to..."

I realize that there isn't really anywhere to go. No malls. No movie theaters. No TV, of course. What do they do for entertainment—visit the horny toads?

"Oh, we have plenty of fun times," Josefina says. "Tía Dolores has brought so many new things from Mexico City. She has a *piano*!"

She says this as if Tía Dolores has a pet giraffe. But I nod vigorously anyway. Pianos must be pretty special around here.

"We can show it to you tonight, if you like. Tía Dolores might play for us." She looks toward her aunt, who smiles. "I'm learning to play too, but I'm not very good," Josefina goes on. "We dance too—and we are learning to read and write! We've been studying with Tía Dolores for almost a year now." She looks very proud, and so do Clara and Francisca.

My mouth drops open, but I shut it with a snap. I don't want to embarrass them. But... Josefina and her sisters are just now learning to *read*?

Get ahold of yourself, I tell myself sternly. This is

a different time. Obviously, they don't go to school. They're busy growing their own food, for heaven's sake!

"There are important tasks too," Tía Dolores says in her brisk way. "Your lessons with Tía Magdalena will one day benefit the whole household."

Josefina must see that I don't know what Tía Dolores is talking about, because she explains. "I've been studying with Tía Magdalena. She's Papá's older sister who lives in the village. She's teaching me to be a *curandera*."

Clara leans over. "A healer," she whispers.

"Oh yes." I nod my head as if I've just remembered.

When we've strung the last sliced squash, Josefina and I carefully carry the *ristras* over to pegs on the wall of the courtyard. Other squash *ristras* are hanging there, already dried. Josefina takes these down and motions for me to hang up the fresh ones. Then we carry the dried *ristras* through one of the other doorways to what I assume must be a storeroom. I can glimpse barrels and bins standing against the walls. This must be where they keep some of their food. Josefina hangs the *ristras* on wooden pegs on the walls.

I follow Josefina through the courtyard into another

large room. It must be the kitchen, but it doesn't look like any kitchen I've ever seen. A big *adobe* fireplace is along one wall, with jars and baskets arranged on a low shelf beside it. Over the fireplace is a long, broad shelf that looks like a bunk bed. A ladder leads up to it and blankets are arranged on top. It looks like someone sleeps there sometimes. A long wooden table is loaded with melons, peppers, and onions in pottery bowls. The air is hot and smells of spices and roasting meat. Carmen, the cook, is bending over the fireplace, stirring something in a big iron pot.

Ana is kneeling on the floor, rubbing some kind of heavy-looking cylinder-shaped stone over another big flat stone. She's smushing a yellow, grainy powder, and it takes me a minute to realize that she's grinding dried corn kernels. She works fast, but the stone must be heavy, because I can see sweat beading at her temples and cords standing out on her forearms.

She smiles at us as we appear in the doorway. "You must be hungry, María. It won't be long until supper. I'm almost ready to make the *tortillas*."

I don't see how she's going to make *tortillas* out of yellow flour anytime soon, so I resign myself to a long wait. "Soon" must mean something different in Josefina's world.

Ana dumps the flour into a bowl and pours in a thin stream of water from a jug. With her fingers, she mixes it all around, and before I even realize what she's doing, she's made several little dough balls. She flattens these out and lays them on a griddle with legs, which is standing over some glowing coals that have been raked out of the fireplace. After a moment, she lifts the little golden *tortillas* off the griddle and piles them on a plate. The whole operation has taken about two minutes.

My mouth is almost hanging open, I realize, and I shut it with a snap. If only Dad were here! Ana could give him a few lessons in New Mexican cooking.

Ana stands up with the full platter. "It's time for our supper," she says.

As she speaks, my stomach gives a loud gurgle. The sisters look at each other and try to hide smiles.

"We must feed our visitor," Josefina says, looping her arm through mine and giggling. "I can hear that your *belly* demands it!"

✱ *Turn to page 68.*

We continue picking, and soon our baskets are almost full. Then I hear a faint bleating coming from behind a stand of prickly bushes, just below us as the land slopes downward. *It's just Sombrita playing,* I think, and I pluck another flower. But something sounds different about her bleating, and I realize that Josefina hears it too. She stops, her hand still on a flower, her whole body listening. Miguel is at the bottom of the slope, breaking up a large branch.

"Something's wrong," Josefina whispers. For an instant, we stare at each other with wide eyes, and then she whirls around, the bright flowers dropping from her hand. We run toward the bleating, pushing our way through the prickly bushes that catch and snag at our clothes as if trying to hold us back.

Suddenly Josefina freezes, and I crash into her back. As I stagger to keep from falling, I see just below us a huge tawny cat—only three feet from Sombrita. The little goat is backed against a boulder and hemmed in on both sides by bushes.

She's trapped!

❀ *Turn to page 72.*

In what looks like a big main room—Josefina calls it the family *sala*—a fire is crackling cheerfully in the *adobe* fireplace in the corner. The sharp aroma of *piñón* smoke fills the room. A servant is loading a long, narrow table with platters of food. But there are no place settings, and there's nowhere to sit. I look around. Is the dining table hiding in a corner somewhere? But none is in sight. Maybe they eat standing up.

Francisca looks at me critically. "María, your sash is tied wrong. Come here and I'll fix it before we eat."

I look down. I've wrapped the piece of fabric three times around my middle, to keep the ends from trailing on the ground. "I wasn't sure—"

"Francisca!" Clara interrupts. "You are unkind to our guest. She's just being practical, aren't you, María?"

"Ah, I—"

"Practical! That's all you ever think of," Francisca shoots back, her hands on her hips. "A sash is supposed to be beautiful."

"It's supposed to help hold up your skirt!" Clara raises her voice.

"Well, *I* think María's sash looks both lovely and practical," Josefina inserts. She puts her arm through mine and lifts her chin, smiling cheerfully at both sisters.

"And I think our guest might appreciate washing up, girls, instead of bickering about sashes," Tía Dolores says, coming into the room with a bowl of cool water with mint leaves floating in it. She hands me a linen hand towel and a bar of lavender soap, and I quickly wash.

Delicate aromas reach my nose as I fold the towel and lay it with the bowl on a nearby bench. Some of the *tortillas* Ana made are steaming hot on a plate in front of me. I take the top one from the stack, only to realize that everyone else is standing around the table with their heads bowed. Whoops. They're going to say grace. I hurriedly replace the *tortilla,* hoping no one saw me, and bow my head too.

"Since your papá is still out with the sheep, I will say grace," Tía Dolores tells us. She says a short prayer, thanking God for the food and for the garden harvest. Her voice is low and soothing. I feel tension I didn't know was there leaving my body. When I open my eyes at the end, I notice that Josefina looks calmer too.

Everyone begins filling their plates with food.

"*Tamales,* María?" Clara says, as she hands me two from the platter. *Tamales!* They actually look just like Dad's.

"*Sí,*" I say, placing the little husk-wrapped bundles on my plate. "*Gracias.*" Dad would be proud of me. There is a bowl of mashed squash, some chicken, and a loaf of bread with a little cross pressed into the middle.

"Try Ana's special cheese," Josefina says, pointing out a bowl. It smells kind of funny, but the last thing I want is to offend my friend, so I spoon a little onto my plate and hesitantly take a small bite. It tastes strong and vaguely familiar—goat's-milk cheese! Just like the goat cheese Mom brings home sometimes. I flash on the goats outside. Wow, this must be made with milk from the family's own goats.

I wait for us all to sit around the table, but there are no chairs in sight. Everyone just takes a plate and sits on the *bancos*—*adobe* benches that are built into the walls. The squash smells delicious, but I don't have a fork—and actually, I realize, neither does anyone else. There are no spoons or knives either. How am I supposed to eat the squash? Then I see Josefina fold the *tortilla* at the side of her plate and use it to neatly scoop up a bite of squash. How handy—it's like edible silverware.

After we're done eating, a servant clears the dishes. Even through the thick walls, I can feel the evening chill. The single tiny window glows red and purple with the setting sun outside. But it's not glass—it's covered with a thin layer of some kind of luminous shimmery stuff, almost like...stone? I get up to move closer to the fire and examine the window on my way. Josefina is watching me. "It's a thin sheet of mica, to let the light in," she explains.

I think of the shiny rocks scattered around our New Mexico house. Dad told us that they were mica when we first moved in, and Henry and I marveled at how easily we could peel off thin shiny layers with our fingernails.

A cold draft blows in around the edges of the window, and I shiver. But here in the *sala,* the fire's warmth bakes my face. I wrap my *rebozo* more snugly around my shoulders as Josefina and her sisters settle on the bench close by.

✸ *Turn to page 73.*

osefina stifles a gasp. I press my hand to my mouth to keep from screaming. "What do we do?" I whisper. Miguel is too far away to help. I am sick with fear.

Josefina's eyes are wide and her face is desperate. She doesn't know what to do either.

"Let's grab her," I whisper.

"No, it's too dangerous!" With her eyes never leaving the mountain lion, Josefina bends down and scoops up a baseball-sized rock at her feet.

The mountain lion turns his head and glances at us. Then he fixes his eyes on Sombrita and crouches, ready to spring.

"We have to do something to save Sombrita," Josefina whispers hoarsely.

❋ *To tell Josefina to throw the rock,*
   turn to page 77.

❋ *To grab Sombrita,*
   turn to page 79.

At home, I'd probably be watching TV on the squishy couch with Mom while Dad grades papers in the recliner.

But Josefina's evening seems cozy, too. Tía Dolores has seated herself at the piano in the corner. With beautiful sweeping motions, she's playing scales up and down.

Josefina looks at me with pride. "Isn't it beautiful?" she murmurs. I nod, trying to look as if I'm hearing a piano for the first time.

Francisca is mending a torn shirt, and Clara has a large piece of cloth spread on her lap. She's using a big needle to embroider flowers all around the edges.

"That's beautiful, Clara," I say, bending nearer to admire it. I can hardly see it in the dim firelight, though. My hands itch to flip on a light switch.

Clara looks up and smiles. "Before your time as a *cautiva,* did you learn *colcha,* María?"

That must be the name of the embroidery. "Ah, no. I've never learned it," I say, careful not to lie.

"Mamá taught us *colcha* before she died." There's just the slightest hint of a catch in Josefina's voice.

"She was very good at it. She even made an altar cloth for the church."

"A flood damaged it badly," Francisca tells me, "but Tía Dolores helped us repair the *colcha*. We added bits of our own designs, too. I embroidered swallows on it—Mamá loved birds."

Clara nods. "Josefina embroidered flowers and leaves that Mamá loved, and I worked on sprigs of lavender—it was Mamá's favorite scent. Tía Dolores says that doing *colcha* keeps us close to Mamá. She loved to do it, and now we do too."

With the tip of my finger, I trace the outline of a flower on Clara's cloth. It makes me think of happy times. I see my room in our apartment back home. It's scattered with Drama Club scripts. Music soars from my speakers, and outside, the skyscrapers tower silvery gray against the blue sky.

Josefina's words float in through the image. "We can show you the altar cloth. We're keeping it safe here at home until next Christmas, when the church will need it again."

"Tía Dolores has helped us remember Mamá by making a memory book, too. It's a little book where she writes down poems and songs that Mamá used to love," Francisca breaks in. "Mamá was her sister, so Tía Dolores has many memories of her. Now we are learning to write in it too, so that we can remember things she used to say."

Tía Dolores turns from the piano, her *rebozo* drooping gracefully from her shoulders. The candles flaring on the wall send ripples of light up and down her dark red hair. She says, "Your mamá knew so many lovely poems and songs." Her smile bathes us in warmth, and I can see all four sisters lean in a little closer to her. Her eyes travel over each of them. "Words can keep special memories alive." She rises and gently caresses Josefina's cheek.

"I'll get the memory book!" Josefina jumps up. "It's lovely, María."

"Oh, I'd love to see it." This book sounds extremely special.

"Prayers are soon, girls," Tía Dolores cautions.

"We don't have much time," Josefina says, looking at me. "Should we see Mamá's altar cloth or look at the memory book?"

Words can keep special memories alive. Tía Dolores's

voice echoes in my mind. The memory book draws me strongly. But I want to see the altar cloth that brings Mamá back so vividly for Josefina, too.

✸ *To see the memory book,*
   turn to page 80.

✸ *To see Mamá's altar cloth,*
   turn to page 86.

o it," I whisper to Josefina.

Her eyes are steely. The mountain lion leaps. Josefina slings the rock at him, and he twists in midair like a spring. The rock catches him hard on the shoulder, and he lands heavily, scrabbling with his back feet for an instant. He stumbles, hesitates, and with one backward glance over his shoulder, lopes away, disappearing over the rise.

We both breathe a huge sigh of relief. Before we even have time to say a word, Miguel comes running up. Quickly, Josefina explains what happened, and once he sees that we are both unharmed, he tracks the cat down the hill to make sure he's really gone.

Josefina scoops up Sombrita in her arms, and we stand a long time, stroking the little goat, feeling her heartbeat return to normal just as ours do.

Finally, Josefina's eyes meet mine, and we burst into nervous giggles. "So much for a relaxing expedition into the hills!" Josefina says.

I place my hand over my heart. "That's okay. My heart needed a good jolt!"

Josefina heaves a big sigh and places Sombrita on the ground. "No more wandering off!" she instructs the little goat. "María and I might not be able to save you a second time." The goat gazes up at Josefina with her yellow eyes, and I wonder if she knew how much danger she was just in.

"Do you want to go back to the house and rest?" Josefina asks me as Sombrita, unconcerned by her brush with death, nibbles at one of her moccasins. "After all, this was a lot of excitement on top of your long journey. Or shall we continue our gathering?"

As the adrenaline ebbs away, I suddenly realize how exhausted I am—between the trip through time and this brush with danger, I feel like I've been running for a week without stopping. I think longingly of the sheepskin bedroll in Josefina's room. But at the same time, we've barely gotten started on our collecting trip. I don't want to let Josefina down by not finishing the task we planned to do together.

❈ *To return to the house,*
turn to page 88.

❈ *To stay in the hills,*
go to **beforever.com/endings**

launch myself into the air, almost colliding with the mountain lion as he springs at Sombrita. For an instant, I smell his musky odor and feel the heat of his body. Then my fingers close on Sombrita's front leg and I jerk her toward me. The mountain lion screams, and a paw flashes out.

I see a burst of red as I pull the little goat underneath me. I can feel her heart pounding along with my own, and I squeeze my eyes shut, waiting for the mountain lion to leap onto my back. I flash on the part in *Little House in the Big Woods* where a panther jumps onto a horse's back and rips it up as the horse runs away into the woods. Now *I'm* the horse.

Something touches my back, and I scream.

❋ *Turn to page 83.*

'd love to see your memory book," I tell Josefina. She jumps up and leaves the room, and then comes back in a moment carrying a little book with soft brown leather covers.

Gently, I turn the pages while she looks over my shoulder. There are little drawings, handwritten poems, quotes. I think about how wrenching losing her mother must have been for Josefina.

Josefina points to a few lines written in careful script. "This is one of the first things I wrote down. It's a song I remember Mamá singing to me when I was a baby." She croons softly:

> *Sleep, my beautiful baby,*
> *Sleep, my grain of gold.*
> *The night is very cold.*
> *The night is very cold.*

She pauses, her face lit by the firelight. "Those are the very same words Mamá used to sing—and they are right here! Written down, so we'll never forget them."

She shakes her head, and I sense her amazement.

She doesn't have a picture of her mother, but she has this. She has her words.

"I remember that song!" Clara exclaims. "She would sing it to you in your cradle, Josefina, and we would all lean on her knees, listening."

Francisca's eyes are shiny. "I remember that too," she says. Her voice is muffled.

My own throat aches a little as I look at the sisters' faces. I've left behind a city I loved, but the people I love are still with me. You can replace a home, but not the people you love.

Josefina looks closely at me. "Would you show us what your old home was like, María? Will you draw it for us?" She turns to her aunt. "Tía Dolores, may we use a scrap of paper from the memory book?"

Tía Dolores flips through the pages. "Here, dears, this last page has an ink stain on it. Use this one." Very carefully, she tears the small page out and hands it to us. From the way they're acting, I'm guessing that paper is pretty rare around here also—along with water and pianos!

Josefina puts something into my hand. It's a big

feather with most of the feather part stripped off. The end is sharpened into a point. She puts a small glass jar of ink beside me. "Here, María. Show us your house."

✸ *Turn to page 89.*

expect blinding pain. Instead, I feel only Josefina's gentle touch on my back. Her voice fills my ears like the sweetest music. "María! He's gone! He ran away!"

"Are you sure?" Shakily, I push myself up. Amazingly, I seem to be fine except for a few scrapes. Then I look down at Sombrita, lying on the ground underneath me. My breath catches in my throat. "Oh, Josefina! She's hurt!"

The little goat lies still, her rib cage rising and falling rapidly. A deep gash gapes in her shoulder like a bloody mouth.

Miguel runs up behind us. "Stay with the goat," he tells us. "I'll track the mountain lion to make sure he's really gone." He trots off the way the mountain lion went.

Josefina and I drop to our knees over the little gray-and-white form. Blood seeps from the wound, staining Sombrita's soft fur and dripping onto the sandy dirt beneath her.

"We need to stop the bleeding," Josefina says. "Quickly, before she loses too much blood." She presses her fingers to her forehead. "Tía Magdalena never told me how to do that, though. María, I don't know what to do." Her voice is starting to rise in panic, and I grab her fingers and pull them away from her face. I kneel down and look right into her eyes. I try to remember the way my drama teacher would talk down kids who were having an attack of stage fright.

"Josefina." I make my voice low and quiet. "You can do this. Remember, you knew how to save Sombrita when she was tiny? Now you can do it again." In truth, my heart is pounding out of my chest, I'm so terrified, but my voice is steady and calm. "You *do* have the skills. I believe in you."

Josefina raises her eyes and looks me in the face, as if searching for the truth there. She must see that I believe what I am saying, because her mouth hardens and her eyes suddenly glitter crystal clear.

"Leaves." Josefina speaks rapidly and points behind me. "Get me some of those mallow leaves. I don't know if this is right, but we're going to try."

Quickly, I grab handfuls of the broad, dark-green leaves sprouting from a low plant nearby. They're covered with soft hairs. Josefina layers the leaves over Sombrita's wound.

"Here!" I take off my *rebozo.* "Tie them on with this." Josefina nods, and twists the shawl into a bandage, wrapping it securely over Sombrita's shoulder and leg. Behind us, Miguel trots up. He nods when I look up at him, and I let out a breath. The mountain lion is gone.

Josefina strokes Sombrita's forehead and bows her own head. I can see her lips moving. She must be saying a prayer. I close my eyes too. My forehead is coated in sweat and my hands are trembling. I find myself praying, too. *Please let her live. Please let her live.*

❀ *Turn to page 91.*

"ill you show me the altar cloth?" I ask Josefina. A smile lights her face, and she jumps up from the bench and disappears through the doorway. In a few moments, she is back, carrying a folded white cloth in her arms. The sisters gather around, and Josefina gently shakes it out.

My breath catches. Richly colored flowers—crimson, indigo blue, golden—are scattered across the top and embroidered thickly around the edges. Green leaves sprinkled throughout make me think of a midsummer meadow. "You all did this?" I ask, tracing my fingertips around the tiny stitches.

Josefina nods. "We put our love for Mamá into every stitch," she says. I hear a little catch in her voice, as if she's holding back tears.

Tía Dolores looks over us all, sitting still, wrapped in our thoughts, and then she goes to the piano. Seating herself on the bench, she begins a quiet tune that winds through the room, swaying and rocking us with its melody.

After a few moments, the tune picks up speed, and Tía Dolores throws us a teasing look over her shoulder. She starts a rollicking dance tune. Josefina's face lights up. The melancholy thoughts scattered, she takes my hands and pulls me up from the *banco.* Clara and Francisca dance together too, and we all spin with our full skirts flying out.

My heart is full, and somehow talking about what she's lost—and thinking about what I've lost—has made me feel *better.* "You know," I whisper to Josefina under cover of the music, "I think, after tonight, that I know my way home now."

Her feet slow and her hands tighten on mine. "Are you sure, María?"

I nod. Mom, Dad, Henry—they're waiting for me back in my own time. They've *been* waiting for me ever since we moved. Maybe I had to lose them first, before I could find them again. And I know where to look— my new Santa Fe home.

❋ *The End* ❋

To read this story another way and see how different choices lead to a different ending, turn back to page 76.

To read this story another way and see how different choices lead to a different ending, turn back to page 76.

think I'm ready to go home," I tell Josefina.

"Are you sure, María?" Josefina asks, her dark eyes concerned.

I nod, but even as I do, I wonder which home I mean. Do I mean Josefina's home? Or my modern *adobe* house with Dad and Mom and Henry inside? Or do I mean Chicago—the only place that ever meant home before?

Then I realize, as Josefina and I make our slow way down the sloping hills, with Sombrita springing ahead, that when I told Josefina I wanted to go home, the image in my mind wasn't the *rancho*—or Chicago. It was our Santa Fe house, with the high desert surrounding it.

I do see what Dad means about the beauty of the desert now, I think to myself as the sun slants low and golden across the sky. This land seems different now—not just too hot, too dusty, too empty. This is Josefina's home, and she loves it—and now it's my home too. I wonder if I can make a life here, the way Josefina has. It's time for me to see. The first chance I get, I'll go back to my own time—back home.

✤ *Turn to page 119.*

I picture our brownstone apartment building. I know every brick and crevice. I fumble with the quill and bend my head close to the paper. How do Josefina and her sisters see anything in this firelight?

Clumsily, I draw our apartment building, and the Chicago skyline behind it. After a few moments, I lay down the quill. "This is hard to draw with," I tell Josefina.

"But you have caught on quickly," she remarks, peering at the paper and kindly ignoring the many blobs and blots. I take another look at the drawing. Something that resembles a humpbacked mountain with a rectangle in front of it tilts across the paper.

Josefina tips her head. "Why, your home looks almost like *our* home. That looks like the mountains just beyond our *rancho.* See?" She points. "You've drawn one hill with a hump, just like the one outside."

"Really?" I look closer. Whatever I drew doesn't look like the Chicago skyline, that's for sure. Actually, it *does* look kind of like the hills around here.

"And these are the pine trees." Josefina indicates the little lines at the bottom of the page.

I squint. "That's supposed to be the fence outside our house."

"And there's the house right in the middle," Josefina goes on, as if she hasn't heard me. "How clever, María."

"Gracias," I say, staring at the paper. She's right. The rectangle looks like our modern Santa Fe home, and the hill could be the same one outside both my house and Josefina's. I started out trying to draw one home, and I wound up with another.

❋ *Turn to page 92.*

osefina opens her eyes. "We must get her back to the house, quickly. Miguel, will you carry her?"

Miguel lifts Sombrita as if she's a toy, and we start off up the slope. I can see the square shape of the house at the top of a hill a few rises away.

My heart is still pounding. I can't believe I've seen an actual mountain lion. "She will live, won't she?" I ask Josefina.

"I hope she will. I couldn't bear to lose her." The little goat's eyes are closed. She lies limply in Miguel's arms.

"Is she breathing?" I gasp, scrambling to keep up with Miguel's trotting. "She's so still."

Josefina rests her hand on Sombrita's ribs as we half-walk, half-run. "She is," she says with relief. "But her heartbeat is weak. We must hurry."

❀ *Turn to page 95.*

eñor Montoya appears in the doorway, and we all rise respectfully to our feet.

Tía Dolores gets up from the piano bench. "It's time for prayers, girls." I follow Josefina and the others to the back of the room, to a narrow table. It must be an altar because everyone kneels in front of it, with Josefina's papá in the center. Ana and Tomás, her husband, slip in at the back, and we all bow our heads.

Señor Montoya prays, and I let his deep, musical voice roll over me as I peek through my almost-closed eyes at the altar. It's covered with a beautifully embroidered cloth. Candles send wisps of smoke to the ceiling, and several brightly painted figures stand on their own special little platform at the back of the altar. They look familiar, and then I remember seeing some at the museum in Santa Fe. Dad told me they were figures of saints carved from wood.

I glance at the faces of the family gathered around me as Josefina's papá prays. They look peaceful, refreshed, as if they've all had a drink of cold water on a hot day. I get the feeling that this is a really important time of day.

I follow Josefina and her sisters toward the doorway after prayers are over. Tía Dolores and Señor Montoya are talking quietly by the altar. Then Señor Montoya says, "I need to check the animals for the night." He leaves the room.

"María," Tía Dolores calls softly, coming over to us. "You know there's a harvest *fandango* tomorrow night in the village. Josefina and her sisters will be going there in the morning to help prepare. Perhaps you'd like to join them."

"Oh, yes!" exclaims Josefina, before I can say anything. "You must, María! *Fandangos* are so much fun."

A party? Oh, this is the party they were talking about earlier. *Yes, please!* I open my mouth to say so, but Tía Dolores keeps talking. "However, Josefina's papá is going to Santa Fe for some business. He will talk with officials there and will also ask if anyone knows of a family in a village somewhere who has lost a child. You and Josefina may accompany him if you'd like, but you'll miss the *fandango.* I will go with you, and we'll take the wagon and stay overnight. If you decide not to go, Josefina's papá will go by horseback and will return for the *fandango* in the evening."

Beside me, Josefina claps her hands. "A party or a trip!" she breathes.

In my mind's eye, I see the downtown streets lined with shops, offices, and cars, and the cathedral soaring over everything. Of course, I know Santa Fe must look different in Josefina's time, but still … it's a city, right? It would be nice to have a taste of big-city life again, even if it's not Chicago. Already the empty black desert is pressing in at the tiny window in the *sala*. There are no sounds except the wind whispering around the *adobe* walls. A city! Streets! Buildings! People bustling around! Color, light!

I almost burst out, "Yes, I want to go to Santa Fe!" But then I waver. I love parties, and I haven't been to one for so long! My body almost aches for laughter and music. After all, I *am* kind of a party girl. I haven't felt much like having fun since we moved, but I do now—having Josefina as a friend must have perked me up.

❀ *To help prepare for the fandango,*
   turn to page 99.

❀ *To go to Santa Fe,*
   turn to page 102.

Tía Dolores rushes toward us as we enter the house. "I will send a servant to the village for Tía Magdalena. You poor girls!" She draws us close to her as Miguel carries Sombrita past us into the courtyard.

We follow Miguel as he gently places Sombrita on a hide. Then we kneel over her anxiously to keep watch. Her eyes are closed, and the *rebozo* is soaked with blood where it covers the wound.

After what seems like an eternity, Tía Magdalena bustles in, followed by Ana and Tía Dolores. We all breathe a sigh of relief at her gray-haired, no-nonsense presence. She nods at me, but there is no time for introductions.

She deftly unties the crusted, dirty *rebozo* and, with confident fingers, gently feels around the wound. The gash is partly closed now, with the edges hardened and the blood around it gummy. Tía Dolores sets a bowl of steaming water at Tía Magdalena's elbow, and the older woman pours in something that smells like vinegar from a small jar she's taken from her pouch. Gently, she bathes the wound over and over, until the blood and dirt are washed away. Then she uncorks another small jar and spreads a thick, strong-smelling salve over the wound. "This will keep it from festering," she says, almost to herself. "It will heal without stitching." She hands a clean white cloth to Josefina. "Bind the wound tightly," she says. "You know how to do it well, I've already seen."

Her mouth pursed in concentration, Josefina carefully winds the bandage around the goat's shoulder, chest, and upper leg, just as she did with the *rebozo.*

Sombrita sighs. Her eyelids flicker and then open, just a little. "Look!" I gasp.

"Do you feel better, little one?" Josefina asks, stroking the goat's head. "You must lie still, to let your shoulder heal." She draws a second hide up over the goat for a blanket. Sombrita almost seems to understand her, because her body relaxes. She pushes her head against Josefina's hand and falls asleep.

We all let out a big breath. Tía Magdalena pats Josefina's hand. "You were right to bind the wound immediately, Josefina," she says. "Your instincts were correct."

Josefina's cheeks grow a little pink, and she nods. "*Sí.* I tried to think of what you would tell me." I can hear the respect in her voice. And she trusts

Tía Magdalena to guide her—I can see that.

Tía Magdalena smiles. "She will get well," she assures us all.

Ana gives Josefina a little hug, and Tía Dolores beams. "We're so glad," Tía Dolores says. Josefina leans forward and kisses Sombrita on the head, and I do too.

Josefina and I tenderly carry the little goat to a wide shelf above the fire in the kitchen. "She'll be warm here," Josefina says. "This is the shepherd's bed—it's not really a bed though. It's the warmest place in the house at night." A tender smile lights her face. "I slept with Sombrita here when I first took care of her." She covers the goat with a sheepskin. "Now I'll watch over you again, little one," she whispers, looking down at the little white head poking from the skin.

We sink down onto the floor and rest our elbows on the still-warm stone hearth. "I'm so tired!" Josefina says. I realize suddenly that I am too—more than tired. Now that all the excitement is over, a great weariness spreads over me. The kitchen is silent and peaceful with its neat rows of clay jars and stacks of pottery bowls. The firewood piled beside the oven gives off the woodsy scent of pine and smoke.

Josefina closes her eyes and rests her head on her arms. I close my eyes, and a sudden longing for home sweeps over me—but strangely, it's not our Chicago apartment I'm thinking of, but our *adobe* house, so much like Josefina's. My family is there, and I want to be with them. I think of the respect and trust Josefina has for Tía Magdalena and how Dad asked me to trust him that life in New Mexico will get better. Maybe I should, as Josefina trusts her elders.

We are silent then, as the minutes unspool in the quiet kitchen. Sombrita's breathing is slow and steady over our heads. She'll be all right now, I know. And I'll be all right. I don't know how I know that, but I just do. It's a sense I'm bringing back from Josefina's world—a feeling that love and trust are waiting for me. All I have to do is go find them.

I slip my other hand into my waist pouch. I squeeze the bird flute, feeling its smooth clay against my palm. It's time to go home.

❋ *The End* ❋

To read this story another way and see how different choices lead to a different ending, turn back to page 72.

"I'd like to go to the *fandango*," I tell Tía Dolores, a little shyly. I look over quickly at Josefina. Is that okay with her? Is she disappointed? But my friend grins. She doesn't look sad.

Tía Dolores smiles as if she understands. "It is good to have a little enjoyment every now and then, especially at the end of the harvest."

"Oh, good!" Josefina claps her hands. "And tonight you can sleep with me, María. It's late, and we must be up early for chores."

Tía Dolores gently traces the sign of the cross on Josefina's forehead, and then on my mine. Her fingers are soft and when she bends close to us, I catch a whiff of a lavender perfume. Then I follow Josefina out into the cold, dark courtyard. The sky is inky black and scattered with a million stars that glitter like diamond dust. I want to stand and stare and stare, but Josefina is leading me across the courtyard to the room where I rested earlier in the day. Clara and Francisca are already there, tucked into their sheepskin beds, and the room is warmly lit with a flickering candle in a sconce on the wall.

Josefina starts untying her sash and taking off her

skirt. I do the same, glancing around at the same time for some pajamas, or even a nightgown.

Josefina neatly folds her skirt and sash and tucks them into a trunk in the corner of the room. I do too. Then, still wearing her white blouse, she unrolls our bedding, folds back the blankets, and climbs in.

Okay. I guess they sleep in their blouses. I can't help wondering what Josefina would think of the purple-striped pajama bottoms and T-shirt I usually sleep in at home.

Josefina sits cross-legged in the bed. From a peg nearby, she takes down something that looks like a whisk broom tied together with a ribbon at one end. She unbraids her hair and starts running this broom through it, like it's a brush. Then I realize—it *is* a brush. Whew. Good thing I didn't ask her why she was combing her hair with a broom.

Josefina helps me comb out my braid and then I comb hers. She has lovely long hair that's wavy and curly at the ends, and the broomy brush does a surprisingly good job pulling out the tangles. Sitting in front of Josefina on her bed on the floor reminds me of sleepovers with Danielle. We'd sleep on the floor then too, in our sleeping bags, and we always did each other's hair. I liked a French braid the best, and Danielle usually wanted me to use the flat-iron on hers. I was a little worried I'd be homesick if I decided to spend the night in this world, but as Josefina blows out the candle and I snuggle down into the soft sheepskin, I feel almost at home.

✸ *Turn to page 103.*

í, *gracias.* I would like to go to Santa Fe very much, as long as Josefina does also," I say respectfully to Tía Dolores.

Josefina makes a little noise that sounds like a squeak and grabs my hand, squeezing it hard. I squeeze back, excitement bubbling up in me as well. Two girls, off to the big city!

I snuggle next to Josefina that night in her soft bed of sheepskins and wool blankets. Francisca's and Clara's quiet breathing fills the room, and cool desert air wafts in through the one tiny window over my head. Far away, a coyote howls. The sound still reminds me of a child screaming, and a brief chill runs down my spine. But my eyelids are heavy and the sheepskins are so soft, and I soon fall asleep.

❋ *Turn to page 109.*

I open my eyes to gray twilight. "Good morning!" Josefina cries as soon as I open my eyes. She's already up and buttoning her skirt over her loose white blouse.

Morning? It's the middle of the night! I push myself up and see the single small window glowing rosy with the sunrise. Ooof. They get up early here.

"We have a busy day, María," Clara says from the corner, where she is combing her hair in front of a small mirror on the wall. "We need to hurry and get the chores done so that we can go over to the village."

"I can't wait until tonight. Dancing!" Francisca says rapturously, closing her eyes and whirling around the room.

Clara frowns. "There's a lot to do first, Francisca," she chides her sister.

Josefina gives me a little sideways smile, as if to say, *There they go again.* "Tía Dolores fixed the tear in your skirt last night, María," she says. "She brought it in while we were asleep. Dress quickly. I need to fetch water from the stream."

I pull on the clean, neatly mended skirt and quickly braid my hair. Josefina and her sisters all put on the same clothes they wore yesterday, too. I guess when you don't have a washer and dryer in the basement, laundry is a bigger deal.

After Josefina returns with the water jug, there are more prayers at the family altar, and then bread and fresh goat cheese for breakfast.

We wave to Señor Montoya as he mounts his horse and sets off for Santa Fe, and then Clara, Ana, Tía Dolores, Josefina, and I all start off for the village, carrying baskets of squash, *chiles,* and even—*eek!*— dead chickens that will soon be turned into stew. Tía Dolores has a small basket of herbs. Francisca stays behind to take care of Ana's little boys and help Teresita, Carmen, and the other servants prepare food for tonight.

We walk briskly along the dusty road leading from the *rancho.* White clouds sail in the blue sky, and the crispy air is scented with wood smoke. Josefina and I trot to keep up with the others.

"It'll be so good to visit with everyone," Josefina says. "I haven't seen Señora Sanchez for a few weeks. She was my mamá's good friend. And the other women too—they all grew up with Mamá, and I've known them since I was a baby. I remember falling over a stool at Señora Sanchez's house and banging my nose when I was just a little girl. They were getting ready for a *fandango* then too!" She smiles with the memory. "The village is like a second home, really."

A powerful ache throbs in my middle. I'd like to feel at home out here. I'd like this place to feel like it's part of my skin and my blood, the way Josefina does.

We walk by plowed fields crowded with cornstalks heavy with ripe ears. Pumpkin vines are growing in between the green rows. A burbling stream runs close to the path, and as we walk along, I can see that little channels have been carved out, leading from the stream to each field. A small wooden gate sits at the opening of each little channel. Some of the gates are lifted, and the water is running through those channels into the field, and some gates are closed. Josefina calls these little channels *acequias*—irrigation ditches. It's like using a garden hose at home—except without the hose. And the faucet. And any pipes, and a city water system. But other than that, it's *just* like using a hose.

Women are kneeling at the edge of the stream. They look up and call out greetings as we pass. Tía Dolores stops to exchange a few words, and I watch a girl about my age scrubbing a shirt in the river water. She's using a handful of some kind of shredded-up plant as a soap, it looks like. Clean shirts and skirts and pants are spread on bushes to dry.

After about twenty minutes of walking, Tía Dolores calls back to me, "You can see the village now." I strain my eyes, expecting to see a bustling little town with shops, and people going in and out. But all I see are a few little *adobe* houses arranged around a square *plaza.* We must be getting near the village.

We walk right into the square of houses, and I realize that this *is* the village. Behind the houses are gardens surrounded by stick fences, and corrals for goats and horses.

That's it. Not a shop in sight. And the bustling crowds consist of a few women talking as they grind corn outside with the same type of stone cylinder and flat stone Ana used yesterday—a *mano* and a *metate,* she called them—and some boys playing some kind of a ball game with long sticks.

"Isn't it lovely?" Josefina says happily, looking around her.

"Oh, yes!" I try to match her enthusiasm. I don't want to hurt her feelings, of course, and it is cute. Just not very...busy. I'm starting to realize that there are just a *lot* fewer people in Josefina's world.

A girl comes up from the stream, carrying a basket of folded laundry. "May God grant you a good day, Montoyas!" she calls.

"And you, Ofelia!" Josefina calls back.

"Señora Sanchez's house is right next to the church," Clara tells me. She points to a small house with the door standing open. Lively chatter, delicious smells, and the sounds of knives chopping come from the doorway.

The church is made of *adobe,* just like the houses, but it's bigger and taller, and a bell is hung high above the door. It looks just like those really old churches Dad showed me in Santa Fe—but newer. The skin on the back of my neck prickles as I picture my own self in my jeans, standing in front of one of those old churches along with a bunch of other sightseers, reading a historical plaque. I really have traveled through time.

"Girls, Señora Sanchez is expecting us, but

I brought along some herbs to deliver to your Tía Magdalena," Tía Dolores says. "She's requested them from the *rancho.* Josefina, would you and María like to take them to your godmother? I can do it myself, though, if you're eager to join in the *fandango* preparations."

"María," Josefina says. "What would you like to do?"

I hesitate. The party preparations sound fun, but I want to meet Josefina's special aunt too. This might be my only chance.

❋ *To meet Tía Magdalena,*
   turn to page 111.

❋ *To go straight to Señora Sanchez's,*
   turn to page 113.

osefina and I are up with the sun. Josefina brings a jug of water from the stream, and after a quick breakfast of *tortillas* and goat cheese, we hurry to help Ana with the dishes.

"Girls! We are ready to go!" Señor Montoya calls to us from outside, and we wipe our hands on dish towels, kiss Ana, who is still washing, and run outside through the big wooden doors at the front of the house. Señor Montoya is standing there beside a wagon. Two mules are hitched to the front. I almost fall over. Of course— why would there be a *car* waiting for us? But for some reason, my modern mind had expected us to climb into the back of a *station* wagon and speed off.

The morning is fresh with a cool breeze left over from the night, and puffy white clouds sail high over-head like ladies holding their skirts up as they cross a room. The bright yellow wood of the wagon is cheerful in the brilliant blue morning, and the mules raise their heads when they see us coming. They look eager to go too. Tía Dolores is already waiting on the front seat. On the ground beside her, Josefina's papá smiles at us and extends his arm. "Ladies," he says with a touch of playfulness. Josefina giggles, and he helps her into the wagon, settling her on a board across the back with a blanket laid on top of it. Then he turns to me. "María, allow me to help you," he says.

I look at the mules, and at Josefina beaming at me from the wagon seat, and at Señor Montoya's strong hand and kind face. This will definitely be an adventure—and haven't I been missing the excitement of my old life? Here's some new excitement! Boldly, I grasp Señor Montoya's hand and haul myself up next to Josefina. Carmen hands up a bundle of food for lunch, Señor Montoya swings up into the seat beside Tía Dolores, the mules toss their heads, and with a jolt, we're off!

"Adiós! Adiós!" We wave to the entire family and the servants, who have all come out to see us off.

"Be careful!" Clara calls behind us.

"Bring us back something pretty!" calls Francisca.

✽ *Turn to page 120.*

'd like to meet Tía Magdalena very much," I say. Josefina smiles as if she's pleased, and Tía Dolores takes a bunch of dried leaves and stems out of her basket. I follow Josefina across the flat, hard-packed *plaza* and past the boys shouting over their stickball game.

"I wish I could have played shinny when I was younger," Josefina says as we pass them. That must be the name of the game. It looks just like field hockey—with even the same curved sticks. "But it's a game for boys only."

We stop at the doorway of a small, tidy *adobe* house. "Hello, children!" Tía Magdalena is standing at the doorway to her house. She's gray-haired and wrinkled, with eyes that crinkle when she smiles.

"Tía Magdalena, please allow me to present María, a new friend who has come to us recently," Josefina says respectfully, with her hands clasped in front of her.

Tía Magdalena gives me a sharp look that makes me drop my eyes. It's as if she can see inside my head. But she merely says, "Welcome, child. Come in."

We duck our heads below the low doorway of the house, and immediately a pungent, dusty smell teases my nose. Through a partly open door leading to a back room, I can see bunches of dried herbs hanging upside down from the ceiling beams. Suddenly I picture the shiny white aisles of the drugstore at home, packed with brightly colored bottles of every kind of medicine you could want. I realize that Tía Magdalena's house must be like the village pharmacy, and these plants are the medicines!

❋ *Turn to page 139.*

I really hope I get to meet Tía Magdalena some-time soon, but right now, I'd love to go join the *fandango* preparations," I tell Tía Dolores and Josefina.

Smiling, Tía Dolores waves us toward Señora Sanchez's, and heads for another little house nearby.

"Buenos días!" voices call out as we stand in the doorway. The little house is buzzing with activity. Some girls are hanging *ristras* of dried peppers, women are peeling onions and squash, and still others are making *tortillas* on a flat iron griddle over coals from the fire in the fireplace. Welcoming faces turn toward us, even as the women's hands never stop working.

I follow Josefina around the room as she greets each woman. They smile at us, and the older ones pat our cheeks. It's like a family reunion.

"My dear Josefina!" A comfortable-looking older woman bustles over to us, her apron dusted with flour. "I'm so glad you are here, and your dear sisters." She catches sight of me, and her eyebrows shoot up in sur-prise. "And you've brought a guest!"

Josefina introduces me to Señora Sanchez and quickly tells her my story.

"A *cautiva*!" Her eyes are tender, and she catches

my hand. "We are so glad you have returned, my child. And we have much to keep you busy today!" She laughs out loud as she looks around the chaotic house. "Clara, Ana, I hope you will help me with the bread. And would you younger girls mind little Luisa, Felipe, and baby Mateo while we work?"

"Of course," Josefina says right away, and I nod. I love baby-sitting—back home in Chicago, I'd just started watching our upstairs neighbors' kids before we moved.

Josefina and I herd the little boy and girl into the corner. There, a baby lies on a kind of a small platform lined with sheepskins. It's hanging from the ceiling with ropes. The baby looks up at us with bright black eyes from his soft bed. A strand of coral beads decorates his fat little neck.

"Hello, little one," I coo, leaning over him.

"Play with us, play with us!" The other two crowd around our legs, tugging on our skirts.

"*Sí, sí*," Josefina says, laughing. "María and I will play with you."

I lift Mateo from the cradle and hold his soft, heavy little body close to my chest. I hum him my mockingbird tune. Felipe is clutching a carved wooden horse, and Luisa has a rag doll, with a lovely little dress and teeny braids. It reminds me of my favorite old doll, Clementine. She was a rag doll, too.

Josefina seats herself on the floor with the children and starts a clapping game with them, going faster and faster until they are screaming with laughter. It reminds me of the clapping games we always used to play on the bus, going on school field trips. I stand watching them, jiggling the baby as he slurps on his fingers.

Finally Josefina holds her hands up. "Enough!" she says, pink-cheeked and breathless from laughing. "Now I will tell you a story. Your mamá wants you to rest, I'm sure."

The children lay their heads in her lap, and I sit down and cradle the baby in mine so that he can listen to the story too.

"I'm going to tell you about *La Jornada del Muerto*— do you know that story?" Josefina asks the children. They shake their heads, their eyes fixed on her face.

"Well, you know that our trading caravans have to travel for many months across mountains and desert to bring us wonderful things from Mexico City,"

Josefina says. "And the desert is hot, and dry. Men have died out there."

Josefina pauses for effect. The children are perfectly still, their large eyes shining. I'm still too, I realize, and even the baby seems to be listening.

Josefina goes on. "One stretch of the desert has been especially terrible to the traders. It has no water, and some call the trail that runs through it 'The Route of the Dead Man.'" She widens her eyes dramatically, and Luisa gasps. "The first Spanish settlers crossed that desert long ago. At first, they drank just a little of the water they brought, to save it. But they became so hot and thirsty that they drank a little more. And then a little more. By the end of the second day, they had only enough water left to moisten their tongues. They thought they would surely die."

She stops, and Felipe pipes up, "Did they die?"

"Well," Josefina says. "The settlers had a little dog with them. The pup would range ahead of them during the day, seeing what he could see. But he would always return to camp at night. At sundown on the second day, he came back to camp as usual. But this time, he had mud on his paws. Mud! The settlers looked at one another with hope in their eyes. If there was mud, there must be water. And they were going to find it.

"With the last of their strength, they followed him to a small spring hidden deep in the desert. They drank the water, which saved their lives and allowed them to continue their journey. From then on, that spring was called *Los Charcos del Perillo* so that people would always remember him," Josefina finishes.

The Pools of the Little Dog, I think. *What a good name.*

We are all quiet an instant, and then Luisa bursts out, "That was a good story!"

"Good, good!" her brother echoes, jumping up and clapping his chubby hands.

Josefina smiles and smooths her hand over the tops of their heads. "I'm glad you liked it," she says. "Now it's time to play quietly with your toys."

The children begin making a stable for the horse out of corncobs, and I turn to Josefina.

"They loved that story—actually, *I* loved that story too." I pause. "You're good with them—I should take lessons from you on caring for children."

Josefina smiles and holds her arms out for the baby. "I learned that story from Mamá. All I have to do is close my eyes, and I can hear her telling it."

I pass Mateo over to her and let my eyes wander around the room. The women are all talking together as they work. Their laughs are those low, familiar ones you hear with people who've known one another all their lives. Outside the small window, I can hear the shouts of the boys as they play a ball game.

Josefina sits peacefully, rocking the baby and humming. She looks utterly content, as comfortable here as at home, surrounded by people who love her. I swallow and pretend to be folding Luisa's handkerchief, which has fallen to the floor. I see myself walking through the crowded halls at school, alone, and sitting solitary on my rock outside the house. People are around me all the time, but I still feel so alone. I wish I could bottle some of what Josefina has here and take it back to my own time with me.

✸ *Turn to page 124.*

he last thing I hear is the trilling notes of my flute, and then everything goes black.

When the blackness lifts, the sun is still hovering just above the horizon, flooding the rocks and sage and *piñón* trees with golden light. Daisy raises her head from gnawing at her paw and laps my hand as if to say *Welcome back.* In the house, I can see Henry holding the paper he's pulled from his backpack, and Mom and Dad bending over it. It's the same moment as when I left. But yet . . . it feels different. Almost as if I've brought some of Josefina's love for this place back with me. I can see it through her eyes now.

I climb down off the rock, and Daisy slips down beside me. I survey the distant hills with my hands on my hips. The three rounded spires point to the sky. Maybe Dad will hike to them with me tomorrow. I have a feeling this desert has a lot more adventures to share. I'm ready to find out what they are.

✹ *The End* ✹

To read this story another way and see how different choices lead to a different ending, turn back to page 26.

hree hours later, I'm hot, cramped, hungry—and still in the wagon. The wagon wheels squeak so loudly that conversation is difficult, and a fine layer of yellow dust has settled over everything and everybody. Rocky hills roll by endlessly, with small, glinting rivers winding their way around the bases. *Piñón* trees. Small *adobe* houses with stick fences like Josefina's. Then, bigger hills—mountains, actually—green and gold and touched with snow at the tops. They look cool. But I'm not.

I'm done with being jolted on the rutted road so hard that the top of my head feels like it's going to come loose. Even the cold *tamales* we've eaten for lunch don't refresh me. I think longingly of zipping into downtown Santa Fe in our car—a quick fifteen minutes, with air-conditioning.

But Josefina and Tía Dolores don't seem to mind the hot, bumpy ride at all. In fact, Josefina leans close to me and chatters on, pointing out landmarks here and there.

"María," she says now, "wait until you see the marketplace in Santa Fe! *Everyone* is there, and you'll see so many things to trade. And we'll visit with Abuelito and

Abuelita. It's been so long since I've seen them!"

She's practically bouncing up and down on the seat. It's pretty clear that Santa Fe is the most exciting place she's ever been. And her excitement is catching. I can feel my heart beating faster as at last Señor Montoya announces that we're not far away.

Already we're seeing more people on the road: other wagons, men on horseback, people walking with bundles on their backs, and big carts drawn by teams of oxen. Their wheels are incredibly squeaky, so loud that I want to cover my ears with my hands. Josefina mouths something at me, but I can't hear her over the racket of those squeaky wheels! I lean closer.

"There are a lot of people on the road because it's market day," she says.

I peer eagerly through the clouds of dust billowing around us. Then Señor Montoya shouts, "Whoa!" and the mules halt. The dust settles. We're at a crossroads. The traffic is flowing down the main road, but a smaller road branches off to the right.

Señor Montoya turns in the wagon seat to face us. "Girls, I'm taking Dolores to her parents' house now.

She wants to visit with Abuelito and Abuelita while I go to the *plaza* to trade and speak to the officials about María."

Tía Dolores twists around also. "Your grandparents will be eager to see you, Josefina. But it's up to you girls—you may go to the house with me now. Or you may go to the *plaza* first and join us later."

Josefina's forehead creases. "Oh, I want to visit with Abuelito and Abuelita! But . . . it's been so long since I've seen the *plaza*! Will Abuelita be disappointed if I don't come to visit with her right away?"

"She may," Tía Dolores says gently. "You know that she has strong opinions about how young ladies should behave. But you have traveled all this way. I know that you are looking forward to the market."

"Oh, I can't decide." Josefina wavers. "María? What would *you* like to do?"

"Um . . . um," I stammer. I don't want to get Josefina in trouble with her grandparents, but I'm dying to see the market she's been talking about, all the people and the trading in the *plaza.* And Josefina doesn't want to miss it either, I can tell.

On the other hand, the thought of getting out of

the hot sun, washing up, and getting something to eat is beyond tempting. And I'm really curious to meet Josefina's *abuelito* and *abuelita.* Josefina has told me that her grandfather tells the best stories she's ever heard.

❋ *To visit Abuelito and Abuelita,*
   turn to page 126.

❋ *To go with Señor Montoya to the plaza,*
   turn to page 132.

The cooks have made a huge stack of *tortillas,* and Señora Sanchez's house is tidy as a mouse's hole, as my grandmother used to say. We all eat a quick meal of stew, and then Tía Dolores announces that it's time to return home for the *siesta.*

The white-hot sun is overhead now and seems to bore a hole straight into my skull as we trudge back along the path back to the *rancho.* The freshness of the morning has worn off, and even the bushes at the side of the path look dusty and tired. Sleeping through the hottest part of the day sounds pretty good in a world without air-conditioning.

But then my thoughts start to turn from sleep to the condition of my stomach. I'm starting to feel kind of queasy. As we keep walking in the blazing sun, I feel worse and worse. Oh boy. My stomach is definitely feeling bad. I think back to the stew I ate, and I almost groan out loud. No one else notices, but Josefina looks over at me quickly and takes my arm. "Are you well, María?" she murmurs, and I just shake my head.

When we finally reach the Montoyas' house, I head straight for the sleeping *sala* and collapse on the bedroll

Josefina spreads out for us. The other girls lie down too, and soon the room is filled with peaceful breathing as everyone takes a nap. But I can't sleep. Instead, I just lie there, nausea rolling in my stomach.

❋ *Turn to page 129.*

'd like to go with you," I say to Tía Dolores. "If that is all right with you, Josefina."

"*Sí*, of course," Josefina says right away. Her face is lit up with the anticipation of seeing her grandparents.

At a large *adobe* house on the outskirts of the city, Señor Montoya halts the mules and helps us down from the wagon.

"Andres, what is this lovely surprise you've brought? We were expecting you alone, and now look at this—three beautiful flowers to brighten our *sala*!" A cheery-looking older man with a big gray mustache hurries from the doorway. "My beautiful daughter." He kisses Tía Dolores and takes Josefina's face in both his hands. "And my littlest granddaughter. You are even more beautiful and grown-up than the last time I saw you."

"Papá, please meet our guest, María," Tía Dolores introduces me. I clasp my hands and bow my head the way I've seen Josefina do. Tía Dolores quickly explains my story, and Josefina's *abuelito* looks at me kindly.

"*Bienvenida*," he says, patting my head. "We welcome you to our house."

Their house is built sort of like Josefina's, with big

thick walls and a central courtyard with rooms surrounding it. In the main *sala,* an elegant gray-haired woman dressed all in black looks up from her sewing as we come in.

"Dolores! What a wonderful surprise!" she exclaims. "My dear daughter, you are covered with dust. Go wash immediately." This has to be Josefina's *abuelita.* Josefina has told me she bosses everyone around.

Josefina's grandmother looks Josefina and me up and down, as Tía Dolores explains who I am all over again. "You must wash also, children," she commands us. "And then we will have refreshments."

The cool water a servant pours into a bowl for us feels wonderful on my dusty face, and I leave some pretty impressive hand and face marks on the towel. Josefina looks refreshed also. When we join Tía Dolores and the grandparents in the *sala,* two cups of cool water with mint leaves are waiting for us.

"How was your journey, Dolores?" Abuelita asks her daughter. "Was the road terribly dusty?"

I straighten up. *Yes!* bubbles behind my lips, but of course I know enough by now not to speak until I'm spoken to.

"Not terribly, Mamá," Tía Dolores replies quietly. "And not too hot, either."

Josefina nods agreement, and I look from one to the other. What? Weren't we all in the same wagon? Or were they on a different trip?

Then I realize—Josefina and Tía Dolores *did* think the journey was dusty and hot and probably just as uncomfortable as I did. But they don't complain. What's the point? There's no other way to get from the *rancho* to Santa Fe. Besides, I've been in Josefina's world long enough to see that they just don't complain, not even when there's something to complain about. Except for Francisca!

❋ *Turn to page 168.*

A late-afternoon sun gathers in the corners of the room, and as a cool breeze blows through the tiny window, the others begin to wake up.

"It's time to dress!" Francisca sings, jumping up from her bed. She goes straight to the trunk and starts searching through the layers of folded clothes. "María, I have a beautiful skirt I can lend you. I think it will fit if we— What's wrong?" She stops rummaging and stares at me.

"Nothing," I try to say, but another wave of nausea rolls through me. "Ooooh." I lie back on the pillow with sweat beading my forehead.

Beside me, Josefina is awake too. She leans over me and feels my head, then my palms. "You're very pale, María," she says. "And your hands are clammy."

"I'm a little sick to my stomach," I confess. "But I don't want to miss the *fandango*."

"You can't miss it!" Francisca cries. "It would be terrible if you had to stay here sick, while everyone else is dancing and listening to lovely music."

Clara frowns at her sister. "Francisca, how can María go, when she can hardly get out of bed?" she says sensibly. "Be practical."

Francisca ignores Clara and pulls a blue-green skirt from the trunk. She lays the lovely soft fabric in my lap. "Look at this, María, and you'll be up in a moment! I'll lend it to you for the evening."

Josefina gently nudges both sisters aside and folds the skirt. "María, you certainly can't go if you're ill," she tells me, sounding as firm as Tía Dolores. "I'll help you feel better, though, don't worry." She climbs off the bed and disappears through the doorway.

Soon she's back, carrying a steaming bowl in both hands. "I made you a settling tea," she says, placing the bowl in my hands. "Tansy mustard. It's what Tía Magdalena always recommends for upset stomachs."

I lean over and sniff. *Whoa.* I can't help wrinkling my nose and backing away. Unlike the chamomile tea Josefina made me when I first arrived, this one smells like burnt rubber.

I don't know what to do. I want to take the medicine—and I don't. That smelly brew is scary, even though I know that Josefina is learning healing. But I'm dying to go to the party, and I'm sure I won't get better in time without treatment.

I look into Josefina's dark eyes. I want to trust her.

She's my friend. Then the room is thrown into sudden darkness as the sun sinks below the window, and a chill settles over me. I suddenly long for home, yet at the same time, I want to stay with Josefina. And my stomach still feels awful.

❋ *To refuse the medicine and go home,*
   turn to page 137.

❋ *To take the medicine,*
   turn to page 156.

'd like to go to the *plaza* with you, Señor Montoya," I say rather shyly.

Josefina squeals and squeezes my hand. "Oh, María, it's the most exciting place in the world!"

"Now, now, girls," Señor Montoya says. "I have a lot of business to do. You may go, but you must keep out of trouble." He gives us a stern look.

I nod hastily. I can't imagine disobeying anyone with eyebrows like that.

We drop Tía Dolores at the door of a big *adobe* house that looks a lot like Josefina's, and she waves as we disappear back into the dust cloud that surrounds the road.

Soon we see more and more wagons and walkers on the road. People leading horses and pack mules are so close on both sides of us, I can almost touch them. In front of us, a woman is carrying a crate of live chickens balanced on her head, and beside her, a man has a huge basket of peppers lashed to his back. The houses are crowded close together now, and they extend as far as I can see.

Then in front of us, I catch a glimpse of a broad open space lined with *adobe* buildings on all sides.

Señor Montoya calls back to us, "There it is, girls—
the Santa Fe *plaza*." He points across the *plaza* to one
of the long, low buildings with a wide, shaded
veranda that takes up one whole side of the square.
He tells me that it's the Palace of the Governors, where
the officials work. An *adobe* palace—I never imagined
such a thing!

"Isn't it wonderful?" Josefina breathes. Her eyes are
shining beneath the *rebozo* draped over her head, and
she clutches the wagon seat in excitement. "So many
people! You can see *everything* in Santa Fe—everyone
comes here."

There's something familiar in her words and the
expression on her face. Then I know—it's just how
I used to feel when I'd go downtown back in Chicago.

*Santa Fe for Josefina is like Chicago was for me—the
big, dramatic center of everything,* I realize. This is the
most sophisticated, modern place she's ever been.
Okay. I'm going to think that way too. I take a deep
breath, wipe the dust off my forehead—it's mostly
mud now, since it's mixed with sweat—and sit up
a little straighter.

We roll right up to the *plaza,* and I gawk. In an

instant, everything I thought about Santa Fe being sleepy and dull is blasted apart. There are so many people and so many things that I hardly know where to look. Chicago's Magnificent Mile has *nothing* on this place.

Josefina can see how wide my eyes are, and she points out the different people and sights as we drive around the edge of the *plaza.* I listen hard to her brief descriptions: priests in sober black robes, and people from the surrounding farms and *ranchos* leading goats, horses, mules, and oxen to sell. Cages of chickens rest on the ground, waiting for buyers, and dogs mill around the ankles of their owners.

Along one side of the *plaza*, horses are lined up. Men are walking around, patting their necks, examining their legs. "Those are horses for trade," Josefina says. "Aren't they beautiful? Maybe we'll go look at them later."

As our wagon rounds a corner of the *plaza,* Josefina says, "These are Pueblo Indians." She points out a group of people sitting on the ground, with melons, pumpkins, and apples spread out on a hide in front of them. Their hair is cut differently from that of Josefina's family, with bangs straight across, and they wear white shirts with shawls draped over one shoulder. "Maybe we'll see Mariana, my friend. She lives at the *pueblo.* Her grandfather Esteban is Papá's good friend. They trade together."

Josefina gazes across the *plaza.* "Oh, look!" she says. "Here comes Señor García, who owns more land than anyone else."

I stare at the elegant man riding into the *plaza* on a bay horse. His saddle is mounted with silver, and he wears odd, tight pants of green silk that have buttons all the way up the leg. He's left half the buttons undone, though, so that his white stockings show. "I think he forgot to button his pants," I say, and Josefina laughs merrily.

"You *have* been away a long time, María! That's just the latest fashion. And there's one of the trappers!" She nods her head at what I first take to be a bear riding a burly horse. Then I realize that it's a man with a bushy beard and long matted hair, wearing clothes made from skins, and with a big pile of furs tied on the horse behind him. "They live alone in the mountains and hunt and trap for months at a time. Then they come down here to trade their furs," she explains.

"Oh." I nod understanding. How could I ever think Josefina's Santa Fe was dull?

✽ *Turn to page 144.*

I set down the bowl of tea I've been cradling, without taking a sip. "*Gracias* for the tea, Josefina, but I don't think I can drink it right now. I should probably stay back and rest," I say.

"Are you sure, María?" Her dark eyes are troubled. "Do you want me to stay with you?"

"No, I don't want you to miss the *fandango* just because I'm sick," I say. "Go, and have a good time for me."

Josefina strokes my hand, her brow furrowed, and then sighs and stands. "Only if you're sure you're not very sick."

"I'm really okay. Just tired, mostly." I push myself up higher in the bedroll. "But you know . . . I think that I'm starting to remember some things about my family."

"Oh, María, that's wonderful!" Josefina beams and pulls the blanket up around me. She tucks in the corners and smooths it out. "Rest now. We must go, but Teresita will be here if you need anything."

"Josefina—" I catch at her hand as she starts to turn away. "I . . . think I remember where my home is now. I must leave you soon to look for it. But I couldn't have remembered without you. So, I wanted to make sure I told you ... *gracias.*"

A grin spreads across my friend's face, and our eyes meet in a bond that I know will last me forever.

When everyone leaves, and the room is in darkness, I raise the flute to my lips and play the special tune. I'm going home.

✸ *Turn to page 147.*

osefina offers Tía Magdalena the herbs, but the healer shakes her head. "Come into the storeroom, and I'll show you how to put them away yourself."

She leads us into the back room. Here, the walls are bright white, and jars of all shapes and sizes line wooden shelves built along one wall. "Take one down," Tía Magdalena says, seeing me eye the jars.

I reach for a small brown jar, lift the lid, and peer inside. It's full of dark, red-brown flakes.

"Deer blood," Tía Magdalena says, and my head jerks up, my eyes wide. Josefina grins at me.

"It's good to help you regain strength after an injury," Josefina says. "You mix it with water and drink it."

I hurriedly replace the jar on the shelf. "Maybe next time," I say, and they both laugh.

Tía Magdalena shows us how to prepare the herbs we've brought. We strip the dried leaves from the stems and crumble them into small bits in a bowl. Then I scrape them into an empty jar, and Josefina caps it with a round wooden plug.

"Now," Tía Magdalena says, smiling at us, "you

are my guests and we must have some tea."

We settle ourselves around the scrubbed wooden table in the front room, and the *curandera* brews a pot of mint tea. It smells delicious, and I hold my cup out toward the teapot.

"What is this cut?" Tía Magdalena pours the tea and sets down the pot. She takes my hand and gently touches a wound on the back. I've noticed it, but I haven't thought much about it. I must have gotten it when I "arrived" here.

"It's nothing," I say. But the skin around it is turning red, and when Tía Magdalena touches it, it hurts.

"You must care for it," Tía Magdalena says sternly. "Josefina, do you remember how to make the vinegar soak?"

"Mix vinegar and water and soak a cloth in the mixture, and then bind the wound with the soaked cloth," Josefina answers.

"Very good!" Tía Magdalena's eyes crinkle and her voice is warm as she praises my friend. "Do you think Josefina will make a good *curandera* someday soon, María?"

I nod and smile, but Tía Magdalena gives me that

intent look again. "You are sad, my child," she says. She makes it a statement, rather than a question. "Tell me what's troubling you."

I look into her wrinkled face and then at Josefina's round, rosy one beside her. All of a sudden, all the tears I've kept back since we moved well up inside me. My throat swells and aches, and I can feel tears gathering at the corners of my eyes, threatening to spill. I know my face is going blotchy, the way it always does when I cry. I shake my head, not trusting my voice.

Tía Magdalena reaches out and puts her hand over mine. Her palm is warm and rough. The tears erupt. "I miss home," I weep, and I can't stop crying. I cradle my head in my arms and sob.

"María has been a *cautiva* until very recently," Josefina explains quietly to Tía Magdalena over my head.

"Ah," the healer says. Through my tears, I feel her callused hand stroke my hair. "Cry, child. Let the sadness flow out."

After a minute, my tears slow. I sit up, gulping. Josefina scoots over so that she is right beside me, and passes me a clean, folded handkerchief. I mop my cheeks. The cloth smells of soap and lavender. She puts her arm around me, and I lean against my friend's shoulder. I feel wrung out but peaceful, the way you do after a good cry.

Tía Magdalena dips Josefina's handkerchief in a bowl of water and bathes my face. It reminds me of the way my mom always wiped my face with a cold washcloth after I'd been crying when I was younger.

"It's a terrible thing, to lose one's home," the healer says. "It can break your heart apart."

Her words feel very true.

"I can't imagine having to leave the *rancho* and Papá and Tía Dolores and my sisters," Josefina says.

"And yet, you too know what it is like to lose something very precious." Tía Magdalena wrings the handkerchief out. "And even though you will never stop remembering your dear mamá, are you happy again, Josefina?"

Josefina looks a little surprised. "I suppose I am," she says, knitting her brows. "I hadn't thought about it that way."

"And you will be happy again too, María," the *curandera* tells me. "The healing power of time can be greater than any medicine I have in my storeroom."

I sit up and take a deep, wavery breath. "I feel a little better now, actually."

Tía Magdalena smiles. "And the healing power of tears should not be forgotten either. Feelings kept inside can fester like a wound."

We chat and drink the mint tea, and eat licorice-flavored cookies Josefina calls *bizcochitos.* The sun traces a path across the yellow wood of the table, and outside the window, swallows swoop and call to one another.

❋ *Turn to page 149.*

eñor Montoya parks the wagon in the central *plaza* and unhitches the mules, who look glad to be resting. While they eat feed out of nosebags, Señor Montoya takes some folded papers out of his satchel and looks them over.

I watch a settler setting up his trade goods just a few feet away. He is arranging stacks of blankets and strings of shiny, dark red *chiles* on a canvas cloth. He has small bags of some kind of nut, too. Josefina says they are pine nuts.

"Josefina!" a voice calls, and I turn around to see a dark-haired girl running up to us. Her heavy bangs fall almost to her eyebrows. She wears moccasins like mine and Josefina's, but hers are white, and she has a blanket draped over one shoulder and tied around her waist with a beautiful woven sash.

"Mariana!" Josefina greets her friend with a big smile. "This is María, who is staying with us."

Mariana has one of those smiles that makes everyone else feel like smiling too. "Come see my grandfather," she invites us. "He's brought some of the best pottery we've made this summer."

"That sounds fun," I say, but then a man steps up

beside us. By now, I can tell that he's a *patrón,* like Señor Montoya.

"*Buenos días,* Señor Montoya," he says.

"*Buenos días,*" Josefina's papá responds. "I hope your harvest has been good, Señor Jaramillo."

"*Sí,* God has blessed us this year," the man replies. "But there is a matter I wanted to discuss with you, about the *acequia* near the edge of the village . . ."

As the two men talk with their heads close together, we hear a voice calling. "Mariana!"

Josefina's friend turns to us.

"That's my grandfather! Shall I tell him you're coming with me?" she asks.

I take a step toward her, but something else catches my eye. Señor Jaramillo has a clay flute strung around his neck on a cord. It's a bird too, but not as fine as mine. It's smaller, and there are no wing or feather markings.

"My friend María has a beautiful flute too," Josefina tells Señor Jaramillo.

I look up, startled. I didn't expect Josefina to mention my flute. It's not that it's a secret, exactly. It's just that I think of it as a sort of private thing.

"Do you?" Señor Jaramillo asks. "May I see your flute? Fellow musicians always like to see new instruments." He smiles, and his eyes are kind.

I untie the pouch Josefina gave me to wear at my waist and bring out my flute. He takes it in his hands and turns it over. "This is skillfully made, María. Finer, perhaps, than my own flutes." He pauses. "Would you consider trading it?"

"Oh, no," I say right away. But Señor Jaramillo has put his hand in his pocket. He pulls out a small blue rock. It's about the size of a quarter, and it gleams bright blue-green. Some parts are flat, and those surfaces shine cool and blue.

"Oooh," I gasp, and beside me, I hear Josefina catch her breath in delight.

"Turquoise," she breathes.

"The turquoise is not valuable, but it is beautiful, as you can see," Señor Jaramillo says. He holds the turquoise out closer to us. It glows in his hand like a piece of the sky fallen to the earth. With his other hand, he reaches for my flute.

❋ *Turn to page 151.*

Birdy!"

I open my eyes. I'm back on my boulder, and Mom is calling from the doorway of the house. Quickly, I sit up, brushing at my T-shirt as she comes over.

"I've been calling and calling," she says. "Were you asleep?"

"Um, sort of . . ." I clamber down from the boulder, and Daisy jumps down behind me.

Mom loops her arm through mine. "Well, let's go in. Dad's *tamales* are almost done."

"Yum," I say, and I realize I already feel better.

She shoots me a curious glance. "I thought you didn't like them, honey. I was going to offer to make you a chicken breast."

I think back to the clay platter on Josefina's table. The steam rising from the husk-wrapped bundles. The faces of Josefina, Clara, Francisca, and Tía Dolores, glowing in the candlelight—loving one another, loving their home.

"Well, maybe I've just realized that there's a lot to love here in New Mexico. More than I thought before," I tell her. We're at the house, and Mom opens the door.

The warm aroma of cooking billows out, riding on a wave of Henry's and Dad's laughter. "Maybe I just needed some time." Like nearly two hundred years.

✸ *The End* ✸

To read this story another way and see how different choices lead to a different ending, turn back to page 131.

We stay so long at Tía Magdalena's that we never make it over to Señora Sanchez's. Tía Dolores has to fetch us to go back home and rest before the *fandango*. She brings us a few *tamales* to eat on the way.

As we leave the little house, my heart feels lighter than it has since the day our moving truck pulled onto the westbound highway out of Chicago. It's amazing that just talking can make me feel so much better. It's like having healing power in your words, I think, as I walk down the dirt path beside Josefina. And all you have to do is notice when someone is feeling sad or lonely—and you can talk with them and help them feel better, just like Tía Magdalena did with me.

We walk quickly, eager to reach home, and my thoughts seem to keep time with our footsteps. I could even do what Tía Magdalena and Josefina have done—I mean, not heal people with medicines, but help them in other ways—just by listening when someone needs to talk. Even people in my own family.

I swallow then, suddenly ashamed of myself. Henry and Mom and Dad seem so happy with our move, but they've had big adjustments too. Even Audrey at school—maybe she's trying to be friends with me because she could use someone to talk to also. I just haven't been paying attention.

I suddenly realize how many times Josefina has noticed when I'm feeling tired or sad. She's lost more than I have, and somehow, she still manages to pay attention to others. And she actually seems to *like* it— it makes her happy. Maybe listening to others a little more and myself a little less would make me happier, too. I don't know—but at least I could try.

❋ *Turn to page 153.*

"**N**o!" I cry suddenly and clutch my flute to me. The spell is broken. My only link to home!

Josefina sees the distress on my face and quickly steps between me and the *patrón*. "We are not interested in trading. *Gracias,*" she tells Señor Jaramillo firmly.

Señor Jaramillo looks at us narrowly but nods and moves over to Josefina's papá to continue the *acequia* discussion.

I'm breathing hard, and my palms are wet with sweat. "I—I think I should sit down," I say.

"*Sí,* let's rest by the wagon," Josefina says right away. "The heat and the dust are too much for anybody."

We walk slowly back toward the wagon and hoist ourselves up to sit on the seat, with our legs dangling. I bow my head and try to gather my thoughts while Josefina pats my back. I squeeze the clay flute tightly.

"Be gentle, María." Josefina delicately loosens my fingers. "You'll shatter your flute if you squeeze it so hard."

I look at the concerned face of my friend, who can see how distressed I am and who is so caring, even when she doesn't know exactly what's wrong.

Josefina, I wish I could explain, I think. *My link to home is more precious than ever now that I've almost lost it.* My *home* is precious, and my family. I love Josefina's world, but I want to go back to my own, I realize suddenly. I can see now how much it means to me—and how much I would miss my family if I couldn't see them again.

✸ *Turn to page 161.*

s soon as we return to the *rancho,* Josefina, Clara, Francisca, and I all curl up on our beds to rest before the *fandango.* When we get up, the sun is setting outside in a beautiful glow of dusky purple and fiery rose-orange. Black clouds are silhouetted against the horizon, and the air is soft and scented with pine and wood smoke. I feel the old party excitement rising, and Josefina and her sisters must feel it too, because Francisca is singing as she twists her braids up onto her head, and Clara is dancing with Josefina in a rare light-hearted moment.

"You must let me help you with your hair, María," Josefina offers. She sits me down on a chair and combs out my mussed braid, carefully untangling the snarls with her fingers. Then deftly, she braids my hair again neatly. "I'll lend you my blue silk ribbon," she says. I get the sense from the way she says this that the ribbon is a special treasure. She gets up and opens the trunk sitting against the wall. Digging carefully through the items inside, she pulls out a little bundle of white cloth. She opens it reverently and pulls out a sky-blue silk ribbon.

"*Gracias,*" I tell her, gently stroking the soft silk

between my fingers. I tie it at the end of my braid. Josefina pulls on a blue-green skirt and a fresh blouse. Then we stand back and admire each other in our party finery.

Tía Dolores looks in at the doorway. "Girls, it's time to go," she says. All talking and laughing, we head out into the twilight, full of the promise of the party.

Inside Señora Sanchez's house, the dancing has already begun. Ladies in full skirts trimmed with ribbons sway with gentlemen in short jackets. At one end of the room, a fiddler and a guitar player fill the air with a rollicking tune that reminds me a little of square-dance music. Candles flicker and flare on the walls, and in a corner, a table is spread with a cloth embroidered with flowers. A painted pottery bowl of flowers sits in the middle.

Francisca is whisked away immediately by a handsome young man, and Tía Dolores laughs and accepts an invitation to dance from Tomás, Ana's husband. My feet are tapping, but I notice that no one my age is waltzing. Instead, Josefina pulls me down to sit on the floor with her. All around us, other kids are sitting on the floor and crowded on the *bancos* with their grandparents, watching the dancers and clapping in time.

Dip-sway-three, one-two-three. I hum with the music. "I think I could play this on my flute," I whisper to Josefina. I take the little bird from my pouch and start to lift it to my lips, but Josefina gently shakes her head "no."

I sigh. It seems like a *fandango* might not be as much fun as I thought. Then Josefina leans over and grins. "Let's go practice the dance steps outside," she says, keeping her voice low.

I jump up right away, but just then, a wonderful fragrance floats toward us. Señora Sanchez is putting *tortillas* and a pot of chicken stew on the table. My stomach is rumbling. It's craving food almost as much as my feet are craving dancing.

❋ *To sample the tortillas and chicken,*
   turn to page 158.

❋ *To go outside and dance,*
   turn to page 173.

close my eyes and take a big swallow. Then my eyes open wide in surprise. It's not that bad!

After a half hour or so, the gurgling in my stomach dies down and the nausea dissolves. I laugh and hug Josefina, and we do a celebratory little dance. "You cured me!" I tell her. "All your lessons with Tía Magdalena have paid off."

"Oh…" Josefina brushes away my praise, but her cheeks are pink with pleasure.

Then Josefina and Francisca help me dress in a white blouse with lace flounces on the sleeves and around the neckline, and Francisca's beautiful blue-green skirt that flies out when I twirl. Josefina ties a long blue fringed sash around my waist, and Francisca tucks a bright yellow flower into my braid. They stand back to admire me, and Clara sighs. "You are beautiful, María. The skirt makes your eyes look green."

"Gracias," I say, trying to imitate Josefina's modest tone.

Tía Dolores and Ana join us. Tía Dolores looks beautiful in a dark red flowered dress, and Ana is wearing a black skirt with yellow bands at the hem. "My dear children, you look lovely," Tía Dolores says, her warm smile lighting her face. She smooths a stray tendril behind Francisca's ear and pats Clara's cheek. "Now, then, we're all ready! We must go—we don't want to be late."

A wagon, with two mules harnessed to it, is waiting for us. Ana's husband, Tomás, helps us climb onto the boards laid across the wagon box, while Tía Dolores sits in the front with Señor Montoya. With a jolt, the wagon starts, and we all set out in the sunset for the village.

✸ *Turn to page 164.*

ancing sounds wonderful, but my stomach is calling louder. "Come! Eat!" Señora Sanchez calls to the room, and the musicians end their music with a flourish. The adults crowd toward the tables, laughing and talking with one another as they pile chicken stew and *tamales* on their plates. A gray-haired man with a big mustache is teasing Señora Sanchez. Josefina's papá helps an older man reach the *tamales.* Their faces are glowing in the candlelight. It feels like a family gathering, even though I know they're not related. But in another way, they kind of are—it feels as if everyone here belongs to one big extended family.

My stomach is gurgling, but I wait politely with Josefina, Clara, and the rest of the children for the adults to finish before we serve ourselves. I heap the delicious-smelling stew, which is full of squash, tomatoes, and peppers, onto my plate and add two *tamales* at the side. Clara and I crowd next to Josefina on a *banco,* set our plates on our laps, and eat quickly, filling our empty stomachs. All around, the other guests are laughing and talking as they eat.

At last, my plate is empty. I mop up the last bits of stew with a *tortilla,* then sigh and set down my plate on the floor beside me. I'm perfectly content with my belly full and my friend beside me here in the bright, warm *sala. There's nothing more I want,* I think to myself—and then I realize that maybe this is a perfect time to leave Josefina's world. Maybe I can bring some of this peace I feel back with me.

I take a deep breath. "Josefina, I . . . I think it's time for me to go," I tell my friend. "Tomorrow, perhaps."

Her eyes widen with surprise and concern. "But María! We haven't found your family yet," she protests. "Where will you go?"

I put my hand over hers. The music has started again and the adults are dancing. The lilting notes swirl around us. I lower my voice. "I know. But . . . I just have this *feeling* that I'll be able to find my family. I . . . can't exactly explain it. It's just a sense I have that I might be able to find my way home now." I look right into her eyes. *I'll be able to find my way home in my heart,* I tell her silently.

Josefina's eyes narrow, and then she nods slowly. "*Sí,* I understand. I know that sometimes you just have to trust that things will be well. Even if you don't know why or how."

I squeeze my friend's hand. "But I do know one thing—I'm awfully glad I met you on my journey. It..." I hesitate, searching for the right words. "It's almost been like coming home. You and Tía Dolores and Teresita and Francisca and Clara—you all gave me the strength I need to find my way home."

"María...in case I forget to tell you in the morning...thank you for being my sister—for a little while." Josefina's eyes are shiny.

I grab her into a hug. "What do you mean, 'for a little while'? I'll always be your sister." My throat swells and I feel my eyes getting wet. "Always," I repeat softly.

❋ The End ❋

To read this story another way and see how different choices lead to a different ending, turn back to page 94.

I realize that Josefina is still watching me, her brows knit. I sit up straighter and swipe at the sweat on my forehead. "I'm all right," I tell her.

"Are you sure?" she asks, and I nod.

"In that case, why don't we go visit with Mariana?" We slide down from the seat of the wagon and cross over to Señor Montoya. "Papá, may we see Mariana?" Josefina asks quietly.

Señor Montoya nods. "Yes. Tell Esteban I will be over soon to greet him," he says.

"Come!" Josefina gives me an eager smile. We weave our way over to Mariana through the piles of goods displayed on hides, and past mules and bleating goats tethered together, waiting for new owners.

"Oh!" A rider with spurs on a big black horse crosses right in front of me. A rifle is stuck into a scabbard on his saddle, and a sword hangs from his hip.

"A soldier," Josefina whispers in my ear. "They travel with the caravans bringing goods from Mexico City, to protect them from bandits."

I follow Josefina over to a hide spread on the ground, where a gray-haired man is sitting calmly. His straight hair hangs to his shoulders, unlike Señor

Montoya's, which is cut short, and he wears a piece
of cloth tied around his forehead. His moccasins are
white, like Mariana's, and he wears a white shirt and
pants with a dark shawl over one shoulder.

Spread out before him are pottery jugs and bowls
in neat rows. They are made of smooth reddish clay.
I've seen jugs just like this at Josefina's house. I wonder
if her papá trades with Esteban for them.

"Grandfather, Josefina has a visitor staying with
her. This is María." Mariana speaks quietly, with her
eyes down, just as Josefina does when she talks to
her papá.

"Welcome, María," Esteban says.

"Gracias." I clasp my hands against my skirt and
cast my eyes down to my moccasins.

Esteban doesn't say anything more, but one by one,
he offers each of us a little open-faced pie, filled with
fruit—some kind of berry.

"Gracias, Grandfather," Mariana says, and Josefina
and I echo her.

Esteban nods in a dignified way, but I think I spot
a small smile crinkling his cheeks.

The pies smell delicious, and I suddenly remember

how hungry I am. We sit on the ground near Esteban and devour them.

"Do you think your grandfather will let you come with us to see the horses for trade at the other side of the *plaza*?" Josefina asks Mariana, as we wipe our sticky fingers on Josefina's handkerchief.

Mariana doesn't reply but catches her grandfather's eye. He nods and smiles, which must mean yes, because Mariana takes one of my hands and Josefina takes the other and they skip me off across the hard-packed dirt to the side of the *plaza* nearest the huge church.

❋ *Turn to page 177.*

Light and music pour from the doorway of Señora Sanchez's house, greeting us. The large main room is transformed from the busy working scene of this morning.

Brightly dressed ladies and their partners are already twirling about to the music of a violin and two guitars played by three musicians in the corner. Older men and women are clustered on the *bancos* around the edges of the room, chatting and watching the dancing, while children play on the floor or sit in their laps. The twirling ladies seem as light as butterflies, their feet barely touching the floor. Francisca and Ana are immediately whirled away to dance. "Come on!" I tug at Josefina's hand. "Let's dance too."

Josefina looks shocked. "Oh no, María. We are too young to dance, of course. We can watch, though—here." She squeezes onto the corner of a *banco,* and I crowd in beside her.

Too young to dance? My hands pat in time to the music, and my body yearns to be out there twirling around. But I've been in Josefina's world long enough now to know that there are a lot of rules about how young girls behave.

At least there's still plenty to see. We take turns picking out the skirts we like best, and Josefina gives me a little background on the different couples. Francisca floats past with a handsome boy, glancing up at him through her eyelashes. Ana and her husband Tomás smile at each other as they dance. Then Josefina sits up a little straighter, and I follow her gaze. Tía Dolores and Señor Montoya are waltzing together. As if carried on the waves of music, they skim around the room.

"They dance so well together," I whisper to Josefina. Tía Dolores's face is lit with a warm smile as Señor Montoya inclines his dark head toward her.

"Yes, they do," Josefina murmurs back. She sounds a little surprised, as if the thought is new to her, and her eyes follow her aunt and her father as they dance in each other's arms.

The candles flicker and flare in their holders, throwing a magical glow over the room, and along one wall, I can see a cloth-covered table loaded with *tortillas,* stew, white cheese, bowls of custard, and *tamales.* The musicians are playing a lively tune, and the men stamp their heavy boots in time and the women clap their hands, their lovely shawls trailing from their arms. Too soon, the musicians put down their instruments for a break.

"Josefina, my dear, your hair is disheveled." Tía Dolores has come up behind us. Josefina raises her hand to her braid. "Here, come let me fix it."

She draws Josefina to a bench in a corner, and I follow. Gently, she loosens the ribbon Josefina has tied at the end of her braid, and with her fingers, she untangles the wavy strands. "Your hair is getting rough," she says softly. "When we're home, I'll give you some lavender oil to comb into it. But you must use it every night." Tía Dolores's face is soft as she braids Josefina's hair again, and Josefina briefly rests against her aunt's shoulder.

The swirl of the party seems to fade as I watch the two of them together. All of a sudden, I wish that my own mother were here—or that I were with her. She used to braid my hair just like that, every morning before school. And I would lean up against her, just as Josefina leans against her aunt. I want to see my own mother and let her braid my hair. With a pang, I realize that I need to go home.

"Tía Dolores, Josefina, the party is wonderful, but

I—I think I need to go back to the house," I say.

"Do you mean you are tired, María?" Tía Dolores says. "I can ask Miguel to accompany you back home."

"Sí, gracias," I say. I'm sure I can find a way to slip off quietly in the dark.

"No, María, don't go yet!" Josefina cries. "There's still the supper to eat."

"The party has stirred up some memories," I tell them. "I'm going to think—to try to remember my family. I'd like to find my way home to them. But I want to say *gracias* to both of you, for taking such good care of me."

Tía Dolores nods and smooths my hair back, just as she did to Josefina earlier. "We are glad you came to us, María," she says simply.

Josefina walks me to the door as Miguel waits just outside. "Good-bye, friend," I say. She hugs me tight, and I squeeze her back. *We're bonded through time,* I tell her silently, and I hope she can hear me in her heart.

✹ *Turn to page 171.*

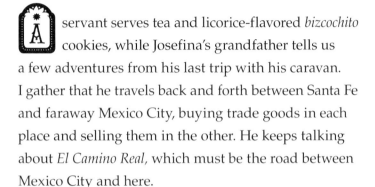 servant serves tea and licorice-flavored *bizcochito* cookies, while Josefina's grandfather tells us a few adventures from his last trip with his caravan. I gather that he travels back and forth between Santa Fe and faraway Mexico City, buying trade goods in each place and selling them in the other. He keeps talking about *El Camino Real,* which must be the road between Mexico City and here.

Josefina recalls a time he brought her and her sisters a cone of the finest chocolate. "When Teresita made hot chocolate from it," she says, her eyes shining with the memory, "it was so creamy. And the taste when it spread across your tongue! Rich and sweet. I dreamed about it all that night."

It sounds odd that Josefina would be so enchanted just by *chocolate,* but even though she doesn't have as many things as I have, and even though she has to take a four-hour dusty wagon ride to Santa Fe, she doesn't seem unhappy. Not at all—actually, she seems *happy.*

Maybe the way you see your life matters more than the things you have. Josefina is just as happy in an adobe *house with no running water as I was in a city apartment,* I think, brushing a few *bizcochito* crumbs from my skirt.

"Abuelita, may I show María my favorite hill?" Josefina asks, finishing her tea.

Josefina's grandmother smiles at us warmly. "*Sí*, children, run along."

Quickly we clear away the teacups, and then I follow Josefina out the front door. There is no dust out here, just clear, sparkling air. Panting, with the wind blowing our hair back, we climb a steep hill behind the house. "Not too much farther," Josefina calls back, noticing that I'm lagging. Her cheeks are pink, and little wisps of hair have fallen from her braid into her face.

"I'm coming!" I call up to her. With a burst of speed, I run to catch up, dirt and small rocks sliding beneath my moccasins.

By the time I reach her, Josefina is standing at the top of the hill with her hands on her hips, looking out. "There! Isn't it beautiful?" she says. "This is my favorite place in all of Santa Fe."

"Oooh," I breathe as I gaze out over the rooftops. We can see all of Santa Fe from here—the low, flat houses with narrow roads between, a silver slash of river, and all around the city, big flat fields of ripe crops. The mountains are dusted with dark green pine trees and sprinkled with golden aspens. The snow on the top seems almost close enough to touch. "It *is* beautiful." And I mean it. It's a different kind of beauty than the lights and soaring skyscrapers and bridges of Chicago. It's quieter, closer to the earth. But for the first time, I can see why Josefina loves this place. I think I could grow to love it too.

I unbutton my waist pouch and draw out my flute. Josefina is still looking out at the city, so I hold the flute down by my side and stroke the soft clay with my thumb. I was Birdy the musical girl once, but I lost her somewhere between here and Chicago. I wonder if maybe, just maybe, I could find her again.

"You know," I say slowly, "I think, from up here, I can almost find my way home."

Josefina looks at me, surprised. "Truly, María?"

"Yes," I tell her. "I . . . think I just had to climb this high first." *I can see it through time,* I tell her silently. And it's time to go back.

✹ *Turn to page 175.*

've barely played the last note of the mocking-bird's song before I find myself sprawled at the base of the rock, with a wet tongue licking my cheek. It's Daisy, and I'm back in my own world. Funny how the hills lit by the sunset look like home now.

I brush myself off and head into the warm, noisy house. My family is still gathered in the kitchen. Their faces look wonderfully familiar. I want to run over and hug them all, but since they think I've just been outside for a few minutes, I settle for pulling myself up to sit on the counter.

"Hey, sis," Henry says. He holds out the piece of paper I saw him showing Mom, right before I zoomed off to Josefina's world. "Check it out—a beginners' rock-climbing class. The outdoors club is putting it on. Do you want to take it with me?"

I study my brother's eager freckled face. Before Josefina, I would have said no right away. But now, exploring the desert doesn't sound so bad. "Yeah," I say slowly, examining the flyer. "That could be fun."

I look up and meet Dad's eyes. He raises his eyebrows as if to say, *Now that's a change.* I shrug.

Mom moves over to the stove and lifts the lid on the

steamer to check the *tamales*. A delicious spicy smell billows out. "Mmm," I inhale and slide down from the counter.

Dad wanders over casually. "Decided to give New Mexico a try, huh?" he murmurs out of the side of his mouth.

"I've been doing some thinking, is all," I tell him.

His forehead knits. "Must have been some serious thinking session."

I slide my fingers around my flute, safe in my pocket. "Oh, it was," I say. "You have no idea."

✹ *The End* ✹

To read this story another way and see how different choices lead to a different ending, turn back to page 108.

y feet can't resist the music. I grab Josefina's hands, and we whirl out into the shadows beside the house. From a window, a square of light and the sounds of music and pounding feet pour out. "One foot forward, step back, step forward," Josefina instructs. I stumble and almost fall on her, and we burst into laughter. I've missed having a friend to clown with, and I've missed being surrounded by music. I don't want to leave these things behind when I leave Josefina's world, I think.

And then the thought strikes me—maybe I don't have to.

Through the window, we hear everyone clap as the music ends with a flourish. Josefina and I look at each other and clap too, in our own little dancing space.

I look at my friend, who is breathlessly rearranging her *rebozo,* and I try to fix her warm face in my mind. I suddenly realize that being friends with Josefina hasn't made me forget Danielle, just like having Tía Dolores in her life hasn't made Josefina forget her mamá. I don't have to lose one friend just because I have another.

"Josefina, it's the oddest thing, but I think I know

how to find my way back to my home now," I tell my friend.

She lets her *rebozo* slide back down to her elbows. "Oh, María, have you remembered?"

I nod. "I've remembered . . . the important things."

"That's wonderful!" Josefina catches me by the arms and we swing around again, bathed in the warm light from the window, our feet carried on the wave of the music itself.

✿ *Turn to page 181.*

M y stomach is fluttering the next morning when I push open the door to school, and it takes me a minute to realize that I'm nervous. *It's the first day of the rest of your life, it's the first day of the rest of your life, it's the first day of the rest of your life.* The old saying that my dad loves runs through my mind like the cars of a freight train going by on a track.

I can almost see Josefina walking beside me—it would be so much fun to show her my world now that I've seen hers! Still, she *is* with me. I've brought some of her strength and fun back with me through time, just like I've brought Chicago to Santa Fe with me in my heart.

I stop at the bulletin board that Audrey and I looked at yesterday. The Skit Club poster is still there. *Auditions on Tuesday!* it trumpets. As I examine it, I suddenly see myself covered in dust, jolting along in that wagon. I almost laugh. If I can embrace *that* experience, then I can handle this one, right? Josefina showed me that I'm a lot stronger than I think—and that Birdy is still inside me.

I turn on my heel and march down the hall. If I hurry, I can get to Mrs. McGlynn's classroom a few minutes before the bell. I have something important to ask Audrey—after all, auditions are next week and I know a great two-person scene we could perform.

Audrey is already at her desk when I hurry into the classroom.

"Hi," I say breathlessly.

She looks up from her book. "Hi." Her voice is neutral. She looks at me, waiting.

"I have this great book of scenes—all for two people." I pull it from my backpack. "Maybe . . . maybe we could practice one together. You know, for the Skit Club auditions." I hold my breath.

Audrey is still silent. Then she says, "Yeah. That would be fun." A smile spreads across her face. It's a warm smile that invites me in. Just like Josefina did.

❈ The End ❈

To read this story another way and see how different choices lead to a different ending, turn back to page 123.

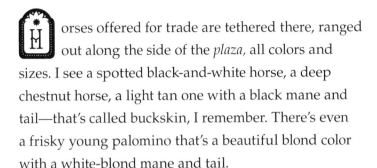orses offered for trade are tethered there, ranged out along the side of the *plaza,* all colors and sizes. I see a spotted black-and-white horse, a deep chestnut horse, a light tan one with a black mane and tail—that's called buckskin, I remember. There's even a frisky young palomino that's a beautiful blond color with a white-blond mane and tail.

Each horse wears a simple rope halter, tethered to a peg in the ground. The traders stand behind them in little knots, talking and waiting for offers. Here and there, men are walking up and down, studying the horses, looking in their mouths, and examining their shoulders and flanks.

"They're so beautiful!" I breathe, staring at their large, intelligent eyes and tossing heads. Their ears are pricked at all the noise and excitement of the *plaza,* and their nostrils flare, breathing in the unusual scents.

"Let's pick out horses for one another!" Josefina proposes. "I'll pick one for Mariana. María, you pick one for me, and Mariana will pick one for you. Then we'll ride our mounts back to our homes!"

We all laugh. "And we can race on the way!" I add. "Pick a fast one for me, Mariana."

"I like slow and steady," Josefina chimes in. "Sturdy too, María."

Mariana tilts her head at the adult horse-buyers and arranges her face into the same serious, brows-lowered expression they have. "Horse trading is serious business," she says in a pretend-deep voice.

Josefina bursts out laughing. "That's just what Papá always says."

"And my grandfather!" Mariana says in her own voice.

We walk up and down the row with our hands clasped behind our backs just like the adult horse-buyers. I look carefully at the big chestnut, who stands calmly with his noble head high, and at a fat, shaggy little pony with black spots like a Dalmatian. Beside him is a coal-black stallion who tosses his head and rolls his eye at me when I get too close. Josefina spends a long time looking at the palomino, and Mariana seems enchanted by a slender bay who snuffles at her hand.

After a few moments, I stop and face my friends. "All right!" I announce. "I've made my choice. How about you two?"

Josefina nods. "I have the perfect horse for Mariana," she says. She gestures toward a perky black mare beside us and makes a little bow toward Mariana. "My friend, I've chosen this fine black pony for you. Her eyes sparkle like yours, her mane is exactly the color of your hair, *and* she's not too tall, so you can mount by yourself."

Mariana grins. "*Gracias,* my friend. I accept my new horse!" We laugh.

Then it's my turn. I stand straight and pretend that I'm reading from a paper. I do a deep voice too, like an adult giving a speech. "My dearest Josefina," I begin. The girls giggle appreciatively. "For you, I have chosen a fine mount. He is bold and swift, yet he is young. He will require much instruction, and you are a skilled teacher." I give Josefina a significant look from under my brows, and she blushes a little and drops her eyes. "May I present—the palomino!" With a flourish, I extend my arm to the beautiful blond horse, who is little more than a colt.

"My beauty!" Josefina strokes the horse's velvety nose.

"María, I have a special horse for you," Mariana

says. "I didn't know which one I would pick until this moment. But now it's clear to me. Even though we just met, María, I hope you will be my friend, as you are Josefina's—so I'm choosing the chestnut horse for you." She nods toward a handsome animal who stands with his head raised, as if he's listening to us. "He's a beautiful brown—halfway between my black horse and Josefina's golden one. Do you see? Your horse joins the other two together. And we are three now, instead of two."

I feel a rush of affection for this girl who just met me, but who has accepted me as a friend. As I stand in the noisy, colorful *plaza,* I think of Audrey and how she wants to be my friend, even though we've just met. I don't want to leave Danielle behind—but maybe I don't have to. Josefina is still friends with Mariana, even though she welcomes me. Maybe being friends with Audrey doesn't mean that I have to lose Danielle.

I don't know. But I'm ready to try. I'm ready to ride the mockingbird's song back home.

✿ *Turn to page 182.*

ack in my own world that night, I curl up on my bed under my down comforter. It's *almost* as comfortable as Josefina's sheepskins. I reach for my phone on my bedside table and thumb through the online school directory. There she is. Audrey Capella. I take a deep breath and touch her number.

It's ringing. My stomach is fluttery.

"Hello?" she answers.

"Audrey, it's Birdy," I say. "You know, from school?"

She doesn't say anything. This is hard. But I think back to Josefina, reaching out to me when I was lost and alone. "I—I've been wondering. Do, um, do you want to come over one day after school? My brother, Henry, can pick us up. We could go for a hike."

She still doesn't say anthing, and my stomach sinks. I wish I'd never called.

"Sure," she says. "That would be fun."

A big grin splits my face. I feel like Josefina is watching me—and applauding.

✹ *The End* ✹

To read this story another way and see how different choices lead to a different ending, turn back to page 155.

The next day, back at school in my own time, I spot Audrey down at the end of the hallway. "Hi!" I call out, hurrying past the row of lockers. Audrey is stuffing a textbook into her backpack. She shuts her locker door and eyes me warily.

"Yeah?"

"I looked for you after English, but I must have missed you." I stop, breathing hard from my sprint down the hall.

She gazes at me steadily, but says nothing.

I swallow. This isn't going to be easy. But I summon up Josefina's face, and Mariana's, in front of me. They made friends with me when I really needed it. Now it's my turn. "Listen, I wasn't being very nice yesterday. I—I'm sorry. Moving here has been kind of hard, you know?"

She nods, just a little.

"I, um, I thought I wouldn't have anything in common with the people here at this school. But... I don't think that anymore," I tell her.

Audrey narrows her eyes. "How come?"

I think of skipping across the *plaza* with Josefina and Mariana, holding hands. "I had a few lessons.

From a very good teacher."

"Okay . . ." She looks a little confused.

"So . . . how about that ice-cream shop you were talking about yesterday? Do they have peach?" I grin at her and she grins back.

"They do! And it's so good."

Side by side, we push open the school doors and head out into the fresh New Mexico afternoon.

❋ *The End* ❋

To read this story another way and see how different choices lead to a different ending, turn back to page 26.

ABOUT Josefina's Time

New Mexico is part of the United States today, but in 1824 it belonged to Mexico, and before that it had belonged to Spain—just like California, Texas, and all the states in the Southwestern U.S. Almost everyone who lived in that region in Josefina's time was Spanish or Native American.

Most New Mexicans lived much the way Josefina and her family do, on *ranchos* or in small farming villages. Raising crops and animals in the high desert was not easy, so everyone, including children, worked hard and depended on one another. Children grew up with very close ties to their extended families and the few neighbors or villagers who lived nearby. The Catholic faith was an important part of people's everyday lives, and children usually had a special bond with their godparents, just as Josefina does with her godmother, Tía Magdalena.

When New Mexicans were sick or injured, they called on a *curandera* like Tía Magdalena for treatment. *Curanderas* knew how to make medicines from many kinds of plants. They were highly respected for their healing skills and their wisdom.

Children were expected to be respectful of grown-ups. To show respect, they kept their head and eyes down and their hands clasped in front of them, and didn't speak until they were spoken to. Still, children had lots of fun, too. Girls enjoyed string games, clapping games, and home-made dolls, and boys played a ball game called *shinny.* And everyone loved to share stories, songs, and riddles as they worked together or relaxed by the fire at night.

The Spanish settlers in New Mexico were allies and trading partners with their Pueblo Indian neighbors, but they were enemies of tribes such as the Navajo, Apache, and Comanche. Both sides raided each other fiercely and took women and children as captives, or *cautivas*. The Spanish used *cautivas* as servants; Indians often used them to do camp work or herd sheep. Torn from their families and their culture, *cautivas* must have suffered greatly. Some escaped and made their way back home, just as the Montoyas think Birdy did. However, most captives did not escape and eventually adjusted to their new lives, as Tía Dolores's servant Teresita did, but they probably never forgot the home they had left behind.

Santa Fe was the only town for hundreds of miles in any direction. As Birdy discovers, Santa Fe was not a big city, but it *was* a lively, exciting place where people from all around came to trade. The *Camino Real* was the wagon trail that connected Santa Fe with towns and cities far to the south. Trading caravans like Abuelito's traveled the *Camino Real* to bring necessities and luxuries from all around the world to Santa Fe, although the trip from Mexico City took months and crossed rugged, dangerous deserts and mountains. In 1821, a new wagon trail opened up between Santa Fe and Missouri. Known as the Santa Fe Trail, it began to draw American traders to New Mexico— the beginning of New Mexico's ties to the United States.

GLOSSARY of Spanish Words

Abuelita *(ah-bweh-LEE-tah)*—Grandma

Abuelito *(ah-bweh-LEE-toh)*—Grandpa

acequia *(ah-SEH-kee-ah)*—a ditch made to carry water to a farmer's fields

adiós *(ah-dee-OHS)*—good-bye

adobe *(ah-DOH-beh)*—a building material made of earth mixed with straw and water

banco *(BAHN-ko)*—a bench built into the wall of a room

bienvenida *(bee-en-veh-NEE-dah)*—welcome (used only to greet girls and women). The greeting for males and mixed groups is *bienvenido.*

bizcochito *(bees-ko-CHEE-toh)*—a kind of sugar cookie flavored with anise

buenos días *(BWEH-nohs DEE-ahs)*—good morning

cautiva *(kaw-TEE-vah)*—a female captive. (A male captive is a *cautivo.*)

chile *(CHEE-leh)*—a chili pepper

colcha *(KOHL-chah)*—a kind of embroidery made with long, flat stitches

curandera *(koo-rahn-DEH-rah)*—a woman who knows how to make medicines from plants and is skilled at healing

El Camino Real *(el kah-MEE-no rey-AHL)*—the main road or trail that ran from Mexico City to New Mexico. Its name means "Royal Road."

fandango *(fahn-DAHNG-go)*—a big celebration or party that includes a lively dance

gracias *(GRAH-see-ahs)*—thank you

La Jornada del Muerto *(lah hor-NAH-dah del MWEHR-toh)*—the name of an especially rugged, waterless part of El Camino Real. The words literally mean "The Route of the Dead Man."

Los Charcos del Perillo *(lohs CHAR-kohs del peh-REE-yo)*—the pools or springs of the little dog

mano *(MAH-no)*—a stone that is held in the hand and used to grind corn. Dried corn is put on a large flat stone called a *metate*, and then the mano is rubbed back and forth over the corn to break it down into flour.

masa *(MAH-sah)*—a dough made with cornmeal that is used in Mexican cooking

metate *(meh-TAH-teh)*—a large flat stone used with a *mano* to grind corn

patrón *(pah-TROHN)*—a man who has earned respect because he owns land and is a good leader of his family and his workers

piñón *(pee-NYOHN)*—a kind of short, scrubby pine that produces delicious nuts

plaza *(PLAH-sah)*—an open square in a village or town

pueblo *(PWEH-blo)*—a village of Pueblo Indians

rancho *(RAHN-cho)*—a ranch or farm where crops are grown and animals are raised

rebozo *(reh-BO-so)*—a long shawl worn by girls and women

ristra *(REE-strah)*—a string of fruit or vegetables that is hung up to dry, preserving the food for the winter

sala *(SAH-lah)*—a room in a house

Santa Fe *(SAHN-tah FEH)*—the capital city of New Mexico. Its name means "Holy Faith."

Señor *(seh-NYOR)*—Mr.

Señora *(seh-NYO-rah)*—Mrs.

sí *(SEE)*—yes

siesta *(see-ES-tah)*—a rest or nap in the afternoon

sombrita *(sohm-BREE-tah)*—little shadow, or an affectionate way to say "shadow." The Spanish word for "shadow" is *sombra*.

tamale *(tah-MAH-leh)*—spicy meat surrounded by cornmeal dough and cooked in a corn-husk wrapping

tía *(TEE-ah)*—aunt

tortilla *(tor-TEE-yah)*—a kind of flat, round bread made of corn or wheat

HOW TO SAY Spanish Names

Ana *(AH-nah)*

Andres *(ahn-DREHS)*

Carmen *(KAR-mehn)*

Clara *(KLAH-rah)*

Dolores *(doh-LO-rehs)*

Esteban *(EHS-teh-bahn)*

Felipe *(feh-LEE-peh)*

Francisca *(frahn-SEES-kah)*

García *(gar-SEE-ah)*

Jaramillo *(hah-rah-MEE-yo)*

Josefina *(ho-seh-FEE-nah)*

Luisa *(loo-EE-sah)*

Magdalena *(mahg-dah-LEH-nah)*

María (*mah-REE-ah)*

Mariana *(mah-ree-AH-nah)*

Mateo *(mah-TEH-o)*

Miguel *(mee-GEHL)*

Ofelia *(o-FEE-lyah)*

Sanchez *(SAHN-chehz)*

Teresita *(teh-reh-SEE-tah)*

Tomás *(toh-MAHS)*

Read more of JOSEFINA'S stories,
available from booksellers and at *americangirl.com*

◈ *Classics* ◈
Josefina's classic series, now in two volumes:

Volume 1:
Sunlight and Shadows
Josefina and her sisters are excited when Tía Dolores comes to their *rancho*, bringing new ideas, new fashions, and new challenges. Can Josefina open her heart to change and still hold on to precious memories of Mamá?

Volume 2:
Second Chances
Josefina makes a wonderful discovery: She has a gift for healing. Can she find the courage and creativity to mend her family's broken trust in an *americano* trader and keep her family whole and happy when Tía Dolores plans to leave?

◈ *Journey in Time* ◈
Travel back in time—and spend a day with Josefina!

Song of the Mockingbird
Spend a cozy evening at the *rancho*, come face-to-face with a snarling mountain lion, or visit the lively market in Santa Fe. Choose your own path through this multiple-ending story!

◈ *Mystery* ◈
Another thrilling adventure with Josefina!

Secrets in the Hills
Josefina has heard tales of treasure buried in the hills, and of a ghostly Weeping Woman who roams at night. But she never imagined the stories might be true—until a mysterious stranger arrives at her *rancho*.

A Sneak Peek at

Sunlight and Shadows

A Josefina Classic

Volume 1

What happens to Josefina?
Find out in the first volume of her classic stories.

osefina had gathered a basketful of onions when suddenly she stood up. Francisca stood up, too, and the girls looked at each other.

"Is it . . . ?" Francisca began.

"Shhh . . ." said Josefina, holding her finger to her lips. She tilted her head and listened hard. Yes! There it was. She could hear the rumble and squeak of wooden wheels that meant only one thing. The caravan was coming!

Francisca heard, too. The girls smiled at each other, grabbed their baskets, and ran as fast as they could back through the gate. "The caravan! It's coming!" they shouted. "Ana! Clara! It's coming!" They dropped their baskets outside the kitchen door as Clara rushed out to join them.

The three girls dashed across the front courtyard and flew up the steps of the tower in the south wall. The window in the tower was narrow, so Josefina knelt and looked out the lower part. Francisca and Clara stood behind her and looked over her head.

At first, all they saw was a cloud of dust stirring on the road from the village. Then the sound of the wheels grew louder and louder. Soon they heard the jingle of harnesses, dogs barking, people shouting, and the village church bell ringing. Next they saw soldiers coming over the hill with the sun glinting on their buttons and guns. Then came mule after mule. It looked like a hundred or more to Josefina. The mules were carrying heavy packs strapped to their backs. She counted thirty carts pulled by plodding oxen. The carts lumbered along on their two big wooden wheels. There were four-wheeled wagons as well. And so many people! Too many to count! There were cart drivers, traders, and whole families of travelers. There were herders driving sheep, goats, and cattle. People from town and Indians from the nearby pueblo village walked along with the caravan to welcome it.

Francisca stood on tiptoe to see better. She put her hands on Josefina's shoulders. "Don't you love to think about all the places the caravan has been?" she asked. "And all the places the things it brings come from, too?"

"Yes," said Josefina. "They come from all over the world, up the Camino Real, right to *our* door!"

Most of the caravan stopped and set up camp

midway between the town and the rancho. But many of the cart drivers camped closer to the house, in a shady area next to the stream. Josefina saw Papá ride his horse up to one of the big, four-wheeled wagons. He waved to its driver.

"That's Abuelito!" Josefina cried. She pointed to the driver of the four-wheeled wagon. "Look! Papá is greeting him. See? There he is!"

Francisca leaned forward. "Who's that tall woman sitting next to Abuelito?" she wondered aloud. "She's greeting Papá as if she knows him."

But Josefina and Clara had already turned away from the window. They hurried down from the tower. Josefina ran to the kitchen and stuck her head in the door. "Come on," she said to Ana. "Papá and Abuelito are on their way up to the house."

"Oh dear, oh dear," fussed Ana as she wiped her hands and smoothed her hair. "There's still so much to do. I'll never be ready for the fandango."

When Papá led Abuelito's big wagon up to the front gate, Josefina was the first to run out and greet it. Francisca, Clara, and Ana were close behind. Josefina thought she'd never seen a sight as wonderful

as Abuelito's happy face. He handed the reins to the
woman next to him and climbed down.

"My beautiful granddaughters!" said Abuelito. He
kissed them as he named them. "Ana, and Francisca!
Clara, and my little Josefina! Oh, God bless you! God
bless you! It is good to see you! This was the finest trip
I've ever made! Oh, the adventures, the adventures!
But I am getting too old for these trips. They make me
old before my time. This is my last trip. My last."

"Oh, Abuelito!" said Francisca, taking his arm and
laughing. "You say that every time!"

Abuelito threw back his head and laughed, too.
"Ah, but this time I mean it," he said. "I've brought
a surprise for you." He turned and held out his hand
to the tall woman on the wagon. "Here she is, your
Tía Dolores. She has come back to live with her mamá
and me in Santa Fe. Now I have no reason to go to
Mexico City ever again!"

Josefina and her sisters looked so surprised, Papá
and Abuelito laughed at them. Tía Dolores took
Abuelito's hand and gracefully swung herself down
from the wagon seat.

Papá smiled at her. "You see, Dolores? You have

surprised my daughters as much as you surprised me," he said. "Welcome to our home."

"Gracias," Tía Dolores answered. She smiled at Papá and then she turned to the sisters. "I've looked forward to this moment for a long time!" she said to them. "I've wanted to see all of you! My dear sister's children!"

She spoke to each one in turn. "You're very like your mamá, Ana," she said. "And Francisca, you've grown so tall and so beautiful! Dear Clara, you were barely three years old when I left. Do you remember?"

Tía Dolores took Josefina's hand in both of her own. She bent forward so that she could look closely at Josefina's face. "At last I meet you, Josefina," she said. "You weren't even born when I left. And look! Here you are! Already a lovely young girl!" Tía Dolores straightened again. Her eyes were bright as she looked at all the sisters. "I'm so happy to see you all. It's good to be back."

The girls were still too surprised to say much, but they smiled shyly at Tía Dolores. Ana was the first to collect herself. "Please, Abuelito and Tía Dolores. Come inside and have a cool drink. I'm sure you're tired and thirsty." She led Tía Dolores inside the gate. "You must excuse us, Tía Dolores," she said. "We haven't prepared any place for you to sleep."

"Goodness, Ana!" said Tía Dolores. "You didn't know I was coming. I didn't know myself, really, until the last minute. I've been caring for my dear aunt in Mexico City all these years. Bless her soul! She died this past spring. It was just before Abuelito's caravan arrived. I had no reason to stay. So, I joined the caravan to come home."

"Yes," Abuelito said to the girls. "Your grandmother will be so pleased! Wait till Dolores and I get to Santa Fe the day after tomorrow! What a surprise, eh?"

Josefina could not take her eyes off Tía Dolores as everyone sat down together in the family sala. The room's thick walls and small windows kept it cool even in the heat of the afternoon.

Francisca whispered, "Isn't Tía Dolores's dress beautiful? Her sleeves must be the latest style from Europe."

But Josefina hadn't noticed Tía Dolores's sleeves, or anything else about her clothes. *This is Tía Dolores,* she kept thinking. *This is Mamá's sister.*

Josefina studied Tía Dolores to see if she looked like Mamá. Mamá had been the older of the two sisters, but Tía Dolores was much taller. She didn't have Mamá's soft, rounded beauty, Josefina decided, nor her pale skin or dark, smooth hair. Everything about Tía Dolores was sharper somehow. Her hands were bigger. Her face was more narrow. She had gray eyes and dark red hair that was springy. Her voice didn't sound like Mamá's, either. Mamá's voice was high and breathy, like notes from a flute. Tía Dolores's voice had a graceful sound. It was as low and clear as notes from a harp string. But when Tía Dolores laughed, Josefina was startled. Her laugh sounded so much like Mamá's! If Josefina closed her eyes, it might be Mamá laughing.

There was a great deal of laughter in the family sala that afternoon as Abuelito told the story of his trip. Josefina sat next to Abuelito, her arms wrapped around her knees. She was happy.

About the Author

First, EMMA CARLSON BERNE
thought she was going to be a college
professor, so she went to graduate school
at Miami University in Ohio. After that,
she taught horseback riding in Boston and
Charleston, South Carolina. *Then* Emma
found out how much she enjoys writing for
children and young adults. Since that time,
she has authored more than two dozen books
and often writes about historical figures such
as Sacagawea, Helen Keller, Christopher
Columbus, and the artist Frida Kahlo.
Emma lives in a hundred-year-old house
in Cincinnati, Ohio, with her two little
boys and her husband.